BOX 991
THE COMPLETE CABALISTIC CASES
OF SEMI DUAL, VOLUME 5

BOOKS IN THE ARGOSY LIBRARY:

DR. SKULL
LEWIS CLAY

ABBEY OF THE DAMNED: THE COMPLETE
CASES OF MIKE AND TRIXIE, VOLUME 3
T.T. FLYNN

THE DEATH MESSENGER: THE COMPLETE
CASES OF JIGGER MASTERS, VOLUME 4
ANTHONY M. RUD

BOX 991: THE COMPLETE CABALISTIC
CASES OF SEMI DUAL, VOLUME 5
J.U. GIESY & JUNIUS B. SMITH

BLIND TRAILS AT TONTO: THE COMPLETE
TALES OF SHERIFF HENRY, VOLUME 8
W.C TUTTLE

IN THE MURDERER'S BRAIN: THE COMPLETE
CASES OF THE SCIENTIFIC CLUB, VOLUME 3
RAY CUMMINGS

THE LEGION OF THE LIVING DEAD: THE
COMPLETE CASES OF MR. STRANG, VOLUME 2
CARROLL JOHN DALY

THE MENTAL MARVEL
FRED MACISAAC

THE ADVENTURE OF THE VOODOO
MOON: THE COMPLETE CASES OF
THE LADY FROM HELL, VOLUME 2
EUGENE THOMAS

MURDER ON THE FILM: THE COMPLETE
CASES OF CANDID JONES, VOLUME 1
RICHARD B. SALE

BOX 991
THE COMPLETE CABALISTIC
CASES OF SEMI DUAL, VOLUME 5

J.U. GIESY &
JUNIUS B. SMITH

POPULAR PUBLICATIONS · 2025

TABLE OF CONTENTS

SNARED

1

COLONEL SHELDON IS JUBILANT

I AM CERTAIN that when Lucile Foote, Semi Dual, Sheldon, and myself left the Hall of Justice, taking with us Lily Lawton, whom Dual had freed from the web of peril in which her false lover, Homer Reich, and Greek Annie, his confederate, had ensnared her, the majority of us felt that the incident was closed and the two white slave agents destined to a well-merited fate.

Those of you who have followed the history of that adventure will admit that we had certainly scored against the organized band of social vampires who prey upon the youth and virtue of their country's womanhood. Reich, who had won her trust and her promise to wed him while acting as a white slave scout, and the woman, wife of a Greek member of the organization who had helped in the girl's capture, we left in charge of the police when we started back to our suite at the St. Francis. With us we took the assurance that the Greek accomplices in Salt Lake would be arrested as soon as the wires could carry the order.

All in all, it was a remarkable victory which Dual had scored against a subtle foe. As Colonel Mac Sheldon put it:

"I reckon we put a kink in that bunch of jaspers this time. My hat's off to Semi Dual."

And those of you who have followed the stories of the

strange man which I, Gordon Glace, have tried to set down from time to time will know of whom he spoke.

You will recognize the name as that of that super-soul who moved other souls of men and women like pawns on the chess-board of life—who sought from time to time to unravel some of the miserable tangles into which those lesser souls had snarled their skeins of life.

The man who studied and used the higher forces of the universal laws, as those lesser men about him used the simpler implements of material forces, and who did all this with a smile that destiny made of him a means to a noble end.

And it was Semi Dual who, when old Colonel Sheldon, of Goldfield, appealed to him for aid, had engaged in a battle of wits with the organization which had stolen the pale-faced girl who now sat opposite me in the taxi, her head resting on the shoulder of Lucile Foote.

Lucile, as you know, was the agent of the police who, in helping Dual to see justice performed, had won her own vengeance against the man Reich—and Reich, three years before, had done her sister to her death.

Oh, it was a triumph for right I had seen that night! And Dual was the high priest of right, always.

The taxi took us back to the hotel where we had engaged our suite such a few crowded hours ago. It hardly seemed possible that this was the same night in the evening of which we had registered at the yellow marble desk and gone forth without delay to free a threatened soul. We went up to the rooms, and I think we all breathed a sigh of relief as we reached them.

Lily Lawton turned to Semi then and would have

spoken save that he waved Lucile to take the girl to their room.

"To-morrow, Miss Lawton," he said not unkindly. "Wait until a little of the strain has passed—for to-night—thank that Power who watches the sparrows and feeds them. Good night!"

"Just the same," erupted Sheldon, when the door was closed behind Lucile and the girl, "there ain't no strings on my expressin' my opinion, an' I reckon this is our night to howl. For downright pure quill queerness, this last thing puts it all over anything I ever heard of. I ain't takin' nuthin' of credit from that Power you speak of, Mr. Dual, but I'm addin' that you played some hand, sir—some hand, and won all the bets that was down. Yessir, this is our night to howl!"

"There will follow a day, which is almost dawning," said Semi. "I shall sleep despite your howling, my friend." A slight smile flicked across his lips.

Colonel Mac and I went to our room, and he kept on talking till I told him to keep still. It had been a pretty strenuous night as I viewed it, and, like Semi, I wanted to rest.

Yet in the morning he took up his sleep interrupted exclamations, like a phonographic record half played through. In fact, an air of congratulatory excitement pervaded our little party when we gathered in the parlor of the suite, where a waiter was spreading a table by Dual's direction.

Lucile was fresh, smiling, with an expression of calm triumph in her deep brown eyes, unlike that vague unrest which had excited my interest in the days since I had known her. She impressed me as one awaking from a dream of things past and opening eyes upon a brighter future as she sat by the window, looking out at the already busy street.

It was one of those golden mornings which often come to the city of San Francisco after a night of fog. Tired as we all were by the events which had held us, we had slept late. At least all of us had except Semi Dual, whom I suspected of having followed his usual custom of rising with the sun.

The warm glow of the outer day streamed into the room, filling its atmosphere with light, while we waited for the serving of our morning's meal.

As for the Lawton girl, she was pale but composed with a sort of pensive composure. She seemed hardly to realize fully her new position, and stood beside Miss Foote, with the elder woman's arm about her supple waist. She was a pretty little thing in her way, with wide eyes which told one why she had fallen so easy a victim to the dapper and plausible Reich.

One could sum her up as an innocent—a creature without experience of men's falsity—one to give trust to the one who spoke kindly—one who had blundered through ignorance into her fate.

Colonel Mac fairly sparkled with good humor this morning, did the colonel, and the whole world was his friend. All his life he had been a man who did nothing by half: and when he took charge of this girl as her protector, he had taken her welfare to heart. That he had her back unscathed, save for the shock of her peril, brought him into a jovial mood.

I glanced at Semi. He was sitting in a large chair,

from where he could command a straight sweep of the down-dropping length of Powell till it jutted into Market. I could see his profile from where I stood. It was quiet, calm, composed, yet with a firmness about it which spoke to me of a mental introspection.

For a man who had done what he had accomplished, he struck me more as a detached spectator than the principal actor in a drama of human passion and pain.

He felt my gaze, as he seemed always to do, when my eyes dwelt upon him, turned his glance to my own, and smiled in a slow, almost enigmatic fashion A moment more and he was once more watching the human ants which scuttered about the streets. Yet I felt sure that he saw them only with his physical eyes, and that his mental vision was turned toward some other point.

In that moment it came to me that our little celebration might be in some way premature—that even as he had led us through the maze of plot and counterplot which had brought us at last to the woman we sought, who now stood with Lucile by the window, so now he might still know more of the final issue than any of us others suspected. It was almost as though that slow smile of his had said as much to me in a voiceless message, unmeant for other ears.

A waiter came in with the breakfast and set it forth with its service. Lucile and Lily whispered by the window, and I saw the girl glance more than once at Semi Dual. It appeared to me that she wanted to thank him for her salvation and hardly knew how to approach him.

After all she was only a child at heart.

"Before we eat, I want to express my feelings," Sheldon began. "This here is one of th' happiest moments of my somewhat busy career. I've lived a long time an' I done some things I thought rather nifty myself, an' I seen some nifty things done, now an' then. But th' thing which skins th' whole lot and caboodle is th' thing which makes it possible for us five to sit here an' be glad we *are* here, an' we all know what it is.

"So before we eat this breakfast I want you to all join me in a toast to Mr. Semi Dual—th' one man livin' who never misses a shot an' always rings th' bell.

"I knowed he could do it when I asked him to help us, but darn me if I see how he done it—now. Here's how!"

Dual fiddled with a glass of milk, which he held in his long, supple fingers. Once more that slow smile twitched his lips as I watched.

"I am glad," he began, "that I have been able to justify Colonel Sheldon's expectations. I am grateful, as we should all be grateful, for a sincere appreciation of our efforts at any time, and I am thankful that by my means the Great One who guides the universal round, has seen fit to preserve the innocence of one who walked unawares."

He lifted his glass and drank.

Lily Lawton raised her blue eyes to his face. "May I thank you now, Mr. Dual, for what you have done for me?" she questioned. "I know that I must seem a very foolish girl to you, to have done as I did, but I really trusted the man who said he loved me. And I didn't know—I didn't dream—that a man—that any man—could be so—so base."

Dual smiled, and now the inscrutable quality which marked the spread of his lips at times was lacking. It was free—open—compassionate—that smile.

"Miss Lawton," he responded, "the action of one who loves truly should never seem foolish to one who knows that sincere love is the mainspring of universal creation. Against the machinations of social parasites there is but one protection, and that society must take.

"It is education. Ignorance is not as once thought, innocence. Miss Lawton. Ignorance is danger unsensed, no more. Innocence is purity of thought and action, linked with knowledge; a trinity which can make the soul blossom like a flower, even in a night of sin."

For a moment no one spoke. For a moment the full, rich tones of Dual's voice seemed to echo in the room. Then Sheldon chuckled slightly. "They used to tell me that ignorance was bliss," said he.

"Ignorance is danger," replied Dual. "Ignorance causes more suffering, bodily and mental, than any other thing. Ignorance of the law makes us a malefactor in its sight. Ignorance of cause makes us the victim of result."

"I reckon," grinned the colonel. "Ignorance of what you was doin' was what put this bunch of rustlers on the blink, all right. Ignorance sure threw a jolt into them they won't get over in a hurry."

I glanced at Lucile and smiled. Despite the wonderful work of Dual I could not help but feel a certain amusement at the personal note which the colonel threw into the matter. She seemed to sense my meaning, for she nodded.

"They are unfortunately a very strong and closely guarded organization," she returned to Sheldon. "I hardly feel that they will be greatly affected by the little we have done."

"Exactly," Dual assented, sprinkling sugar over his

breakfast of berries. "Our little engagement is a mere skirmish. Our victory here will be no more than the slightest pin-prick to their evil might. They have lost one or two of their mercenary soldiers, no more."

I started. I wondered what he meant. But even then I did not dream. A sob from Lily Lawton changed the tenor of my thoughts.

She was sitting with downcast eyes, eating practically nothing. Lucile put out a hand and patted her arm.

"We ought not to talk any more about it," she suggested. "But here is something for you to consider, Colonel Sheldon. This little girl must have some clothing before she starts home. I think I'll take her shopping this afternoon."

"You bet," agreed Sheldon, thrusting a hand into his pocket and dragging out a plethoric wallet. "Get her anything she needs, an' if this ain't enough, I got more. She's my girl from now on, an' you get her whatever is right, Miss Foote." With the air of a lord conferring largess, he tossed the wallet to Lucile.

For the second time Lily sobbed "You're all—so—so—good," she burst out. "I never dreamed there were men like Homer Reich! And now Colonel Mac says I'm to go home with him—but how can I? Everybody who knew me will point at me and say I was the girl these people stole. Oh, I don't know what to do!"

She paused and dropped her face against Lucile.

"Do?" roared Sheldon. "You'll go home, an' if anybody with a loose tongue lets it get to waggin', I'll put pepper on it 'fore they can close their trap. An' as fer your havin' done anything to deserve this here trouble, you didn't. Things jest happen sometimes, an'—"

"You are wrong, colonel." Dual interrupted. "Things do *not* just happen, and Miss Lawton has done something to bring her fate upon her. She has created a Karma, which induced just this thing."

"She's what?" exclaimed Sheldon.

Lucile Foote laughed—a soft little laugh of delight. "You delicious being," she said softly, with her eyes on Semi's face.

He smiled. Some way those two always seemed to understand each other from first to last.

"Created a Karma," he repeated to the colonel's open-mouthed interrogation. "In other words, she has set into operation certain forces, which have produced equally certain effects. Karma is after all but another name for the Book of Judgment, of which orthodox ministers of the orthodox gospel sometimes speak in their endeavors to *frighten* souls into a better manner of living.

"Karma is but the astral record of the things we do, good or bad. Karma is the Universal Ledger in which Universal Law sets down the account for and against us. We create it ourselves, building it up from moment to moment, from hour to hour, from day to day, from birth to death, and its final balance is the thing which determines the state unto which we shall go after that death of the flesh occurs."

Lily had ceased her weeping and was staring wide-eyed upon him while she listened. "But what did I do? How did I create this—this thing you spoke of? I always tried to do what was right." Her voice trembled.

Dual addressed her directly.

"And by always trying to do what was right you also created other Karma, which made your escape from the peril which threatened a possible thing. Your fault lay like that of mankind at large, in not learning the law of your own self-need. Your fault was a fault of ignorance.

"That very ignorance it was which made you a possible victim of one more learned in the ways of the world and men. Because you knew little of the guile which wraps a mantle of seeming probity about its evil body, you took the surface seeming for the reality itself. You gave your trust before its deserving was proven.

"In that you created Karma, and, because the one whom you trusted was unworthy of trust, he availed himself of the chance to betray you for his own selfish enrichment."

He paused, drew a deep breath, and resumed in the voice of a judge pronouncing sentence:

"And in so doing that one who betrayed you created a Karma, which will certainly be his undoing. Already its evil effects have begun to overtake him. And they shall continue to overtake him, to buffet his body and spirit, to torture his days and his nights, until the last item on the Karmic scrolls against him shall have been paid in full.

"But you, child in error, rather than in sin, shall profit by the lesson you have learned. So shall you walk safely and be not afraid."

"Well, my Lord!" sighed Colonel MacDonahue Sheldon, "I reckon you said a mouthful that time. Lily, my girl, that's about the best sermon on common sense I ever heard in my life. Summed up it comes out jes' about like this, I reckon: Do the best you kin, an' leave the rest up to th' Great Accountant—eh, Dual?"

"That, and endeavor to learn while you act," said Semi. "And, colonel, there is a very large question, both in your

mind and in that of my friend Glace, as to why the success
of our adventure has not wakened a greater satisfaction in
my mind—"

The telephone whirred sharply. I saw Dual draw his
watch and take the time.

Sheldon, as the one nearest the instrument, rose and
answered the call: "Hello! Who?" He paused a moment
and listened. "Oh, you want Miss Foote? All right, wait
just a minute." He turned and held the receiver out on its
cord toward Lucile. "Somebody wants you, ma'am," he
announced.

Lucile rose and took his place at the phone. "Yes, this is
Miss Foote—" she began, and evidently awaited the pleasure of the one who was speaking. Gradually as I watched
her I saw the color sink in her face, and she leaned slightly
forward. After a bit she put up a hand and rested it on the
telephone-box, as though seeking a partial support. Still
later she spoke in a tense, low voice: "Yes, yes; I understand.
I will speak to him at once, and we will let you hear later.
Yes, captain, at once; I understand the need of immediate
action. Yes."

She slipped the receiver into its catch and turned back
toward the table, and her eyes were deeper and darker at
that moment than I had ever known them. Perhaps it was
because her face had gone white to the lips and had lost
the look of happy content it had worn throughout the
morning.

"That was Captain of Detectives Connel, speaking from
the Hall of Justice," she whispered." He tells me that Mr.
McKabe disappeared between the time he left us last night
and this morning.

"Just now Captain Connel has received an anonymous communication, demanding the release of Reich and the woman Greek Annie within twenty-four hours, with the alternative of Mr. McKabe's death and his body's return."

2

SEMI DUAL DISAPPEARS

DUAL SNAPPED HIS watch. "Ten-twenty-seven," said he.

"Lucile," whispered Lily Lawton—" Lucile, what does it mean?"

"It means," said Miss Foote, "that a brave than is in danger of his life for giving us the help we needed last night."

I mentally applauded her control. Shocked as she was at the turn of affairs, she said no word of personal reproach to the girl.

So many would have made McKabe's actions in the path of his duty appear rather a matter of personal obligation at such a time.

"It means," declared Sheldon in a fighting voice he sometimes used, "that these jaspers are piling up a heap of Karma. Somebody's apt to get hurt when it falls over on him. Karma's a good thing to stand from under."

Dual smiled slightly. "I agree with you," said he. Watching his face, I saw it change and settle into lines of purpose, and my heart leaped within me.

Once more I knew that he was about to answer that half-spoken appeal of Lucile's. And some way I felt that he had known all the morning that that appeal was going to be made.

"Gordon, take Miss Lucile and go to Connel's office," he said to me. "Learn all you can of the particulars surrounding this affair. Verify the fact that McKabe is really a prisoner of these people. Learn also how well his connection with the police was known to any or all persons in the Chinatown district. When you have learned all you can return here at once. Call a taxi."

I sprang to attention and hurried to the phone to engage the cab, as he ordered. Already Lucile had run into her room for her jacket and hat. Hardly had I put through my demand when she came back, her pale face tense with impending action. I turned from the phone and went to get my own hat and coat.

"And what do I do?" Sheldon was saying as I came back.

"Keep a watchful eye upon Miss Lawton," said Semi. He had risen and crossed to a small writing-table placed between two windows. I saw his open watch lying upon it and a sheet of the hotel's paper.

A thrill went through me at the sight. Time and again I had seen him at the inception of some puzzling case, thus begin his operations by an abstruse calculation, involving the influence of planetary positions.

I joined Lucile, opened the door of the suite, waited till she had preceded me into the hall, and followed.

Together we trailed across the red-and-yellow foyer to a porter, who led us to the taxi I had ordered.

Then we were off. Lucile facing me as we swung into Geary and turned east. She was still pale, but I saw set purpose in the eyes which looked into mine.

She was breathing slowly and deeply, and one hand, resting in her lap, was clenched into a hard, little fist.

"Did Connel tell you what time McKabe is supposed to have been taken?" I asked as we lurched forward.

She shook her head "No. I didn't ask, you know. He just told me the salient facts, and asked me to tell Dual and explain it to him.

"I think Mr. Dual made a very great impression on Captain Connel."

"And you," said I on impulse, "have made a great impression on Semi Dual."

She leaned forward. Her lips parted.

"I— Mr. Glace, just what do you mean?"

"I mean," I told her, still following some compelling impulse to give her an encouragement at the beginning, "that now and then he meets some one whom he recognizes as what he calls a soul-seeking attainment—some one who sincerely desires to learn and grow, and that then he will do anything in his power to help such a one, just as he answered your appeal for his help for McKabe this morning."

"Mr. McKabe deserves help," she flung out quickly. "His fate came on him through us. And it was I who brought him into the danger—I went on the errand which resulted in his being detailed. I—"

She paused abruptly.

I might have suspected it before, but now I felt sure.

Why not? I asked myself. The girl was young—strong—daring.

McKabe, too, was a soul which lived and throve on

adventure. Why should not these two spirits find each other congenial?

Why should not some rapid course of events, such as had held us all last night, work the results of months in other circumstances and wake them to their mutual attraction?

The girl who sat opposite me in the taxi loved Dan McKabe.

"And Mr. McKabe will have all the help which Dual can give him," I gave her assurance. "Can you doubt it, Miss Lucile?"

"He is a brave man," she said softly, and I knew she meant McKabe. "And your friend, and mine—yes, mine, I am sure; is the most wonderful person I have ever known. Yes, I am sure he will do all he can, Mr. Glace.

"But, oh"—she struck her knee to emphasize her speaking—"he is fighting such a terrible power of evil! I know. I fought it, too, for years. How can we be sure?"

"Don't try." I responded. "Trust him. Do as I do. Go where he says. Do what he says. Leave the rest to him. Even now we are acting by his direction. See, we are at our destination."

The cab stopped.

Lucile straightened, and her parted lips grew firm. "You are right. He is the captain—we the soldiers. Thank you, Mr. Glace, for showing me the necessity for remaining calm.

"And do you know"—she fastened me with her eyes—"I believe in some way he looked for this move of theirs? I knew it this morning for a minute after I came back from the phone. He was not surprised."

I told the driver to wait, and we passed into the massive entrance of the Hall of Justice.

Last night had taught me the way to Connel's office, and I lost no time in seeking admittance.

My name and that of my companion brought us a ready entrance.

We came into the same room where we had sat in the early hours of this same morning, and found Connel, grim-faced, sitting at his desk.

He looked up and sprang to his feet.

"Miss Foote, Glace," he began quickly, "this is prompt-ness with a vengeance, and I'm glad to see you."

Himself he handed Lucile a chair.

"Dual sent us," I informed him. "He wants the verifi-cation of everything you told us. First, are you certain that McKabe is really in their hands, and that the thing is not a plant?"

"It's no plant," said Connel." Do you suppose Dan McKabe would hole up anywhere if he could get here to report? And if there was any doubt, this alone would make it certain.

"You must know, Glace, that there are two things a policeman never gives up while he can retain them—his revolver and his badge.

"Look at these."

In a manner almost dramatic he tossed a service revolver and a gold-and-silver badge toward me across the desk.

"McKabe's," he declared." Sent in this morning with their demand for the release of their jackals."

I heard Lucile Foote gasp sharply.

In a moment she was bending over the weapon and badge. Her finger touched the latter gently.

It had been worn by the man she had met last night for the first time. Even I thrilled at the sight of the "offices" of the captured man.

If I had hoped there might be a mistake, I knew now there was none.

"Who brought them?" I asked.

"Nobody knows," said Connel. "The cleaners found them wrapped up in the hall. The bundle was addressed to me. Here. It also contained this note."

He handed us a sheet of paper, covered with a penciled scrawl.

We read it, Lucile and I.

CAPTAIN CONNEL,

Detective Bureau,

Hall of Justice.

SIR:

Reference to your records will doubtless convince you that the enclosed are the regulation weapon and the official badge of authority of Detective Daniel McKabe, late of the China-town squad.

We regret the necessity of curtailing the activities of Mr. McKabe, but through circumstances with which he was connected, which resulted in your apprehension of the man, Homer Reich, and the woman, Anna Paulos, commonly known as "Greek Annie," we find ourselves obliged to do so.

We would beg to suggest that the matter can be arranged agreeably to both sides by the release of Reich and the woman within twenty-four hours. Failing this, we shall not

be responsible for the safety of Mr. McKabe. We hope that
you will be amenable to our argument as we realize that
McKabe is a man whose sudden death might be a serious
loss to your force.

At the same time, should you decide to attempt any
counter stroke, we shall feel compelled to return his body to
your doors as a sign that we mean exactly what we say.

I glanced at Lucile. She was pale as death.

I swung my eyes to Connel.

"There doesn't seem any chance for doubt," I began.

"None at all. They've got Dan," he said shortly. "They
picked him up somewhere around four-thirty as far as I
can find out."

"Then you have word from him as late as that?" I
inquired. Lucile had sunk into a chair.

"He spoke to a roundsman on Washington and Dupont
at four-twenty," said Connel.

"What sent him back there after we left? I thought he
was done for the night," I remarked.

"He was. That is, he should have been," Connel admitted. "I don't know why he went back. I suppose, though,
he wanted to see just how much of a dust the night's work
had kicked up.

"I'll say one thing for Dan, when he was on a case he
had no hours; he'd run on a scent till he dropped. I guess
he wanted to feel out the lay of things up there. You know
he posed as a Chinatown guide."

"But," Lucile cut in for the first time, speaking quickly,
"was his connection with your office really a secret? Don't
you suppose some of them knew he was a detective?"

"It looks like it." Connel smiled grimly as he replied.

"That isn't what I mean, exactly," said the girl. "I mean, didn't some of them know it for a long time? Are you sure about it? You know how subtle those yellow men are."

Connel nodded. A frown grew between his brows.

"There was one, and just one, chink up there who was wise to Dan's lay, Miss Foote," he responded. "But I hardly think he'd have been likely to tip it off."

"Why not? You know they're clannish. How do you know he wouldn't give Mr. McKabe's connection with you away?"

Lucile's voice quivered with insistent demand.

"I don't," said Connel, "but I don't believe it. Admitting all that you say as true. I would add that they are like our own American Indians in the return of a debt, either of good or evil. The man I mean is indebted deeply to McKabe."

Again my heart leaped.

I remembered Dual's instructions to learn if the missing man had been known as an official to any of the Orientals.

Here already things were leading up to that point.

I don't know if the fact struck Lucile or not, but she asked an immediate question.

"Who is he?"

"He's Kim Lee," said Connel slowly. "To be frank with you, Miss Foote, he is regarded by us as a mighty white man."

"Then he has no connection with the white slave organization?"

"Kim Lee? Good Lord, no! Say—I forgot you'd not been here for a long time.

"The man is a cosmopolitan, Miss Foote—educated, wealthy—a sort of merchant prince. Of course you know that none of those people use their real names for trade, but between you and me, Kim Lee is the main owner of the big shop on the northwest corner of Grant and Clay.

"The man's a millionaire and a philanthropist in his way. I think we are safe in saying he is not mixed up with the cutthroats who have made away with Danny McKabe."

"Good," I exclaimed. "That was another thing Dual wanted us to find out—whether McKabe was really known as a man of yours to anybody up there."

But Lucile asked the more personal question:

"How did a man like this Kim Lee become indebted to Mr. McKabe?"

Connel paused a minute and considered. "I may as well tell you the whole thing," he began at length. "I can't see how it will help Dan, but if Dual told you folks to ask—

"It was like this—Kim Lee has one kid—a boy—couple of years old. It wasn't born till the old boy had about given up hope of an heir, and he thinks more of that baby than of anything else, I guess, Chinese are great for boys, you know.

"There is one of Kim's hangers-on—a sort of body-servant—whose whole duty is to look after Kim's boy when he goes out. Well, one night when Mac was guiding a bunch of sightseers around town a half-shot chauffeur tried to drive his car from the Fairmount up above down Clay Street, and something went wrong with the brakes. Autos aren't very common in Chinatown, as you know, and the chinks don't keep an eye out like we do on Market.

"This old male granny and the kid were coming across Clay just as the cab came down the hill like a streak of grease. The old un lost his head, and for just a moment it looked like good night for the little feller.

"But Mac happened to be there. He made a jump, got the youngster, and just then the fender hit him.

"It rolled him across the street, and he hit his head and went out for a minute or two.

"Old Kim was inside his shop when it happened, looking out, and he saw it. He ran out, had Mac picked up, and carried into his own quarters.

"By the time he came to they had pretty well undressed him, and of course Kim got wise to the shield.

"Just the same, he told Mac that there was nothing he wouldn't do to pay him for saving the kid, and Mac told him to forget it.

"But that's why I don't believe he'd squeal on the boy."

I looked at Lucile and found her eyes on me. I think we both had the same thought—that here was the thing we had been sent to find out.

Here was a man—a Chinaman himself—who owed a life-debt to the man we were seeking to aid.

A warm little glow of courage woke up in my breast. I nodded to the girl, and for just a moment the merest smile flitted across her face.

She voiced a part of my thought at least:

"Would this Kim Lee be willing to help in this matter?"

"I hardly think so," Connel decided. "It would be going pretty strong to ask him to turn on his own people. So you can see where we are.

"I've taken every man from every case I could and sent him out. I'm doing all I can; but if they don't make good before it's too late, I'm going to spring this Reich and the woman.

"I don't care what they've done, Mac's life is worth a blamed sight more than getting them five or six years of a stretch."

He paused, rather red of face, and breathing hard.

"You mean you'll liberate that man Reich?" Lucile took him up.

"You bet," said Connel. "Strikes you pretty raw, I guess; but Danny McKabe is worth more to me living than Reich is in jail. I've known that boy for years. He's one of the best men we got."

He paused for breath and resumed more calmly:

"That's why I phoned you this morning. Your man, Dual, struck me as having put over a pretty smooth bit of work, and I thought maybe he could do something to help us before our hand is forced."

"He's going to," I cut in.

Connel looked somewhat relieved.

"This thing has got on my nerves," he said. "I'm sort of fond of Danny; he's a good boy. And, by God, he don't die if I have to spring a dozen 'cadets' to save him!"

He struck the desk with his fist.

To this day I don't know why I did it, but I rose and beckoned to Lucile. "Don't 'spring' anybody or anything till Dual tells you." I suggested to Connel as I started for the door.

Lucile rose and followed, and I held it open for her.

Just as we passed from the room I heard the telephone ring. Looking back I saw Connel lift the receiver from the hook.

We went back to our cab, and I told our driver to return to the hotel.

Lucile sat silent, apparently wrapped in study. I lighted a cigarette and smoked. I knew she didn't mind it.

Presently she spoke:

"Mr. Glace, I think I shall leave you when we cross Grant Street. What Captain Connel told us appeals strongly to me in a way. I think I shall go up to the store of this Kim Lee and see if I can find him.

"I have a feeling that if he knew of the danger to Mr. McKabe, he might be willing to help. A blood-debt is something no true Oriental ever forgets."

I shook my head.

"I hardly think I'd go up there alone." I objected.

"Nonsense," she retorted. "I know my San Francisco. It's broad daylight, and I want to see this Kim Lee."

"But Dual told us to return."

I didn't approve of this sudden determination of hers.

"He told *you* to return," she corrected.

I yielded.

After all, I thought, she had followed the game for a long time. She was no simple-minded girl, but a woman who had pitted her wits against criminal circles for years.

At Grant she got down, and I saw her melt in the crowd. Myself, I went on up Geary, dismissed my driver, and went up to our suite in the cage.

I entered to find Sheldon reading a paper, smoking one of his long, black panatellas.

"Where's Dual?" I asked even as I pushed shut the door.

"I don't know," said Sheldon. "He went out about five or ten minutes ago."

"Where to?" I tossed my hat on a couch and sat down beside it.

"He didn't say," said the colonel. "But he did say you was to stick around till you heard from him."

"Heard from him?" I repeated. "Mac, did he leave the hotel? I thought he told me to come back here and report."

"So did I," Sheldon admitted. "But after you left he sat down here and drew some cart-wheels on some paper, put spokes into 'em, and set down a lot of curlimecues around the rims.

"Then all at once he jumps up and looks at his watch an' goes into his bedroom, comes back with his hat, an' beats it out, after tellin' me to tell you to stick around. An', say, what have you done with Lucile?"

I told him briefly.

He eyed me with positive reproach.

"You let that leetle gal go chasin' off up there alone?" he demanded. "Son, I don't reckon you ought to have done that noways."

A rap fell on the door. I rose and set it open.

A boy stood before me with a package.

"Suite 205? Sign here," he said in a breath and shoved a receipt-book into my hands.

I signed and brought the package inside.

"What you got there?" Sheldon wanted to know.

I shook my head.

The package was large, and felt soft and bulky.

I began untying the strings, and presently had them loosened.

I laid the bundle on the table in the center of the room and pulled back the wrappings, and then I stood staring, while Sheldon came out of his chair with a strangled imprecation.

Inside of the strong manila paper which had concealed them were the suit, shirt, hat, and shoes which I had last seen on the person of Semi Dual himself, less than two hours before!

3

LUCILE IS TRAPPED

FOR A MOMENT I confess the thing gave me a distinct mental jar.

When I had left Dual sitting at the little writing-desk, and taken Lucile with me to the Hall of Justice, he had been wearing this same suit of gray tweeds, the gray silk shirt and the shoes with the gray cloth facings.

The hat I knew as his, of soft gray felt. Gray was a color he loved and often used in his wearing apparel.

Now they lay before me, with their wrappings curling up about them—but—they were neatly folded and showed no signs of violence in their handling.

So much I saw and then—

"Well, my Lord!" rasped Sheldon. "If they are Dual's rags, what in the name of time is he wearing?"

"He didn't change his suit before he went out, did he?" I asked in turn.

"Not unless he came back through a different door after he left here," said Sheldon. "I always thought I was a pretty good hand to notice a lot of little things, and I know he went in and got that there hat, just before he told me to have you wait around, and went out."

"And you don't know whether he left the hotel or not?"

It came to me that perhaps Semi might merely have taken a different room, for some purpose of his own—perhaps to secure absolute privacy.

"I don't know nuthin'," Sheldon almost whispered.

His face was drawn and worried.

"But if he did or didn't, why should he send back his clothes? He didn't take anything with him. My Lord, Glace—you don't suppose anything can have hap—"

"Quit that, colonel," I snapped. "No, I don't think anything can have happened to Semi Dual—not such as you mean. He hasn't been kidnaped or anything like that. If he had, why would they send back his clothes?"

"For the same reason they sent McKabe's shield and gun, like you said they done. They wanted to make us sure they had him. Now I suppose they'll be sendin' us in a note. Damn them! If they've done anything to Dual— Say! Don't you care a cuss about this business? You stand there and don't bat an eye."

I had been thinking. After the first shock of the thing I felt little fear for the man I had known for years.

Of course on its face it had a mighty funny look, yet I felt that if I were to look beneath the surface I would find rather some message of assurance than dread in this new turn of Semi's actions.

I knew from long experience that this strange man did nothing except from purpose well thought out.

Now, to all surface seeming he might be either a victim of the power he fought, or running about the streets of a city in an extremely light attire, or—he might be wearing some other form of apparel.

Right there I stopped.

Sheldon had said that Dual had set up several astrological figures, after I had left, had acted suddenly at the end of his calculations, and had left word for me to await a message from him.

On top of that he had sent back the suit he had worn when he left. The thing then was plain. Save for the surprise, I would have seen it before, as he doubtless intended that I should.

That pile of neatly folded apparel was a message to me— that Dual was moving, because necessity urged—that he was following what he deemed a most important clue— and that he was gone somewhere—in disguise.

I turned to Sheldon and smiled.

"Sheldon," said I, "after last night, when he stopped that mob of yellow fiends in the tunnel by the mere words he spoke, is he likely to walk out of here in daylight and be picked up and carted away? Something must have shown him that he could do more in the matter himself than he could accomplish by waiting."

"Showed him, how?" Sheldon inquired.

"Through the figures he set up after Lucile and I left."

"Them pictures he drew?" said Colonel Mac. "Honest, Glace, it gets my goat to see him set down and draw a few pinwheels an' then get up an' hand out the dope that something is due to come off. Holy smoke! He sort of makes a problem in figures of life.

"I asked him this morning what two funny things he set down stood for.

" 'Mercury and Venus,' says he.

" 'And what about them?' says I.

" 'They are in conjunction,' he said.

" 'And what does that mean?' I asked him.

"He looked up and smiled and said:

" 'That means that McKabe has an astral life insurance, colonel,' says he, an' just after that he goes out. Now, what do you reckon he meant by that?"

I laughed. I felt like laughing. I wondered if Semi had meant for the old mine-owner to tell me that.

"Mean?" I mimicked. "Lord! don't you see it, colonel? He meant that McKabe would come back safe and sound, and because there was some need of rapid action he went out to take hold himself."

A smile rippled the colonel's face. "Sure!" he agreed softly. "That's what I hoped he meant."

"Colonel." I explained, "the Mercury and Venus Dual spoke of are stars—planets. Roughly, Mercury stands for mind, intellect—or a person whose qualities are good. Venus stands for woman, or for womanly attributes. In conjunction they would mean that a woman would play a big part in McKabe's destiny, I think."

"Oh," said Sheldon. He lapsed into silence, which after a time he broke "Just the same I wish we knew where he went to. Waitin' always did get me all fussed up."

He slammed his cigar down on the end of the desk, where it sent up a thin curl of smoke.

"Where's Lily?" I asked, for the first time.

"In the next room. I made her lie down. Guess she's asleep," returned the colonel. "An' that reminds me. Where'd you say Lucile was going?"

"To see a man named Kim Lee."

"Chink, of course?"

Yes."

"I don't like it," he grunted. "An' I don't see as Lily needs two able-bodied men to stand guard over her, while that other girl goes it alone. I got to stretch a leg or go batty. What's the matter with your watching out here while I take a hike around. I kin try an' see if I can light on Lucile while I'm out. You got to wait for Dual anyway, son."

"Dual told you to watch Miss Lawton," I reminded.

"But you're here." He got up and reached for his soft Stetson hat.

"And I may be called away at any time at all," said I.

"Well, if you are, tell her to lock all the doors an' not let any one in," said the colonel. "I simply got to get out or bust."

"How do you expect to find Miss Foote?" I inquired.

He paused with a hand on the knob. "I'll just go up where you said, and scout about a bit," he explained. "I'll find it all right, an' if I can't I'll ask a policeman."

He opened the door and was gone.

I crossed to the little writing-table and looked down at the circle-marked sheets of paper Dual had left. I wished I could read them as he did, and know on what thread of meaning his action hung.

I looked out at the busy streets of the city, and all at once I thought of Connie. This was our honeymoon.

I smiled a bit ruefully at the thought. A fine honeymoon indeed, with my bride in Goldfield, Nevada, and myself standing here twiddling my thumbs!

I got out of my chair, went over to the phone, and asked for the Hall of Justice and Connel's office. I had determined at least to find out if anything more had developed.

After a slight delay the captain's voice came back to me.

"Hello!"

"This is Glace talking, captain," I told him. "Has anything new developed since I left?"

"No," he said shortly. "Your friend called me up just as you were leaving, but I suppose you know that."

"No, I didn't." Even as I spoke I remembered his lifting his receiver as I left his office. "What did he want?"

"Say, where are you?" Connel demanded.

"At the St. Francis," I returned.

"And where's Dual?"

"I don't know. He—"

"You don't know!" The wire fairly writhed under the captain's tone.

"Say, aren't you folks moving at all? He called up here and I gave him the same dope I gave you. What have you been doing?"

"I've been waiting," I explained. "When I got back here he had gone, and left word for me to wait. Just what did you tell him?"

"Why, about Danny's badge and gun, and that Kim Lee, and the rest of it," said Connel.

Kim Lee again. Dual now knew about Kim Lee beyond doubt. "Miss Foote went to see Kim Lee," I told Connel.

"Well?" He paused and I could hear him breathing harshly. I could picture him listening intently, his florid face more florid than before, under the anxiety and impatience he felt.

"She hasn't returned yet," I began.

"Hell!" Connel's phone snapped viciously into place, so that it rattled in my ear.

A sound from the bedroom, where the woman had slept, roused my attention.

I turned to find Lily Lawton, her face flushed with sleep, standing in the doorway, sweeping the room with her eyes.

"Oh, Mr. Glace, where is Colonel Mac?" she questioned, "and have they heard anything more about poor Mr. McKabe?"

"No," I told her. "I was just talking to Captain Connel. Colonel Sheldon went out some time ago. He got restless sitting still and waiting."

"It is so dreadful," she said, sitting down and dropping her clasped hands in her lap. "Mr. McKabe seemed like such a fine, brave young man, and I can't bear to think that he is likely to be killed for helping me. Isn't there anything, we can do?"

"Mr. Dual is working in his behalf right now," I explained.

"Oh, I'm so glad. Then we needn't worry, need we? Mr. Dual will save him and everything will be all right."

I found myself recalling something about the "faith of a little child."

Miss Lawton was childlike enough in all conscience for a woman of her years, and her faith seemed to be of the unqualified sort one finds rarely enough save in children. I could only add my sincere hope it would be justified.

"And where is Lucile—Miss Foote?" she wanted to know. "She is the dearest thing, Mr. Glace. She's so awfully good and kind. I might have been her own little sister, the way she talked to me last night. I'm not going to forget some of the things she told me, ever."

"She is working for Mr. McKabe, too," said I.

"I wish I could *do* things," she went on. "I feel so awfully useless, sitting here like this. I'm just a big baby, that has to be taken care of. I wish I could be a woman like Lucile and do things like she does, and not be afraid. But I know I'd be awfully scared, even to try. Why, I'm even afraid to go home and face the people who know me."

I had to admit that I could hardly blame her when I thought of gossip's tongue.

I drew my watch. It was three and after. Rather to divert her attention than anything else I asked if she would like some lunch. She accepted.

I put through the luncheon order and turned back from the phone. Lily had risen and approached the bundle of clothing on the table. As I turned she lifted the coat and inspected it closely.

"Why, this looks like Mr. Dual's," said she.

"It is," I replied in absent fashion.

"But he was wearing it this morning," she objected.

Briefly I told her about its coming back to Sheldon and me while she slept. She heard me with open-eyed wonder.

"And he didn't send any word with it?" she cried at my ending. "Not a single thing to say what he had done or where he'd gone?"

I shook my head.

She thrust a slim hand into pocket after pocket, took up the vest, the trousers, and shoes.

It shows what a state I had been in, not to have done it myself, but frankly I hadn't even thought of doing it at all. I stood and watched her, and saw her draw something from down in the toe of a shoe.

I was beside her before she had it unfolded and spread out—a small slip of paper on which were written words:

"Behold the Karma of Kim Lee."

I caught my breath. I had seen that firm script too many times to doubt the hand which wrote it.

All this time it had lain here for me, and I had been too blind to see it. It had taken the curiosity of a child to spread it for my reading.

Yet it told me all I wanted to know. Beyond doubt Dual had gone, like Lucile, to ask the payment of a Karmic debt.

"Is it a message?" inquired Miss Lawton as I stood with the slip in my hand.

I nodded.

"Good!" he exclaimed. "Then even I helped a little bit by finding it, didn't I, Mr. Glace?"

Again I nodded. To tell the truth I was disgusted to think of the hours I had sat with the thing unfound.

The luncheon came up and we ate. Lily prattled of any number of things, to which I replied without a great deal of interest.

We were still dallying at our meal when the door swung open without any warning and Colonel Sheldon came in, looking warm and worried.

He threw himself into a chair, drew out a kerchief and mopped his face of a slight dew of perspiration.

"I don't like it!" he burst out, "There's something funny about the whole blamed business. I went out of here an' I went up where you said. I kept an eye out, but I couldn't see any sign of Lucile.

"Then I went into the store you told me about and I asked a clerk for Kim Lee.

" 'I want to see your boss,' I said.

"She called a little sawed-off shrimp, an' I says, 'Are you Kim Lee?'

" 'Kim Lee?' says he. 'Oh, no—there is some mistake.'

" 'No, there ain't no mistake,' says I. 'I want to see Kim Lee, who owns this joint. Where is he? Lead me to him.' He looks kinder funny and shakes his head. 'There is no Kim Lee.' says he.

"Well. I chinned a bit, an' then I left an' I was mad. After a bit, though, I thinks maybe one of the other shops will wise me up, so I goes to two or three.

"An say, Glace—honest, not one of them places ever heard of this party. I reckon somebody gave Connel a mighty bad steer. I reckon there ain't no such man."

I thought of the paper in my pocket.

Of course Dual had obtained the name from Connel, as I had, but surely he must have found this man, or else where was he?

I took out the bit of paper and handed it to Sheldon.

"There may not be any Kim Lee," I retorted, "but Lily found this in one of Dual's shoes a little while ago."

The colonel studied it for a moment.

"More Karma," he said slowly at length. "Dual seems to have had this Kim Lee tip, too."

"And you saw nothing of Miss Foote?" I questioned.

"Nary hide or hair," said the colonel," but I found the shoofer who drove Dual away from here, an' where do you suppose he went?"

I shook my head.

"To a barber-shop!" The colonel lifted his hat and cast it on the floor.

"But there's a shop in the hotel," I exclaimed.

"I know it," rasped the old Westerner quickly." But he takes a cab, goes down the street to a shop, gets out, and sends the man back up here, an' he don't even go toward chink town, but *away* from it.

"An' that ain't all, either. When I was comin' back from up there, there was a yellow-faced mutt trailed me clear down to this here leetle park in front of the hotel. Then I gets tired an' I turns round an' tells him to take his foot in his hand an' beat it back the way he come.

"He pretended he didn't savvy, like they do, but he stayed where he was when I come on. I tell you I don't like it, Glace. I don't like it at all."

It seemed to me that the telephone snarled rather than rang.

I reached it on the run, caught up the receiver, and answered the call.

Connel's voice came back to me at once.

"Hello! That you, Glace? Say, have you heard from your man, Dual?"

"No, captain, I haven't," I confessed.

"Didn't expect you had," said the captain, and the tone he used held a sneer.

"Well, listen: You folks sure have made a hash of things to-day. A roundsman just sent in a package, which fell on his head from the second-story window of an empty building. It contained a watch with Miss Foote's name engraved inside, and a note to the effect that the girl has been grabbed by the same bunch that got McKabe!"

Like Lucile before me, I laid a steadying hand on the telephone-box.

Then, with exceeding care, I put the receiver back on its hook.

4

LUCILE TAKES UP THE STORY

MR. GORDON GLACE has asked me to take up the story of those strange events which took place during the day when that wonderful man, Semi Dual, fought the secret power of one of the most vicious bands of organized evil, and carry it on from that point where he ceased to be an eye-witness, until he comes into the action again.

I shall try to set down each important incident as nearly as it occurred, though of course, not being a writer, I shall probably not do it justice.

All my life, until I took up police work, I lived in San Francisco.

I knew my city, and I may add that in a sense I knew my Chinese.

Much of my first work was in my home city, among the people I was now fighting again. As a result I felt competent to begin the search for this high-caste Oriental who might hold the life of the captured man in his hands, if Connel were correct.

My knowledge of the Chinese customs and ethics, if one may call them so—told me that a man of that type would be the last on earth to forget such a service as McKabe seemed to have rendered, the more so since the child he had saved was an heir, arrived after it was well-nigh despaired of by its father.

There was one queer thing which made me decided upon the step I took in leaving Mr. Glace to go back to the hotel with his report alone.

Shortly after we had left Connel, and while I was debating the likelihood of Kim Lee's granting a request for aid, it seemed as though something began urging me to act at once. It was as if something actually led me to do what I did.

I know some people scoff at telepathic communication, but I have come to believe in it myself, and I know Mr. Dual says that it can be accomplished by those who know the proper methods, or by any one—unconsciously—under the stress of some driving circumstance or emotion.

And Mr. Dual has since told me frankly that he sent me a telepathic direction that morning. In view of all that happened, I would be the last one on earth to doubt.

Therefore, after becoming assured that it was the best I could do, I told Mr. Glace of my determination, overruled his objections, and left the taxi on the corner of Grant and Geary.

I stood for a moment until I saw him go on up toward Union Square and the hotel, and then turned to the long slope at the top of which Chinatown began.

It was a beautiful day, soft, and actually warm for San Francisco. All about me were the crowds of the busy city— people like myself, hurrying this way and that.

Girls and women passed me in street costume, wearing great bunches of violets and carnations and little "baby" roses, from the flower markets down on Kearny and Market.

Men of my own race pushed by on errands of their own forming. I stood for still another moment watching.

It seemed hard to realize even then that a few blocks north from here would plunge me into a maelstrom of foreign life—a totally different atmosphere of life—where the current of living flowed with a sluggish surface, which masked a seething passion of intrigue and plotting too deep to be discovered by any casual glance.

And it seemed doubly hard to believe that a man had been snatched from his every-day round last night, and now lay shut in some secret dungeon awaiting a fast-approaching doom.

That last thought set my feet in motion.

I don't know whether at that time I loved Danny McKabe or not. I am sure that the man's personality had taken a strong hold upon me the night before.

At first I had regarded him only as the ordinary city detective. It was only later, when we had won our point and were back at the Hall of Justice, and I saw him straightened from his assumed stoop, and met the full fire of his exultant eyes, that something waked in my heart and answered his look, in a way I had never known before.

Also I knew that when I heard of his capture, for just a moment I felt dizzy, and feared I would fall.

And from that time until I saw him again. I am sure he was never fully out of my mind.

And then, when I saw him—as I saw him—I knew— that there would never be any other man who would mean what he did to me, and that whether he cared or not it would be the same with me, in my heart, and I would never be quite the same woman again, unless he did care as I wanted him to.

Anyway, I began to walk up the slope of Grant Street, toward Clay and the great emporium of Oriental goods, which Connel had said was owned principally by Kim Lee.

I didn't hurry, for the simple reason that I did not wish to attract attention.

There was every probability, I knew, that some agent of the people who had captured Danny would be keeping an eye upon the movements of Semi Dual and those with him. They would hardly neglect so obvious a point.

I kept purposely in the most crowded part of the street, therefore, and slipped along without any apparent purpose, acting more as though waiting for some one to meet me than anything else.

Yet all the time I was keeping a keen put look, as I had learned to do, to see if I could detect any one who seemed interested in my movements.

I felt sure that our visit to Connel would be known. They would certainly keep the Hall of Justice under observation.

But I had left there with Glace in the taxi, and I had left it quickly of purpose. I hoped that if it had been kept under surveillance my movements might have escaped detection.

I went on up the hill, crossing street after street, losing little by little the touch of Occidental life and coming gradually into the fringe where the two edges of east and west met and mingled.

Then all at once, as it seemed, the faces on the sidewalks took on a yellow cast.

Slant eyes gazed out of them upon me, and the singsong of speech, the shuffle of slipper-shod feet, replaced the sharper accentuation of voice and step which marked the course of the race I had left.

So far as I could I now adopted the air of a sightseer merely walking along the narrow pavement, pausing now and then to stare through a window at the wares of the East on exhibition. I even went in one place and purchased a few little things to carry out the simulation, and came out carrying them in my hands.

After a time I came to the corner I had made my destination. The three-storied building of the store I sought rose with pagoda—like roof and tower before me.

The sunlight glinted from its great windows, behind which a wealth of beautiful things from the East found place.

I knew it well. To all intents and purposes it was a great department-store.

Its interior arrangement was mostly Occidental. Its saleswomen wrote your order or purchase in a duplicate book, and kept record of their sales as precisely as any shop-girl down on Kearny.

Its floor-walker—small, dapper, Occidental clad— would direct you to anything you might desire. It maintained a magnificent tea-room upon the second floor.

I had been in it dozens of times now and then, but never before had I heard of Kim Lee as the governing spirit of the place. That shows you how secretive those people are.

I wondered as I stood for a moment before it what luck I would have in reaching him today.

Then I pressed my lips and made up my mind that reach

him I would in one way or another. In a way, I put it up to
fate to lead me on from this point to the end.

I went inside the great plate-glass and bronzed-front
doors, and approached the dapper little genius who walked
here and there with clasped hands behind his hack.

"One moment, please," I said.

He paused, glanced up, and allowed a bland smile to
grow upon his otherwise impassive face. In a moment he
was all attention to what I might require.

"Yes, madam," he returned in excellent English.

"I have a message—a message of importance—to
deliver," I told him, endeavoring to impress him at the
outset, so that he might perhaps tell me what I wished. "It
is a message which I cannot deliver except in person. It is
a message for Kim Lee."

If I had asked for a paper of pins it would have been all
the same, I suppose. Not one muscle in the yellow face
changed under my scrutiny.

Yet I fancied that deep down in the brown eyes which
met mine fully a little something stirred, looked up quickly,
and dropped its head.

"Kim Lee, madam," he questioned softly—"who is Kim
Lee?"

"Surely *you* must know," I suggested, smiling as though
very certain of what I was saying. "He is the man who
controls this great business."

He shook his head.

"I am afraid there is some mistake," he responded. "I am
sorry. Madam must have the wrong store in mind."

But those narrow-lidded eyes were not quite steady, and
I knew he was lying.

"See," I said quickly. "I understand that Kim Lee is not known as the owner of this business; but *I* know, for I was told before I was sent, and the message is one of importance."

Even your Oriental has the human failing of curiosity. I thought the little man wavered.

"And did not the one who sent, madam, tell her how to reach this Kim Lee?" he inquired.

"Only to come here and say what I have," I returned. "Also, that it might be denied that there was a Kim Lee, but that I was to insist that I be taken to his presence."

He smiled faintly and shook his head.

"I do not know. I am sorry," he repeated.

Duty had, dragonlike, swallowed his curiosity.

But I was sure now, even though my heart failed. I had spoken on impulse, fitted my answers to his questions, gathered facts for my replies from his very actions themselves, and still he barred my way.

Yet I was sure that there was a Kim Lee and that this was his place, if only I could come upon a way to reach him. But it was not through this man. Forbidden to admit the slightest knowledge of the overlord, he would maintain his steady denial.

What, I asked myself, was I to do?

"It is the wrong store, I think, madam," he suggested when I did not speak.

After all, it was a combination of senility and childhood which stepped in to save the situation.

There was a stairway leading to the second floor and the tea-room, coming down on the central aisle of the main floor, where I stood with the man I had questioned.

Down these stairs as I waited, striving desperately to find some final argument to gain me my point, there came a small child in gaudy silken blouse and breeches and a small satin cap.

Behind him, shuffling from step to step, came an old man, at whose appearance I gasped. I was sure I had seen him before.

Hardly had the partial recognition filled my thought when the child cried out gaily.

Taking the last two steps at a bound, he rushed upon me and threw himself against me, clasping my thigh with two little, circling arms and smiling up into my face.

Recollection became complete. On the night before, when Mr. McKabe, Semi Dual, and the rest of us had walked down this same street, and later when Mr. Glace and I had strolled by while McKabe waited for Greek Annie to appear, I had seen this same old man and this same little child as I passed.

More, the baby then, as now, had run out and thrown himself against me, holding me fast; and I had opened my purse and given him a piece of money, and I had spoken to the old man, who had seemed to be watching the child.

Now beyond any doubt the little one seemed to recognize me, to judge by the smile on his face.

At the time it seemed to me that I acted purely on impulse in what I did. At least I am certain that I did not plan in any way to take advantage of the situation to further my own cause, because I did not dream that it could.

But I have always loved children, and the little midget, with his shining brown eyes, was in a way appealing.

"Baby!" I exclaimed, stooped, and lifted him into my arms. "Why, whose baby are you?"

He laughed and laid a hand on my face, while the old man paused just above the foot of the stairs and watched with a grin on his toothless mouth.

"Him like you velly well, maybe," he mumbled after a moment.

"Whose baby is he?" I asked, little expecting what was to follow.

The old man smiled and, without noticing a hasty gesture of the little man who had denied me, answered my question.

"O-o-h, him baby b'long Kim Lee. Kim Lee him papa."

If looks could have stricken him dumb I am sure his tongue would have ceased right then to wag.

The little man I had questioned at first shot him a glance which was black with anger, and burst into a rapid fire of speech.

The old man listened for a minute, drew himself up, and waved him to silence. He turned on me with a question.

"What for you wan' see Kim Lee, maybe? What for you come this house?"

"I have a message for Kim Lee," I told him, despite the frowns of the man beside me.

The ancient nodded. He came down, shuffled to my side, and took the baby from my arms.

"I go look, see?" he suggested. "I tell Kim Lee maybe so one white lady want see him. I tell him white lady what baby velly much like. You wait."

He turned back to the stairs with the child in his arms.

I think the man beside me called to him to stop, for

half-way up to the turn of a landing the old nurse paused and poured out a few guttural phrases in a tone which left nothing to the imagination.

Then he was gone, and I was left standing there beside the crestfallen little dandy, who had been exposed in the deception he had tried.

I walked over to a showcase and began looking at the articles it held. After a moment my companion took himself away.

Still, though fate had been kind, I was hardly prepared for what followed. Standing there waiting. I was surprised to hear a soft, resilient step come down the stairs.

I turned to confront the figure of a very striking man. He was tall, well built, with excellent head and features. His forehead was high and his nose distinctly bridged, and his lips firm in repose. Beneath his heavy brows his eyes were almost black and piercing.

He was wearing a loose blouse heavily embroidered in gold thread, a pair of snow-white trousers, white silk stockings, and white-and-gold slippers, and over his head was drawn a black silk cap, crowned by a scarlet button.

As I turned he was coming directly toward where I stood. Behind him shuffled the old man, still with the child in his arms.

He paused part way down the stairs, and stood looking on.

The newcomer advanced directly to me, paused, and spoke in well-nigh faultless English.

"You are perhaps the young woman who desired to speak with Kim Lee?"

I bowed. Some way it seemed the most fitting answer to the dignified accents of his question.

"I am Kim Lee," he replied. "My servant told me one waited below with a message. You are she?"

I inclined my head again.

"And I am Miss Foote. I was denied access to you," I explained. "I was about to give up the endeavor to see you when your little son came down and saw me and seemed to remember having seen me last night."

Kim Lee smiled slightly.

"I know," he replied. "Wah Lee has told me that last night little Kim ran to you on the sidewalk, and that he repeated it to-day. He forms sudden likes and dislikes."

He turned his face and smiled up at his son.

"But the message—what is it?"

"I must speak to you of it alone," I said.

"Indeed?" His heavy eyebrows were lifted just a little. "Then—"

He paused for a moment, stepped back, and bowed. "If you will precede me up the stairs."

Success! My heart leaped in my bosom. I had won my point, and I had seen the glance he threw to his child.

It was a glance which said more than my words could have done of love for the little Kim Lee.

As he requested, I turned and mounted the stairs, and he followed close behind me, old Wah Lee going ahead with little Kim looking back over his shoulder.

So we reached the third floor at last, and the old servant opened a door and led me into a small reception closet.

I caught my breath at that room.

Walls and ceiling—it was all done in blue-and-gold

lacquer, paneled and inlaid, and the floor was a blue-and-golden rug, across which writhed tangled dragons.

The furniture was of teak, inlaid with mother-of-pearl. It was gorgeous, magnificent, in keeping with the quarters of the man at my back, with his air of the man of the world and his well-modeled Manchu face.

Kim Lee passed me.

"Your pardon," he murmured, opened a door on the far side of the room, and stood back for me to proceed.

I entered a wonderful room. Unlike the abodes of the lower-caste Orientals, this place was lofty, airy, full of light.

Its floors were of polished woods in arabesque of inlay. Its walls supported wonderful works of tapestry art. Its windows flooded it with the gold of the outside day.

Swinging lanterns of metal worked in every conceivable design of fancy, surrounded the globes of the electrics which gave it light. The rugs on its floor were of the finest Persian and Turkestan. Cushions stiff with golden thread were piled about it.

Tabourets held jardinieres of cut and growing flowers and plants, and dwarfed varieties of vegetation brought from the distant East. Its furniture was of teak, for the most part massive and heavily carved, some of it plain, some of it trimmed with inlay of what seemed ivory to me.

Kim Lee led me to an immense chair of carved-out teak, and waited until I was seated. He took a place at a wonderful table of the same wood and raised his inquiring eyes to mine.

"And now the message, Miss Foote, if you please," he said.

I rushed into the story.

I told it all from the very beginning up to my coming to him. I gave him every detail of the action, even to my meeting with little Kim the previous night, and my speaking to old Wah Lee. And at the end I asked his aid in saving Danny McKabe.

He heard me through without so much as a quiver of an eyelid—just sat at the great desk-like table and toyed with a gilded paper-knife with a jade handle, and held his deep eyes on my face, as though to verify the truth of what I was saying by my expression.

Even after I had finished he did not speak for a moment, but sat still, tapping the paper-knife on the top of the table.

"And little Kim ran to you on the street, and to-day he came down as you were leaving and recognized you again," he remarked at length.

"Yes," I reaffirmed. "If he hadn't chanced to come just then I fear your man would have kept me from reaching to you."

"Kismet!" said Kim Lee. "It was more than chance, Miss Foote. It was fate which led you to me. I think it was fitting for fate to use the child which Mr. McKabe once saved."

My heart leaped. "Then you—" I began. A queer, little whistling squeak filled the room.

"Your pardon a moment," said Kim as he reached down and lifted a bronze mouthpiece from beneath the table and set it to his lips before lifting it to his ear. I saw it was a sort of artistic speaking-tube.

In a moment, still holding the tube in his hand, he swung back to me and fastened his eyes on my face.

"Miss Foote," he inquired, "do you by any chance know a Prince Abdul of Teheran?"

I am sure my face answered him before I spoke, but I told him the truth.

"I certainly do not know any one by that name," I replied.

"Because," he went on, "some one of that name is below stairs, asking to see me and inquiring if you are here. My identity seems to be growing well known."

"Yet I am sure I know no one by that name," I repeated.

Kim Lee considered thoughtfully for a few moments, swept his eyes about the apartment and back to my face, then lifted the tube to his lips and spoke shortly, and put the tube back beneath the table.

"I have directed them to bring him up," he told me. "At least he seems to be aware of your presence. His coming may have a bearing on your case."

He sat back and waited, picked up the little paper-knife, and began tapping the table once more.

Myself I sat in a state of mental confusion, asking myself what this new turn in affairs could mean, who Prince Abdul could be, and how he could know of me.

Had I then, I wondered, been shadowed to Kim Lee's door, after all? Was my mission known thus early? And, if so, how far could I trust the man who sat tapping on the desk with the jade-handled knife?

5

A DANGEROUS MISSION

AND THEN THE door opened and there entered a tall figure of a man in flowing robes of gold and purple. His head and smooth-shaven face was crowned by a purple turban, from which gleamed a great crimson ruby, holding a pure white aigret aloft. His face was strong, high browed, with aquiline nose and strong, firm lips and chin.

He paused just inside the door and bowed in slow dignity to Kim Lee, who had risen.

"Greetings, son of the Manchu," he said in English, paused slightly, and went on in a rapid flow of Chinese. A moment more and he had turned to me, smiling. "And to you, Miss Lucile. You have done well and prepared my way."

For a moment my senses reeled at the sound of his voice. Then I caught myself, and I wanted to laugh in the vast relief and elation which swept through my being. For I knew those soft bell-like tones as the voice of the man on whom so much depended, and, therefore, I knew that Prince Abdul of Teheran was none other than Semi Dual.

Kim Lee turned his eyes from Dual to myself and back to the tall figure before him. He bowed in as grand a manner as his guest.

"Welcome, Abdul of Teheran," he greeted. "Thou art from the East?"

I noticed the slightest movement of Semi Dual's hand before he replied. "I am from the East, Kim Lee, and I have traveled in the East. In the West, however, I am known as Semi Dual, of whom Miss Foote has told you ere this."

"And what brings Abdul to my humble place of dwelling?" queried the mandarin by the table.

"A duty," said Semi Dual. "An act of justice, and a demand for justice. I require thine assistance in a matter concerning the life of another. It is my desire to teach the wrong-doer that the lion's paw is as much to be feared as the jaw of the lion, and more." Again he made a sign.

Kim Lee started slightly. For just a moment his face showed a decided sense of surprise and he drew himself up to his fullest height. Quite slowly he bowed.

"Justice is eternal, and cannot be denied," he made answer. "The master has spoken, let the master speak."

"And this I shall tell thee, Kim Lee," said Semi Dual, resuming. "Thy name is in the stars and the stars change not in their rounds. The destiny of a man is linked with others, as the power of the stars is mixed and intermingled. On the scrolls of Karma there stands a debt against thee. Wilt thou pay?"

Watching him closely it seemed to me that the face of the Manchu twitched slightly. I am certain at least that he drew a deep breath before he answered, "I will pay."

"It is well." Dual advanced further into the room, gathered his purple robes about him, and sank into a chair across the table from Kim Lee. "The stars say that thou shalt repay, Kim Lee, and that all shall be well. Dost believe in the stars, my friend?"

"I believe," the Manchu responded. He also sank down in his seat, and I saw he was breathing quickly, as one shaken in his inmost being. He began to speak rapidly in Chinese.

I leaned back in my great teak-wood chair and a feeling of absolute assurance came upon me. I remember that as a child I have dreamed a bad dream and waked to find my mother above me, and felt strangely comforted and safe. In a way the feeling which flooded my mind now was like that, and I think, too, it was something like that which inspires the breast of a soldier in a crisis of warfare; when some beloved leader of a corps or brigade throws himself to the head of his men and cries them forward. It was a feeling of calm, undoubting confidence in the success of Semi Dual. Even the dramatic manner of his coming had contributed to it.

Now, as I listened to the voice of Kim Lee, and the calm, quiet answers of the strange personality who faced him, I recalled that Mr. Glace had told me that the man's father was really a high-caste Persian, and his mother a Russian princess, and that his father's first name had been Abdul; so that Semi Dual was in reality the Prince Abdul as whom he had been announced.

I had to admit that as he sat before me, clean shaven, clothed in the garments of the Orient, he certainly looked the part.

And there was something else. I recalled his entrance, the words he had spoken, the signs, barely noticed, which he had made, and one set of words he had used. To Kim

Lee's question he had answered, "I have traveled in the East."

Suddenly the meaning flooded my mind with the light of understanding. I knew that those words were sometimes used by members of a worldwide secret-order; that they constituted a sort of sign manual of membership; were both a question and an assurance. I saw now why Kim Lee had given that slight start of recognition, and had later addressed Dual as "the master." Both the Manchu and Dual were members of that order, and Kim Lee recognized Dual as a brother, and one, if I were to judge from his words, of a degree superior to his own.

I glanced at the two men bending toward each other across the great teak table. Dual had drawn some papers from his garments and spread them out on the top. He was pointing out various signs, which were drawn upon their surface, and Kim Lee was following his words and gestures with the closest attention. Suddenly, as I watched, he sat back and lifted his face to Dual's.

"Kismet! It is fate," he said for the second time since I had entered the room.

Dual smiled. "It is the mathematical precision of orbital motion, Kim Lee," he returned.

"Which is fate," said the other, with the very faintest of smiles.

"Also," said Dual with meaning, "it is the balance of the Karma which McKabe has built."

"You are an excellent collector of Karma, friend Abdul." Kim Lee shrugged slightly, "and your plan?"

"To inspire overconfidence and strike before it is shattered," said Semi softly.

A glance passed between the two men. In it I sensed the subtlety of the East, which makes the straightforward Western mind a thing of little avail against its scheming.

"And this you will do?" the Manchu inquired.

"By seeming to yield, while not yielding, by seeming to be overreached, while overreaching; by placing two souls in pawn, in order to redeem one, by striking in two spots at once, while seemingly bound hand and foot; by watching while seemingly blind, and hearing when no one seems to speak. Do I convey any meaning to your mind, Kim Lee?"

"I would hazard that I must supply the ears and eyes, at least."

"A good hazard," Semi assented. "Have you not several pairs to your hand at need?"

"And even fifty, if you need them," Kim Lee smiled grimly.

"Say half a dozen at first," said Dual.

The Manchu nodded and rose. "Excuse me, until I arrange the matter," he suggested, turned away and walked to another room, the door of which was veiled by a bit of golden tapestry.

Dual swung directly to me. "Mr. Glace went back to the hotel?" he inquired.

"Of course," I responded, surprised. "Haven't you seen him?"

He shook his head. "I left word for him to wait until I communicated with him. After you left I discovered that my own presence was needed in handling this." He paused and smiled slightly. "Hence the masquerade, which is not all masquerading. Back where I was born I am entitled to dress like this.

"But I donned these garments today, and sacrificed my beard and mustache that I might appear as an Oriental to any eyes which were watching, and the Prince Abdul did not drive here from the St. Francis Hotel."

"Mr. Glace didn't want me to come up here, but something simply drove me," I told him.

Again he smiled in quiet understanding. "That something was your fate, and my desire that you do so," he said slowly.

"Your desire?" I repeated. Here he was confirming what I had half suspected.

"Exactly," he returned. "Glace has told you how I call him at times by a telepathic power. This morning I sent you such a message to come on up here. Instead of calling, I drove, that is all. I wanted you to come here and tell your story, and begin the working on the mind of the man who must help us. You did your part well, Miss Lucile."

"And how will it end? Do you know?" I cried out, leaning toward him. "Have your stars told you the end of it all, Mr. Dual?"

He lifted his gray eyes and gazed fully into mine. In that gaze it seemed to me there was a knowledge too deep for words; a confidence, a purpose, which darted out and fell over me like a mantle, wrapping me in a blind faith of assurance, which held me from then to the end.

"Thou shalt gain thy heart's desire, Lucile," he said very softly, yet so that each word seemed to sing into my very soul and find lodgment, and live and echo long after he had spoken. "Be thou of good courage to the end."

The golden tapestry lifted from over the door and Kim Lee came back before I could speak further. But I took his words to my heart and felt them send a warm glow throughout me. Surely I knew that Dual would not speak such words without a full consciousness of their ultimate meaning. I sank back in my chair again and gave myself up to wondering what Danny McKabe was thinking about; and after a bit I found myself asking myself the question if perhaps he was thinking of me.

I felt the blood rise in my cheeks, and the thought was not at all displeasing.

Kim Lee was speaking to Semi Dual. So far as I could judge from the expression of the latter's face the former was detailing to him what action he had taken toward furthering the progress of the matter.

Once or twice, while he spoke, Mr. Dual nodded as though satisfied with the things Kim Lee had done. Abruptly at the end he turned and glanced once more in my direction.

"Miss Foote, have you eaten since breakfast?" he inquired.

I shook my head. To tell the truth I had not even given a thought to food in my desire to gain the help of this merchant prince of Chinatown.

Dual smiled, in the way I had grown used to. "You had better," he advised. "You may need food before this matter is ended. Unless one knows how to conserve his strength, the vital forces ebb fast."

He spoke to Kim Lee, and I felt the eyes of the merchant swing to me quickly and as quickly drop away. At the end of Semi Dual's request, as I judged it to be, he nodded, rose and again disappeared behind the golden tapestry.

Mr. Dual took me into his confidence to an extent. "Kim Lee has summoned some of his dependents, men bound to him in one way or another, who will do what he says and ask no questions. You of the Occident can know little of the absolute obedience which the servants or dependents of an Oriental will render to him, with no reason save his verbal command.

"It is a remnant of the old vassalage which used to obtain even in Europe in the middle ages, when the overlord held the right of the high justice, the middle and the low. To these men whom Kim Lee has summoned his word is the supreme law. They will do what he tells them in defiance of any or all other laws. He is their lord, and they are his slaves in duty at least.

"A bit ago I spoke to Kim Lee of the way in which I intended to strike for Mr. McKabe's freedom. I shall use these men of his to find out all details for me, to carry word, to act as spies. There could be no better agents to watch the band we are opposing than these yellow men of their own race, who may pass and repass and be unsuspected of aiding us in our work.

"Now Kim Lee has gone to order you a bite of luncheon, and I want you to fortify yourself against my need of using you further before a great time has passed. From now on I want you to do only as I shall direct you, and feel neither fear nor surprise at what it may be."

"I will do anything—anything within my power to help save Mr. McKabe," I told him quickly. At that moment I felt buoyed, uplifted, unafraid.

"Spoken like a true woman," said he. "You will be of great service ere long. For a vital reason I cannot tell you more at present. In a sense I must ask you to blindly obey."

He made almost a question out of the last phrase, by inflection. I raised my eyes and looked into his once more.

I will obey any order you give me," I promised. "I will be like one of Kim Lee's coolies. I shall do what you say without question."

"Child," said he very softly, "in that way I give you my promise; the stars themselves shall lead you to your heart's desire."

"And what is my heart's desire?" I asked on impulse.

"The life and freedom of the man you love," said Dual.

Again the blood mounted to my face. The assurance with which he spoke was disconcerting to say the least. Dual smiled softly at my confusion. "Peace. You are the chief instrument of his saving. Remember my words and be strong."

Kim Lee came back, followed by a servant with a tray. This he placed on a small table and carried to my side. It was a luncheon of cold meats, a salad, some cakes, and a pot of tea.

The servant bowed and retired backward out of the room. I turned to the food and ate, and found I was hungry. I think it was Semi Dual's assurance which allowed my appetite to assert itself, for up to then I had not felt any conscious need of food.

While I ate there came the sound of feet in the little reception closet. A rap fell on the door. Kim Lee spoke shortly and I glanced up to see the door open and admit six men. They were Chinamen, such as we associate with the word in this country.

Seen together there was little in common between them and the man who sat at the teak-wood table. They were flat faced, flat nosed, slant eyed, clad in nondescript apparel. For the most part they were of small stature and thin boned. Only the last of all was large, big framed, with a stronger cast of feature than the others.

They came in and bowed low before Kim Lee, who sat impassive at the table until one and all they stood before him, awaiting his pleasure.

These I knew were the men he had sent for; his retainers, if one might call them by such a name. They were the men who bowed to his word in all things, went where he told them, and did what he said and looked to him for protection in their acts.

Kim Lee's men! Seen on the street no one would have thought them other than the many Chinamen who thronged the district. There was nothing about them of distinction. Only here in this room they bowed themselves to the floor and stood in silence waiting the word of command from the one who had called them. There was something almost sinister about it to me.

Suddenly it came over me that these men would go out from this room and rob or kill or kidnap with the same unquestioning calm with which they stood waiting—because the overlord had so directed.

Kim Lee waved his hand to their little group. "Here, O Abdul, are your ears and eyes," said he.

Dual swept them with a slow glance, before which they ducked their faces, half minded to bow to him also.

"They will suffice for the present," he accepted. "And the larger man, Kim Lee; is he fit at the need to seize another and still his outcry before it is uttered?"

"He is a veteran of wars," said Kim Lee. "He is one of my tong."

I repressed a shudder. I knew the half-spoken meaning of those words. I looked into the sinister face of the big man who stood silent beneath the scrutiny of his master and Dual. It was a cruel face in every line of its features, even down to its little snaky eyes, and the thin, pallid lips which lay together in an almost colorless line.

This I felt sure was one of the hatchet men of the tongs; one of those paid mercenaries of the Chinese who slay by order in the most cowardly of fashions. They live on the quarrels of the various societies of their race, and live by taking life for a price. In that light a terrible sort of humor seemed to lie in the question of Semi Dual.

Dual nodded. "Good," he made comment. "If there is need, he may prove his strength." He turned to the men and began to address them in their own language. Once or twice he paused as if for answer, and received a servile assurance in a sing-song whine. Seemingly he told off three men to some task, for they bowed low to him and their master and fled crabwise from the room.

There remained two of the others and the grim-faced hatchet man.

Dual spoke to the two coolies. To my utter surprise he directed their gaze to me. By his direction, as it seemed, they came closer to where I sat, stood and stared at my face, as if fixing it in their minds beyond any chance of forgetting. I lifted my head and gazed back into their beady brown eyes.

"If you will stand now, Miss Foote," Semi Dual prompted.

I gave him the obedience I had promised.

Full of wonder at the request, and his purpose in having these two men study my face and figure, I raised myself from my seat and stood while they walked about me, studied me, as a modern woman might inspect a manikin in a new-style creation, and finally retreated to their places.

I glanced at Dual, and he nodded me back to my seat. I sank into my chair, filled a cup of tea, and drank it.

Dual was addressing the two again. His voice ran on, rose and sank, drooned and strengthened, in every seemingly possible inflection of the difficult Chinese tongue. I found myself marveling at his mastery of the language, and told myself that after all it was but another manifestation of the unbelievable things this incomprehensible man could do.

In the brief time I had known him, days merely since I had met him in Salt Lake, I had found that he understood and spoke English, Italian, Greek, and now Chinese.

The two men he was addressing whined what I took to be an affirmative assurance. Dual nodded to Kim Lee, and their master waved his men from the room. At a further word from Dual the hatchet man also made his exit and left us three alone.

I didn't understand a word of what had been said, but I felt sure that the first steps in the program Dual had mapped out had been taken. He met my eyes and smiled and nodded.

"We are beginning to act at last," he said.

Again he spoke to Kim Lee. The merchant listened closely, frowned slightly, and made a short response of what I took to be objection, because Semi Dual leaned toward him and replied in hurried accents which seemed charged with driving force.

For perhaps a moment the Manchu drew back before the volley of words. At the end, however, a slow smile creased his stern face, and he nodded in acquiescence.

While I watched he drew a massive signet from a finger of his left hand, and cast it on the table between Dual and himself.

"Will that do, Abdul?" he questioned in English. "To one who knows it means no little, as you may observe."

Dual lifted the bauble and inspected it closely. He laid it down and nodded. "Yet it should be certified beyond doubt. Kim Lee—say a bit of writing."

Kim Lee pondered a moment. His eyes lifted from the ring to the calm face before him, and I thought something like admiration was lurking in their brown, black depths. Without a word of spoken reply he opened a drawer in the table, took out paper, a cake of India ink, and a pencil-brush.

Moistening the latter in a glass of water, which he poured from a carafe, he took a long slip of paper and began marking a column of ideographs down its length. At the end, he lifted it and waved it to dry it of moisture, reached out his arm, and laid it face up before Dual.

Semi read it, or seemed to read it, bowed a grave acceptance picked up the ring, and wrapped the paper about it. It lay on the table between them. Kim Lee in turn took it up.

He rose and crossed to where I was sitting. He held out the tiny packet. "Take it, Miss Foote," said he in a voice which seemed heavy with meaning. "Take it, and keep it, and guard it as you have guarded your virtue. Conceal it in a place of safety about you, and use it only should your life appear to be in actual danger. Few women have been so honored. Be discreet in its use."

I wanted to ask him what it was, but something held my tongue. I remembered that Mr. Dual had said I must act blindly. I took the packet he extended and laid it in my lap. Then I took off my hat and loosened my hair. I have heavy hair, thank goodness, and I gave thanks for it then. I loosened a braid and laid the paper and the ring within it, and braided it up again while the two men watched. Then I coiled up my hair and pinned it, and turned the back of my head to their view.

"Does it show?" I inquired.

"Not at all," said Semi Dual.

"A woman of wit," said Kim Lee.

"And of purpose," Semi added. "For three years she trailed this man Reich, of whom she told you."

"You choose your tools as a master builder," the Manchu responded. "Good tools assure good ends."

Dual smiled. "If properly used, Kim Lee."

He rose, and in turn came over and faced me. His hand, thrust into the breast of his robes, came forth and brought an ugly little automatic pistol into view. He handed it to me.

"Lucile, my child," he announced, "the hour is at hand for you to act. Take this and carry it with you. Hide it where you may keep it under any ordinary search. Use it only in case it is a final resort. I give it to you only to give you a sense of safety—that you may feel prepared.

"What you are to do I may not tell you fully; you must act on trust of me. But this much I shall say in order to assure your success. You will leave here and go into the street. When you get there act as one distressed. Let your face, your walk, your figure itself, express failure in your mission. Walk slowly along the street in any direction your fancy takes you. At the same time seem to be watching— seeking—trying to find some leading, which you almost despair of finding.

"Lucile, are you brave enough, are you strong enough, to do this thing and not falter?"

I rose and stood before him, and looked up to his face. "Yes," I declared, and put out my hand. "Give me the gun."

In that moment I had made up my mind to follow his directions and meet whatever might come with a faith in his ultimate success. But I did not accept on impulse. I had seen enough, heard enough to realize that I was being deliberately sent out on a dangerous mission. Just what or where I did not know.

Right now there seemed to be little "where." But I saw that the men who sent me had taken what seemed like great precautions to insure my safely and success, and I did not hesitate in my mood of the moment to trust life itself in the hands of Dual.

He smiled. I felt the cool metal of the weapon in my palm. "You are brave, Lucile," he said gently. "Continue to be brave."

I was wearing a dress with a low throat. I turned away from Dual and Kim Lee, opened the neck still farther, and thrust the little automatic down inside my waist. My experience with the police had shown me that it was a place where a cursory search would miss it. I had known money and jewels to be so concealed by female thieves.

In a moment I turned back and picked up my hat. "I'm ready," I announced.

"Venus and Mercury draw to conjunction," said Semi to Kim Lee. He took me by the hand and led me to the door which gave into the little reception closet. "You go to the destiny of woman," he whispered, and set the door ajar.

I passed out. In the closet itself I found the grim-faced hatchet man still waiting, sitting silent, his arms folded on his breast. He neither looked up nor glanced in my direction. I opened the outer door and let myself through.

Down-stairs I looked at my watch. It was almost three o'clock.

6

LUCILE IS CAPTURED

I PAUSED INSIDE the main entrance of the store and looked out.

Now that I was about to take the first steps upon the blind mission to which I stood pledged, I confess that I found my breath coming with an unwonted quickness. It was not that I doubted, but just that the uncertainty of what I was expected to do hurried my pulses and keyed my nervous system to a higher tension.

Presently I drew a deep breath, pushed the door open, and let myself out.

Just what was I going to do? I glanced to right and left.

"Walk in any direction you fancy," Dual had said, and that was all. I recalled his direction to appear uneasy and partly discouraged. I let a droop creep into my shoulders and glanced furtively about me again, in keeping with the part I was to play. Then I turned to the left and moved off north toward Washington Street.

As I walked along I thought busily to myself. Beyond any doubting, it seemed to me, I was playing, the part of a decoy. Dual and Kim Lee were from deliberate purpose throwing me out to the street in order that I might be observed by any who were watching.

Therefore, I was to seem confused and act as though I were blindly searching for something to give me a leading to the person I sought. I remembered what Semi Dual had said about creating an overconfidence in the minds of those he fought, and then striking before it was shattered. Surely then my attitude was to be used to speak to those others of a discouraged endeavor on our part in the matter of Danny McKabe.

I went slowly with drooping shoulders and downcast eyes, but all the time I was watching to see if any one had seemed to observe me. All about me were the slant-eyed denizens of that part of the city, with a sprinkling of the slum element on whites. But there was nothing to excite suspicion.

The sun of a mellow afternoon lay over the district, painting its gaudy squalor with a painful distinctness.

I reached the doors of the restaurant where we had first picked up Greek Annie the night before. Its gilded entrance, its dead lanterns and streamers looked tawdry in the open light of day. Only the flowers on its balconies high up were the same as on the night before.

I paused before its doors and looked around. Strive as I would, I could see no one who seemed to take any interest in my proceedings.

Of what use was this aimless strolling? I asked myself. Yet Dual had directed my footstep. I answered my own question, and surely he had a definite purpose in what he did.

It came to me that somewhere in my near vicinity the two followers of Kim Lee, who had taken their mental photograph of myself, must be lurking. I set myself the task of picking them out, and I failed. Nowhere in the faces of those who shuffled past me could I find one I could recognize, or who seemed to recognize me.

Yet I felt them. Subconsciously I knew that they were trailing my course, and I felt also that it was by Semi Dual's orders that they did so.

In that moment it came to me that, perhaps, I might be a guide as well as a decoy. What if the two were to follow my course and see where I went and report back to Kim Lee? What—and my heart leaped at the thought—if I were to guide them to the prison of Danny McKabe itself? Yet, how could I? I of all people had little idea where he might be hidden; in what warren digging of this place he might be held.

Still, the thought set me moving. At last I could inspect the course over which we had traveled last night. There was the theater through which we had entered the underground tunnel, and the place lower down on Washington Street where we had emerged through a shop and come out once more to the surface.

Some impulse beyond any reason urged me to go down toward that shop and see what it looked like to-day. I yielded.

As well go that way as any other, I reasoned. I had been assigned no direction. I turned and walked on in the way I had been going, and hardly had I turned when I knew I was under observation.

You may know how it is. You may not be able to see the one whose eyes are fastened on you, and yet some strange, latent sense seems to wake and cognize the fact of another's inspection. You can actually feel the glance impinging on the back of your brain, as it seems.

That was the feeling which swept me as I went forward now.

I paused and looked back. The life of the sidewalk was the same as a moment before. I turned and went on, and again I felt it—the sensation of hostile eyes fastened upon me as I walked.

All at once I began to tremble. I wasn't afraid. I am sure of that. Time and again I had been in more perilous situations, so far as I could see. I think in was the unknown quality of the entire affair, the air a mysterious undercurrent of intent, the sense of going somewhere and doing something, outside of my conscious volition, which gripped me and made me shiver as I walked along, and felt those unseen eyes which watched me as I went.

I reached the corner of Washington, and paused again. Then I crossed the street and went on down the hill toward the door of the shop where we had come out last night. It was just ahead of me when I stopped and stood staring on down to where the great gray pile of the Hall of Justice reared itself at the foot of the slope on Kearny. It was only half a block away.

I could see its shadow falling across the street I stood on as the sun struck it slantwise to east and north. I wondered what Connel might be thinking of now, and if he had held Reich and Greek Annie until this hour or turned them loose, as he had threatened.

A step sounded behind me, and I whirled. But I faced nothing more startling than a young man, nattily clad, even to a small, swagger cane which he carried. He was of a round-headed, florid type, with a stubby mustache over full red lips, and close-cropped, reddish-brown hair. All in all, he reminded me of an English type of manhood, and his words seemed to confirm the surmise.

"Pardon me, miss." He lifted his hat with a neatly gloved hand. "Are you acquainted up here? You see, I was looking for the Chinese telephone exchange, and I can't understand the beastly pidgin these chaps speak at all. I rather wanted to see the place. They tell me it is unique in its way for this side."

Inwardly I laughed at my nervous starting. The man's manner was deference itself. I pointed back up the way I had come.

You can hardly miss it," I replied. "If you'll just go up nearly to the corner—"

The man I was directing lurched against me. Apparently in seeking to turn and follow the line of my hand's indication he had slipped or stumbled. He staggered diagonally forward and struck me so that I, in turn, lost my balance and must have fallen save that he caught me quickly, even as he recovered himself.

And in that moment, as he seized me and seemed to be dragging me back to a secure footing, I saw a smaller figure rush forward, dragging a flapping something from underneath its blouse.

It had all come so quickly. It was so totally unexpected that for just a moment I did not understand. The shock of the man's impact against me, the lift of his hands as they held me upright, the darting attack of the smaller assailant, seemed for an instant to deprive me of the proper power of action, of which I stood in need. And by then it was too late.

The flapping object which I had seen swung up and descended in the choking, smothering folds of a cloth about my head and face.

I sought to ward it off, and found that my arms were held beyond freeing. I sought to cry out, and tense fingers gripped my throat. I felt myself lifted in muscular arms and borne swiftly upward. A door slammed smartly shut. The sound of board flooring came to my ears as I was carried onward.

There was a pause, another door shut more softly, and I felt myself lowered to a sitting position, with strong hands on my shoulders, holding me fast. "Got her, all right," said a voice, speaking in English.

"Tally," said some one else with a chuckle. "The score stands even."

A singsong broke in with a rapid chatter.

"And that's right, too," said the first speaker. "We haven't any time to stand here chinnin', an' this ain't the place for it. This dame goes to the chief for a little third degreein'. Wait a mo'."

The cloth was shoved up from my face slightly so that a faint glimmer of artificial light came to my eyes from below its edge. Some one forced my mouth open and slipped a cloth gag into my jaws, tying it behind my neck. The cloth was pulled down, some one seized my wrists and secured them behind me, thrust a hand under my arms, and lifted me to my feet.

"Come on," directed a voice shortly. "Mind the steps."

We went forward and downward, along what seemed

to me like a steep flight of stairs. Presently we reached the bottom, and I felt earth beneath my feet. I knew that once more I was in the underground tunnel through which we had come last night, or at least in a similar one. The man who held me walked forward quickly, and almost dragged me along.

I suppose you think that now I was really frightened. But, strange as it may appear, I was perfectly cool. Hardly had I felt the hands upon me, felt myself lifted and carried away, than it came upon me that this was a part of Semi Dual's design.

Something within me seemed to cry out: "This is the thing that was to happen. Thus shall you serve the end desired."

An, I remembered the words Dual had spoken. "Be of good courage, to the end." Also I recalled what he had said of appearing to be overreached while over reaching. It certainly looked to me as though his plans were working as he wished, for most surely those who had seized me must regard my capture as a most important move.

As a result I went forward along the underground passage without any sensation other than a firm determination to meet each fresh event with a bold front and see to baffle my captors in every way I could.

I had hardly reached this conclusion when the man who led me spoke.

"Well, this is far enough for us, Sing. You take her on to the chief. If she gives you the slip she can't get out till you grab her. Tell the chief this skirt seems to be th' only one of their bunch who was trying to put anything over. That old wild West guy scouted about a bit, but Wong followed him back to the hotel. S'-long!"

There was a change of hands on my arm. I heard two pairs of feet retreat, and then a more talonlike grip was urging me forward. I went without resistance. At least I had learned a little. They were in ignorance yet as to Dual's actions, and Colonel Sheldon had evidently made a trip to Chinatown.

A little chuckle of delight at this proof of their lack of knowledge welled up in my throat and died without a sound. I walked forward as fast as my guide could lead me.

We twisted and turned, and after a while we paused once more. I heard the sound of knuckles on wood, and after a time it appeared that a door was opened and we entered a carpeted room, to judge by the feel of the surface beneath my feet.

The one who led me pushed me into a chair and spoke to some one else.

We waited. There was no sound whatever. I could hear the faint breathing of the man who stood above me. Then a door closed and footsteps came nearer. Some one, who, I fancied, must be the one referred to as the chief, addressed the one who had brought me:

"Have you searched her, Sing? Is she armed?"

"I do," grunted my guide. I felt his hands sweep over my body, pressing and patting, drop to my hips and the edge of my skirt, lift the latter, and examine the tops of my shoes.

"No fin'," he announced at the end.

"Ungag her," the newcomer directed.

The strings at the back of my neck were loosened and the gag dragged out of my jaws. I closed them with a very marked relief. Things were not going so badly. I had been searched, and the weapon and the package were still in my possession. I settled myself more comfortably in the chair, so as to ease my bound wrists, and waited.

"And so your mission proved a failure, Miss Foote," said the voice of the man who had entered.

I held to my resolution to meet him boldly. "Did it?" I returned.

"So it appears," said he.

"It may to you," I responded quickly. "If you'd have your servant remove this strangling cloth, I might be able to view the matter better."

He chuckled. "Kept your nerve, eh?" he remarked. "Good! Well—under the circumstances I fancy it can be arranged. I rather liked your looks the only time I saw you. Just a minute."

There was a pause; then hands fumbled at the cloth and dragged it off. I looked about me.

I sat in a well-furnished room, lighted by a great opalescent globe above a central desk. About the walls of the apartment were chests of drawers and filing cabinets. A typewriter stood on a special table, and behind it was the door of a vault with a combination knob. Save that there were no windows, I might have been in a modern office.

In a chair against one wall a figure sat huddled. It was that of a good-sized Chinaman, and I fancied it was the man called Sing.

A footfall came from behind me, and a tall man, slender, lithe, with iron-gray hair brushed straight back from a high, narrow brow, came around to the desk and sank into a swivel chair beside it. He had drawn a white silk kerchief about the lower part of his face, and above it a pair of greenish-yellow eyes peered directly at me.

He was immaculately dressed, even to a pallid tuberose, which lay on his coat's lapel and at which he now and then sniffed, inhaling its heavy perfume. He sank down and lay back in his chair, which tilted beneath him.

"And how does the situation appear to you now?" he inquired.

"Not exactly what I expected," I replied.

"Enough quibbling!" he snapped sharply. "I have been at some pains to gain your presence. Now I want answers to my questions, not evasions. What did you seek to accomplish in that store to-day?"

"I was after information," I told him as quietly as I knew how.

"Did you get it?" He leaned forward and shot it at me.

I shook my head.

The flesh about his greenish eyes wrinkled. I fancied he was smiling beneath the masking silk of the handkerchief.

"My reports led me to imagine as much," he rejoined. "And did you learn anything from Connel?"

"Just how do you mean?" I asked.

"Did Connel tell you what he intended to do—or what he knew? Speak up, girl. I'm not in the habit of asking a question twice, and you want to remember you're no more than any other piece of female flesh in my eyes, despite your exceedingly pretty face. Now, come across, if you know what's best for you. I know you for the police agent you are, and I know you saw Connel this morning. Now, what did he say, and what is he trying to do?"

My mind was busy while he was speaking. Into it there

flashed Dual's words about overconfidence. On the instant I saw a way to help this man to an unwarranted sense of security and triumph.

"I don't think Mr. Connel knows anything at all," I made answer. "I did see him, and I did have a talk with him. He told me that unless something turned up he would release Reich and Creek Annie before the time limit expired."

The man chuckled. Once more he tilted back in his chair.

"Connel knows what he is up against," he said. "And what is this wonderful friend of yours who grabbed Reich and Annie doing? Come, girl, let's have it all."

"When I saw him last he was sitting in a room with a luncheon tray, and talking about seeming to be bound hand and foot," I returned slowly. It wasn't exactly the truth, but it was near enough.

The man actually laughed. "And so you tried to go it alone? In a way, I admire your nerve. Well, if Connel adheres to his sensible resolve, everything may end very well. If he does, McKabe and you will go free."

"And if not?" I questioned.

"People who stand in our way must take their chances," he answered me softly. "Your one chance would be to throw in with us."

"I'd die first!" I hissed out, before I gave my answer a thought. "Why, it was you who dragged my sister to her death—you and your Reich!"

"As you will," he said without any apparent feeling. He turned to the Chinaman in the chair. "Sing, isn't that a watch at Miss Foote's belt? Get it. I may want to use it as confirmatory evidence for Connel."

The Chinaman rose, came over, and tore my watch, with

its fob and safety clip, from my waist. Crossing, he laid it on the desk. The man in the swivel chair spoke again.

"I shall have to detain you until Connel makes up his mind," he announced. "I may as well advise you that resistance is vain. Permit me to wish you good day."

He rose, spoke to Sing in Chinese, and turned through a door on the other side of the room.

Sing came back to my side, stooped and picked up the cloth which had muffled my head and face, thrust the gag back into my mouth till it sent a wave of clammy sickness through me and I retched with a nausea beyond my controlling, threw the cloth over my gasping features, and tied all fast.

I heard other footsteps approaching. Some one dropped at my feet and bound my ankles. I was picked up and carried I knew not where.

After a time I was laid down, and I heard a sound as of something hollow being dragged toward me. I was picked up and lowered into something. My senses told me that a narrow wall confined me. I thrust out my elbows and touched what seemed like wooden walls. What little light seeped through the cloth on my face, faded. I heard the sound of a hammer driving on wood above me. And I knew that I was being nailed up in a box, or a case of some sort.

A guttural command followed the blows of the hammer. There came a grunting and straining. The box which held me moved. I felt it sway and swing as it was carried by what I supposed was a band of coolies. There came a sliding, grating sound, on the heels of a surging upward heave, and then more jolting motion. Through the cracks of the box I caught a breath of fresher air.

The jolting and rattling of wheels went on. I became convinced that I was being taken somewhere in a wagon—probably one of those nondescript express-carts which stand about the quarter, picking up a living as best they may.

It was the most trying thing I had ever known. To be there, with each jolt and jar cutting the cords on my wrists and ankles into my flesh, powerless to move or turn, unknowing to what fate I was being driven, taxed all the faith I had felt in the words of Dual. The instinctive love of life, which is animal impulse, cried out and asked if, after all, this was what could have been intended when I was sent out from the abode of Kim Lee.

The belief that I might have been meant to act as a guide for Kim Lee's men faded to a more uncertain thing than ever. How, I reasoned, could any one follow the body of a woman nailed into a case and carted through the streets?

I bit my lips on my resolve not to falter. I tried to clench my hands and stopped at the pain in my wrists. I wanted to cry out, and could not for the gag. Without knowing that I was crying, I found my hot checks wet with tears of pain and discouraged emotion. In that moment I cried out in my soul to Dual, the man who had sent me, and after that I cried out to the God I had seldom appealed to before.

After a bit the first sick shock of my position passed and a calmer mood came on me. What sort of actions, I asked myself, were these for a woman who had promised to be strong and of good courage? Was this the bravery Dual had praised? Had I, when I followed him in his rescue of the girl Lily Lawton, known any more fully than now what plans he had formed in his brain?

And he had told me that everything would be well—that by doing as he said I would reach to the man whom I loved. Was I to doubt? Surely he had known I was going into danger. He had shown me so much. The little automatic, still safe in my waist, said so. The package Kim Lee had given into my keeping spoke of a knowledge far deeper than mine.

I eased myself on my jolting bed as best I could, and fought back by degrees to something like my former resolve to be calm and meet things as they came.

After a long time I felt the cart slow and then stop. So far as I could tell, it was backing. There came a sound of whining voices, and a squeaky tone, speaking in English, inquiring if this was the place where a packing case was expected.

My case moved again. It was dragged out, and swung and swayed as it was caried—somewhere. It was laid down. A hammer hit the wood above my head. A nail shrieked as it was withdrawn from the wood. Many hands, as it seemed, seized upon me and lifted me out. The cords on my ankles parted, and I was placed on my feet. With a sense of immense relief I felt my wrists untied.

Quite unexpectedly the cloth was torn from my face. I glimpsed a circle of yellow faces grouped around me. I looked about.

So far as I could see, I stood in the vast interior of a deserted warehouse. The debris of years of disuse was scattered all about me. Old packing-cases, old boxes, old packing refuse, littered the floors. A faint light of late afternoon filtered through cracks in the walls. High up, the girders of the roof spanned the distance from wall to wall.

So much I saw, and then one of the men about me laid hold of my arm. Surrounded by the others, I moved down the length of the littered floor toward the farther end. As I neared it I saw what looked like a heavy door set into the wall. Before this my captors paused. The one who held me fumbled in his garments and brought forth a key.

At a sign from him, another produced a small, dark lantern and set it alight. The key was thrust into the lock, turned, and withdrawn. The door itself was set open. A gust of cool, musty air rushed out. The man who led me and one other—the one with the lantern—passed through. The door was closed.

We stood in what seemed to be a tunnel dug straight back into the ground. The faint beams of the lantern showed me the damp-streaked sides of the place and the earthen floor under my feet.

We went forward again—perhaps for a hundred feet. Again a door barred our progress. It was small and set into a heavy framework, its surface reinforced with iron bars and the heads of bolts. A great padlock held it fast by a staple. It was also secured by a bar dropped into sockets.

The man with the light handed it over to the one who held me, lifted the bar and set it aside, took a second key from the hand of my guard, and unfastened the heavy padlock.

Leaning back against its weight, he drew the door open.

My guard led me through. I heard a sound which sent my heart into my throat. It was the sharp, metallic clanking of a chain and the motion of a body of some sort disturbed by our arrival.

My guard paused. The ray of his lantern darted beyond us and struck the farther wall.

I think that save for the gag I would have screamed aloud. Before me in the dim circle of light I saw Danny McKabe, crouched down on the floor, staring with wide, wild eyes into the gleam of the lantern. And he was chained by the throat!

About his neck was a collar of metal, from which ran a chain to a staple in the wall. Not five feet from where he crouched was a second metal collar, hanging empty. Toward this my guard led me.

The second man ran forward, drew a long, wicked knife from his sleeve, and stood, half bending forward, between the empty collar and McKabe.

7

LOVE IN A CELL

MY GUARD LIFTED the collar, adjusted it about my neck, and stepped back. Both he and the man with the knife turned away. The door clanged behind them, shutting us in. The darkness came down in an impenetrable pall. I tore the gag from my mouth.

The sound of a breath slowly exhaled came to my ears then:

"Miss Foote—what does it mean? What in God's name does it mean? How did they get you here? What has happened?"

Briefly I told him of our learning of his disappearance and my own capture.

The fiends!" he exclaimed. "The foul-souled fiends!" His chain clanked, and I felt that he had edged nearer to where I sat on the floor of the cell.

"But how did you ever come to let them get you? What took you up there to-day?" he went on.

"I went up there to see a certain man and ask his aid in gaining your freedom," I told him.

"Some one up there—in Chinatown?" he questioned. "Who, Miss Foote?"

"Can anyone hear us?" I asked softly.

"I don't think so," said he. "If they can, they've heard some mighty nasty opinions expressed about themselves."

"Then," I spoke in a lowered tone, "I went to see Kim Lee."

McKabe whistled softly "Kim Lee! How did you learn about *him?*"

"From Connel," I explained.

For a time he said nothing; then: "I see. And did Connel say what he meant to do?"

"Unless he gets some lead which will win your freedom, he intends to turn Reich and Greek Annie loose," I replied.

"I hope he does," said McKabe. "Oh, not for myself, Miss Foote, but for you. Now that they have laid you fast, I hope to God Jim Connel didn't call their bluff and try to hold on."

"Is it a bluff?" I questioned.

"Hardly," he gritted. "I know them. Our lives aren't worth a bean if Jim holds out. That is, mine isn't. I don't know what they may do with you."

"Don't!" I cried out. His words brought a suggestion of things worse than any death to me.

"Forgive me," he begged. "You can't know how I blame myself in this whole matter. But for my blundering work you would be safe, instead of here in this hole. It is all my fault that you *are* here."

"Nonsense," I retorted. "Just how did they get you? You haven't told me."

"As simply as they did you," he returned. "I went back up there to see how things lay, after the run in, and I scouted around. I was leaving the district. I spoke to an officer on post and walked down the street. I was passing an alley, and something hit me in the back. It was a man—half a dozen men, as it seemed. They knocked me down and dragged me into the alley, tied me up, and ran me over here."

"And do you have any faintest idea of where 'over here' is?" I inquired.

"Not at all," he admitted. "I was blindfolded and gagged. Still I know I smelled tide-water just before we came in, so I fancy we are somewhere near the water-front. That don't help any, though. Whatever made you mix into this, Miss Foote?"

"A desire to see you set free, of course, Mr. McKabe," I said.

"But why *you?* You had never even seen me until last night. Why should you interest yourself in my behalf?" he persisted.

Some way, in the darkness, it seemed to me that a meaning deeper than the words he spoke lay in his tones. Something reached out to me and sent a little warm flutter up from my heart, and inspired a greater frankness in my answer.

"Mr. McKabe," I said, "I don't want to flatter, and I want you to feel that I mean it when I say that last night you impressed me as being very much of a man. As such I wanted to help you."

"I see," came his voice. "I hardly felt that your actions could have been inspired by a purely impersonal interest in the situation. Since you have said what you have, I hope that I may return your compliment by saying that last night you impressed me as a more than usually well-balanced woman."

I laughed. Yes; there in the darkness of the cell I laughed out loud. "Mr. McKabe," I remarked, "does it not strike you that there is a ludicrous side to this matter? Here we sit, chained by the neck like two dogs, and bandy the small talk of a conversation."

"It but proves the correctness of my judgment that you are able to sense humor in the situation," he retorted. "How many women would take the thing as you do?"

"My three years with the police removed some of the feminine emotionalism from my make-up," I returned.

"Perhaps," said he. "Just the same, I think you must have always been different—a law to yourself. I felt it last night, and to-day you have proved it by seeking to help save a stranger."

"Hardly that," I objected. "You must remember that you fell into danger through helping us. There was a certain amount of obligation."

"Nothing more?" Again his words sent a thrill to my heart. Almost they sounded regretful.

I took advantage of the darkness to play with a hope they awakened within me, as a woman ever will. "Just what do you mean?" I inquired.

"You'll probably think me a fool," he replied. "I know what I am going to say will sound mawkish—like the ravings of a hero of romance—but, frankly, I hoped there was another reason. Oh, yes, I did. I—well, you said I made a good impression on you—I hoped—I dared to hope that might have had something to do with your taking the risk."

"I think I intimated that," I replied.

"Not as I mean it," he answered quickly. "Miss Foote, I've seen a lot in my life, but I never saw a woman who impressed me quite as you did last night. It's a good thing it's dark in here, or I wouldn't dare tell you that I thought you my ideal woman. Hang it, I'm only a cop, but I made up my mind to try and see more of you sometime. I didn't expect it to be this way, but I may never have another chance to tell you just what I feel. May I go on?"

His last words drove the last shreds of resistance, of dallying, from me. I might never have another chance to hear the speaking of the words any woman wants to listen to at least once in a lifetime. Why, I asked myself, should I put off their saying merely because I had known this man to whom my heart and soul cried out so small a time? If the end came here in this cell, at least I would know what he felt for me, and he should know that my heart answered the call of his own.

"Go on," I let myself whisper.

"It is this, then," he continued. "I love you. It is a funny place to say it, isn't it, Lucile? But I love you. And I hoped when you said I had made a good impression on you last night that there might be more to the thing than you said. Oh, it was nervy, and all that, but I hoped—that—you could find it in your heart to—"

"Love you?" I questioned. I moved toward him in the darkness, swinging my chain along the wall.

"Yes," said Danny softly. "Could you, Lucile? If this is to be the end of us, could you give me your love for the hours we have left?"

My throat ached. I felt my eyes wet without knowing exactly why I was weeping. I put out my hands and groped toward the sound of his voice, and my hand touched his arm and lay there, clutching the cloth of his coat.

"Danny," I began, and faltered. "Danny—Danny, dear—"

His hands seized my arm. He came toward me, creeping forward. His hands groped for my face and took it between his palms.

"Lucile!" he answered my sob with his breath on my throat. "Sweetheart!"

I felt his lips as he kissed me on the mouth. My hands found his shoulders and I clung to him and trembled. So, for a time we clung fast together in the darkness, not moving or speaking—just feeling the wild sweet thrill of a mutual love steal through us.

"Girl," said the man who held me, hoarsely, after a moment. "Oh, girl, I want to see your face!"

I felt him move. A tiny speck of light flared before me. A match! In its flickering light I gazed into the eyes of the man who loved me, and he into mine. I forced myself to smile.

So we sat and looked upon one another till the little light died and the darkness came back.

"My last match," said Danny. "But its light has served to show me the most beautiful thing in the world—the face of the woman I love." He reached out and gathered me to him. Again we sat silent, while I listened to the beating of Danny's heart, where he held me against his breast. I was almost startled when he spoke.

"My God!" he cried in a voice gone savage. "There must be some way to get out of this hellish place. It can't end like this, Lucile. It can't, I tell you. To find you and lose you like this—"

He paused as abruptly as he had spoken I could hear his breath coming in panting respiration.

I crept as closely to him as I could—as the chain would let me. Despite everything else, I was supremely happy at that moment. It was one of the supreme moments of my life. I forgot the collar about my neck, the ache of my wrists, the peril of our position.

Danny loved me. Just for a moment that was enough. All the love hunger of my sex seized me and swept me up to a height of sublime emotion. Danny loved me, what more did I desire; what more could my heart desire?

And it seemed that the thought evoked a recollection. Dual had said to me when I left him that if I did as I promised, the stars themselves would lead me to my heart's desire; and he had said that I went to the destiny of woman.

How plain his meaning was now that the thing had happened. Had I not come to my heart's desire, the destiny of woman, the arms of the man I loved, whose first kiss was hot on my mouth? Dual had said truly. Said truly—I paused in my quiver of womanly exaltation at the thought. If he had been right in this, then why not in all else?

If so, then all that had happened had happened as he had planned; was all a part of his planning—foreseen by him. A blinding inner light of new courage flooded my soul.

"Listen, Danny," I whispered as I pressed against him. "I feel sure we will get out. Even if we have to stay here awhile longer, I feel sure. And Danny, I have a weapon—an automatic!"

"You have?" he exclaimed. "Good Lord!"

I fumbled for the gun and drew it out and laid it in his hand.

"Here it is," I said. "Mr. Dual gave it to me himself, and told me not to use it unless it was a last resort. Be careful of it, Dan."

"Use it?" he muttered. "All I'd like is a chance. Maybe I'll get it." Abruptly I heard him chuckle. "What a surprised bunch of ginks they'll be if I let loose into the bunch without warning. Lord, but you're a wonder, little woman, to smuggle this thing in. You say Dual gave it to you? Is he working on this case of mine?"

"It was Dual who sent Glace and me to Connel," I told him, and went on and described all that had been done up to the time I had been accosted and captured.

When I had finished, Danny sat still for a time without a word.

"And this package Kim Lee gave you?" he questioned at length: "Have you any idea what it is?"

"Not exactly," I answered. "But I learned this much. Both Kim Lee and Dual belong to a secret order. I have an idea that the package has something to do with its secrets; that in some way it is a thing another member might recognize and respect."

"Holy smoke!" exclaimed Dan. "I wonder. Lucile, dear, I don't 'make' your friend Dual at all. Last night he did some things which didn't appear possible to a head like mine. He uses a method of working I never saw anything like. Do you really suppose he had you trailed up here?"

"I don't know, Dan," I confessed. "I hope so. I believe he meant to do so. If he did, he knows where we both are now."

"Gee!" said Danny. "I hope Kim Lee's scout made good. Anyway, that gives us a second chance. It's up to Dual and Connel now. I suppose the folks who grabbed you are sure to send word to Jim. When he gets that I think he'll 'spring' that precious pair. Oh, things might be worse, little girl. At a pinch we've got the gun to boot. Now, if only I could get out of this cursed collar, I never knew how to sympathize with a dog before."

"Some way, Danny," I whispered, "I feel that we will get out of this thing quite safely." I told him all that Semi Dual had said to me, even about my reaching to my heart's desire. "And I have done that, Danny McKabe," I finished. "I knew it when I felt your lips on mine."

"If that's all—" said Danny. For a moment my hot face was glad of the darkness. And for some time after that we were still.

By and by Danny began to speak, and told me all about himself from the time he was a boy. When he was done I gave him my own story, and under his questions I told him all about the work of Dual on the Lawton girl's case so far as I knew it, and at his request, of all that had happened to me from the time I left Kim Lee's until I was led in and chained fast beside him.

While I spoke he slipped his arm about me, moved over as far as he could in my direction, and drew me back so that I sat leaning against him. At the end he said nothing, and I closed my eyes and sat silent in the warm darkness of the cell, strangely happy in the pressure of his arm about my waist.

It seemed a long time before I heard him mutter:

"Poor little girl. Poor little girl! God, what a risk! To send a woman out like that to be captured. Girl, you went through a terrible danger to win to your heart's desire."

"Wasn't it worth it, Danny?" I whispered.

"Sweetheart!" The arm about me tightened. "I thought you were asleep," he said.

"No," I told him, "I was merely thinking."

"Of what?" asked Dan.

"Of how I used to want a dog-collar when they were in fashion," I answered, driven by a whimsical impulse. "I was wondering if the love which laughs at locksmiths could work up a smile over these things we are wearing."

Dan snorted. "You're the limit, Lucile," he remarked. "I wish you'd smuggled in a bottle of water along with that gun."

"Water?" I repeated. "Danny, haven't they given you a drink?"

"They haven't even let me wash my face," he returned.

"Or a bite to eat?" I continued.

"My stomach's as empty as my heart is full." The Irish in my lover was coming to the surface.

"You poor boy," I murmured. "Dual made me eat before he sent me out."

"That man certainly crosses my wires," Danny averred. "I wish I could get hep to the way he does things. How in time did he know that you loved me? I hadn't told him. Did you? And yet he pulled that stuff about it.

"Lucile, there's something unnatural about that man. It isn't possible to do the things he does. What man in his right senses would have sent you out like he did? The thing was just about criminal in my eyes. Yet he does it without batting an eye, and tells you to keep up your nerve and everything will come out right. And some way, after last night, I am just soft enough to believe it. That same, hard-headed Danny McKabe. Well, if we get out of here he's got to tell me how he knew we loved each other. I think he reads minds."

We sat on. Time in the dark seems doubly long. To me it seemed that many hours had passed since I was led into that room. There was nothing to mark the passage of time save the beating of our hearts. No sound save that of our words or our breathing came into the place where we lay, with the metal bands locked fast about our throats.

So once more we lapsed into silence, busy with our own thoughts, each turning over his own problems and hopes in his mind. Yet I am sure that the main thought of us both was of the thing which had come to us in the darkness, and made us grope for each other blindly with our hands, and seek each other's lips by the sense of touch alone.

I know that for myself I felt no regret for the things which had happened, and I told myself that no matter what didn't happen, whether the end Dual had predicted, or its reverse came as the final issue, these few hours spent by the side of the man who had waked the latent woman within me would be worth to me all it cost.

I think something like this must have passed through the mind of Danny, for after a time he bent and whispered:

"And you aren't sorry then, Lucile?"

"Sorry?" I told him. "Danny, I'd rather lie here with you this way than anywhere else. And whether we get out or not, at least if we go, I shall know that we go together. I want it to be that way after this, Dan—together—always."

"My dear," he said slowly, and after a while still more slowly, "My dear—I wish I could feel that I deserved a thing like this."

"But we will get out, Dan," I reassured. "We will. I think it is fate."

"If I could only do something," he cried out in a tone of exasperation. "If I could do something to show you my real feelings, if I could get out of this infernal collar. If I could get up and fight—fight your way to freedom!"

He lifted his hands from about me and I knew from the clank of the chain that he was tugging at the metal band which held him.

"Don't, Danny," I begged him. "Don't, dear. Wait. Try and be patient. Those who are wiser than you or I are working. They will not fail."

"God—if you're right!" he choked coarsely. "*If* you're right, Lucile. A man hates to cut such a sorry show before the woman he loves."

Another long time went by. How long I do not know, because I do not know when I was led into the cell, or how long had elapsed until the end of the whole matter came. By intervals Danny and I spoke together, and I kept reasserting my belief in Dual's success in our rescue.

The longer I thought of the matter the more convinced I became that all that had happened had been of his scheming. Sitting there in the dark with my man mate's arm about me. I felt my shaken courage rouse itself and take control of my spirit once more.

Little by little I won Dan to a more quiet endurance and a greater faith in the end of the thing.

Again for long moments we sat silent, and I mused on how odd a wooing had been mine. Had there ever been another like it, I wondered. Yet it was sweet—sweet as the telling of love between man and woman must always be while the plan of creation lasts and man and woman turn their faces to each other in a God-ordained attraction.

I found little delightful tremors of pure harmony of spirit running throughout my body and limbs as I sat there and waited for what might come. Alone there in the night of the tunnel my womanhood seemed to have opened and flowered to a fuller potential feeling than I had ever dreamed I was capable of.

The end came abruptly when it did come. Without warning we both heard some one at the door. In a moment it was pulled open and left standing ajar. In the light of a reflector lantern, held up by a talonlike yellow hand. I saw three men in the passage beyond it. It was the second of these held the lantern. The last stood silent behind him, with his head cocked to one side as though he listened. The foremost was crouched down in a tense posture. He held a long, curved knife in his hand.

From somewhere a long way off it seemed to me I heard a sound of shouting. It came for just a moment and died. But it seemed a signal.

The man with the knife sprang through the door directly toward us. He with the lantern trained its rays full upon us, advancing just inside the cell.

8

GLACE RESUMES THE NARRATIVE

FOR A MINUTE after I heard Connel's message over the wire I felt sick and dizzy, and my senses reeled.

Of course, you have read Miss Foote's story of what happened; but at that time I could not know how much of the thing was a part of the inscrutable plans of Dual.

Coming as it did on top of an afternoon full of uncertainty inspired by Semi's most unusual actions, the information from Connel pretty nearly knocked me off my feet.

I slid the receiver back onto its hook, turned, and walked slowly to a chair and sank down.

Sheldon shot me a glance and jumped up. "What's the matter?" he rasped. "What's happened now? Glace, what ails you, man?"

I told him as best I could, and he swore.

Lily Lawton put down her head and began to weep in nervous terror.

"My God, Gordon!" the colonel burst out, "do you see what that means? I told you you hadn't ought to have let that leetle girl go up there the way you done. 'Course they saw you and her go to the police station, an' when you come back here an' she went up there, they laid for her an' roped her fust off.

"Well, that ends it, I reckon. You phone to Connel, an' tell him to kick them two out. Let 'em have their dirty scum, if that will git Lucile and McKabe turned loose."

He paused, breathing hard.

"Please, Mr. Glace," Lily sobbed brokenly, "if there is any way to help poor Miss Lucile, you will take it, won't you? Oh, she was so good to me! I can't bear it to think those people have caught her."

She resumed her tears.

I didn't answer for a moment. Some way, it seemed that the excited outcries of my companions served to steady my own disturbed balance, and show me the need of cool thought and action in this new crisis.

On the face, it looked pretty bad.

First McKabe, old hand at the game, had been taken; then Lucile, a woman who for three years had matched wits with this very society of banded evil, had been seized in broad daylight, if I was to accept Connel's statement at full value.

To cap all, Dual had gone off and left me sitting idle, with orders to await a message. And as yet no message had come.

Against that, however, was my knowledge, now several years old, of the man whose gray suit had come back to us with the cryptic bit of writing stuffed into a shoe.

True, Sheldon had failed to pick up any trail leading to the mysterious Kim Lee; but I could only admit in fairness that the colonel's methods savored too much of brute directness to avail against the secretiveness of the people he had questioned. Certainly Semi Dual would not have written that name without a well-founded knowledge upon which to proceed.

The best answer I could find, then, was that there really *was* a Kim Lee, and that Semi Dual and he were somewhere under cover, with hands on the pulse of affairs.

The thought steadied me yet further. I looked up at the flushed face of the old fire-eater before me and shook my head.

"Colonel," said I, "I do not believe this is the time for us to mix in. The Lord knows I wouldn't spare any effort to save that girl who gave us such noble assistance; but if turning Reich and the woman loose will save her, they have doubtless told Connel as much, and he will do it without any urging from me. He said as much this morning."

"But, my Lord," he questioned, "why don't Dual do something? Do you suppose he knows about this last thing they've put over?"

"I can't say," I replied. "There isn't any way for me to tell unless—"

Suddenly I stopped. One of the most peculiar thoughts I had ever had flashed into my brain.

I sat and studied the thing, and the longer I did so the more like a bit of my friend's uncanny work it appeared.

"Unless what?" prompted Sheldon with impatience.

"Unless Mercury and Venus reached their conjunction a little bit ago," I remarked.

It seemed to me that something back in my brain applauded the words.

I thrilled as I spoke. At last I seemed to be picking up a well-nigh intangible thread of meaning in the jumble.

It came on me that back of this second seemingly crushing blow was the unseen hand of Dual. If that were so—

"I don't get you," said the colonel; "and I wish you'd talk so a man could understand you."

The old man's nerves were palpably ragged.

I smiled. "I'm not sure myself yet, colonel," I told him; "but I think I see light."

"Well, I don't!" he snapped. "Anyway, call up Connel and ask him if he's goin' to turn them two loose. If I was sure of that I'd feel better. Gad, if this was in Goldfield, we'd have had a posse out after these here folks inside an hour; but in a town like this a feller don't know where to hunt first."

More to quiet him down than anything else, I got Connel on the phone and asked if the capture of Lucile had been used to strengthen the demands for our prisoners' release.

"Well, what do you think they used it for?" he threw back sarcastically. "As for 'springin'' them two, I'll do it if I have to.

"I can tell you this much, though. A report just came in from a feller who says he saw Mac grabbed. We're following it up. If we can't land in time, I'll kiss your pair good-by."

"I think that would be best unless something more develops," I responded.

"Thanks," said Connel. "That helps me a lot." He hung up.

He was in a savage humor, and I couldn't blame him myself.

I turned back and gave Sheldon the assurance he wished for.

"Well, thank the Lord!" he accepted with relief. "At least,

now we know one way to save her. Why should we give a hang, anyway, Glace? We got Lily, an' them two will get their comeuppance sooner or later if they keep on rustlin' round."

"Yes; and they won't rustle long if what I think is right, either," I gave him back.

"Eh?" He had been fumbling for one of his black cigars.

Now he glanced up from trimming its end and eyed me closely.

"What d'ye mean by that son?"

"I mean," said I, "that I think Dual is back of this whole business. I mean"—I spat out the thing in my mind—"that I think he knew Lucile was going to be taken before he left this hotel."

The colonel's jaw dropped open, held so for a moment, and closed with a snap.

"If anybody but you had spilled that I'd ring for a couple of guards," he made comment, "An' if any man but Dual done a thing like that—knew about it an' let it happen—I'd take a gun an' go after him myself. But—I reckon I ain't wise enough to th' game to take a hand. All I can say is, I hope to the Lord you're right."

He thrust his cigar into his mouth, sighed deeply, and set it alight.

It was at that particular moment that a rap sounded from the door for the second time.

I fairly leaped to answer the summons, and even in leaping I knew that at last the thing I had awaited was about to happen.

I set the door wide and confronted a district messenger-boy.

"Mr. Glace?" said he.

I nodded.

He handed me a note. I turned back to the room and tore it open.

One glance sufficed. I knew the writing as well as my own.

"Dual," I muttered in relief, as I began to read it. I heard Sheldon grunt in surprise at the word.

I sent my eyes along the lines. They were clear enough in themselves, but they filled me with a certain surprise:

GORDON:

Read this closely and make no mistakes.

Go down quickly and take a taxicab. Drive to the Palace Hotel and ask of the clerk for a package addressed to you. In it you will find the key to a room.

Go to it, take the house phone and call Bryant 2128. When they answer, give your name—just that and hang up.

After a time a man will come to you. Do what he says and ask no questions. Answer none either.

When he has finished what he has to do, take a taxi—a different one, Gordon, and drive to the corner of Grant and Clay.

Leave the cab boldly and enter the store on the northwest corner. A man will be waiting for you.

Ask for Prince Abdul, and he will direct you. Before leaving, impress on the mind of Colonel Sheldon that he must remain with Miss Lawton, and under no circumstances leave the hotel until we return.

I folded it up and lifted my eyes to find Colonel MacDo-

nahue Sheldon, sitting forward in his chair, his face a
picture of amaze.

"Was that from Dual?" he shot out in a gulp of excited
question.

"That was from Dual," I assured him, smiling. "He told
me what to do, and he told me what to tell you to do. He
told me to tell you to stay here with Lily until we get back.
He means that, colonel."

The old eyes squinted into mine.

"I reckon," he accepted, "I'll stay put. You goin' somewhere, son?"

I nodded, picked up my hat and coat, and went out. I
walked down the red-carpeted hall and rang for an elevator cage. It rose, and I stepped inside.

My taxi put me down at the Montgomery Street
entrance to the Palace. I dismissed it and went rapidly in
to the desk.

I asked for a package addressed to "Glace." The clerk
produced it. I tore it open. Inside was a numbered key.

I called a bell-boy and handed it to him. At his heels, I
entered one of the bank of cages and left it to follow him
to a room. Once inside, I went to the phone and asked for
my connection with Bryant 2128.

A voice came back after a time.

"This is Glace," I said distinctly.

"With you at once," the voice assured. I heard the
connection cut.

I sank down in a chair and waited for what was to
happen next. I didn't know what it was, but I was sure it
was going to enable me to reach back to Dual's side, and
I was content.

The mental unrest which had bothered me throughout the day departed, and I felt confident again.

All that time Semi had been somewhere, working. He had not called me, because he did not need me; but he had very plainly arranged to call me when he should be ready to use me.

As always before, he had foreseen the course of this matter. Beyond doubt then, he knew that Lucile was taken—and in that light I lost my anxiety for her.

Semi would not have allowed her capture to occur if any material injury to her must result. The idea which had come to me just before he called me gained strength while I sat there waiting for the unknown person I had summoned to arrive.

I no longer doubted that Semi Dual had planned the whole matter as it had happened. If so, he knew where Lucile Foote was held a captive, and would free her in good time. I wished the unknown would come.

I was growing anxious to get back into the game.

Footsteps paused outside. A rap fell on the door.

I called a reply, and the door swung inward. There entered a man who impressed me as being a member of the theatrical profession, or one who had been. He looked like a second-rate actor, at any event.

"You Mr. Glace—Mr. Gordon Glace?" he inquired.

"Correct," said I.

He came over and deposited a flat, black case which he carried on the bed. Without delay, he began loosening a couple of clasps which held its two sides together.

"Take off your coat and collar, an' roll up your sleeves above the elbow," he directed.

I saw the whole proposition. I was to be made up. The flat case was a huge make-up outfit.

He had it open now and was taking out various articles of apparel, mostly of silk or satin, as it seemed to me. These he tossed on the bed.

He took up a bottle and a small sponge, and approached me where I stood in my shirt-sleeves.

"Sit down, if you please," he required.

I complied.

"A little picric acid for your skin, sir," he went on, pulling the cork and wetting the sponge. " 'Tain't strong, an' 'twill give your skin just about th' right touch of yellow. Better shut your eyes for a minute."

He began to sweep the sponge over my face and on down my neck to well below the band of my shirt. The stuff prickled slightly, but dried quickly.

I sat with my eyes fast shut till he finished my face and picked up a hand; then I looked on, while a delicate yellowish shade took the place of the natural color of my skin.

In a way, the man was an artist. For instance, he shaded his staining to simulate nature, making it dark and even spotted on the outer and upper sides of the forearms, lighter on the bottoms and insides, and lighter still in the palms, where he merely touched lightly with the well-nigh dried sponge.

"An' now for your hair," he remarked as he put up the bottle of stain.

He took up another flask and moistened a small comb in the fluid. He began to comb my hair quickly.

"It should be several shades darker," he explained, "an'

this will do it in a few minutes, though you'll have to have it cut later, as the color won't fade none to speak of."

"Never mind that," I urged.

He finished my hair and went once more to his case. He came back with yet another bottle.

With a small brush he touched the outer corners of my eyelids slightly. I felt the stuff draw and pucker, giving my lids a tense, uplifted feeling.

He nodded in apparent satisfaction, caught up a stick of paste, and attacked my lips; stood back and viewed me, made a final touch here and there, and tossed the cosmetic back into the case.

"And now, sir, if you'll take off your clothes an' put on these others—" He indicated the silken garments.

I lost no time in following his directions. I slipped out of my shirt, trousers, shoes and socks, and lifted the clothing from the bed. In the mean time the man was gathering up my discarded apparel and folding it up to put in his case.

"It will be sent to the hotel," he told me as he packed it away.

I smiled. I saw now how Dual's suit and hat and shoes had come back to us.

I slipped into the socks and Oriental slippers I discovered, drew on a pair of flapping pantaloons, and thrust my arms through the sleeves of a silken jacket, which hung loosely down below my waist. Lastly I added a cap, and then I walked over to the mirror-filled door of a closet in the room and had a good look at myself.

The yellowish face of a seeming Oriental was thrown back to my eyes.

Even the eyes themselves seemed slightly slanted by the

contracting pull of the stuff the man had placed at their outer corners. My yellowed hands and wrists stuck out of the jacket's flowing sleeves.

I was a pretty fair counterfeit of a Chinaman as I saw it.

I went to the phone again and asked for a taxi. I gave the key of the room to the man with the case and left the room.

I felt rather bizarre, in a way, as I walked across the foyer of the hotel.

I had entered as Gordon Glace, and I was leaving as the apparent servant of an Oriental prince. I wondered if any watching eyes would detect the connection. I rather fancied not.

My taxi was waiting, and I entered it at once, giving my driver the directions in a singsong voice through the tube.

We were off.

I leaned back and let myself relax as we darted through the traffic of Market, and I chuckled. The adventure took hold and swept me along.

Once, years before, when I first knew him, Dual had disguised me as his personal attendant, and we had gone to the rescue of the daughter of the same old Colonel Sheldon who was now mounting guard over the girl in the St. Francis Hotel.

The present circumstance brought back the former, and with it the thrill of that other masquerade. Then, as now, Semi Dual had led and I had followed.

Then, as now. Sheldon had been left to wait with what patience he could when the final movements of the game were to be played out. Then, as now, he had taken me with him in the end of the venture and made me his lieutenant—the witness of his skilful playing on the strings of fate.

Then, as now, he had posed as Prince Abdul.

I smiled. I fancied how I would find him now, dressed, no doubt, as some Eastern potentate in flowing robes which seemed to fit him as to the manner born.

The evening glow was lying over the city, flinging the streets into shadow as we turned up the hill toward my destination. From the windows of the cab I glimpsed the hurrying crowds as they jostled along.

Again I smiled. Not one of them, I fancied, would dream in their routine round that the spirit of adventure was abroad in their midst.

They led their lives from day to day in the selfsame manner. They went their ways and minded their business, and saw only what was on the surface. They couldn't see deeper to the soul of things.

To them, if they saw me, I was a Chinese driving in a hired taxi. In a whimsical way, I paraphrased an old verse I once had heard:

> A Chinee in a taxicab,
> A Chinee was to him, by Grab,
>> And he was nothing more.

And I grinned. Since Dual and I had been friends, the spirit of adventure had grown familiar to me. People said adventure was dead in these commercial days.

Well, then, people didn't know. A tingling thrill of impatience laid hold of me as in the old days of our early acquaintance, and I mentally urged the wheels of my cab as we climbed the long hill.

Adventure dead! What a fallacy.

It was no more dead to-day than a thousand years ago.

It could not die as long as men and women loved and gave life to their children, and reared them with hopes and aspirations of what they, too, were to become.

Life itself was the great adventure, and to-day Dual, and now I, were engaging in the task of saving life.

What more could there be than that—to save life itself—the life of a man and a woman who loved, and if I was to believe the words of my paradox-speaking friend, would mate and give yet another life to the world.

What an adventure! To save life!

And before Dual had left our hotel he had known. He had read it from the stars themselves, and told Sheldon that Mercury and Venus were drawing to conjunction.

He was a strange man, an odd man, who spoke plainly in riddles—which became plain after the things they predicted had happened, so that you wondered why you had not seen his deeper meaning instead of being confused by mere words.

Yet what chance did a man like Connel, trained in the technical methods of the police, stand of comprehending?

Poor Connel! He was worried. I felt sorry for him in his worry, because I knew from his words, and their tone of this morning, that a sincere friendship for McKabe lay back of the anxiety he felt.

Well, I told myself, after a bit now, when Dual really went into action Connel might give over worry and take up rejoicing instead.

And surely, now that the evening fingers were feeling across the landscape, Dual must be getting ready to strike.

All the long day he had been laying his threads of leading, knotting each to the other to form a strong net of holding.

By now he should be almost ready to begin drawing up that net with its catch of poor, blind, distorted human souls.

And when it was done, like the true Oriental, he would say:

"Kismet! It is fate—a debt of Karma—a man's misdeeds have overtaken him at last."

And he would glory that the right had triumphed, and that he had once more been made an instrument to that end.

The cab lurched to a standstill.

"Here we are, John," called my driver.

I made no answer. I merely opened the door, climbed down, backwards as a Chinaman will always leave a vehicle, much as a woman leaves a trolley—against the rules; fumbled in my baggy trousers for some coin I had placed there when changing, and paid him his fare.

He took it, grinned, and rattled away.

I turned about and faced the great store I had been told to enter. Without hesitation or any effort at concealment I went up its steps and pushed open the door.

A small man hurried forward on my entrance.

"Prince Abdul," I said to him softly. He turned with a sign to me to follow, and led me back to a stairs.

We mounted, turned, and again went upward; came out on a second floor and attacked a second flight of stairs.

At their top he opened a door and I entered a little reception-room of great beauty. Miss Foote has described it, so I shall not try, save to mention that as I entered I saw a very large man, as Chinamen go, lounging back in a heavy carved chair.

He was dark, with an oily skin. His eyes were little, and set close under a high narrow brow. His lips were thin, loose, and almost without color.

He was idly smoking a cigarette, and I noticed the hand which held it. It was long fingered, sinewy, and the nails of the fingers were like talons—thick, horny, and sharpened till they looked like claws.

He gave no notice to my entrance save by his eyes.

For one instant they rested piercingly upon me, and turned away. Yet in that instant's inspection I felt the soul of a brooding hawk rest upon me.

The eyes were cold, without feeling, yet with a shrewd intelligence behind them. Without glancing toward me again he lifted his cigarette and set it to his mouth.

I crossed the room and tapped upon a door.

"Come," said a voice I knew.

I thrust the door before me and stepped into a gorgeous apartment. On opposite sides of a massive table two men were sitting.

Their eyes were upon me as I entered. The one I felt sure was Kim Lee. The other I knew for Dual.

"You made good time," he greeted.

I smiled. I felt all my old assurance come back to me now in his presence.

"Did you know Venus had met her conjunction?" I retorted.

Dual allowed a flicker of amusement to twitch his lips.

"Miss Foote left here at nine minutes to three. She was taken by a white slave agent at five minutes past three," he replied. "Allow me to make you acquainted with Kim Lee."

9

THE HAMMER OF GOD

THE MAN ACROSS the table and I exchanged salutations.

"Then you know where Miss Foote is at present?" I asked, with no attempt to mask my eagerness.

"She is with McKabe," said Dual evasively.

"And that—" I began.

"I expect to learn very shortly," Semi finished. "At present my very good friend, Kim Lee, and myself, are waiting a report from some of his agents as to the exact whereabouts of the place where these people have confined the two. Sit down and tell us what has happened at your end of the line while we wait."

I took a chair and drew it across to an end of the table.

"Nothing much has happened," I replied. "Sheldon insisted on coming here and trying to find Miss Lucile and Kim Lee. He failed, and was shadowed to the hotel. Connel phoned just before you called and said we had made a hash of things in general. That was after he was sent word of Miss Foote's capture. He also said he was going to turn Reich and the woman loose as a last resort."

"I shall advise him to do so after a time," said Dual.

I gasped. I turned my eyes to his face and sought to read his meaning.

A cold hand seemed to seize my heart and squeeze it slowly until it beat with a palpable effort.

"Turn them loose?" I stammered. Were we beaten then, I wondered? Had Dual failed at last, and was he about to admit it, and set free the ones they demanded in order to save the man and the girl he had sent to her fate?

He met my gaze fully. In his eyes there was nothing to answer my question. They were clear, deep, calm, as two gray shadowed forest fountains.

There was neither discouragement nor elation in their strange, inscrutable glance. Yet they seemed to read the unspoken question in my mind before he answered:

"Patience, Gordon. The time is not yet, my friend. Reich and the woman shall go free at a time already decided. I shall advise Connel by and by."

A rap came on the door of the reception cabinet. Kim Lee seemed to bark his answer, and leaned forward in an almost un-Oriental excitement. I saw that his dark eyes glistened.

A man pushed open the door and entered in a hurried manner. His face showed traces of exertion, and his breathing was that of one who has spared no labor in arriving.

He sprang into the room, paused, and bowed low before breaking into a rapid stream of speech which I had no chance to follow. Unlike Semi Dual, I had no knowledge of tongues save my own, and the man was speaking in Chinese.

Therefore I confined my efforts to watching the face of Dual.

I saw a quick fire light it at the words the messenger uttered. He listened without interruption until the fellow paused, and then snapped into question after question, which the Chinaman seemed to answer without hesitation.

At the end, Semi turned to Kim Lee and spoke in English:

"Is there such a place as this, Kim Lee?"

"Most certainly, Abdul," the merchant assured him.

Dual smiled. He thrust a hand into his garments and dragged out some pieces of gold. With an outward flip of his hand he cast them at the fellow's feet.

"A reward of service, Kim Lee," he said to the other. "He is a valuable man. We shall use him again. Bid him wait."

Kim Lee spoke to the man, who not until then bowed himself before Semi, and picked up the gold. I admitted to myself that the servants of this merchant were trained exceedingly well.

Dual turned to me.

"I shall translate," he began. "Above the basin where the Italians keep their little fishing boats, between here and the northeastern shore of the bay, there is a place known as Telegraph Hill. To the north of this, near the shore of the bay, there stands an empty warehouse. It is now disused, and has been for years. It is built over the mouth of a tunnel.

"Within this tunnel McKabe and Miss Foote are detained. These are the main facts which this agent of Kim Lee has reported. It was to learn this that I permitted Miss Foote to be captured to-day. I knew that her taking would be used as additional pressure on Connel, and that the people who took her would almost surely carry her to the same place where McKabe was held.

"I arranged to have her followed by Kim Lee's agents. You can see how well they have done their work. There was no one else could have done it, because no one else was so well fitted for the undertaking. They know this district, its entrances and its exits. They knew where to watch and what to watch for, and they have succeeded, as it was fated they should."

The man had picked up his gold and gone softly back to the reception-room while Dual was speaking.

"Then all we have to do is go get them," I cried in relieved conviction.

"I think I shall let Connel 'go get them,'" said Dual.

I nodded.

"And you let them take Miss Foote so these men could follow her course as a guide," I summed up.

"For that, and because unless Venus reached their conjunction, Mr. McKabe cannot be rescued alive," said Dual. "She is the main agent of his rescue, Gordon. Her presence preserves his life, my friend."

He turned to Kim Lee.

"Speaking of exits and entrances; may I use yet other ears and eyes of thine?" he inquired.

The Chinese nodded. He rose and went to the door to the reception-room, spoke briefly, and came back to his chair, after drawing the curtains at the windows and switching on the lights.

He spoke to Semi and was answered. They plunged into a conversation in which I found no part.

I listened, and ever I was puzzled as I had been puzzled for the greater part of this day. These two men, ten minutes after learning the place where the man they desired to save and the woman they had so calmly sent to share his prison, were lying, had plunged into a general discussion of Eastern philosophy.

Part of the time they spoke in English, and then I could dimly follow. Again they fell rapidly into Kim Lee's own language, to which I could only listen.

Why, I asked myself—why in the name of all things in the world did Dual not take some action toward setting free those two souls he had labored all day to save, if I was any judge of his actions?

After some time, Kim Lee turned in my direction.

"Your friend is a very remarkable man, Mr. Glace," he observed. "In fact, the most remarkable man I have ever known. I have lived for some years, and studied and known many men, and I know some things, but he seems to me to have met all men, and to know all things in himself.

"You are fortunate to call him friend. To a man like him there is no line of race or creed. Life is a simple equation in good and evil to such a one. I regret that in this wrong you are fighting you run adverse to some of my people—that like some of your own, they have been lured into this vicious traffic by a love of material wealth.

"I believe with your friend here, that he who injures another incurs not only a physical debt, but a debt of the soul. Because of that, when your friend Abdul came to me to-day and told me of a soul obligation, which stood against me, I was willing to give the assistance he desired.

"I have studied deeply of these things. For years I have kept myself apart from the bickerings of factions, the wars of tongs. I have sought to make of myself a man, rather than a native of a race or a subscriber to a creed. Yet, to do this, and maintain my station in peace, it has been necessary for me to collect a certain band of my own people about me.

"I have done this. But, while I used them, I have also watched over and taken care of them as well, and sought to see that they kept the law of man, and the common good. Some of these men will come here ere long at my bidding. They are the ears and eyes your friend Abdul spoke of. They will go out and see and hear the things we must know in order that we may keep our hand on the helm of affairs and steer a true course this night.

"One of them you heard report, and his report was good. He did his duty well. The man in the reception-room yonder is not one of mine. I do not employ his sort myself, but because the need might arise, I called him to us, and we shall use him as the physician uses one poison to fight another."

He paused and smiled slightly.

"I hope we may even say that he will be administered in homeopathic doses. And now, perhaps you understand the situation better."

I bowed. I felt that I did. It was all coming to me in flash after flash. To-day these two had sat here and planned, while these vicarious ears and eyes of theirs ran here and there and told what they saw and heard.

Surely I was beholding the workings of Kim Lee's Karma now. I saw what it meant, and I saw that the Chinese was no common man himself.

"I think," I said, "that I may now add another unusual man to my list of acquaintances."

His eyes lighted slightly.

"Abdul has told me much of you to-day," he replied. "I should be glad to call you also, friend."

Kim Lee's men tapped on the door and entered.

Like those Miss Foote has described in her story, they were plain men of the streets; but with their master's words of explanation in my mind, they took on the seeming of something more.

They stood while Dual spoke to them in direction. Their stolid faces betrayed no emotion at what he said. Only at the end their eyes sought out Kim Lee's like those of dogs seeking confirmation of the order.

Kim nodded, and they left the room in wordless acquiescence. They would go where they were sent, and see what they were to see, hear what they might and come back.

I found myself aquiver with the realization of how subtly Dual had been fighting; of how completely he had masked his movements and led the ones he fought into a false security—a false belief in his inaction.

Their capture of Lucile must have seemed the last blow of the battle to them. No doubt they were full of elation. And all the time these impassive eyes and ears ran the streets, spying, listening, reporting to the master mind which directed their movements as a general moves his commands as need requires.

The subcurrent of the matter took me up and swept me along in an enthusiastic admiration for the thing which had been done.

"Dual," I exclaimed; "this is the most wonderful of anything yet."

Semi Dual turned his eyes upon me and smiled. "And I shut you out, Gordon," he said slowly. "My friend, there was need. It was a thing for my handling alone—I and Kim Lee. I see Sheldon told you of my words to him about Venus in conjunction. I fancied that that and the return of my suit would show you something of my actions."

"The return of the suit nearly drove Sheldon distracted," I returned, "and I confess I was worried for a moment."

"Until you found the note, in fact," Dual smiled.

I shook my head.

"Lily found that," I explained.

Dual's smile widened.

"Unlike you, Gordon," he observed. "Suppose while we wait I tell you something of the invisible currents which have flowed steadily forward to-day."

"One moment," I interrupted. "You say 'while we wait.' I thought possibly you had sent these men just now to Connel to tell him to strike."

I paused, and my question looked foolish. He had said Reich and Annie were to be set free.

"Or maybe you told him to let his prisoners out," I finished, and had to admit that that was foolish, too, because Dual now knew where to strike, himself, without setting any one free. I think my face showed that I saw where I had entangled myself, for Semi nodded, his eyes lighting.

"I intend to lighten some of your burden of non-comprehension, friend Glace. To begin with, in the rescue of Miss Lawton I went deeply into the astrological aspects of the case. In so doing I looked further than the mere rescue of the woman and the apprehension of Homer Reich and the woman who helped him abduct the girl.

"I saw that there would be attempted retaliation on the part of this organization. Therefore, I did not last night regard the incident as closed, which will explain my lack of enthusiasm which you noticed this morning, and my lack of surprise at Connel's telephone call. You will remember that I took the time of the call.

"After you went with Miss Foote I set up a figure on that time as a basis. It was then Sheldon questioned, and I gave him the answer I knew he would retail to you."

"About McKabe's astral life insurance?" I cut in.

Dual nodded, and Kim Lee flashed me a dry sort of smile.

"Yes. I sent you and Miss Foote to Connel to keep him busy while I set up my figures. Later I called him up myself and told him I would go to work on the case. I then left the hotel, went to a barber-shop and was shaved, left the shop and walked down to the Palace Hotel.

"I there arranged to register as Prince Abdul and suite, and have any inquiries as to the name confirmed by the management and desk. I called a costumer from my room—the same you used—and had him send me what I required, save for my ruby and aigret which I suppose you recognize. I also arranged matters for you.

"After that I came at once to this place, and have remained. Miss Foote arrived here before I did myself. I had commanded her to come, which was easily done, as her mind was centered upon my ability to help her, and I could sway it telepathically as I wished. For that reason she insisted on leaving you to go back to the hotel alone.

"My astrological figures had shown me that Miss Foote was a very necessary agent in locating McKabe's place of detention, and also of saving his life at the time of their rescue. For that purpose I gave her a weapon before I permitted her to go forth to the fate which called her. I had also learned of the debt Kim Lee owed to McKabe in saving the life of his son. I knew that he would never ignore such a Karmic debt, so that I was sure of his assistance.

"I came. I presented the debt, and like a soul of honor, he is paying on the nail.

"His men have to-day been my ears and my eyes, as you heard me call them. From this room they have gone out, and to this room they will come back, as one has come already, and what they shall bring shall enable me to do what I desire.

"You think it strange that with a knowledge of the place where Miss Foote and McKabe lie imprisoned, I hold my hand from the blow which shall free them. Gordon, last night and to-day should have taught you how little a wound we inflicted upon them when we seized the two agents last night.

"Back of those vile machinations which have robbed homes of their daughters, have robbed those daughters of their birthright of virtue, and unborn children of the God-ordained right to be born of clean mothers, there lies an evil brain.

"In that brain are held the reins of control of this local organization. Its identity is unknown save to the agents of his work.

"He moves disguised by a surface seeming, and lays his snares and sends his hunters out to capture the victims, whose barter and sale, to sickness, lust and death, keep his pockets filled with the price of happiness, and purity, of youth and innocence—of blood money, Gordon, soul money—"

He paused, with eyes flashing and head uplifted.

"And the hour of such a one draws near," he resumed in a voice which rang through the apartment.

"For that hour I hold my hand, and permit two other souls to draw nearer to each other in a secret prison. For that I delay. For that I sit in this room and send forth the ears and eyes of those who can return here and tell me at what point to seek for the one who lies in a fancied safety and gloats over the blood-stained gold in his hand—to whose ears no cry of maimed souls has meaning—for whose eyes no sight of blasted lives, of ruined beauty, of suffering flesh has any power of compassion.

"And at that hour I shall strike—my hand shall be the hammer which strikes the hour of his debt to Karma."

"Bravo!" cried the voice of the merchant. "You shall strike as the hammer of God."

It was all clear at last. I saw it.

While I chafed for a minor victory in the matter, Dual had been planning to strike not a puny, but a more or less crushing blow against the power of evil he fought.

I remembered once before when he had held his hand in similar fashion, in a case involving murder itself, in order to snare the master mind of the matter and bring home to him the justice of his deeds.

"The hammer of God, yes," said Dual slowly. "The hammer of Eternal Justice, the hammer—the agent. It is a divine privilege, Kim Lee, to be an agent of that justice which the Power of Life has decreed must be. It is the one thing in life which still thrills me deeply.

"At such times I feel the nearness of that Spirit of Love which ordains the rounds of the planets, and holds all life on its hands. At such times I feel that my spirit is open to the sun of that Spirit's approval, as a flower is flooded by the orb of day. At such times I feel myself in harmony with the Infinite, indeed."

He paused again and controlled his temporary flash of emotion.

"In all other things save this, I have learned the lesson of impassivity," he said. "This alone can shake me to those other days when lesser things could move me as this does.

"Enough. When the hour shall approach, Glace and I and the man with the eyes of a hawk, who sits in the anteroom yonder, shall go out from here and walk—three Orientals—through the streets. It is simple. What is there in three men of the East, walking through the streets?

"Its simplicity is its strength, even as the simple is ever strongest, as truth is stronger than lies."

" 'The wise men came out of the East,' " Kim Lee said softly.

Dual smiled slightly.

Again some one was rapping on the door. Through it in answer to the master's summons, came one of the last three men to leave.

Quite in a matter-of-fact tone he gave his report, was rewarded as his fellow had been, and then took his departure.

Dual turned to Kim Lee and myself with a smile.

"The hour draws near," said he. "Gordon, you are apt with a pen or pencil. Take paper Kim Lee will give you and prepare to write."

Kim Lee handed me pen and paper and in silence, not yet understanding, I drew them to me.

"Address this to Captain Connel," Dual directed. "I shall send it to him by one of Kim's men and messenger boy, as I sent the note to you at the hotel. To telephone would be too great a chance, but a man may carry a note and send it forward from a messenger station, and not be suspected, provided he is well known in a district.

"Now write:

"Captain Connel:

"I am writing you by Mr. Dual's direction. Throughout this day, while you have doubted, Mr. Dual has worked. To complete the work it is needful to ask your assistance.

"You are perhaps aware that some time in the eighties there was a project to build a tunnel beneath the bay, somewhat as they have tunneled the Hudson in New York. Work was actually begun, and a tunnel was driven into the elevation known as Telegraph Hill. Financial backing failing, the work was abandoned. Later a warehouse was built over the mouth of the tunnel. For years even the warehouse has been abandoned, and is commonly believed to be unused.

"This warehouse stands above the basin where the Italian fishing boats are now kept. Doubtless you know the place.

"Attend to the rest with close care, captain. Take an armed squad, one provided with axes, to this warehouse at exactly 8:01 o'clock to-night. Do not arrive at one minute of eight, nor at eight—but at one minute after. Much depends on this.

"At that time, break into the warehouse and go to the end next the hill. Break into the tunnel and follow it until you come to the place where Miss Foote and your man McKabe are kept in confinement. Liberate them, and seize any men who may oppose you.

"Have a strong squad of your men ready for instant service at the Hall of Justice. Instruct their leader to give obedience to Mr. Dual's directions. At such time as word shall be conveyed to them, have them divide into three sections. One will go to the Chinese theater through which Mr. McKabe and we others entered the tunnels last night. One will go to a place midway of the built-up portion of Clay below Grant where a man—a Chinese—will meet and lead them to another tunnel entrance.

"The third will wait exactly five minutes after the first two have left the hall, and then march to the shop on Washington, which we told you last night concealed an exit from the underground tunnels. They will there enter the tunnels and follow a trail they will find until it leads them to Mr. Dual and myself. The other squads will sweep the tunnels they enter and work inward until they meet this last.

"One other thing you will do. At seven-thirty you will set free the man, Reich, and the woman, Greek Annie. You may do this with the certain conviction that they will be followed by our agents and later be reapprehended.

"This is all, save to add to it the caution that upon your complete compliance rests the fate of your officer, Mr. McKabe, and that of Miss Foote, as well as the completion of Mr. Dual's efforts. You will, therefore, give a verbal assurance to the boy who brings this that you will comply.

"Upon receipt of such a message from you, we shall be ready to strike so soon as our agents send word that Reich and the woman have been trailed. You can see from this that the whole matter lies in your hands.

"Most sincerely yours,
      "GORDON GLACE.

"And now the man who brought the report from the warehouse," said Semi.

Kim Lee in person summoned the man. To him the message was given, with directions for its sending forward.

He stuffed it inside his blouse and departed. I looked at my watch. It was seven o'clock.

Dual drew the balance of the paper I had been using to him and began tearing it into little, irregular bits. A pile of the stuff grew before him. He swept it up and stuffed it into some inner pocket of his robes. His eyes met mine and he smiled.

"Do you see it now, friend Gordon?" he inquired.

"I see it," I responded. "It is like all the other things I have known you do—plain enough at the end. Yet I can imagine that Connel will be vastly puzzled. Will he agree?"

"He will agree," said Semi Dual. "He will remember last night and he will want to save McKabe. He will agree."

He gathered a last bit of paper from the floor where it had fallen.

"Kim Lee," he went on. "It has been a great pleasure to meet you. On that Karmic debt which was yours, so much has depended—the life of a man—the love of a woman—the bringing of justice to the guilty. Truly it is written that no man lives to himself alone. The destiny of each is interwoven with the destiny of the whole.

"Soon the account against you will have been discharged. For those others who shall gain from it, I thank you—for the rest I leave your own soul to repay by the knowledge of a good deed done."

He thrust a hand once more into his robe and drew out a heavy purse.

"But for those who have run and returned, divide this among them, as I have rewarded their fellows."

He laid the purse on the table and leaned back.

"You are a prince indeed, of a princely action, O Abdul," said the merchant. "In all things I shall obey your counsel, and ask only that you call me friend."

"Friend and brother," Semi responded.

He lifted his arm and extended his palm. The two men clasped hands.

Silence came down on the room where we waited. One by one the minutes dragged by, ten, fifteen, twenty—twenty-five.

Kim Lee's man came with Connel's answer. It was:

"On the job."

I smiled.

Thirty minutes, forty-five.

There came the sound of footsteps from the little ante-chamber, a hurried rap, and the door swung open. A man sprang in and began speaking even as he entered, in hurried gasps.

He paused. Semi Dual rose from his chair. He spoke to the man. The fellow turned and ran out, and Semi addressed Kim Lee.

"Call now the hawk-eyed man, my brother, and bid him do as was agreed between us."

Kim Lee crossed and bade the giant I had seen as I entered, come in. He came, tall, saturnine, impassive. Kim

Lee spoke to him shortly. He waved a hand to Dual and to me.

The man he addressed bowed his head in understanding and acceptance.

Dual was holding a weapon out to me. I took it and covered it in my hand as I dropped it to a pocket in my baggy pantaloons. Kim Lee was still standing as we three moved toward the door.

Dual gripped his hand, and I followed. Behind us stalked the great bulk of the hawk-eyed man.

So we passed out and down the stairs to the street— three men who wore the garb of the Eastern people, and walked slowly, and without apparent haste.

10

REYNARD IS CAUGHT

YET IF THE haste was not in the seeming, it was in my heart at least as we trailed along, Dual in the lead, then myself, flapping baggy-legged garments; behind me the great, gray mercenary of the tongs.

Dual led the way, in a wordless dignity of slow advance. To one passing he must have seemed some power of the Eastern world, with his tail of attendants, in order of nearness to his person.

At the corner of Washington we turned east and passed steadily forward down the hill. Somewhere far away, as it seemed, I heard a clock begin to strike. It was eight o'clock!

"In a minute now!"

The thought flashed in my brain. In one minute, if Connel had been as he said, "on the job," he would strike for the freedom of Lucile and his man McKabe.

In one minute, sixty seconds—

Dual paused before me, so that I trod well nigh on his heels.

I looked up to find that we stood before the dingy front of a small shop. In an instant it was familiar as the one through which we had led Lily Lawton and Annie and Reich the night before.

Back of its grimy windows dim electrics cast a reddish-yellow light about a squalid interior of wooden counter and half-filled shelves, where sat one or two denizens of the quarter, holding long bamboo pipes and smoking in a passive sort of enjoyment.

So much I saw and then Dual turned to the great man who followed behind me and spoke quickly in the native tongue.

In response he advanced, passed to the front and set his hand on the latch of the door, swinging it before him and stepping inside.

Dual and I followed. In a moment we were in the shop.

The same little keeper of the place, who had shown such palpable fear and surprise at our advent of the night before, showed before me.

Like his fellows, he glanced up as we entered, and began to chatter in what seemed questioning to me.

For the first time in my presence the grim-faced giant opened his mouth and spoke. He snapped forth his words in a torrent of deep-toned phrases, seemingly addressing the several occupants of the place in collective fashion.

At the end of his speech he waved his arm in a gesture which seemed to clear the room. They rose from before him—those stolid-faced sons of the East, and slunk out of the door, all save the little keeper of the shop, who glanced here and there in a furtive manner, while his companions scuttered away.

Of course, I understood no word of what the hawk-eyed man had said, but even without I could see that they seemed to have carried terror to all those present.

I glanced from the little shop-man, whose face showed

fear and a sort of desperate determination, to the man who faced him, and surprised on his thin-lipped mouth a sort of awful smile.

Again he waved an arm; this time toward the door at the rear of the room which led back to the entrance to the tunnel, as I knew.

Very slowly and as one driven by superior force, the proprietor of the shop sidled along back of his counter before the other's advance.

So we reached the rear of the room and passed through its door to another apartment behind it.

And first of us all walked the keeper of the shop.

He seemed cowed, overawed, but he was still not without a sort of cornered courage, such as the weak things show at times in unescapable places.

Of a sudden, and before I had dreamed of the action, he sprang forward, cried out in a shrill sort of scream and threw himself toward a second door beyond us.

As I followed that mad leap my eyes distinctly saw an electric button set into the frame of the door.

I saw it and found my gaze fastened upon it as a target toward which the little man had launched himself in a wild chance of sounding an alarm.

But he never reached it.

Have you ever seen a hawk strike a running rabbit? I have, and to this day I always liken that scene to the other which transpired now.

As the little figure hurled itself forward the man with the hawk eyes acted, as quickly even as the hawk itself sweeps down.

He lunged from his position at the other's heels. His

great arm with its long talon-like nails reached out, its fingers spreading like the claws of the bird itself.

They spread out and closed with a grasping, prehensile motion, and—they closed on the throat of the man who leaped before.

The little man screamed again—screamed as the rabbit cries out when the hawk's claws pierce it.

The great hand dragged him back. I caught a glimpse of his face, drawn and distorted with pain and terror. Then I looked at the claw-like hand.

It had caught him just under the chin. Its long nails seemed buried in the flesh of his scrawny neck and while I looked, tiny trickles of blood started from beneath the strangling, tearing fingers and ran down over the yellow-brown skin of the puny thing they held.

With a heave the great arm raised and held him striking and struggling as the rabbit struggles, and the threads of blood widened and deepened, and the eyes in his face started and rolled backward like the rabbit's.

"Dual!" I cried out. "Semi! He will kill him."

My friend shook his head.

Very slowly the great arm lowered the writhing thing it held, to the floor, and released it. It lifted skinny hands to its torn throat and moaned and whimpered.

The great hand seized it again, this time by the back of the neck, and turned it toward the rear of the room and the door it had sought to reach.

We passed through that door and down a ladderlike flight of steps.

Damp earth was at the bottom. A dim light came from a row of incandescents which hung from a line of open

wiring at the top of the tunnel. They led off and disappeared at a turn.

Semi Dual thrust a hand into his robes and brought it
out filled with bits of tom paper. He let a few fragments
fall to the floor.

"It was necessary to gain a guide," he said softly to me.
"The man is not seriously injured, but he knows death waits
if he disobeys."

I nodded. I could well believe the terror of death in the
warped little brain under the stiff, black hair.

I could fancy how well I myself would recognize the
potential death in that gaunt, talonlike hand, the nails
of which were holding him helpless on either side of his
yellow-brown neck, provided the neck were mine.

I felt a sort of compassion for the fellow, thug and white
slaver though he was, as he shuffled ahead, while his blood
welled slowly from beneath the gripping nails.

So we went forward—along the dim length of the
tunnel, where the light showed the sheen of moisture, and
the earth was sodden and fetid beneath our feet.

Little by little, as we advanced, the bits of torn paper
fluttered and dropped; to the floor from the fingers of
Semi Dual. He was laying a paper trail to guide the steps
of those who came after.

I began to tingle with a nervous sort of elation as we
pushed deeper and deeper into the crooked channels
beneath the upper city. I thrilled as I saw how completely
it had all been thought out and arranged. Nothing had
been left to chance.

Pushing forward toward the end of the matter, to the
laying hands on the central mind of the whole loathsome

aggregation, Dual laid a paper chase for his hounds of the law to follow.

It was a game of hare and hounds, and the little rabbit held by the claw of the hawk was the guide who should lead us to the heart of the warren. I wondered just what we should find at the end.

Dual spoke again.

"The liberty of Reich and his ally is of short duration, my friend. They came from the station and entered this place. By and by, like Nemesis, we shall overtake them and hale them back from whence they came."

"You used them as you used Lucile then?" I whispered.

He nodded. "The hounds must have a scent," he said shortly. "When the fox has gone to earth, one seals his burrow before digging him out."

Well, Dual had sealed the burrow.

If his orders had been obeyed, by now strong squads of police were in the other leads of the tunnels, working inward toward us as we went forward.

Let the fox try for another exit than the one we were threading and he would merely fall into other hands than ours. The result would be the same—capture.

I smiled somewhat grimly as I walked. The whole thing was so extremely simple in a way, yet so unexpected.

I looked back over the day. I saw how Dual had led these people to think him inactive, baffled, beaten, by their counter stroke. He had led them to think only of their own success.

He had thrown them a second captive and used their seizing of the bait to expose a secret they still believed to be safe. He had yielded, as it seemed, to their demands and used the ones they demanded to lay the trail, which should lead to their absolute undoing.

"Whom the gods destroy they first make mad," I muttered as I walked.

Semi heard me. He turned his head and smiled with a quick flash of understanding in the half light of the tunnel.

"Or overconfident at least," said he.

We went on. We twisted and turned. We took cross tunnels, and turned again into longer, and at last we came to a door.

It was set in the side of what seemed to me to be a wall of concrete. It was made of steel like the door of a vault, and in its center it held the button of a bell.

Above the button was a small circle of glass, to judge by the fact that it showed light. It was a peep-hole beyond any doubt.

I wondered how we were to pass this barrier to our progress. Surely, if we rang and they looked forth, they would never admit us.

Dual settled the matter. He reached up and partly unscrewed the bulb of an incandescent so that its filament ceased to glow.

The dimness of the tunnel increased. It was as though this light had burned out and left only its more distant fellow to lighten the gloom of the place.

On soft feet we advanced, and at a sign from Dual I knelt down, close to the steel leaf of the door, so that the line of vision from the peephole passed above my head.

I drew out my weapon and held it ready. I found my heart beating quickly so that the little pistol quivered and jumped in my hand.

On the other side Semi sank down also. He whispered to the man of the tongs, who, in turn, addressed his captive briefly.

At the end he shoved him up to the door, and then sank slowly behind him, using his body as a blind. In the faint glow of the distant light he was no more than a shadowy outline.

He muttered hoarsely. The hand of our guide went up and rang the bell, paused, and rang again.

The light from the peephole fell on his face. I saw it livid and drawn with a double fear. He was caught between two fates, as he saw it, with small escape from either.

Yet he dared the one in the near future to be spared the present menace of the man who had driven him here.

The light in the peephole died. I knew now that those within were seeking identification of the one who rang.

Evidently they could not see distinctly in the absence of light in the tunnel. There was a click as of something falling into a socket, and some one spoke abruptly.

I sensed that the glass had been turned back, and left space for a voice.

The man we had captured hissed sharply, as against his volition. I knew that once more the clawlike hand was biting into his flesh. He spoke quickly immediately after.

The voice from the inside answered. Again the glass clicked into place, and a light streamed through it.

Then, while I listened to my pulses hammering loudly, while I strained forward, waiting, I saw the steel door move slightly and swing partly ajar.

"Now!" barked Dual.

We three hurled ourselves against it, the shopkeeper shoved before us and adding his weight to ours.

For a second a surprised resistance met us, and then the door yielded.

We plunged into a room brilliant with the soft light of modern electrics; the same room which Miss Foote has described.

I saw its equipment of office fixtures in the first glance of entry, and then my eyes flashed to the occupants of that strange underground place of business.

In a way it was strangely in keeping with the business transacted, that it was done underground, away from the light of day.

A smothered oath struck my ears, and I whirled.

Half-way between a large desk in the center of the room and the door, at a place where our inward rush had hurled him, a man with reddish-brown hair and mustache, and full red lips, was glaring upon us.

I threw down my hand, holding the automatic, and waved him backward from our front.

My eyes followed his movements.

Dimly, as we entered, I had heard a woman scream. As my man retreated before the menace of my weapon I saw two women.

One was Greek Annie. She was sitting in a chair and staring with unbelieving eyes full into my own.

Back of her was Reich, who had leaped to his feet.

From him my eyes turned to a man—tall, thin—with hair, brushed back from his forehead, and narrow, deep-set eyes.

He sat at the desk itself, or had been sitting. Now he had

half risen and was leaning forward, his hands gripping the edge of the desk's top, as he viewed our unexpected arrival.

In the brilliant light his eyes glowed and glistened with what seemed a sort of catlike sheen to me—a sort of greenish yellow, as though they might be slightly phosphorescent in the dark.

But it was the second woman who made me fairly gasp. I have never seen anything like her.

I may as well describe her as a gorgeous rose in a vase of gold. Even in that moment it was the thought which came to me.

She was dark—one of those clear-skinned brunettes one sometimes finds with skins like pale wax. Her hair was black, and into its dusky masses were thrust on each side in front of the ears the fresh flowers of two crimson peonies.

Her eyes were dark, and darkened underneath until they looked like pools of midnight blackness. Her skin, as I have said, was waxen; but her cheeks and lips were rouged until they made whirls and a red slit of crimson in the mask of white.

She lay back in a great padded chair of crimson, and she had not moved at our entrance save to turn her eyes; yet every line of her supple body was tense.

And she was dressed in gold. Her entire dress, which fitted her like the sheath of a flower, was of some golden fabric, which glinted and flashed with a thousand tiny points of brilliance under the lights.

She was like a great exotic flower, set to the calyx in a golden tube.

All these things I saw in a flash, while the red-lipped, brown-haired man retreated from me.

There came the sound of a fall. I caught a fleeting glimpse of the shopkeeper lifted and flung to the floor between the door and the desk where the cat-eyed man was leaning.

The man of the tongs had hurled him into a huddled, groveling heap. Now he calmly drew a huge weapon from his clothing and added its threat to my support.

I looked for Dual. He was standing just inside of the door, which was closed once more.

He had drawn himself up to his full six feet of height and was calmly returning the stare of the man at the desk.

The light sparkled and shone from the facets of the huge ruby he was wearing in his turban, and it glowed like a living flame of menace above the other menace of his eyes.

"Who—who the devil are you?" spoke the man at the desk.

"Call me Nemesis," came his answer in tones deep, full, vibrant, which seemed to carry a hint of immutable truth.

"Nemesis?" stammered the other.

For one moment he seemed unable to gather his wits fully before our sudden apparition.

"Nemesis," Dual repeated, and it seemed to me that now he played for time—sought to add to the other's startled surprise.

"The sum total of the misdeeds a man commits. The thing he creates for himself—by which he is pursued, and by which each is some day overtaken. Call me the incarnation of the souls you have crushed, come to crush you in turn."

"What balderdash is this?" snapped the man at the desk. "I don't know who the devil you are, but I fancy the best thing is to call some of my servants and have you thrown out. By what right do you break in here, and what do you want? Is this a hold-up? Who led you here?"

"Fate," said Dual.

The man sneered.

"Do you call that thing on the floor there fate?"

He pointed to the shopman, who still lay where he had fallen, the blood of his torn flesh drying on his skin.

"I perceive that you tortured that carrion into leading you here. When I have attended to you he will die."

"Stop!" said Dual softly as the hand of the man crept out toward a button on the end of the desk.

"You will call no one. You will kill no one. You will listen to me, and do as I say—and, failing in that, *you* will die if *I* speak the word. The nails of Wong Sing are strong and your neck is slender. Can you picture yourself like the thing on the floor?"

The creeping hand drew back. I saw the green eyes turn, as against their will, to the torn throat of his servant. A sort of involuntary shudder shook him.

"You—you seem to have the drop," he said with an effort. Dual's pose appeared to have shaken him deeply.

"What do you want?"

"Sit down," Semi directed. "And bid your two men sit down behind you."

He gestured to Reich and the red-lipped man.

"You cursed devil—you bloodhound!" shrieked the former, breaking the tenseness of his posture. "Nemesis is a good name for you, you hound of the law! Maybe Reynard don't know you, but you bet I do. You're Semi Dual. I make you for all your fake rags!"

He turned swiftly to the man by the desk.

"It's a frame-up, and by God they've got us!" he went on in half-hysterical excitement.

"They 'sprung' Annie and me for a shadow, an' they got by with the thing. You thought you had them beaten, you did. You, the wise guy—you, Reynard, the fox, as you call yourself. You was just tellin' us how you'd put it all over Connel an' this bunch who grabbed the Lawton kid. You was rubbin' it in on us for that fall down. An' now—"

He pointed a finger toward Semi.

"That man is workin' with Connel—he's a fly cop. He's the fliest cop I ever saw. You thought I was easy to let him use me—didn't you, Bill? Well, now you're up against the guy yourself. It's up to you, old fox!

"That's Semi Dual and a hatchet man, and the other guinea is Glace for a thousand any day! You told us we was safe in here, that nobody could reach us. Well, are we— are we? Why, you ain't even safe yourself—you're grabbed. Who's made a fall down now?"

His voice rose to a shrill yell of question. He sank into a chair, and shook and shivered.

"Oh, hell!" he exclaimed, and fumbled in his pocket to draw out a cigarette, while I watched his hand to see that it wasn't a gun.

The man at the desk, Reynard, turned his eyes slowly from Reich to Dual. For a minute he seemed to be completely confused, and in that moment the strange creature in the golden dress sat up and spoke.

She lifted a hand to her left breast and clutched the golden fabric which sheathed it. She lifted herself from the depths of the crimson seat in which she sat, and I saw from the rise and fall of her bosom that she panted.

"Are you of the police?" she cried out, leaning forward toward Semi. "Are you? Oh, for God's sake, tell me!"

"Mr. Reich is correct in his recognition," said Dual.

She rose to her feet and threw out her arms in a wide-flung gesture, as one who tears loose from bonds.

"Thank God—oh, thank God!" she cried and turned to Reynard.

"At last! At last!" she went on; "the hour has come that I prayed for. Your hour, Reynard—yours—and mine. At last the God I have prayed to has answered and sent the help I asked. I have prayed and prayed. I have hoped and doubted, and now I am answered—at last.

"Ever since you had me trapped and brought here to this den of your building to be the plaything of your passions I have prayed for this time to come.

"It's two years, isn't it, Reynard, you have kept me in prison—two years you have made me your toy—two years you have painted my face and clothed my body to please your eyes—two years of bondage—two years of hell—two years when I never saw the sun by day nor the moon by night—two years you have kept me in a padded prison, lined with rose-colored satin, watched over by your jackals that I might not escape—even from life—two years since you had me fooled from my home and caught in your trap and brought here, because you had seen me and wanted to make me your creature to take the place of that one you had tired of before you saw me?

"And this is the end. God has heard and sent these men to free me because, no matter what you have done to me, Bill Reynard, my soul is as pure as the day you stole an innocent girl and dragged her away from God's light to this hell-hole of yours!

"And God hears the prayers of a clean soul, sooner or later, Reynard. It is my time now. It is you who shall go into prison.

"For two years you have fancied me doomed to your pleasure forever; for two years, you have told me your plans, and your sins, and even the names of some of those poor girls you have captured and caged and sold to your buyers of flesh!

"I know! I know, Reynard, and I shall tell. And with every word I say I shall give thanks that I know and can swear to the things I shall say. Those things shall send you to prison, Reynard.

"I shall tell of murder—of the death of those girls who would not submit. I shall tell how you slew with your own cruel hands. And you shall go to prison, and I shall go back where the sun shines once more. I shall go back to the light, Reynard—back to the light—the—"

Reynard sprang from his chair.

"Quit it!" he screamed. "Hold your tongue, you fool—you!"

His hands lifted on tensely flexed arms, as though he longed to choke the words in her beautiful throat, beautiful yet for all the two years she had been shut in his sensuous dungeon.

"Steady, Reynard!" came the voice of Dual. "What will it avail to add another count to the score? You are taken. Listen!"

With a quick motion he threw open the door.

From the tunnel beyond it there came a sound of running feet.

"Your hour is at hand," Dual went on. "That is the sound of the lawpack running on your trail. They are sweeping your tunnels, Reynard, from three directions. They are almost here."

The woman in gold laughed shrilly. She stood, tall and gleaming, in the light of the lamps. Her breath was coming in great, quivering sobs. The flowers in her hair were red and meaty, as clotted drops of blood.

Reynard turned to the sound of racing footsteps.

Without warning he leaped over the desk and struck the floor near the still huddled form of his henchman. He struck, running like a gaunt cat, and launched himself for the door Dual had set wide, as a cornered animal will sometimes chance all on one dash for the open.

The hawk swooped for the second time that night. The great hands reached out and seized him.

He cried out shrilly once, and hung in the grip of the talons which clutched and circled his throat. His own hands came up and clawed in an effort to break that grip. He struggled and writhed and turned.

For the second time the slave laughed at the spectacle of her master.

The pound of feet grew nearer. Some one cried out. There was a rush of blue and brass from the tunnel, and the room filled quickly with the forms of the police.

"By Jove!" said the red-lipped man I held covered.

Reich swore softly. Greek Annie sneered.

Dual addressed the lieutenant in charge of the squad.

"Take all here, with the exception of the dark girl in

gold. She is a witness of value. With her evidence and that of Miss Foote, the conviction of all is assured. Send your prisoners to the hall, lieutenant. Wait here until your other squads have swept the other tunnels. That is, I think, the end of your duties. Good night."

With a sign to the man of the tongs and myself, he turned and stepped into the tunnel, walking swiftly back along the trail which he himself had laid.

11

THE KARMA

THE HAWK-EYED MAN and myself walked after.

Outside in the shop we had entered not so very long before, Semi paused. Once more he drew money from his person and placed it in the sinewy blood-stained hands.

He spoke briefly to the man, who bowed and smiled slightly for the second time that night; and, having smiled, pocketed the gold Dual had given and stalked out of the door to the street.

Dual watched him in silence, and turned to me.

"Come, Gordon," he said, "the matter is ended. Let us return to the hotel."

"But Miss Foote?" I questioned. "And McKabe?"

"Do you doubt they are safe?" said Semi.

"Doubt? Great Heavens, no!" I assured him quickly. "I was merely wondering where they were and just what had happened."

"We can learn that at the hotel, I fancy," said Semi, and led the way to the door.

If I had felt bizarre when I walked out of the Palace Hotel, I surely felt more so when I followed Dual in his purple and golden robes from the taxi which put us down in and across the lobby of the St. Francis.

Our advent caused almost a commotion, and the boy in the cage we entered stared until he well-nigh forgot to start his car, and was spoken to sharply by the captain, who had signaled him twice.

I think it was in a mood of whimsy that Semi rapped on the door of the suite. Once in a while my strange friend gave way to a sort of playful manner.

Sheldon himself answered our summons. He stared into our faces without recognition.

"Hello!" he began. "I reckon you've made some mistake, ain't you, mister?"

"I hardly agree with you, colonel," said Dual.

The old man started.

"Well, my Lord!" he exclaimed. "I'm wise to that voice, but—well, by golly, was that what you put on when you shed your clothes? Say, I remember you pulled that sort of a stunt once before, though I didn't see it. That was the time you was Prince Abdul of Teheran. Come on in. Say, folks—here's Semi Dual an' Glace."

We entered, and I started to see Lily, McKabe, and Lucile Foote staring toward our entrance.

Dual smiled at my surprise, and spoke to the latter.

"Did Abdul say truly, Miss Foote? Didst reach to thy heart's desire?"

A flush swept the face of the girl. In an effort to mask her confusion she answered lightly:

"Abdul is a man of truth, O Abdul!"

"She was just telling us about it," said Colonel Sheldon. "And what happened then, Lucile?"

The girl went on with her narrative much as it is set down in preceding chapters.

"And then the man with the knife sprang through the door at us. The one with the lantern turned it on us, coming just inside the cell.

"'Stop!' It was Danny's voice.

"I turned my eyes to see him level the little automatic on the man with the knife.

"'Come any farther and I'll drill you, you rat!'

"The crouching figure paused in its advance and stared at the gun trained upon it. A snarl grew on the yellow mask.

"'No good,' he said on the instant, in English. 'You kill me, others kill you allee same, McKabe.'

"'You'll kill nobody!' I cried, adding my voice. I reached up and dragged at my hair, tearing out the package Kim Lee had given.

"'You look this—you see you kill or no!' I called to the man and tossed the package to him where he crouched.

"He caught it deftly in the uncertain light, unwrapped it, and gave it a glance, started, and nearly dropped it.

"After a bit he gave it a second inspection, spread out the strip of paper, and seemed to read it. His eyes lifted to mine, and the snarl had left his face.

"'Where you get?' he questioned, with the savage menace gone from his tones:

"Something seemed to force me to answer:

"'From the master.'

"He gave me another glance. Abruptly he turned with the signet and the paper to the man who held the lantern.

"The two bent above it, uttering excited sibilants of speech.

"'Well, I'm darned!' breathed Danny, beside me. 'Wouldn't that jolt you?'

" 'S-s-sh!' I whispered.

"The two by the lantern conferred briefly; then the one who had threatened turned back.

" 'You live,' he addressed me. 'Boss say kill McKabe; anybody come get him. I do. You get out, maybe.'

" 'Not with my permission will you kill me, you scut!' said Danny. He leveled the gun once more.

"The yellow man leered, rolled up his sleeve, and seized his knife.

"Again I heard the shouting. It was louder. There came a shot—several shots.

"I heard the sound of crashing blows and confused babble of voices. I strained forward in my collar to listen.

"The man with the knife had edged out of the ray of the lantern, which still played fully on Danny.

" 'Get him, Dan—get him!' I found myself crying.

"My companion was leaning forward, also, peering toward the spot where the yellow assassin had disappeared.

"Again came resounding blows, the sound of axes striking and tearing wood. A rending crash followed, and a bull-like bellow filled the tunnel.

"I heard the sound of many feet running. The man back of the lantern-bearer cried out. I saw him turn like a trapped rat to escape.

"A wave of life seemed to seize him and bear him down. The man with the lantern wavered. He dropped the lantern. It lay flickering weirdly on its side as its light flared and died.

"A vicious crack of powder came from beside me. In the last of the dying flame of the lantern I saw a shadowy figure stagger back from beyond Danny.

"And then the room was full of excited Caucasian faces, lighted by the glow of electric torches.

" 'McKabe—Dan—are you here, boy?' I heard a voice calling.

"Through the mists of a wild relief I saw the drawn face of Connel peering toward where we stood.

" 'All right, Jim,' I sensed Danny speaking. 'Look sharp! There's a rat in here somewhere with a knife. I think I winged him. Dig him out and then get a blacksmith. They've got us chained up by the necks.'

"At that I began to laugh in a manner beyond my control—and I guess that's all," she ended. "We got out, thanks to Abdul."

"Abdul is a holy wonder!" Sheldon exploded. "If I hadn't seen it, I wouldn't believe it! An' as for Glace, he's no slouch of a chink himself."

"Just the same," I retorted, "I'll feel a bit more like myself when I get something else on. Did my clothes come back here, colonel?"

He nodded.

"Oh, yes; they came back. Folks have been makin' a sort of second-hand clothing-shop of this 'sweet' all day. I was worried when Dual's duds arrived; but when yours came up, I was wise that it was getting to be a habit. I went in an' locked up my suit-case, to make sure all my things was here."

"Thanks for the information," I told him. "If you don't mind, I'll go get into Western attire."

I was back in five minutes, to find McKabe speaking.

"As for myself," he was saying, "I can only express a deep appreciation for your work, Mr. Dual. It has brought me out of a pretty tight position. I don't pretend to understand your methods, but they surely seem to give results.

"And that brings me to the point that Connel said he was coming up here after a while to apologize to you. He went back to the hall first to see what his other squads had caught."

"They caught a good deal," returned Semi. "They caught Reich and Annie, and another male agent, and also William Reynard—"

"Bill Reynard!" exclaimed McKabe, sitting upright tensely.

"Exactly," said Dual.

"I've had my eye on that chap," McKabe asserted. "Lord! Did you get him with the goods?"

"Very much with the goods."

"Connel will have a fit!" McKabe chuckled. "Say, he'll simply have to eat crow now."

Dual shook his head. "I have no desire to have Captain Connel humble himself in any way," he responded. "There was no chance for him to understand my efforts. My methods are the result of years of experience and much study, Mr. McKabe."

Dan McKabe nodded.

"They sure show it! But look here! We're all friends, and I want to ask a question. How did you know that Lucile and I were going to find ourselves locked up together, and how did you know that about—about that heart's desire stuff that you told her before you sent her out?"

He paused, flushed, and turned to Lucile.

"I told you I was going to ask him," he said.

Dual smiled softly.

"I learned that in the same way that I learned that you would be set free at eight one o'clock," he returned; "from my calculations. It would not require them to tell it now."

Lucile's flushed face swung from her lover to Semi.

"You are the most wonderful man I have ever known—shall ever know," she said in a voice of emotion. "You have given me a little insight into what a man may become—you have given to me—the greatest thing—which has ever come to me—perhaps which ever will. I shall never forget, and I shall try to be worthy—and"—she smiled out of eyes which were wet by sudden tears—"I shall try to build up the right sort of Karma."

"In such you shall tread the path of attainment," Semi replied.

"Lucile—I have looked into your soul, since I met you, as I looked into your eyes the first day that we met. I have found both clear and steadfast. Walk forward, and be not afraid."

Sheldon, who had been sitting silent, appeared to wake up.

"An' when do we go back to Goldfield?" he queried. "I gather that McKabe an' Miss Lucile here have about decided to play partners, an' I say 'Amen'; but I reckon Glace would sorter like to see a certain little woman he's left back there where we come from."

"We will start to-morrow," said Semi. "Gordon's honeymoon has been sadly interrupted. The matter here is ended, and we can return at once."

I was glad. As he said, my honeymoon had been severely broken. I looked at Lucile and McKabe, whose eyes turned ever toward each other; and I thought of Connie, waiting and worrying, no doubt, back there in old Sheldon's home.

I would be glad to get back and take a few days' quiet in her company and love. I would have a lot to tell her—

The telephone rang.

"Oh, shut up!" grinned Sheldon as he rose to answer. I laughed.

The colonel turned back from the phone.

"There's a fellow down-stairs named Connel. He wants to come up," he announced, and winked at McKabe.

Dual nodded, and the colonel instructed the office to let the captain proceed.

He tapped on the door, which I opened. He came in, his florid face wearing a half puzzled, half abashed expression. Dual rose and extended his hand.

"Come in, captain; we are glad to see you," he began.

"An' I had to see you," said Connel. "When I'm in wrong I'm not the man to deny it. I had you wrong to-day, Mr. Dual, an' I want to say so. You pulled off what we've wanted to put over for a good long while. I don't know how you did it, and I don't expect to, but I want to just say that it was a mighty big thing—the biggest I ever saw."

He turned his eyes to McKabe.

"You was right about that Reynard guy, Mac. An' that ain't all. Who do you suppose come in with him?"

McKabe shook his head, though he seemed to sense the suppressed excitement in his superior's tones.

"You remember the Morena case, two years ago?" Connel continued.

McKabe started.

"Morena?" he repeated. "You mean the society girl who disappeared one night on her way to a ball an' was never heard of since?"

Connel nodded.

"Just. I mean little Lola Morena. Reynard grabbed her, an' has held her for two years. She'll be the star witness against him. If her story is right, we got him for murder."

"Her story is right," said Dual.

Connel shook his head slowly.

"I don't know how you do it," he muttered. "I don't see how you did it last night, and I don't 'make' your actions to-day. But I'll have to admit that you've been right all along. If it's a fair question, what gave you the edge on these folks, Mr. Dual?"

"That, captain," said Semi Dual, "was merely a matter of Karma."

"Karma," Connel repeated. "I don't, get you, I'm afraid."

"No?" Dual smiled slightly. "If you are not familiar with the subject, captain, permit me to advise you to look it up some time. It is one which might very well be worth any man's investigation."

Sheldon chuckled.

"Karma is the same thing as the kick of a twenty-horse-power mule, Connel," he cut in. "Karma is the joker in the deck, an' it's always trumps."

That night, after we retired, the colonel surprised me by speaking aloud, as though completing a half-voiced sentence. "Karma," said Colonel Sheldon, "is all to the good. I got a new motter for life:

"Play the game straight, an' don't try to use a hold-out. Any man who does that can walk up an' kiss Karma when he meets her, an' not get a poke in the jaw.

"Ain't I right?"

I told him I thought he was.

BOX 991

1

FARR?

I WAS STANDING beside the railing, chatting to Dick Sheldon, assistant cashier of the Fourth National Bank, when I first saw Joe Hood.

Having dropped in that morning in early November to attend to a little business, I had stopped for a word with Dick, whom I had known for some time.

His quarters on the floor were inside of a low rail set between the passage which led to the vault and the built-in rooms of President Carlton and Cashier Gibson in the front. Back of the passage to the vault began the various cages of the several tellers, which ran on down that side, crossed at the rear and continued up the other side. From Dick's station one could command a view of the entire main floor.

My business hadn't taken over ten minutes and I had arrived on the stroke of ten. It must therefore have been a quarter past when I saw a broad-shouldered, well-set-up individual clad in a rough-finish suit of gray come out of the vault passage rather quickly and turn down the line of cages to that of Paying-teller Mack.

Years in the newspaper business and later in the detective game with my partner, Bryce, have taught me to see a good deal in a glance. Something in the fleeting glimpse of the man's face as he passed me, an indefinable manner in his walk, indicating haste and strained intention, attracted my interest so that I followed his back with my eyes. That was how I saw him stop at Fred Mack's window and apparently speak to the teller.

Then, after a word, he swung about and came straight back along the floor.

As he approached I could appraise him as an open-air type from his bronzed skin and his free carriage that held a hint of conscious self-sufficiency in its bearing. And as he drew nearer still I saw that his eyes, now slightly narrowed, gleamed gray from between the lids. His hair, neatly trimmed, was brown, and showed evidences of a recent trip to the barber's, and his jaw, now firmly set, was square.

He passed me not three feet away, and again entered the passage between the cages and Sheldon's railing, pausing there until suddenly Mack emerged from the alley back of the cages themselves.

Business with the bank had caused me to know Fred Mack, A to G teller, quite well by sight. He was a man who was likely to attract attention.

Square-faced one might call him, with reddish-brown hair, just frosted with gray at the temples, a ruddy skin and a red, almost pouting lower lip, partly masked by a short red-brown mustache. I think, though, that the thing I had always noted mainly about him was his absolutely punctilious dress—his bandbox appearance. Never in my life had I seen him when he did not look as though he had just been groomed.

BOX 991   163

Ordinarily I wouldn't have paid any attention. It was the subtle something in the manner of the gray-clad stranger which made me watch the two men out of the corner of my eye and lose the thread of Sheldon's remarks.

Mack advanced directly to where the other stood, and they spoke in low tones together. Mack seemed protesting; the stranger continued to insist. Abruptly the teller seized him by the arm and faced him toward Sheldon, forcing him up to the rail.

"Mr. Sheldon," he said tensely, with a glance toward me.

Sheldon turned toward them in his swivel chair, and the teller went on: "This is Mr. Hood—Mr. Joe Hood. He's—well, he's just been in the vault, and he says somebody's been at his box."

"Impossible!" That was all Sheldon said, and I saw his eyes narrow as he said it.

"That's what I've just been telling him, sir," Mack continued, speaking softly. "But—Mr. Sheldon, I've known Joe since we were boys, and—well, something must have happened. I thought it best to speak to you at once."

"That's right," said Dick, and turned to the man Mack had called Hood. "When were you in your box last?"

"Two years ago—the day I rented the thing," Hood replied.

"Not since?" Sheldon's tone was a bit sharp.

"No."

"And what's wrong—missing?"

"Everything." Hood shot his jaw still farther forward as he ground out the word.

For a minute the assistant cashier said nothing. The line of his lids grew even closer. He appeared studying the man before him even as I was now. So far as I could see the fellow bore the stare well.

"You must know," Dick spoke after the pause, "that it is practically impossible for any one to get into these boxes."

Hood came closer to the rail, pressing against it. He threw out an arm and laid a hand over on Sheldon's desk.

"That's what I *did* think when I rented the thing," he returned. "But, impossible or not, you don't have to take my word for the matter. Come into the vault and see for yourself. I don't care a hang how impossible it is, it's happened and I'm short just twenty-five thousand worth of securities. That's the main point as I see it."

Sheldon got out of his chair without a word, and then his eyes came back to me. I think he had forgotten my presence for the moment. Certainly one could excuse him. What he had heard was enough to fill his mind completely. Now, however, he hesitated for barely a second.

"You come too, Glace," he requested, turned and stepped through a gate into the passage to the vault.

I followed. My interest was developing swiftly, despite the fact that Sheldon alleged that what Hood claimed was out of the question. Still, strange things do happen, and this looting of a vault box seemed likely to present a pretty tangle to me.

Mack knew me, of course, and nodded in salutation as Dick led us up to the metal grill and spoke to the custodian of the vault, who sat at a desk on its far side. The attendant rose and opened the door to admit us. We slipped through and the door clanged shut.

"Which box?" Sheldon spoke then for the first time.

"Nine ninety-one," said Hood.

BOX 991   165

Sheldon nodded and strode into the vault. I saw the box before we reached it. It had been unlocked and stood half drawn out of its compartment. Dick put up a hand and dragged it clear out. He lifted the lid and glanced inside, turned it upside down and shook it. Then he held it out for Mack and me to see.

"It's empty now, all right, he admitted. "Now just what is your story, Mr. Hood?"

Hood fished a cigar out of his coat, bit the end with strong teeth and set it alight.

"Not very long," he replied. "When my father died he left me some cash and twenty-five thousand worth of salable stocks in paying concerns. Mack, here, can tell you I'm a mining engineer and was two years ago. Just after Dad died I got in with a syndicate who intended exploiting some Alaska holdings. They sent me up there. Before I went I came here and rented this box. Fred knows that, because he introduced me and attended to the preliminary arrangements. I chose this bank largely because I knew him and had for years. I put the stocks in this drawer and paid the rent for a year. Then I went away.

"I haven't been back until to-day. You've changed your vault man since. Fred, here, had to identify me to the new one. After that I came in and opened the box. It was just as you see it now, I left it and came out and spoke to Fred. That's all."

Sheldon turned to Mack.

"You introduced Mr. Hood here?"

"Yes, sir," replied the teller.

"Do you know that he put the stocks into this box?"

"No, sir—that is, I didn't see him. But—"

"Rubbish!" Hood caught the box out of Sheldon's hands and tapped its hollow body with a heavy knuckle. "I tell you I put them in this box. Look at it now. You folks don't supervise what a patron puts in a box or takes out, do you? Well, then—I say I put twenty-five thousand worth of securities in here two years ago and left them. If you think there's any funny work about it, I've a list on my person of those certificates and their numbers. That's all I have got. Call your bank policeman and have him go through me, if you think this is a plant."

Sheldon shook his head.

"We haven't intended to convey any such thought, Mr. Hood. Mr. Glace here is a detective, as it happens." He waved a hand at me.

Hood grinned. Suddenly he jammed the box back into its compartment, seized his coat with a hand on each flap and stretched it open.

"Go on, Glace, and frisk me, just to be sure," he said. "Wish you would. I'm simply desirous of getting to the bottom of this thing and we want to start right. It isn't the money so much. I've cleaned up a pile up North for myself, but I want to get the man who slipped this over on me. And I'll be hanged if I lay down till I do. 'Tain't revenge—it's—a sort of self-defense."

I stepped forward.

"This is at your own suggestion and request, Mr. Hood," I remarked, as I began my search.

He grinned again and nodded.

"Sure. Hope you find 'em. It would save time."

But I didn't find anything save the list he mentioned, and

BOX 991   167

some personal note books and papers and such. I stepped back with a shake of my head for Sheldon and Mack.

Hood shrugged his shoulders into his coat.

"No," he said. "I don't want you folks to think I'm laying any blame any place—yet. But I do want to find out about this, and I intend to, and I think it's up to you to help. What do *you* think?"

"We'll help all we can, of course." Sheldon agreed. "I can't see how the thing could happen. We believed our safeguards effective—"

"I can get your viewpoint there, too," Hood took him up. "If it was as hard for a stranger to get to my full box as it was for me to get to it empty this morning, you're—"

Mack interrupted. He had been standing silent, pulling at his full under lip, while I made the search of Hood.

"There's just one way I can see that it might have happened. Supposing it wasn't a stranger. Several of the boys here have boxes in the vault."

Hood's eyes squinted.

"Yes. Who?"

Mack laughed slightly.

"Well, I have, and so has Sheldon."

We were still standing in the vault. Hood reached over and slapped him on the shoulder.

"You old josher, quit it. This isn't a joking matter," he said, and then to Sheldon: "Well, what do we do, tell the police or get a detective? I suppose you belong to the Bankers' Association, or something like that?"

Sheldon was staring at the box just inside its still open door. Now, he walked over, pushed the door shut and locked it, withdrawing the key from the lock and inspecting it closely. His eyes came up and met mine in question. He looked badly worried.

I couldn't blame him, either. This was the third time in a few years there had been trouble at the Fourth National. In fact, it was through former happenings I had come to know the assistant cashier so well. I made no move, however, but merely waited. He turned his glance away after a second.

"This yours?" he inquired of Hood, extending the key.

The engineer nodded and took it, and Sheldon went on:

"I don't think that in this case I'd advise either course you mention. I'm going to ask a favor of you, Mr. Hood, right at the start. I do not believe that in any detail we are guilty of negligence in this affair; and, while I do not deny that you are loser in the matter, I am going to suggest that instead of calling in the regular operatives of our protective association, you allow me to suggest a private investigation of the case. I am convinced that there are elements about it which will require a more than ordinarily careful search for their finding, and, to be perfectly frank, I want to avoid all the publicity possible in the matter. You know such publicity hurts a bank immensely."

Hood frowned.

"You mean get a private detective, I suppose. I've read a lot about them, but I never saw one worth his salt."

"Like all other callings, there are good and bad ones," said Sheldon. "The man I had in mind is here now—Mr. Glace of Glace & Bryce."

I had half expected it after Sheldon's glance, and I think Mack had, too. I remembered the look he had thrown me when he first told Sheldon what had happened outside. But Hood evidently had not. Perhaps he had thought of

BOX 991   169

me as someone attached to the bank. He turned and met my eye squarely.

"You?" he remarked. "Want to take it on?"

I couldn't well fail Sheldon, and, I confess, the thing interested me. As Dick Sheldon had said, it looked very peculiar.

"That's my business, Mr. Hood," I replied.

He nodded.

"All right, let it go at that, then. What do we do first?"

"First," I said, "you give me that list of stocks I found when I searched you."

Sheldon nodded. I saw his eye light briefly. Hood produced the list.

"Sign it with your usual signature," I directed, and waited until he had done so before taking it and putting it away in my pocket folder. "I'll have our stenographer make you a copy of this and return it," I continued. "And now, Sheldon, tell me just how a customer goes about gaining access to the vault."

Hood answered instead, however.

Oh, I can vouch for the completeness of that, Mr. Glace. You have to give a password to the guard, then sign a card after you are let through the barrier, and then he goes with you and uses a master key before yours will work. It was the password queered me this morning. Not every bank uses that, and I had forgotten all about it and what it was. I had to get Fred for that very reason."

"How many keys does a patron have?" I next inquired.

"Two," said Hood. "I have both of mine, one on my ring and one in my trunk. No clue there."

"Then, for the sake of verification, let's see what your card says." I suggested. "You signed it this morning?"

"I certainly did. Come on and I'll show you." He turned toward the door of the vault.

We all followed, and Sheldon asked the custodian to show us Hood's card. The man produced it, and we bent above it. As stated, it showed a signature under date of two years before, and below that a fresh duplicate dated for the present day. I drew out the listing I had just taken from Hood and compared his writing with that on the card. So far as I could see they were identically the same.

Putting the listing away, I considered the matter swiftly. There was surely a kink in it somewhere. On its face it couldn't have happened, and yet it had, and I couldn't doubt Joe Hood. There was something open, frank, roughly likable about the fellow that inspired a full belief in his story. Then how—I thought of something.

"Look here, I resumed. "You say you paid a year's rental for that box. Now, you've been gone for two years nearly. Could that have had any bearing on the matter—would the box have been held in the meantime in your name? How about it, Sheldon?"

Again Hood interrupted before Dick could answer.

"Nothing in that. You see, I paid the rent at the end of the year. Last fall I came down to Seattle. I half expected to get on here, but it so happened that I didn't. I even wrote Fred that I might get over to see him. We've kept up a hit-and-miss correspondence since I've been away. I came down to Seattle, and it was there I closed up the deal which has put me on what looks like the road to a real fortune. But it took longer than I thought it would, and I didn't

BOX 991   171

get through in time to run over here. So I sent the money for the box through Mack and he sent me my receipt. You remember that, don't you, Fred?"

"Yes; I think I've even got your letter, if I'm not mistaken."

"There you are," said Hood. "I wrote Fred this time that I was coming. I doubt if he'd have known me himself if he hadn't been expecting me to arrive. I've changed a good bit. I used to be as slender and as good a dresser as he is. Folks even said we looked a little alike when we were a pair of young bucks together. But Alaska changed me. It's a great country up there. A man finds himself out in more ways than one. It peels off the outer skin and leaves a man just naked before himself."

I grinned.

"You seem bound to knock all my little simple explanations into a cocked hat," I remarked.

Hood frowned slightly.

"Honest, Glace, I don't think simple little explanations will fit this business."

"No," I admitted, "I don't really think so either; but I want to eliminate them at the start. I've a friend who says that in order to harmonize the possible with the impossible you must find not the new but the unexpected angle through which cosmic force has been caused to work."

I was thinking of Semi Dual when I spoke. More and more this thing began to look to me like a case for my strange friend to find pleasure in solving. Of course Hood knew nothing of Semi Dual, but my words seemed to arrest his attention. He smiled slowly.

"Your friend must be a philosopher," he made comment.

I nodded. Again I saw Dick Sheldon's eyes lighten. He

knew to whom I referred. He had reason, and good reason, to know how effective Dual's peculiar methods were. It came to me suddenly that he had half hoped I would enlist Dual's aid in the present matter when he had asked that I handle the case. In a flash I saw the trend of his intention, and I smiled slightly as I caught the look of relief on his face, and knew that he knew I had thought of the man in the Urania's tower, even as he had. I felt more certain of my surmise when he spoke.

"It wouldn't be any use to examine that box for finger-prints, would it, Glace?"

Then I *did* know of what he was thinking. There had been a time when I had done that very thing and found the right marks. Now, however. I shook my head.

"Too much handling this morning. Sheldon, and too long a time since the thing was done, most likely," I replied.

But his remark had given me another thought. I turned again to Hood.

"When you opened the box this morning, you didn't notice any evidence of its having been tampered with, did you?"

"You mean the lock? No," he said promptly. "It worked all right."

And then I directed myself to Mack.

"Mr. Mack, you say you have a box in the vault; just where is it?"

"Way below Joe's," he answered. "On the one-hundred tier."

"Have you in any of your visits to it during the past two years noticed any sign of his box having been tampered with in any way?"

BOX 991   173

"Never." He shook his head in decided denial.

"You know," I went on, following my new line, "there might be something in your joking suggestion of a few moments ago. Although a customer must give a password and sign a card to get into the vault, I don't suppose a regular employee of the bank—a man known to the vault guard here—would have to do that."

It was the guard who answered this time.

"He'd have to sign the card, sir, just the same."

Mack nodded.

"You'll find my card signed and dated with the day, hour and minute of each of my visits to my box," he declared.

Hood spread his hands palms up.

"And there you are," he said.

"Wait a bit," I returned. "Now, Mr. Mack, you said you had a box, and so had Sheldon. Who else has one among the regular force of the bank?"

Mack flushed.

"Well—really, Mr. Glace, you embarrass me by that question," he blurted. "My remark was not well considered, I am afraid. I wouldn't like it said that I had intimated—"

"You intimate nothing," I told him. "I ask you a question and you can answer it or not. If you do not, I can gain the information elsewhere."

He kept pulling at his lip.

"Well, there's Baird, I believe, and Johnny Powell and young Sidney, and Neville Farr. So far as I know, that's all."

I looked at the custodian, and he nodded.

"That's all, sir," he said.

"Are they all here this morning?" I questioned Sheldon. He frowned.

"Oh, look here, Glace," he began. "All those boys have been here quite a time. I hardly think there's any use in taking up Fred's fool remark like this. There isn't one of those kids would try a thing like that. They just have boxes to keep a few little things in. Powell's got his mother's silver in one, as he told me. Sidney has some mining stock he hopes will be worth a fortune some day, and some life insurance papers and his grandfather's watch.

"Baird, you know. His honesty has been proven by fire. I sha'n't speak of myself save to say that you, who were largely instrumental in proving me square, can judge for yourself. As for Neville Farr, the lad's a nice boy, and as far as I know he keeps mainly the deeds to some real estate left him by his mother, in his box."

Hood's interest was palpably growing as he listened. I caught his eyes on me with a new expression, and I am sure he had not sensed how closely in touch I was with Sheldon. Then he turned them on Mack.

"You weren't serious, were you, Fred?" he inquired.

Mack shook his head.

"I wasn't at the time," he said slowly, "but—"

I cut in:

Just the same, and no matter what I know or don't know, Sheldon, you haven't answered my question. Are all those box-holders here now—this minute?"

"All but Farr," he replied shortly. "He asked me for a few days' leave as we were closing yesterday afternoon. He had some business he wanted to attend to—connected with the real estate I spoke of. What do you want to do, search the boy's boxes?"

The vault guard spoke as he paused.

BOX 991   175

"Mr. Farr took everything out of his box last evening, Mr. Sheldon."

For a minute nobody said a word. Then it was Dick who broke the somewhat tense silence.

"How's that, Edgar?"

"Why," said the guard, "he come in here in a rush and wanted his box. I unlocked it, an' he just reached in, grabbed out a bundle of some sort wrapped in brown papers, and slammed the box bank and locked it. Then he said 'Good-by, Ed,' to me, an' went out shoving the bundle into his pocket."

Again for a minute we five stood and looked at one another. I saw trouble deepen in Sheldon's eyes. Mack was frowning and fingering his lip. Hood's jaw had come forward again.

"Did he tell you where he was going, Dick?" I asked.

Sheldon shook his head.

"No. But I'd stake my reputation that kid is straight. What he took was probably the deeds I just spoke of. There was only one bundle, Ed?"

The guard nodded.

"Yes, sir. His box is low down, an' I could look right into it. He just grabbed one bundle—all there was in the drawer. I wouldn't have mentioned it only for what has happened."

"Oh, you did right enough," Sheldon assured him.

"Did he sign his card?" I asked, from a sudden inner prompting.

By common consent we all stared at Edgar. The man fidgeted, flushed under the staring.

"Did he?" I related.

Very slowly he shook his head.

"No, sir. He was in a hurry, as I've told you, an'—an'—well, I wrote his name on the card myself."

"Good Lord!" Sheldon sighed, rather than spoke it. Then he straightened his shoulders. "What's the use of precautions?" he ground out, and turned toward the grilling. "Let us out of here, Edgar. We'll take up your matter later. This thing has got to go before Mr. Gibson and President Carlton if they've come in while we were here."

The custodian let us through in crestfallen silence, and we retraced our steps toward the main floor of the bank. Sheldon left us in a knot while he went to the door of the cashier's room and rapped, then tested the knob and found it still locked. Next he tried the president's room with equal success. He returned to us.

"Get back to your cage, Fred," he directed Mack. "As soon as Mr. Gibson or Mr. Carlton comes, we'll have you in if we need you."

And just then the front door opened and two people came in.

The one in advance, for whom her companion held the door back, was a girl of striking appearance, dark, piquant of feature, perfectly costumed, and wearing her clothing with that air which graced both it and herself which the French call *chic*. She was a beauty beyond any question, and I recognised her as Miss Gertrude Gibson, the daughter of the cashier.

Passing through the door, she was followed by her father, a man heavy set, without any hint of corpulence, iron gray as to his closely clipped hair and mustache, heavy featured, with small dewlaps of skin along the lines of his lower jaw.

They came straight across the floor toward where we

BOX 991   177

were standing, with the evident intention of reaching Gibson's room through Sheldon's section. But as they neared us the girl caught sight of Mack and spoke quickly to her father.

I saw a question leap into the cashier's eyes at sight of the teller on the floor at this hour of the morning. Then be was upon us. Sheldon addressed him and arrested his course. The girl turned off and put out her hand to Mack.

"Hello, Fred," she said, with utter freedom, drew him a little to one side and began talking with him in the manner a woman of that age adopts only toward an intimate acquaintance.

2

SEMI DUAL ANTICIPATES

HOOD AND I stood and waited, while Sheldon spoke in lowered tones to the cashier. Abruptly Gibson lifted a hand in a sort of silencing gesture.

"That's enough out here, Sheldon. Come into my room," he said in authoritative growl. Then he glanced toward his daughter and Mack. "You'll have to excuse Fred, my dear," he told her, "and you'd better come into Sheldon's place and sit down for a few moments. There's a matter I must 'tend to at once."

She turned and gave him a smile from a charming pair of lips.

"I'll run over and talk to Mr. Farr, then, I think. You won't be long, will you, Dad?"

I saw Mack lean forward. He spoke softly to her. Her head turned quickly in the direction of the cages across the floor and then back. Plainly she asked Mack a question. He shook his head. Miss Gibson turned toward the railed section beside which Hood and I were standing. I saw surprise written in her eyes. Her father held the gate open for her passage, and she spoke to him again as she stepped through. He nodded toward a chair. She went over

BOX 991   179

and sank into it without further response. Once more she glanced toward the cages across the sweep of the floor.

Gibson walked quickly to his door and unlocked it. We followed him into his room. He threw himself into his chair and lifted his gaze to Sheldon.

"Now," he prompted sharply.

Sheldon presented Hood, and rapidly put his superior in possession of the events of the morning. Throughout his narrative Gibson said nothing, merely sat and tapped softly with the point of his index finger on the top of his desk. At the end he addressed Hood rather than the assistant cashier.

"We shall, of course, do all we can to uncover this matter, Mr. Hood, I assure you. I have had experience with Mr. Glace's work in the past, and I think him a good man as any to take care of the case in hand. Along that line, it appears to me that since young Farr is absent, one of the first moves should be to find out where he is, since Sheldon doesn't know. How about it, Mr. Glace?"

"It could do no harm, of course," I agreed. "Perhaps he told Sheldon when he would be back."

"He asked for leave until Monday," said Dick.

"And this is Thursday," said Gibson. "Too long to wait without knowing what he's up to."

Mack cleared his throat. He had not taken a seat, as had Sheldon, Hood and I, but had remained standing at the end of Gibson's desk, close to the door of the room.

"There's a thing I should possibly mention," he began. "Joe has said that he wrote me he was coming home, and that is correct. It wouldn't matter, except that yesterday morning I was speaking to Farr about it. That is"—he paused and seemed to hesitate a moment—"that is, we were talking about men making fortunes, getting ahead, and things like that, and I cited Joe as an example, and said he had written me he was coming back now that he had made good. I don't really know that it has any bearing at all, and I wouldn't speak of it except that as I induced Joe to put his papers in our vault. I would like to do anything I can to help him, in view of what has happened."

Gibson nodded slowly and pursed his lips.

"You dropped that remark to Farr yesterday morning, Fred?" he inquired.

"To Farr and several of the other fellows," Mack amended.

"And Farr cleared out, after telling Sheldon a tale about personal business." Gibson's face darkened swiftly. He lifted his hand and brought it crashing down on his desk. "That settles that part of the thing at least We'll swear out a warrant for the arrest of Farr!"

There came a tap on the door in the slight pause which followed the rather loud decision. Mack swung around and drew it slightly open.

Gertrude Gibson's face showed plainly as the light from the front windows of the room struck upon it, but she made no move to enter. Instead she spoke past Mack to her father, and all she said was:

"I don't think I'll wait any longer, Dad, if you're busy."

She turned away before Gibson could reply, and Mack shut the door. Gibson turned his glance to me.

"Don't you agree with that, Glace?"

"I hardly know," I made answer. "While circumstances seem, in a measure, to have combined to throw suspicion

BOX 991   181

on Farr, still it may be merely that and nothing else. He
may have told Sheldon the truth, and to order his arrest
is a more or less serious step. Personally, I wouldn't take it
at this time without more to go on. Sheldon tells me he's
always seemed a nice boy."

"Sheldon's too quick with his friendships," Gibson
retorted. "I've got to know a man before I trust him. If
you don't want to take the responsibility for ordering the
warrant, I will. I think you'll find the answer to this business when you find Farr, I suppose you *will* try to find him."

"Certainly," I declared.

"Well, then, when you do you'll want authority to arrest
or have him arrested. I'll swear out the papers."

"Very well," I assented. "Now, is there anything else? If
not, I should like Mr. Hood to go with me and meet my
partner. There's a lot to be done in this matter, and we want
to get at it. Besides tracing Farr, we want to find out what
has been done with the stock—or if anything has been
done with it yet."

Gibson sat frowning for a moment. Then he shook his
head.

"No. That's all, I guess," he decided. "Put this through,
Glace. I'm leaving it to you, though it means a lot to us, as
you must see."

I nodded. Sheldon, Mack, Hood and myself left the
room. As we came out I glanced about. Evidently Miss
Gibson had kept her word. She was nowhere in sight.
Mack went back to his cage, and, asking Hood to take a
seat, I led Sheldon to one side.

"Just what has Gibson against Farr?" I asked, because I

had noted more than a purely impersonal something in the cashier's tones when he spoke of the missing man.

Dick nodded.

"Got it, did you?" he said. "Gibson doesn't like the boy. If it weren't for Carlton and myself, I don't believe Farr would be in our employ. Be careful, Gordon. I don't really think he's guilty of this, and if not, it's a bad thing for him. Good Lord, I know what it is to be wrongfully accused. It—well—it hurts."

I nodded.

"And, on the other side, Mack's pretty solid with Gibson, isn't he, Dick?" I had noted that the cashier addressed the man by his first name.

"Ye-es," he returned. "There's a pretty reliable rumor that Mack is apt to be son-in-law before long."

"O-ho? I said—and saw it. That would explain the free-dom of Miss Gibson's greeting to the teller, the familiarity of her manner while she stood and chatted with him just after she came in. And it was quite plain that Gibson was in sympathy with the situation between the girl and the man. Well, I seemed to have gained all I could for the present. I shook hands with Sheldon, got Hood and set out for our offices and Bryce.

Any one who has followed the adventures of my friend Semi Dual and myself since those days when, as a reporter on the *Record,* I first met the strange man, will recall that it was on his advice I left the paper and formed the partner-ship with former inspector of police, James Bryce.

That was just before my marriage with Connie Baird and the exciting honeymoon which followed, with Semi Dual as a sort of fairy godfather to us two newly-weds, yet,

BOX 991 183

even so, seemingly unable to escape those storm centers of tangled human threads which were always involving his peculiar abilities for their straightening out.

Under the circumstances, however, it will seem but natural that the new firm of Glace & Bryce—Private Investigators—took offices in the Urania Building, on the seventh floor.

Dual, you know, had *his* unique quarters on the roof and in the tower of that structure. It was there he had constructed that odd garden, roofed in winter by yellow-green glass, where his shrubs and flowers bloomed the whole year long and birds twittered and a little fountain tinkled softly. It was there, one having ascended the great marble and bronze staircase from the twentieth floor, came upon the annunciator plate of glass inlay which I have described before—and, setting foot upon it, found all the air of the place full of mellow chimes to herald his coming.

One hears talk of the god from the machine. To Bryce and me Semi Dual was that. I have been praised more than once for what was deemed my work in clearing up mysteries of various sorts, and I have at times felt a sense of obtaining credit under false pretenses.

Yet what could I do? Dual was peculiar about things of that sort. The main price of his assistance in my work was that he remain—the god from the machine—his connection with the affairs in hand unknown, save to the necessary few directly involved, and not always to them unless from need.

And there was something godlike at times about the man, with his splendid physique, his olive skin, his strong mouth and chin and nose—something godlike in his calm, unemotional analysis of the perplexities which Bryce and I laid before him, and in the way he said this or that will happen when he had applied to them the unusual means he employed to gain his results.

Modern metaphysician, believer in and user of those higher laws of universal nature so often deemed but superstitions by men of lesser comprehension; astrologer, if you like, but one who read the stars rightly and saw his predictions come to pass—that was Semi Dual as I had come to know and love him—the Occult Detector, as Smithson, my old city editor on the *Record*, had dubbed him in the past.

Nor in his rough-and-ready fashion was my partner in any way behind me in his regard for Dual. At first openly skeptical, he had become in the end a convert to Semi's ability in handling the so-called "occult" laws.

"He's took my angora into camp," was the way he once expressed his change of attitude to me. In substance, at least, that was his creed of faith.

Naturally, then, when the matter of an office came up we decided to get into the Urania, where we could appeal to Semi directly. Indeed, we even had a private service 'phone from our suite to his quarters, over which we could communicate with him at need.

We picked up Danny Quinn, whom Bryce christened the "young sleuth," and installed him as office boy, put Miss Eleanor Newell at the typewriter and 'phone, and announced ourselves ready for business. Besides the reception-room and that in which Miss Newell worked, we had two smaller private consulting-rooms partitioned off, one for Bryce and one for myself. Up to the present we had done pretty well.

BOX 991   185

Hood and I took a taxi from the bank, but I learned nothing new on the way to the Urania entrance. In fact, there was nothing more Hood could tell me, but we got to feel more at home with each other. He was still chewing on the stub of his cigar as we started. Removing it from his mouth he tossed it out of the window.

"That was an awful jolt you threw into them about the signing of the card," he began.

"The whole affair is an awful jolt to Sheldon," I made answer.

Hood nodded.

"That's the trouble with help," he resumed. "They act on their own responsibility, the deuce is to pay and you have to pay him. Sheldon was telling us how careful they were, and you shot it all to pieces with one question."

I smiled.

"You're a good bit more liberal in your judgment than most men would be under such a loss, Mr. Hood," I remarked.

For a moment he said nothing, then—

"The side of the matter is, Glace, that I've a notion that both the bank and myself are associated victims. I've known Fred Mack since we were kids, and that man Sheldon impresses me as a good sort—no pretense—just all man, you know. That's why I'm willing to grant his request to try and keep things quiet. I was sorry for him when you pulled that on the vault man. It *was* pretty rotten, and it hit him all of a heap. D'ye know anything about this Farr?"

I shook my head.

"Nothing, beyond what you heard Sheldon say. He doesn't really believe him guilty."

Hood frowned.

"You've got to admit it does look suspicious, though," he returned. Then he grinned in the way I had already come to like. "Old Gibson is some quick on the trigger, too, isn't he? Still—oh, I don't know."

The cab stopped and we got out and entered the Urania foyer. I led Hood to a cage and we went up to the seventh floor. There I piloted him to our door and inside.

Danny sat on a chair, reading a paper. From the room beyond I could hear Bryce dictating to Miss Newell. I went toward the sound.

"Oh, Bryce," I said as we entered. "I want you to meet Mr. Hood."

"Yours very truly. Write that up at once and bring it to me to sign, Nellie. Glad to meet you, Mr. Hood," said Bryce all together.

I gave Nellie the list of stocks to copy and went on into my private room, where I gave Hood a chair while I put my partner in touch with the case.

Years on the police had taught Bryce to listen as well as ask questions. He sat with fingers locked across his somewhat bulging paunch, chin sunk toward his chest, until I had finished my account of events at the bank. Save for a blinking of his eyes, his face never changed expression. But I sensed that his eyes were on Hood far more of the time than on me.

But he turned them back to me when I finished, and he voiced something like Sheldon's first comment:

"Viewed from a first slant it don't look like it could have happened, does it?"

Hood spoke up.

BOX 991   187

"What's the matter with you fellows here in the East? Sheldon said that and now—you. You've got so used to the routine of life you can't grasp a variation right at first. If you'd been where I have you'd be more ready to look for things a bit out of the ordinary run.

"Hold Up," said Bryce. "Nobody's said it *didn't* happen, Mr. Hood. I reckon people in the detective game meet a few of these variations you mention. I said it didn't look like it could have happened—but it did. Now that means just that whoever put it across was slick enough to dope out a way of doing what couldn't be done. What's known about this Farr?"

I told him all Sheldon had told me.

"And Gibson said he'd swear out th' warrant?"

"Yes. Sheldon, though, doesn't appear inclined to think the boy guilty."

"An' it looks like an inside job," Bryce went on. "Can't say that I blame Gibson. Hood puts his papers away and goes off. He comes back an' finds them gone, an' the box all right. Farr hears that he is coming an' jumps out of town th' night before, taking *something* out of his box. Th' vault guard admits he signed Farr's card for him, 'cause he was in a hurry." He turned his eyes again toward me. "Maybe that vault man was in it with Farr. Thought of that?"

I hadn't. Neither had Hood. I could tell that by the sudden expression which swept his face.

"By Jove!" he exclaimed. "But, why did he admit his action then, when Glace asked him?"

Bryce grinned.

"No use to deny it. Th' card would have showed it. He'd fess up and trust to the bank just thinkin' he'd tried to do something to save the kid time. Nobody could prove anything else, so far as he can see, or I can—yet. Could they sell those stocks without trouble, Mr. Hood?"

Joe Hood considered.

"I don't know," he returned after a bit. "The only trouble would be about the transfer on the books of the company. Of course any broker could deliver the shares and the holder would have actual possession, but the transfers would have to be made out to place their stock in their own names."

"They could be endorsed in blank," said Bryce.

Nellie tapped on my door and handed in the original list and her copy. I gave the latter to Hood and the former to Bryce. He scanned it briefly, and once more glanced at Hood.

"Well?" he remarked.

"Well what?" said the engineer.

"Was they—endorsed in blank?"

"No. Of course not."

"An' this list is what they was an' in your own writin', I take it?"

"Yes, I made it when I put them away, and signed it this morning for Glace."

"The beautiful part of the whole thing is," Bryce went on as though half to himself, "that if the guard was in it with Farr, he could have made a duplicate key to this box 991, got th' papers, guv'em to Farr, an' never left a sign. It could have been done that way easy. We got to watch that guard, I imagine. An' we got to find out where Farr went, an' we want to see if anybody's tried to sell any of this stock."

Hood eyed him with a sort of respect.

BOX 991   189

"Holy smoke!" he said. "If the guard was in it, our impossibility becomes just a kid's game, don't it? Mr. Bryce, I've a notion you've hit it. We don't even know that it was Farr's box he took the stuff out of yesterday afternoon. Maybe it was mine. Maybe when Farr learned I was coming back, he yielded to a sudden temptation, induced the guard to help him and—"

Bryce shook his head.

"You're forgettin' you got both your keys," he objected. "They couldn't have fixed a duplicate that quick. No, they been at it for some time, I reckon. Maybe though Mack's sayin' you was comin' forced Farr's get-away all right. I wouldn't be surprised if what they meant to do was peddle 'em out a little at a time, except for that."

I had to admit there was something in what he said. And there was another thing. I had seen enough at the bank to realize that Gertrude Gibson was acquainted with Farr. The fellow was young. What if, like Mack, he was enamored of the dainty little beauty, without having the inside track?

Sheldon had said there was a rumor of Mack's standing there, and certainly Miss Gibson was friendly enough with the teller, but a rumor wasn't an announcement. What if Farr had formed some wild scheme of taking these idle stocks, and using them to gain sudden riches which would give him a better chance with Gibson's daughter?

Many a youth has dreamed of things like that—dreamed and gone to ruin in attempting to realize his dream. And Mack had said they were speaking of those very things the day before Farr had asked for leave until Monday. He would figure on that giving him ample time for escape. How, though, had he planned for his return if he succeeded? Or had his youth not looked that far before he leaped? At least Bryce's suggestion about the guard removed all the seeming difficulties in the actual looting of the box. I looked at Hood and smiled.

"I think we'll begin work on it along that line," I remarked.

He rose.

"I think you've got the right lead," he agreed. "Now I'll get out and let you get busy. I'm stopping at the Kenton. Get me on the 'phone if there's anything I can do. I'll keep in touch, but if I have to go out, I'll not be long, and I'll ask for a message every time I come in. I hope that fool boy hasn't sold the stocks. If he hasn't and you get him, all I want to do is throw a good scare into his soul and let him go. So get busy as soon as you can."

"Of course," said Bryce. "An' if we want you, we'll get in touch, Mr. Hood."

Hood nodded as though satisfied with that, shook hands and walked out.

Bryce looked at me.

"Son," he remarked, "if ever there was a guy who could tumble into tangles of trouble, you're it. This is a peach."

I grinned.

"Which end of it do you want to take?" I questioned. "Running down this list of stocks at the brokers' offices or trailing Farr?"

Bryce took a cigar out of his pocket, looked it over, licked a crack in the wrapper, and finally bit off the end and struck a match.

BOX 991   191

"The first thing," he said between puffs—"are there any securities to run down, old boy?"

"What?" I exclaimed.

"Meanin' did this Hood ever put anything in his box?" Bryce explained.

"He says so," I returned rather weakly, as I recalled the same point Sheldon had partly brought up.

"I know he does," Bryce returned, "but nobody *knows*— 'cept him. Th' next question is, did Farr have any real estate like he told Sheldon? The Recorder's office can probably tell us that, and also where it was. Call 'em up and find out, eh?"

He reached for the phone.

There was one thing made Bryce an invaluable partner. His years on the police had caused him to be very well known and gave him a sort of semi-official entrée still in a great many places.

Police, detectives of the Central Office and municipal and county officials still remembered the days when he had been a wearer of blue and brass, so he found small difficulty now in getting in touch with the people he wanted, or about inducing them to tell him all he wished to know. After about some fifteen minutes he hung up and swung around.

"He's got it," he announced. "Most of it is up near Little Falls, where his dad lived before he died. Th' stuff came to him through his mother 'bout a year ago—transfers on record shows that. The clerk knows me pretty well, an' he slipped me a tip on th' side. Farr's dad was killed in th' Spanish war. He was in a guard regiment an' went. Got his at San Juan. Always was well thought of, too. Anyway, there's deeds to about a dozen good pieces of ground up there standin' in th' name of Neville Farr, Jr., right now, so that much of the story's straight."

"We've that much to go on, then." I accepted his information. "Now, about that vault guard, Edgar. Give me the 'phone. I'm going to call up the bank and tell Sheldon to have him watched."

Bryce handed the instrument over. I got the bank and Sheldon himself after a moment, and told him what we had decided.

"Gibson has anticipated you a bit there," he said promptly, when I was through. "He had Edgar into his room and tried to make him admit knowing what Farr was up to. When he persisted in a denial, he had our own officer here take him over and lodge him in a cell. Have you heard anything about Farr?"

"We've verified his real estate holdings, but that's all," I told him, hung up, and informed Bryce of what the cashier had done.

He frowned.

"Th' old boy's right on th' job, ain't he?" he remarked. "Still—I don't know."

"You don't know?" I repeated in some surprise. "Why, you suggested the same thing yourself."

He nodded.

"I know it. I've suggested a lot of things when I was younger, too, an' some of 'em was rotten. I reckon I'm gettin' cautious in my old age. It looks to me like my guess was too simple for a wise guy to make from the other side. But I had to say something to Hood."

"Farr's only a boy," I reminded.

BOX 991   193

Bryce shook his head.

"Give me that list of stocks," I said, "and I'll call up the local concerns on the list I see there are one or two—Dunn's Milling Company, and—"

Bryce grinned.

"Give that 'phone a rest and use the one on the wall," he advised.

I sat back and stared.

"You mean call Dual?" I questioned. "Don't you think we'd better wait until we learn what we can about this case?"

"We'll learn faster that way," he grunted. "Honest, I've a hunch there's going to be something funny in this before we run it out to th' end."

I looked at the private 'phone box behind his head. To tell the truth, I wasn't sure but that he was right. Already there was something "funny," as he expressed it, about the whole business. I had been thinking now and then about Dual all morning.

"Well"—I hesitated—"if you think so, it can do no harm, only you and I don't want to get into the habit of depending too much on him, Jim. We—"

"We've done pretty well on straight work," he interrupted. "But I don't believe this is straight. That's all."

"Well, then, call him up," I agreed.

Bryce got out of his chair, put out his hand to make the call, and jerked it back. The 'phone had rung, even as he turned toward it.

I jumped. It was so sudden, so totally the reverse of what I was expecting, that it came like a shock. It was seldom indeed that Dual called us. Even with me, for whom he had proven his liking, he maintained the same attitude of aloofness he adopted toward all the world. Yet more than once he had come to my aid.

Whatever the world at large may think or say about telepathy and its falsity or truth. Dual used it, and I knew that he could read thought waves as correctly with his wonderfully sensitive brain, as ordinary mortals read print or sense a spoken word. And not only could he read, but send such messages as well. Many a time he had called me to him in the past simply by willing my presence. And no matter where I might be, I would suddenly feel the urge to go to him, and going find that he had wished me to come.

So really, there was nothing so remarkable after all in his ringing our call just after we had been sitting there talking about him. Yet in a way it seemed almost uncanny. Bryce had stepped back and was standing there, staring at the instrument in dumb amazement. It rang again.

I sprang up, shoved Jim out of the way, and grabbed the receiver.

"Dual?" I cried.

There was something like a quiet amusement in the low-pitched tone which came back to me along the wire.

"Why don't you come up and talk it over here, my friend?"

I gasped. Often as I had known him to do it before, it always upset me for the moment.

"I—we—all right," I stammered, and hung up. Then I turned to Bryce. "He called up to tell us to come up there," I reported.

Jim was still standing there staring, his eyes bulging out, his jaw dropped slightly so that his cigar slanted down from

BOX 991

195

his lips. As I spoke he clamped his teeth into the tobacco and a grin stretched his lips wide.

"I reckon my hunch was a pretty good one," he said slowly. "But—can you beat it? He picked it right out of the air. That man sure is the limit. Come along up where he is."

3

WHO SIGNED THEM?

THAT WAS THE manner in which Semi Dual entered the tangle about box 991.

It was no more remarkable, however, than other instances I have mentioned. The very first time I ever met him he had told me that Smithson wanted me at the office of the *Record,* and I had gone there and found a big murder story "breaking" and myself the only available man.

That time Semi had sensed Smithson's thought wave calling for some one to send on the assignment. At another time he had told me a woman was dead, and sent me to call up the paper and verify his words. Again he had sent me half across the country to find a man he had never seen, and I had gone and found him where Semi said he would be.

One can imagine, therefore, with what a feeling of relief I followed Bryce out of my private room, told Nellie where we were going, and went on toward the elevator shaft to press an "up" signal for a cage.

There was nothing of the meddler about Semi Dual. The trivial Crimes did not arouse his interest. It was only the gripping climaxes of human life that he cared to exert his power in solving. As he once said to me:

"Property chattels are nothing—ephemeral things of a

BOX 991   197

fleeting existence—the chimera of material moment. It is the soul of which man should think. It is the one eternal, immortal verity of life which carries from plane to plane the marks of each step of existence, be they good or bad.

"The only real sin is a sin against a soul—because that is the only sin which can have more than a transitory effect. If, then, by my efforts, I can prevent such a thing, or lighten its effect—if I can spare suffering or sorrow—if I can lighten the burden any soul must bear in its climb to the heights—I have in so much performed my immortal duty and acquired a modicum of merit which shall make me happier in the soul which is my own."

As a result, when Bryce and I entered the car which presently came up, I felt sure of two things. First, there was something in this affair of more than ordinary interest, and secondly, that whatever it was the guiding hand of Dual would direct the matter to the end. The old feeling of the old days when Semi had sent me forth as his ally in unraveling crime, took hold and gripped me as the car ran swiftly up the shaft.

We left the cage on the twentieth floor and turned toward the massive staircase with its bronze rail and its great bronze figures on the newel posts with their opalescent globes of glass. We went up and came out into the garden.

The green-yellow glass was up, and although a cold wind was now sweeping on all sides of the Urania, here, twenty stories in the air, was soft, even warmth, and the odor of growing vegetation. I saw some monthly roses nodding their delicate heads on slender stems in a nearby bed.

Yes, it was the same quiet air of solitude, of peace with the world of strife shut out, I had always found here since I had known it. It breathed through the place like an emanation from the very soul of the man who dwelt there, an expression of his personality itself.

As by common consent, we both paused before the metal plate at the head of the stairs, with its glass inlay of letters:

> Pause and consider, oh, stranger. For he who cometh against me with evil intent shall live to rue it until the uttermost part of his debt shall have been paid; yet he who cometh in peace, and with a pure heart, shall surely find that which he shall seek.

Bryce turned his eyes to mine.

"It's always different, some way, up here," he said, softly growling the words. "Funny, ain't it? But it always gets me, every time I come. 'Tain t like no place else I go. Feels sorter like a church. Well, come on."

We set foot on the plate. From the tower soft chimes filled all the air under the green-yellow roof of glass. We went on up the path toward the tower itself, and Henri, Semi's man, met us at the door of the tower, smiling.

"The master is waiting, *messieurs*," he said, bowing, and waved us across the ante-room to the well-known quarters beyond, with its door standing half ajar.

We crossed and passed the portal. Dual, clad in a loose house robe of blue and white, looked up from beside his great desk and greeted us with a smile.

"Ah—my friends."

It was good to hear him say it—like that.

"Good morning, Mr Dual," returned Bryce, with a slow grin.

BOX 991   199

"Semi," I cried, "you know, but—how—"

He shook his head.

"Do you need ask, Gordon? I chanced to be having a very quiet morning. Some time ago I sensed your thought of myself. Later still the thing was repeated. I rang you up. It has occurred before. Just what has happened now at the Fourth National Bank?"

He knew even that. Bryce sat down abruptly on a chair.

"Go on an' tell him," he admonished. "If you don't he'll get it all for himself."

Dual smiled.

"It is easy for me to read the thoughts of those with whom I am in harmony," he explained. "For that very reason I sensed Sheldon's hope that I would lend my aid in this, even as I contacted Gordon's thought of myself, and your desire to ring me up, Mr. Bryce."

Bryce nodded.

"I reckon," he mumbled. "I was just reachin' for the 'phone when you beat me to it and guv me a whale of a jolt."

Semi nodded toward my usual chair by the end of the desk.

"Come, Gordon," he said.

I sank down. I looked into his eyes, gray, deep, alive with the fathomless fires of his spirit, the eyes of wisdom, of knowledge, of purity and its strength, and I began to speak.

And I told the story of the morning. I told it all, each and every little detail, so far as I could remember, everything essential at least. I had done it many times before.

Save for the presence of Bryce, the scene was the same— Semi Dual lying back in his chair, his fine eyes closed now, his hands folded, scarcely seeming to breath, centering all his wonderful concentration on my words, and myself, sitting there talking to the keen intelligence of his mind. And at the end I produced Hood's list of his stocks and laid it on his desk before him.

He sat up and took it into his hand.

"The man who wrote the listing signed it at the bottom. This signature is genuine?"

He had swept it at a glance.

"I saw Hood sign it," I replied.

"A man's man," said Semi. "Good vitality, strong self-assurance, open nature of a rough-and-ready sort, inclined to be generous on the whole—would become an easy victim to one he trusted. His writing shows that."

"So does his talk," grinned Bryce.

Dual smiled again at the outspoken agreement. He drew a sheet of paper toward him and made a notation upon it after a glance at the huge clock in one corner of the room.

"Taking this matter at a first inspection," he began, "I would say that we are likely to find some unusual qualities running through it from first to last. I would, therefore, warn you that in your investigations you be prepared for things of that nature, and be not misled by what may be a surface seeming at the first."

"What did I tell you?" Bryce fairly howled it. "Mr. Dual, I was arguing that very thing when I was wantin' to call you up. I said this case had somethin' funny about it."

Dual eyed him.

"You sensed it subconsciously, no doubt, Mr. Bryce. It is a recognised fact that what you would call a 'hunch' is frequently the prompting of the subconsciousness, from

BOX 991   201

which no real knowledge is hidden, provided one knows how to listen to its voice."

Bryce smirked. He seemed vastly pleased all of a sudden.

"Then I was right?" he demanded.

"Unquestionably, I should say," said Dual. "The astrological signs ruling the present period would predicate a double leading in this matter. Everything indicates instability at present. We are under a zodiacal sign of water—Scorpio rules. Sagittarius is rising. Uranus is retrograde in position. The influence of several other planets also combine to ambush the path of fate."

Bryce sat up. Of course he didn't understand save in a general way, but be sat there and listened with all ears.

"An' how does it come out in the end?" he queried when Semi paused. One would have said he thought the man he questioned knew the end already.

Dual smiled.

"I have not gone into that myself as yet, Mr. Bryce," he responded. "But so much as this I can tell you. In the end as always—justice will be done—the immutable justice of universal law, from which no man escapes, no matter how long he defies the lesser law of man."

"I know," said Jim, looking puzzled. "But do we pinch the right guy who lifted those papers?"

"I trust so. I shall endeavor to bring about that conclusion," said Semi. "Along that line, just what action had you two proposed, before I introduced myself into the case?"

"We was goin' to trail Farr, an' find out what was done with that stock," Bryce told him, before I could answer. "Gordon an' I was goin' to split it up between us and see what we could find out along those lines. If any of that stock was sold, we might be able to find out somethin' about how it was done an' run it back to who done it from that."

Dual turned his eyes to me. I nodded.

"That was just about as far as we had gone into the thing, when we began to argue about bringing the matter before you. So far we have nothing to indicate what became of the stock, save the mere fact that it is gone, and that Farr has left town."

"Those," said Semi, "are essential points, and will be necessary to the final solution of the matter. Suppose you follow your first intentions, and gain such information covering upon them as you can. In the meantime I shall follow my own methods toward a similar end."

Bryce rose.

"What gets my goat," he grunted, "is that while we fellows have to run around all over the map, you can just sit here and figure a bit on a piece of paper and find out more than we have when we get back."

Dual's eyes twinkled.

"And just because most men are like you, my friend, mankind at large will not accept my knowledge, unless your running around brings me back material facts with which to verify my conclusions." Abruptly he chuckled softly. "Hence, take your 'goat' out and let it run around."

"Come on, Gordon," said Bryce, grinning.

"Am I *thy* goat?" I countered. Suddenly I felt almost happy. This was like the old days. "Semi," I queried, "where are the cigarettes?"

He waved a hand to the drawer where he used to keep my brand—just for me. I drew it out and found a pack-

BOX 991

203

age still there. I thrust it into my pocket after slipping one from the wrapper, and, striking a match, drew in a whiff of fragrant smoke.

"Now', I'm off," I averred, and waved Bryce to the door.

The last thing I saw of Semi he had picked up a drawing compass and was spinning a circle on a sheet of paper. Like Bryce and I, he, too, was starting his work. He would cut that circle into twelve segments, and chart upon it symbols and signs. And from that he would set up his figures and his equations, and after a time decide calmly what forces were working and what their influence was on the case in hand.

We went down and rung for a cage, then stood and waited. The cable hummed in the shaft; the cage rose; its door clanged open. Bryce sighed.

Once more we were back in the every-day world, its atmosphere of hurry and strife, so different from that room above us now, where a man sat and drew circles and gazed upon them to learn what destiny drove this or that tiny atom of human life this way or that in the ebb and flow of life.

We stopped at the office to get our outer coats and leave word that we'd be back when we got there, and then we went down to the street.

"Which end of the thing do you want?" I asked.

"You take the stock part," said Bryce. "You ought to be better there. I'll be more at home tryin' to pick up Farr's trail. I know all the boys on depot posts and things like that."

That was the way we usually worked things. Each took the line of investigation best suited to his earlier training and ran it out. In the end we compared notes and matched up. So far we had scored not a few successes to the credit of our office. As I left Semi I had picked up Hood's list. Now I felt in my pocket to assure myself that it was still there, and as Bryce ran out to hop on a depot car, I turned up the street the opposite way.

Dunn's Mills lay a little way out of town, on the banks of the river. I caught a car when it came along, and sank into a seat for the ride, and, as one will, I ran over in my mind a bit of the history of the place toward which I was heading.

Originally the mills had been started by the grandfather of the present Dunn. At that time it had depended on the river for its motive power and was merely an old-fashioned private grist mill. Young Dunn's father had enlarged the place, erected a small elevator and extended the business, putting in steam to replace the water power and gradually enlarging the plant as the need arose. In the last ten years, since the present head of the concern had been in control, it had been enlarged on a much greater scale, incorporated and organised on extensive lines and was a paying institution with its stock selling well above par, and none offered.

According to the list in my pocket. Hood had placed some twenty shares of that stock in the Fourth National vault. At its face valuation that would mean two thousand dollars at least. I figured that if the thief had sold any of the stuff, whoever bought it might have made at least an attempt to have it put in his own name, which would entail transfer on the company's books, and as I knew Frank Burke, the secretary of the Milling Corporation. I felt perfectly sure I could find out.

The wind which had been rising all day still whistled

BOX 991   205

around the car after we got out of the built-in streets. I could see the trees here and there in the fields bending bare branches under a gray sky. In a way it struck me that it was a fit day for the beginning of what Dual had already predicted would be a matter involving much of cross purpose and confusion of clues before it reached its end. It was a day when one might expect almost anything to happen.

There was something cheerless and depressing in the very prospect of Nature—as chilling and gloomy as the knowledge of human crime must ever be in its seeming. Like the passions of man, the elements to-day seemed at war with each other, and little dead leaves rattled now and then against the windows of the car in the gusts.

So at last I came to a point where, from a turn in the track, I could see the tall stacks of the milling plant, with the long streamers of smoke whipping like black froth from their metal lips, and the dull flour-grayed brown of the buildings clustered about their base. I punched the button to stop the car, rose and swung off as it slowed.

Before me was an arch rising from stone pillars and bearing the words, "Dunn's Mills, Incorporated," on a gilt-lettered sign. I passed through into the yard and made my way toward a one-story brick building also labeled "Office," beyond any possible mistake.

Young Dunn had ideas of his own. Where his grandfather had kept his rough and ready accounts on a box desk against one wall of the original shack, and his father had used a railed-off enclosure roughly carpentered together, the grandson had built a modern office suite, and fitted it with mahogany and plate glass and gilded grillwork, in quite modern style.

I went in and presented my request for Mr. Frank Burke to a young man who sat at a desk back of a massive rail. He took my card and disappeared through the door of a mahogany partition between the front and the regions beyond.

Presently he came back, held open the gate in the railing and invited me to follow him through the same door. He led me down a short hall and tapped before throwing open a second, whose glass bore the name of my acquaintance.

I passed inside. Frank rose as I entered. We shook hands and he gave me a chair.

"Haven't seen you for a coon's age," he began. "What brings you out here to-day?"

"A desire for information," I told him. "Frank, is there any of your stock on the market nowadays?"

He grinned and shook his head.

"Thinking of investing? If so you're a bit late. Now if you'd been in touch with the right parties just about this time last year, you might have picked up a little. There were a few shares sold then. First I've known of for a long time, too."

"Nothing more recent than that?" I queried, with a feeling of disappointment. Here was an obstacle rising up right at the start, where I had hoped for luck.

He shook his head again.

"Nope. The stuff is too good, Glace, as you ought to know. Dunn's Incorporated is paying dividends, old man. This stock I mentioned brought a hundred fifteen on a forced sale, and the parties buying it in were glad to get it

BOX 991

207

at that. I ought to know, because George Graham, our trea-
surer, and myself split up the twenty shares between us."

I felt an odd sort of thrill run through me. I reached into
my pocket and brought out Hood's list.

"Twenty shares," I remarked. "Were their serial numbers
something like these?" I began reading rapidly from the
list.

"Hold on!" Burke exclaimed before I was half through.
"Where'd you get those numbers? See here, Glace, what's
this all about?"

"Those were the numbers, then?" I questioned.

"Yes, they were," said Burke. "The things were part of an
issue made at the time of the reorganization ten years ago,
to take up the outstanding stock of the old concern. They
stood on the books in the name of young Joe Hood. Old
John, his father, who has since died, had put them in the
kid's name as a sort of investment, I believe."

"So that, at his death, Joe inherited without any trouble
about transfers?" I suggested.

Burke nodded.

"I guess that's about it."

"Then," I followed the thing up, "how did you and
Graham get hold of them?"

He smiled agreeably.

"Saved my wages and bought them, old man."

"Yes, I know. But from whom?"

"Pearson & Co.," he said, naming a firm of brokers with
an excellent reputation. "I told them once that if they ever
had a chance to pick up any of our stock they should tip
it to me and I'd grab it. About a year ago they called me
up—Pearson himself it was—and said they had twenty

shares of this Hood stock—that Hood had to raise money and had put it in their hands for sale. Graham and I split it between us. Why?"

His eyes puckered slightly as he asked the question.

"What did you do, just buy it to hold till Hood could take it up again?" I returned without other reply.

"Good Lord, no! We bought it to have and to hold," he said, almost with impatience.

"How could you do that without having it in your own name?" I demanded in a tone to match.

Burke leaned forward.

"Do you know what you're talking about?" he rapped out. "Who said it wasn't in our own names? We bought it. Couldn't I cancel Hood's shares and issue new certificates to Graham and myself?"

"You could, but for one *trivial* detail?" I returned.

"And that?" He threw out a hand and pointed its finger straight at me.

"Hood's shares would have to be signed over, either to you or in blank."

"They were. In blank," he declared. "What's the matter with you, Glace?"

I didn't answer that, either. I stared.

"You mean those shares you bought were endorsed?" I said somewhat weakly at last.

"Yes." He growled it at me, frowning.

"But—who signed them?" I was feeling rather peculiar just about then.

Burke snorted.

"Who signed them?" he repeated. "Glace, you're dippy. *Hood* signed them, of course."

4

HOOD'S SIGNATURE, BUT—

"HOOD?" I EXCLAIMED, AND stopped aghast.

As I have said I had known Frank Burke for years—not intimately, but well enough to know his reputation. There had never been a breath against it. His father was a heavy stockholder in Dunn's Mills. That was how the younger Burke had come to fall into the secretary's job. He was married, had a charming wife and a nice little girl. All around, he was rated one of the sterling younger business men of the city.

Yet here he was telling me that he had purchased these shares, and that Hood had signed them, and he had transferred them on the company's books to Graham and himself. The shock of the thing jarred me completely.

As for Burke, he came completely out of his chair, reached over and seized me by the shoulder and shook me.

"Glace," he growled, "what is it? What is the matter with you? Stop looking like I'd bowled you over and tell me what your visit here has to do with that stock. What's wrong with the stuff?"

I got a grip on myself then.

"Go sit down," I said, more calmly. Then I gave him the list Hood had signed.

"Whose signature is that?" I asked.

He gave it a glance.

"Hood's," he declared.

I leaned toward him.

"Is it like the signature on these shares?"

"Yes," he retorted, his voice rising. "I told you he signed them. Who signed this?"

I grinned.

"Hood," I said.

Burke sighed. There was pity in his look.

"Then what's all the row about?" he wanted to know.

The thing began to take hold of me really now. Something was mightily wrong and no mistake.

"Frank," I began, "do you know that Hood was in either Alaska or Seattle when you bought those shares?"

He shook his head.

"I didn't know where he was. Pearson just said he had the stock. But if Hood was out there, that explains why he sent it here for sale. He probably knew he could get a letter price here than out there. I wondered a bit about that, too."

"And the only trouble with your explanation," I cut in, "is that at the time you bought it Hood thought it was lying in box 991 of the Fourth National's vault."

That got him.

"What?" he yelled, staring in his turn. "You—you mean that he didn't know it was being sold—that somebody stole it?"

"Something like that, Frank," I said.

He shifted his gaze back to the list.

"But—how?"

"That's what I'm trying to find out," I explained, and

BOX 991　　　　　　　　　211

went on to give him a definite idea of the situation. "You can see now why your statements gave me something of a jolt."

"Good Lord, yes," he assented, and while I had been talking his face had gradually grown more and more worried in expression. "Of course, when Pearson told me he had the stuff and I found it was Hood's, which had been on the books for years, I never doubted but that it was all right. I don't believe Pearson had any doubts, either. He's rated careful. And the signature on the shares was exactly like that on this list of yours, Gordon. Why—hang it all— the things must have been forged or else Hood lies."

"Wait a bit," I checked his rising excitement. "Do you happen to have those canceled shares about? if you have, let's see how the signatures really do match up."

He nodded.

"Y-e-s," he said, slowly. "We can do that." He rose and went toward a vault in one end of the room, twirled the combination, pulled open the door and disappeared inside.

While he was gone I pushed back some papers on his desk to clear a space, and when he came back with a bundle of rubber-banded papers in his hand we spread them out so that the transfer forms were exposed. Then, with the list I had brought between us, we bent over the canceled shares.

Frank looked at me, and I started to look at him in time to meet his eyes. And for a minute we continued to stare at each other, because, line for line, shading for shading, in each and every detail, so far as one could say from an ordinary examination, the signature on each and every share of stock and that on my list were the work of the self-same hand.

"If those are forgeries, they're a darned good job," said Frank Burke at last.

"And if they aren't—" I began, to have him cut me short.

"Look out for a double-cross somewheres. That's all."

I turned the shares over and compared their numbers. They filled the twenty serials on my list without exception. "Look here, Frank," I decided. "I want to take these things with me. Do you care?"

"I don't know about that," he objected frowning. "Under the circumstances—"

"You know Dick Sheldon of the Fourth National, don't you?" I interrupted.

"Yes. We bank there a good deal."

"Then get him on the wire and convince yourself that I'm telling you the truth. If he vouches for me, I'll give you a receipt for the certificates and take them with me. You'll get them back after the thing is settled up."

He ran his hand over his chin, nodded abruptly and turned to the phone on his desk. After a bit, he began talking swiftly, with occasional pauses to listen. In the end he slammed the phone down.

"I'll do it," he said in a voice which grated. "It's devilish irregular and all that, but I want you to get to the bottom of this and I want to know where Graham and I stand. Make out your receipt."

I sat down at the desk and wrote out a statement as to why the shares were being placed in my hands, signed it and gave it to Burke. Then I gathered up the certificates, snapped the band about them and put them in my pocket with Hood's list. I rose.

BOX 991   213

"And now I'm going down and see Pearson," I announced.

Burke nodded. He had been watching me in silence. Now, however, he scowled as he spoke.

"Go ahead, and for Heaven's sake get to the bottom of this. I'll tell Graham what's—"

"Don't do that," I advised. "Keep quiet. The fewer people talking about this the better. I know you boys bought this in good faith. Just lay low till I find out where the kink is."

He kept on scowling.

"Well—have it your own way," he assented at length. "I'll keep still till I hear from you at least."

I put on my hat and went out to get a car back to town, and when it came along I got aboard.

My trip had produced most unexpected results. If it weren't for Hood's statement that he had not endorsed the shares, it wouldn't have seemed so peculiar, but I had heard him deny it to Bryce—and I remembered that he had seemed to hesitate about that, too. Jim had asked him twice, but at the time I had attributed that to Nellie's interruption in bringing in her copy of the list. Now, however—I began to wonder.

I didn't know Hood, really. Save for Mack's identification, he might be any one else on earth unknown to me. Against that he had signed the list in the manner of one who writes his own name—easily, without hesitation and Dual had said the signature indicated an honest man. However, so did the endorsements on the certificates in my pocket—and I knew that either they were forged or Hood was deceiving us about having signed them.

He couldn't have forgotten. A man doesn't sign away

twenty shares of dividend stock and suffer a mental lapse immediately after. And the signatures were certainly Hood's, provided that that on the list was his. At least I knew the man posing as Hood had signed the latter. Then—I was back where I started. I had reasoned around in a circle.

Wondering what Bryce might have learned about Farr, I, strangely enough, saw again in my mind's eye the glance Gertrude Gibson had thrown across the bank floor from Sheldon's section to the opposite cages.

If I was any judge of expression the girl had been surprised to find Farr absent. In fact her remarks at the time about going across to talk with him, while waiting for Gibson, showed the same thing. Evidently then she knew the missing man pretty well, and according to Sheldon and my own observations, Gibson did not like Farr himself.

At this point in my musings the car approached my crossing and the locality of the broker's office; but as I swung off my mind was still full of Bryce, Farr and the endeavor my partner was making to pick up the trail of the latter.

I made my way first to a public 'phone booth and called up our office. There was nothing to be learned there, however. Nellie said she had heard nothing from Bryce, and that save for a couple of 'phone calls from a woman who left no name there had been nothing of importance.

I hung up, left the booth and made my way to Pearson & Company's place of business without any more delay.

I think I have described their offices before. They were the usual type of such places, with a customers' room, a blackboard and a marker who chalked the market trans-

BOX 991   215

actions on the board as he received them over a telephone cord and harness strapped to his head, so that he looked very much like a monkey on a string as he scampered back and forth in front of the board.

Back of the customers' room was a mahogany series of private rooms where I was bent. I slipped another card to a uniformed page and waited. The page vanished and, then returning, nodded and I followed him back. He threw open a door and stood aside for me to enter.

I knew Pearson by sight and he knew me by reputation. There had been an occasion when he had known of my work—that other time when fate involved Dick Sheldon, and his brother, Colonel MacDonahue Sheldon, in a snarl which Dual had untangled. So now I nodded as I met his steady dark eyes across his desk.

"How do you do, Mr. Pearson?"

"How'r'yuh Glace?" he returned, running it all together.

He was a man with a quick, almost abrupt manner, known as a shrewd manipulator in his line. Jerking a hand toward a chair, he inquired brusquely.

"What can I do for you?"

I took the bundle of certificates from my pocket and tossed them onto his desk.

"You can tell me if you remember selling those shares," I returned.

He gave me a quick glance, picked up the stock and rapidly ran them through his fingers, much as a man might riffle a pack of cards. Then he looked at me again without any particular expression.

"These are the Hood shares. We sold them to Burke and Graham of the Dunn's Milling Corporation, a year ago this month. I forget the exact date, but can find it for you if you wish."

"You sold them," I repeated.

He nodded and tossed the certificates back toward me. "Yes."

"Where did you get them?" I asked.

Once more he showed no sign of interest, as he answered.

"From Hood, of course. You can see they stand in his name."

"That's the way it looks," I admitted. "But did he send them to you from Alaska or Seattle?"

This time his answer came slower.

"He sent them to us from Little Falls, Mr. Glace."

Once more that odd thrill which had shaken me at the Mills ran through me. Little Falls was the name of the town where Farr had his real estate holdings—where the boy had lived as a youth. This stock had been stolen and sold a year before, and it had been sent in for sale from Little Falls. And now Farr was gone. It began to look as if Gibson had not been so premature in his swearing out of warrants after all. I glanced back at Pearson.

"Did he send it to you—just mail it in and tell you to sell it?" I queried. "Or what?"

A thin smile stretched the broker's lips.

"I think I had better ask a few questions of my own, before we go any farther, Mr. Glace," he returned. "I know your reputation, both for cleverness and as a man, and I think I see that there is some tangle over this stock. To start with, let me say that our connection with the sale was purely that of a broker selling on commission for a client, entirely regular in every way as the correspondence on file

BOX 991   217

in our office will show. But before we go into the matter, suppose you explain why you want to know. What's this about Hood's being in Seattle or Alaska?"

His question was natural enough, and I decided I would have to answer to establish my claim to information. I put him briefly in touch with the facts.

"Now you see those shares are apparently signed quite regularly enough by Hood," I concluded. "But if he was in Seattle or the North at the time they were sold, and if he did not indorse the stuff before putting it in the vault, how could he send it to you for sale from a town an hour's ride away by train or trolley?"

Pearson's eyes contracted the least bit. He tapped the shares with a finger.

"The signature on these is identical with that on the letters we received from Little Falls," he said. "So far as I can recollect there is no difference, nothing to excite suspicion."

I tossed him Hood's list.

"That is Hood's signature written this morning," I told him. "You will see it is the same."

He picked up the list and scanned it closely. Then he placed it with the certificates themselves. His eyes came back and met mine.

"Exactly the same," he agreed. "You say Hood denies that he signed the shares?"

"He denies having anything to do with them, after he left them in the bank drawer," I returned.

Pearson leaned both elbows on his desk.

"Then if he tells the truth, the signatures on the transfers are forgeries," he said.

"If they are, they are remarkable examples," I returned. He frowned.

"This is a disagreeable surprise," he resumed softly. "I don't see just where we can be blamed, but it is always a disadvantage to a firm to have trouble over any of their transactions, and I may as well tell you first as last that these Hood shares are not all the stock we have sold for our Little Falls client."

I felt myself start. For the time, since my interview with Burke, I had half forgotten the other securities on the list. But now I remembered. "You handled other blocks of the stocks on that list?" I exclaimed.

Pearson nodded. He kept his dark eyes steadily on my face.

"Yes, practically all of them, so far as I can recollect. The business dragged out over a good part of the past year, with these securities coming in for sale from time to time. We sold, deducted our commission and remitted to Hood at Little Falls. Our drafts came back properly endorsed. There was never any question till you walked in here to-day."

I'd got it all in a lump, it appeared. At least, then, I knew where the securities from box 991 had gone. Pearson's records of sales would show me.

"And have you any idea what this Hood or his double did with the money?" I asked from a sudden prompting.

Pearson shrugged.

"He lost a good bit of it, at least, by bad judgment as to the market. We handled some of his deals and can account for that much of it, at least."

Stolen and gambled away. The work of a fool—or a boy. The thought flashed through my mind.

BOX 991   219

"Pearson," I said, "would you let me see some of that correspondence?"

"Surest thing." He reached out and pressed a button, and we waited until a clerk appeared. Pearson directed him to bring the Hood records from the files.

"You'll find everything ship-shape," the broker, told me. "We aren't a bucket-shop, Glace. We've a reputation, and I'll be glad to help you all I can to get to the bottom of this. It will be to our advantage. You say Hood is in town now?"

"He's stopping at the Kenton."

"I knew his father very well," said Pearson. "He traded with us quite a bit. In fact I knew he held blocks of these very stocks. That was one thing made me less apt to suspect anything wrong. Indeed, the only thing about it which made me give it any thought was the rotten market sense young Joe appeared to exhibit. He wasn't even a lamb. He was"—again he smiled thinly—"well, he was a goat."

The clerk came back with the files. Pearson motioned me to come around beside him and we looked them over.

There was the first letter authorizing the sale of the Hood shares in the Dunn Mills, and after that a rather voluminous correspondence covering various sales and stock market gambling operations in which the writer had apparently made more and more desperate efforts to rescue his steadily growing losses.

And each and every letter was typewritten and signed with the same signature appearing on my list and on the canceled shares I had obtained from Burke. As Pearson said, so far as any one could see, there was nothing out of the way from first to last. And, by the correspondence dates, the last sale and the last market loss were not over a month old.

"What did I tell you?" the broker queried. "He had no market sense at all. Why, I even wrote him a letter of protest once or twice, giving him advice. I felt I owed his father's son that much, at least. It made no difference to us, only I hated to see the boy drop it like that."

"Oh, you're in the clear," I told him. "But I've got to uncover this affair. Say, Pearson, would you let me take some of these letters?"

He nodded slowly.

"I see what you want—or I think I do," he returned, and frowned again before he went on. "I'll tell you—I know how you cleared things up for old Sheldon and the Fourth National's junior cashier. You pick out what you want, and give me a line that you have them and I'll help you that much."

I turned to the files. The first letter I took was the one authorizing the sale of the Dunn's Mills stock. It was dated in November of the previous year and gave the return address of "Room 22, Dawson Block, Little Falls." And like my list, it was signed "Joseph J. Hood." After that I picked out some others covering various transactions and laid them with the first.

Then I sat down and gave Pearson a statement of each letter, covering its chief items, and signed it. Placing the letters with the list and the stock, I put out my hand.

"This is mighty good of you, Mr. Pearson," I said.

"Glad if it helps dig out the nigger who seems to be about somewhere," he told me, shaking my hand heartily.

BOX 991   221

"Let me know what turns up. The thing begins to smell pretty rotten all right."

I left him closing up the remaining letters in the files, and went out.

It was between three and four and I had eaten nothing since morning. I decided to lunch and hunted a short order house in a hurry; while I ate I turned things again in my mind. It would bear a deal of turning, I saw.

But strive as I could, only two things would come plainly to the front. Either Farr was guilty and had done the whole thing as Gibson suspected, or else Joe Hood was one of the boldest crooks I had ever met and was deliberately trying to recoup himself for his losses at the expense of the bank. And some way, neither of these ideas seemed to satisfy my conception of the case.

In the end, however, and acting more from natural impulse than from any other purpose or reason, I decided that I would go and see Hood. I would go over to his hotel and get him before me, face to face, and then I would tell him what I had found out and show him his signature on the letters and shares in my possession and see how he looked and acted and what he said.

Sometimes a man faced with something he thinks no one else knows will involuntarily betray his own guilty knowledge at the very first. I decided to try the experiment on Hood. I left the restaurant and made my way to the Kenton.

My old friend Jeffrys was still the clerk there and I made my inquiries about Hood from him in person.

"Sure," he said, when I had made my wants known. "He's here an' waitin' for you. Left word to get him on th' wire quick if you rung up. He's from the West ain't he? Looks like a regular story book type. What's wrong?"

"Never mind," I grinned. "What you don't know won't be spilled, old man. You hotel clerks are worse than a bunch of gossips. I shall ask Angelique over here to announce my presence."

I went over and told the switch board girl to ring Hood's number.

She plugged his room, spoke after a moment, then broke the connection and turned to me.

"Mr. Hood says to come right up. Room 530."

I lost no time about taking him at his word, and he bawled a strong "Come in," to my rap. I pushed open the door and stepped inside.

Clad in shirt and belted trousers. Hood sat smoking a short bull dog pipe. He removed it from his mouth as I entered and closed the door behind me.

"Hello," he remarked in greeting, and waved the pipe stem toward a chair. "Sit down. D'ye mean to say you've turned up something already? If you have, you're a wonder."

In his offhanded way he was cordial enough. The first impression of liking I had felt for the fellow began to come back. I sat down and intimated casually:

"I've turned up considerable!"

"You have?" He sat up in his chair. "Really? Fine business!" He grinned. "Well, go on and spit it out. You must have got right on the job."

"I've found out what broker sold your stock, and what became of a part of the money." I looked him full in the eye and shot it at him.

"What! Sold my stock!" If ever genuine surprise looked

BOX 991   223

out of a man's eyes it did out of his. "Say!" He leaned forward. "You really mean you found out something like that? Why—how could anybody sell that—"

"I'm coming to that," I interrupted. "I've some of the canceled shares in my pocket."

He shot out his jaw.

"Which ones?" he growled.

"The Dunn's Mills stock," I told him.

"And who sold it? Where'd they get it for sale? D'ye mean you know who stole it out of my box?" He was plainly growing excited.

"No," I said, "I don't. But I can tell you the name of the brokers. It was Pearson & Company handled the stuff; in fact they handled all of your missing stock."

He simply stared. Abruptly he jammed his pipe back into his mouth.

"Do you know all this or are you guessing?" he demanded. "Honest, Glace, it's pretty hard for me to sit here and believe that any broker would take that stock and be able to find a buyer for it. But if you've dug up anything like this, it's just about as funny as how the box was looted in the first place. Why how could they sell the stuff. I was in the West—Alaska or Seattle when the thing was done. How—"

"See, here," I checked him once more. "Have you any way of proving that you *were* in Seattle last November?"

Once more his expression was one of surprise.

"Proving it? Why yes, but what for?"

"What's your proof?" I added the question.

"Why—why any of a dozen people will verify that. There's the folks with whom I closed up my deal."

Either he was vastly puzzled or a splendid actor, I had to admit.

"Anything else?" I urged. "It will take time to hunt up those persons and get their statements in the matter. Haven't you something else to show?"

He frowned.

"You remember what I told you about paying the box rent through Mack? Well, as it happens I've a letter he wrote me at that time. Wait a bit and I'll get it." He rose, went over to a trunk and began rummaging through it. He turned back after a bit with an envelope in his hand. "Here," he said, extending it to me. "I guess that might fill the bill as evidence of my whereabouts at that time."

I drew out the letter enclosed in the cover after inspecting the postmarks with care. They showed the thing to have been mailed in our own city in November of the previous year, and received at Seattle some five days later. The letter bore the same date as the mailing stamp, was addressed to Hood and signed by Frederick Mack. I slid it back into the envelope and returned it.

"Corroborative, at least," I declared.

Then I reached into my pocket and brought out Hood's own list of the stocks.

"You signed this, didn't you?"

I kept my eyes on his face. Surely if guilty of any deceit he must, I thought, see now that I was pressing him close.

"Of course I signed it," he retorted. "You saw me. You asked me to, in fact. But what has that got to do with the sale of those stocks? I didn't sign them. You heard me say it this morning. Just what are you driving at? It strikes me you're acting darned funny."

BOX 991 225

I put the list away and selected the letter, ordering the sale of the Milling Corporation stock. Folding it so that only the "Yours very truly" and the signature showed, I held it toward him.

"Who signed that?" I inquired.

He gave it one glance.

"I did, so far as I can see," he replied without hesitation. "But where in time did you pick up a letter of mine?"

"From Pearson." I threw it at him quickly.

He stood there and stared straight into my face. There wasn't any mistake. He was puzzled, and yet his eyes never wavered nor shifted. Presently he grinned slowly.

"Get out," he said. "What is this—a joke or what? I never wrote them a letter in my life. Dad traded with them but not yours truly."

"Perhaps you'd better read this one then," I suggested.

He fairly snatched it out of my hand and shot his eyes along its lines. Watching, I saw amazed surprise grow swiftly on his features. He had been standing since coming back from his trunk, but now he slumped down into a chair, and stared at me.

"Well—I'm damned," he muttered half to himself in the manner of one slightly dazed.

I thought it time to follow up my attack. If there was anything for me to learn, there would never be a better chance than this. I took out the canceled shares and tossed them over.

"You were asking about how those shares were sold, a few moments ago," I observed. "Take a glance at the transfers on these and see if they don't answer your question, Mr. Hood."

He took them and ran them over. I saw his jaw come half open and then close slowly. He appeared to be making a supreme effort at self control.

"Good God!" he said softly, after a time, and sat on holding the certificates and the letter in his hands.

Abruptly he sprang to his feet. His eyes came back to mine. They were wide open, frank, steady. He thrust the shares and the letter into my hands.

"Take 'em," he cried. "I see how it looks and I guess I see what you think. Well—I don't blame you. It's natural enough. That's my signature—on the letter and on the shares. It's mine. There isn't the shadow of a doubt about that. I'd admit it anywhere, if I saw it. I'd have to. Barring the fact that it's smaller, it's the same as the one I wrote for you this morning.

"And yet, just as sure as you and I are here in this room together at this minute, Mr. Glace, I'm ready to take my oath before God that I *never signed one of the things in my life!*"

5

THAT WOMAN AGAIN

WHEN I LEFT Hood I was convinced, so far as I myself was concerned, that the man was sincere in his somewhat dramatic denial. The more I saw of him the more he impressed me as an open-hearted, naturally honest young fellow, and the better I liked him.

I showed him all of the correspondence I had brought with me from Pearson's office; and by degrees I saw his first startled amazement give way to baffled rage, which manifested in the bulldog set of his jaw and the grate which crept into his tones.

"You've got quite a collection," he said at length as I was gathering up the letters after his inspection. "Maybe you'd better take this missive which shows where I was at that time." He held out Mack's letter to me.

"Maybe I had," I returned.

"Ain't it the blamedest snarl?" he exclaimed. "Ain't it completely crazy? I tell you it's got me running around in circles. Don't mind if I begin picking the bed clothes or singing to myself, will you?"

I shook my head, smiling at the somewhat boyish outbreak.

"Just now it goes nowhere," I admitted. "But wait, Mr Hood."

When I came out of the Kenton I had just one idea in my mind. That was to get back to the Urania and Dual as fast as I could.

As Hood had said, the case on which I had stumbled had developed into a lovely snarl and one I felt Bryce had been right in thinking would require the master mind of my peculiar friend to unravel. As I swung on a car which passed the Urania on its route I thought I had at least eliminated any question of double dealing on the part of Hood. The man was a victim beyond any doubt. That left Farr.

And then I grinned. Dual's prediction that the case would show a baffling and confusing complex was verified already. What had he said?

"Scorpio rules—Sagittarius is rising. Uranus is retrograde at present."

Scorpio was a water sign, and Sagittarius one of the trinity of fire. My grin widened. Fire and water made steam and the case was surely getting misty. That was whimsy of course, but a good simile all the same. Uranus stood for the higher faculties of mind. Retrograde, it would throw a damning influence—where? On the criminal brain, I hoped. Had Dual had some such idea in mind?

Constant association and conversation with him had taught me to follow him sometimes to a certain degree. Not that I understood fully, but that instead of being wholly baffled by his words and actions, I now at times saw dimly at least some of the basal elements from which he proceeded to evolve his conclusions and results. It came to me that perhaps now he was banking on the position of

BOX 991   229

that very planet he had mentioned to throw a fatal influence over the scheming brain which had evolved the clever plan of theft we confronted, and cause it to take some betraying step at this time. I began to wonder what he had discovered by his computations up there in the tower, while I unearthed the material facts concerning the sale of the stocks.

And then the Urania loomed ahead in the early dusk of the evening and I left the car, to make my way inside its massive entrance and go up to my office as quickly as I could.

Miss Newell reported that the unknown woman had called up again and she had told her I would surely be in before our closing hour of six. Bryce hadn't shown up as yet. I told Nellie I was going up to see Semi, and was just turning away, when my partner opened the door.

"Hello, there," he accosted me at once. "What did you find out?"

"Same to you and many of 'em," I retorted.

He flushed.

"That's soon answered. I didn't find out nuthin'. Farr seems to have gone away from here in an airship. Nobody around any of the depots knows a thing about it. I run a leg off tryin' to get a line an' I blamed near blistered my tongue. Nuthin' doin'. If Gibson swore out that warrant, though, I reckon he'll be picked up somewhere after a bit. D'you have any luck?"

"Some."

"Well?" He took off his hat and wiped his forehead.

"Come up-stairs," I said, "and I'll only have to tell it once."

He nodded and turned toward the door.

"If that woman calls again?" Nellie began.

"Bother the woman," I flung back on my way after Bryce.

We lost no time in going up, mounting the stairs and threading the central path to the tower. Its door was ajar, and we passed in and across the anteroom toward that other beyond it. Dual sat still at his desk, which was littered now with papers, covered with his odd symbols and calculations. But he was not working any longer. He lay back in his chair in the early twilight, in an attitude of relaxation.

Yet he opened his eyes at the sound of our coming, sat up and touched a button, which illumined the room. The golden apple, in the hands of the life-sized bronze Venus which held it, glowed softly on the far side of the desk He had not been asleep, as he seemed at first glance, for his eyes showed no traces of slumber as they lifted in silent question to mine.

I felt that question as plainly as though spoken. I nodded, reached into my pocket and brought out all I had collected on my round. I laid them on the desk before him, and sank into my chair, while Bryce found himself a seat. And all the while there was not one word spoken.

Still in silence, Semi took the stock, the letters from Pearson, and the one I had obtained from Hood. He spread them out on the desk and ran them over. I saw his eyes light slightly once or twice. He even nodded his head. I glanced at Bryce. He spread out his hands and shook a negation. I thought of his favorite expression concerning Semi—"Can you beat it?"—and smiled in reply.

"And now, Gordon, your part of the story," said Dual.

BOX 991   231

I nodded.

"Be careful," he said. "I told you this affair would present puzzling aspects, and already they are appearing. Overlook nothing in your detail, however trivial it may seem. Proceed."

And, as earlier in the day, I complied, running briefly through the events since I left him, but touching on each point, as Dual himself had taught me to do in the past, when first I came into his life and he gave his friendship and help to me. And this time, instead of lying back in his chair, I found him sitting wide-eyed, with his eyes on me.

After a bit it seemed to me that I saw a little flame way down in their gray depths—a little living flame which glowed and glowed and held me as by a spell while I spoke to the spirit for which I felt instinctively that it stood. That little flame seemed to draw my words and thoughts to itself as a fire draws air in a rushing draught.

I found myself speaking without any effort, like the air flows toward the fire, and every now and then as I made some point in my narration the little flame seemed to leap up and glow more brightly, until quite suddenly, at the end, it went out, and Dual was not looking at me any longer, while Bryce was sitting forward in his chair and staring.

"Gosh, Glace, but you're some talker when you get started," he remarked. "Did you really dig up all that?"

I nodded, glanced at Dual and caught his eyes again for a moment. He smiled.

"In this case I deemed it necessary to drain our friend's mind, both objective and subconscious, of all the salient information it might hold," he said, as if in explanation to Bryce. "Now, what have you learned on your round?"

Jim grinned.

"You can drain me without hypnotizin' me or nothin'," he responded. "I didn't get even a look-in anywhere at all."

I felt odd. It was the first time Dual had ever affected me like that directly. I turned my gaze back to him.

"Did you really influence me as Bryce suggests?" I asked softly.

He smiled.

"It is essential to have all we can obtain to begin with," he told me. "Therefore I merely concentrated your mind on the story you were telling, to the exclusion of all extraneous distraction whatsoever, in order to learn everything you might know."

I shook my head.

"I feel mentally empty."

Bryce chuckled.

"He pumped you dry. That's what's the matter with you."

Dual drew his chair nearer to his desk.

"Come closer, Mr. Bryce," he said. "What Gordon has obtained to-day is of the greatest value. He has done exceedingly well and acted with admirable judgment in the steps he has taken thus far. From what he has learned and what I myself have determined through my own means, I feel that we are now ready to begin a serious consideration of the matter."

Bryce dragged his chair over. His face was slightly distorted with mingled emotions.

"Maybe," he returned as he sat down; "but the only thing I can see now is that Hood seems to be trying a double cross on the bank, no matter what he says about it. Did he really sign those shares?"

BOX 991   233

Dual extended a certificate toward him.

"He appears to have signed them," he said.

"Then he wasn't in Seattle last November." Bryce studied the signed transfer. "This is his writin', all right."

"The letter addressed to him by Mr. Mack would indicate that he *was* in Seattle," said Dual.

"Easy," Bryce grinned. "A confederate could have fixed that."

"There was no confederate in this case," said Semi Dual.

"Eh?" Bryce put down the share of stock and stared.

Dual smiled slightly.

"Every participant in an action shows in an astrological figure dealing with the event, Mr. Bryce. In the case in hand, my figures, erected to-day while Gordon and you were absent, show no evidence whatever of any person cooperating with Hood in regard to the theft of these stocks."

"Er—well—but—" Bryce subsided. "You make it. I pass," he said.

"This morning I mentioned that Mr. Hood's writing showed honesty as his basal characteristic," Dual resumed. "My later investigations support the evidence of his handwriting. Character shows in the work of our hands, as you have known me to prove before. Also my figures, while showing him plainly, also contain him not in the position of the one guilty of the theft from the bank drawer, but in that of the one who has been robbed. Once and for all: Joseph J. Hood did not commit any wrong, no matter how things may look. I warned you this morning that we must beware of just such appearances as this. On the other hand, aside from Hood, my calculations indicate two men as mainly implicated in the circumstances surrounding the theft."

"Farr and th' vault guard, for a thousand. Gibson was right, by granny!" Bryce hitched his chair even nearer. "Go on. I see what you mean."

But Semi paid small attention to the interruption directly. Instead he turned to me with a question.

"Just what is Farr's personal appearance?" he inquired.

"I don't know," I told him. "I never saw the chap to know him. From what Mack and Sheldon said, I imagine he is a young fellow, however. In fact, I'm sure of that."

"Because," Dual went on when I paused, "in my figure there appears a man I might describe as being light haired, blue eyed, of a rather nervous temperament, and a generally pleasing manner—impulsive in action at times, a man of the nervo-sanguine type."

"That fits Farr," Bryce cut in. "I know 'cause, before I started huntin' how he left town, I stopped at th' bank and got Sheldon to describe him. He's got light hair, blue eyes an'—"

"A small colorless mole near the corner of his right eye," said Dual, glancing at a sheet of paper he had picked up.

"Holy smoke!" exclaimed Bryce. "You got that down too?"

Semi Dual nodded.

"There is another man closely involved with this other," he continued. "He is dark, in his general type. Between the two there is really no definite relation, save that Venus is very prominently involved in the destinies of each, and exerts her influence upon them, not only now but through-

BOX 991   235

out a considerable period of time past. That would indicate a woman in the matter, beyond any possible doubt."

"A woman!" said Bryce.

Dual nodded.

"Yes. She also is dark."

Jim nodded.

"All right. Put her in too," he grinned. "Now where are we at?"

"At the beginning of the solution," said Dual, with the least possible twinkle in his eyes.

My irrepressible partner always afforded Semi a quiet sort of amusement. Now he laid down the paper he had been holding and went on.

"So far as finding the actual agent of the theft, there is in this case no difficulty at all. Our main endeavor need not be directed toward determining the identity of the thief. What we must do is to collect still further evidence which will prove his identity to be correct, rather than anything else, and I am reasonably sure that will not entail so much difficulty, in fact, as it will merely the effort of gathering it together. Gordon, to-day, has made an excellent start. Let us consider what he has brought back as a beginning."

He turned and picked up one of the letters I had obtained from Pearson.

"In looking this correspondence over I am struck first by one thing. Each and every one of these letters was written on the same typewriting machine—presumably either a second-hand purchase or a machine used for a considerable time. I presume that you know there is an individuality about writing machines, even aside from the essential differences in machines of different makes, and also about the writing of different operators as well.

"That fact has been made use of ere this in detection, as you probably know. Take the last statement first. The man who wrote these letters is perfectly well acquainted with the work. He uses the professional touch, one might say—but what is unusual, he appears to prefer a six-point margin, rather than the customary ten or five. So much for that.

"Again, one who is familiar with the work of the different makes of machines can state with care which particular type of machine was used in composing any specific specimen of writing. Taking the concrete example I hold in my hand, and speaking from my knowledge of such things I will hazard the opinion that it was written upon an old model Coroya in none too good condition, with some distinguishing features about it."

This was in Bryce's field. He leaned forward.

"Such as?"

"Such as the letter 'd'," said Semi. "You will notice that in the small 'd' throughout these letters, the stem of the letter is very poorly printed. That might indicate a poor or ragged ribbon, save for the fact that the 'I', the 'b' and the 't' are clearly struck. This machine, therefore, had a battered 'd' on its type shuttle.

"You will notice, also, that the lower loop of the small 'e' is very faint. 'E' is a letter used a great deal in writing. The upper part, supported by the cross bar in the small letter, wears less fast than the thin lower loop. Hence the condition of the 'e' here supports my contention of the old machine. The more so, as the main predominating feature

BOX 991　　　　　　　　　　　　　　　**237**

of the Coroya is its permanent alignment and uniformity of work, due to the hammer stroke from a spring release on the key. Because of that very feature, the fact that the 'd' and 'e' are uniformly defective, proves the fault to lie in the type itself."

"And the other letter," Bryce suggested.

Dual picked up Mack's letter written to Hood in Seattle.

"This will also support my claim," he returned. "It is written on a different make of machine. You see the 'd's' even in the address on the cover are perfect, but it is an old machine also unless I am mistaken. Take the address again for example."

"The 'Joseph' is faint, the 'J' quite plain and also the 'Hood'. Suppose this was written on a machine not equipped with the automatic ribbon reverse. Such machines require manual reversing. When the ribbon ran to the end it stood stationary, and the type, striking through the same point many times, wore the ink more completely. A touch then, and the ribbon running back would give a darker impression.

"Suppose, again, that the writer of this finished his letter and his ribbon length at the same time, and you will notice that the last four words of this letter are quite faint—and then slid the envelope into the machine to address it, without shifting the reverse. The first word would be faint as it is, but perfectly legible as you see. But the writer, noting the fact, threw the reverse into play and finished the address with the ribbon again turning backward, giving us a clearer impression because of that very fact."

"And what sort of a machine was this wrote on?" Bryce asked.

"From its general appearance, a Zenith, I think," said Dual.

"Well, by granny! that's cutting it fine, but I wouldn't say you was wrong," Bryce made comment. "Now if you can tell us where these machines are."

"That is a question which answers itself," said Semi. "The Zenith is here in the city. The Coroya is, I fancy, in Little Falls."

Bryce chuckled.

"I reckon I'm rattled. Honest, there isn't any head or tail to this case so far as I can see."

"And yet," said Semi, "it should really offer no particular difficulties in its solution."

Bryce appeared restless.

"That's the second time you've said something like that," he burst out. "Maybe that's how it looks to you but hanged if I see it. I reckon you'd better go right on and tell us what to do."

"I agree with you, Mr. Bryce," Dual took him up. "As I remarked, that necessary to the solution is the collection of more data, before we confront the thief with our proof. Toward that end I am going to suggest that Glace go to Little Falls this evening, and I think that perhaps he had better take the man Hood with him when he goes. It can do no harm to investigate the place from which these letters were sent to the broker. The address is plainly given, and it should be an easy matter to discover some information at that end "

I looked him full in the face, remembering another time when he had told me to go to a supposedly empty storeroom and seek what I might find. I had gone without the

BOX 991 239

least suspicion of what it would be and I had picked up the essential thread which led into the heart of all the mystifying tangle. Now, however, I felt a desire to know just what I was after.

"What do you expect me to find over there?" I inquired.

"A Coroya typewriter with a busted 'd'," said Bryce, slapping his knee.

Dual gave him a glance. It wasn't one of scorn, or contempt, or anger. I think Semi seldom felt such emotions. Rather it seemed to me that the lightning flash of his eyes was one of compelling command. Anyway, Bryce's grin faded very swiftly and he dropped his own eyes toward the floor and sank into an abashed attitude, comically like that of an impertinent child awaiting deserved rebuke.

"Honest, I meant it," he mumbled after a moment. "Th' trouble is I'm a chump."

"The trouble is you were a policeman so long, that the thing became a habit, Mr. Bryce," said Dual. "A flat foot leaves a different trail of approach than does a high sprung arch. As it happens, however, I am inclined to consider your deduction correct so far as the machine is concerned."

He turned his eyes back to me and I found them as smiling as I fancy Bryce had found them impersonally cold.

"You will take Hood with you and go over there, Gordon, tonight. Once on the ground, follow your own instinctive leading as to what you shall do. You have done that in the past and arrived at the goal which you sought. Open your soul to the influences which are working in this matter; let them have full sway upon you. You are one of the appointed agents, who shall aid the sweep of justice. Upon the criminal mind there has come a blight. Those very forces which will lead you, shall upon him exert a wholly blasting power. The clever scheme of his building is being even now undermined. Question not, therefore, anything which shall happen, but go forward to the appointed end, when all shall be explained and the soul of guilt unveiled."

And suddenly I thrilled. The promise of the day was fulfilled and as Semi Dual ceased there was a dash of rain against the tower's window at the end of the room. It rattled and slashed on the pane, and I remember I heard it but dimly.

Dual had spoken like the old Dual—as he had spoken other times to me, before sending me forth to do battle with the forces of unexposed evil, and drag them to the light. There had been command and a note of prophecy in his voice and his words, and a confidence which showed me, in my present understanding of the man, that already he had picked out of the nebulous mass of detail, the germ of truth—that he knew.

Abruptly, all question, all doubt fled away and left me ready and anxious to follow his instructions—to go where he sent me, and find what I now knew would be there. No need to ask how he knew—that he knew was sufficient— that he sent me was, in itself, sufficient proof that he knew. Because, always before he acted, Semi Dual was—sure.

Just as I leaned forward to rise from my chair, Bryce came out of the somewhat depressed silence into which he had fallen.

"And what do I do?" he said in an almost forlornly humble manner.

"You, Mr. Bryce, will take the list of Hood's shares, and go to Mr. Pearson, and ask him to give you a record of the

BOX 991   241

sales they have made of those stocks. It will be as well to be able to locate the securities at the end."

"Is that all?" I felt sorry for Jim. Honestly, I think he believed right then that Dual was giving him a mere routine task rather than anything essential to the final outcome.

"That is all," said Semi.

Jim nodded.

"All right," he agreed. And then he looked at me. "Farr used to live in Little Falls," he observed.

As I have said, there was something irrepressible about James Bryce.

But I had been thinking the very same thing and I nodded back by way of answer, just before Dual spoke.

"Let me explain to you, Bryce—I do not wish you to misunderstand me, and I perceive that you do. You have seen more than one instance to prove that I can use telepathy at will—one as recent as this morning. But the ability is not one possessed alone by me. In the matter in hand we are facing a mind which has formed a cunning scheme; a mind shrewd and alert, which has dwelt upon the final outcome of this affair in all its several phases, so far as it could see. If that mind be left at this time unwarned, my calculations show me that fate—planetary influence—universal justice—call it what you may—will cause that mind, despite all its cunning, to take one false step which shall bring about its complete undoing. For that very reason, I do not desire to put into definite form any statement of what the final outcome of this matter shall be; for the less minds there are to project possible thought waves from themselves into the surrounding ether, the less chance can there be for that cunning seat of evil to contact such a wave and find that his plans are going other than in the way he wills."

"You—you reckon he knows anything about what's going on now?" Bryce stammered as he paused.

"Assuredly," said Dual. "For that very reason, I desire him to feel that what he desires, is what is being done."

"What he desires? Oh, the dickens!" mouthed Jim.

Just what he desires," said Dual, and smiled.

"Is that why you're sending Gordon to Little Falls?" my partner queried.

"Partly, yes. At least he will expect it."

Jim shifted.

"I reckon I'm a mutt," he growled, "but let me ask you one question. Do you know the end of this? Did them figures of yours show you? Did you dope it all out from them an' what Glace turned up?"

"Exactly," said Semi, and glanced at the clock in the corner. "I am as sure of what will be the final end as I am that before six o'clock a new interest will be introduced into the situation. It is now five minutes to. Before six, Venus will—"

The bell of the little service 'phone from our office, thirteen floors below, began to ring. He gave me a glance as he turned toward it, lifted the receiver from its hook and answered:

"Yes—yes, Mr. Glace is here. One moment, please."

He held the receiver toward me and I took it. I spoke into the little box. It was Nellie's voice which reached my ear.

"Oh, Mr. Glace, that lady I told you had been calling has

BOX 991   243

come up here in person. She insists upon seeing you yet, to-night. I left her out in the other room, came in here and closed the door. What shall I tell her, please?"

The persistency of the woman, whoever she was, annoyed me. It was on the tip of my tongue to tell Nellie to say she would not be able to see me to-night; and to close up the office and go home. And then Dual, who had gone back to his chair at the desk, gave another illustration of his uncanny ability to snatch a person's thoughts out of his head.

"Gordon, tell Miss Newell to have the lady come up here," he said.

6

THE OPINION OF MISS GIBSON

IT APPEARED TO be my day for shocks. It was wholly out of the rule for Dual to bring strangers to the roof. Of course he had done it before, but it was not the usual thing, and the very fact that he was now overstepping custom indicated plainly that he deemed the presence of the unknown woman important at this time.

With the feeling that almost anything might be expected from now on, I gave Nellie the answer he had directed, and turned away from the 'phone.

"The influence of Venus comes fully into the equation from now on," he remarked quite calmly. "If you don't mind, Gordon, suppose you go out and meet her at the foot of the stairs. She may feel a bit puzzled else, and one may presume her to be already more or less disturbed."

Of course, I knew he was acting from a knowledge as yet hidden from me, and yet it seemed weird, eery, to hear him speak like that of a person none of us had thus far seen. I made no comment, however, though I was sure from his smile that he sensed my mental condition, as his finger crept toward a button on the end of his desk, and I moved toward the door.

I knew that button turned on the lights in the garden

BOX 991   245

and on the staircase, and even as I reached the anteroom they flashed in the outer dusk. I went out and down the path, and so to the foot of the stairs on the twentieth floor.

A cage came up. The door of the shaft clanged back and a woman came out.

She was clad in what appeared a dark blue tailored costume, and wore some sort of dark fur over her shoulders and turned up about her face. I saw her glance around in an unfamiliar fashion, catch sight of the stairs and turn in my direction. From her manner of approach I judged her to be young, and then as she came nearer I was certain. More, I knew her beyond any shadow of a doubt. I put out a hand and laid it on one of the bronze newels for a sort of support and stared straight at her with the rudeness of surprise. There was no mistaking her storm-heightened beauty or the outlines of face and figure. I waited until she was quite close.

"Good evening, Miss Gibson," I said.

The daughter of the Fourth National's cashier swept my face with stormy eyes.

"You are Mr. Glace?" she questioned. "You were at the bank this morning?"

I bowed and motioned her toward the stairway.

"Shall we go up?" I suggested.

Again her eyes questioned. "Up here?" she said, and I saw amazed appreciation of the marble steps in her face even then.

I nodded and we began the ascent, walking side by side, and not speaking further, until we reached the top, when abruptly, she paused.

At that one could hardly blame her. After the storm

driven dusk she had left when she entered the Urania some time before, the softly lighted warmth of that beautiful garden, sweet with the perfume of flowers, must have come as a shock. She stopped short just in front of the now prismatically glowing letters of the annunciator plate and gave me a wholly startled glance.

"Why—why—just where are you taking me, Mr. Glace?" she stammered.

"I'm taking you into the presence of the man who lives here, Miss Gibson," I told her. "The presence of a man who knows more of detection in a minute than I, a professional detective, have learned in all my life. I was with him when my office girl called me on a private 'phone. I had placed the matter of the bank before him. I often consult him in puzzling cases. He asked me to have you come up."

She was staring at the flashing letters of the plate. But when I paused she lifted her eyes to mine once more.

"Shall surely find that which he shall seek," she quoted, and I knew she had read the message inlaid before us in glass. "Just who and what is this man?" she questioned.

"I have told you what I can briefly, Miss Gibson," I returned. "Come, and you shall see him."

She nodded. Her eyes, wide and dark, did not seem to look directly at me, but beyond me now. Suddenly I saw her shiver.

"And I am one who comes seeking," she murmured as to herself. "How did he know? Did you tell him who I was, Mr. Glace?"

"I didn't know," I confessed. "The girl didn't give your name. Mr. Dual told me to have you come up. I never

BOX 991   247

suspected your identity till I saw you leave the cage just now."

She frowned.

"And he told you, Mr. Glace, I—I think I am a little afraid. You say this man with the strange name told you to have me come up, without knowing who I was; how, then, did he know I should come up? What is this—modern witchcraft?"

I shook my head.

"Nothing like that. All I can tell you now that you must not be surprised at anything he says or does, and that for you to be admitted here is a signal recognition of the urgency of your claim upon him. It is those who seek who find Semi Dual. Come, Miss Gibson."

Abruptly she put a hand on my arm.

"Semi Dual," she repeated, and her eyes began to glow darkly. "Mr. Glace, isn't he the man who saved Billy Baird from being suspected of that murder some time ago? Billy and his wife told me a little about it. Is this man the same?"

I bowed my head.

"The same, Miss Gibson."

Her whole face lighted.

"And now I come seeking—and I shall find. Take me to him quickly—quickly—Mr. Glace."

We stepped out on the glowing plate. From the tower soft chimes pulsed out the message of our coming. The lips of the girl beside me parted.

"Beautiful," she whispered, with a catch of breath. "Billy told me he owed his freedom, perhaps his life, to this man and you," she said softly. "Who is he, Mr. Glace? Will he help me, do you think—if my need seems great?"

"He will help you," I assured her, looking into her eyes. "But as to who he is, I cannot tell you—save just that he is Dual."

Something like awe crept into her face as we went on to the tower and inside and across to the room where Bryce and Dual waited our coming.

I threw open the door and stood aside. Gertrude Gibson entered, and as she came in Dual met her, standing beside his desk, with the golden glow of the Venus held light behind him. Bryce rose heavily to his feet.

For a moment the eyes of Dual and the woman met and held, and then Dual smiled.

"You come at the appointed time," he said softly, yet so that the words filled the room over the lash of the storm. "You come to seek—with a pure heart—and you shall find. And in finding you shall aid the march of that justice which is eternal and not to be denied ever, but to be feared only by those who do a wrongful act. Pray take this chair," He moved to push forward a huge padded seat.

I don't know just what Gertrude Gibson felt, but as for myself, the atmosphere of the place changed suddenly from commonplace to something subtly compelling, like the holy spell of a shrine. And as more than once before, Dual, in his robes of white and blue, was the priest in that peaceful place where immortal truth and right and justice held sway. For a moment, however, the girl said nothing. Her eyes still clung to Dual as she sank into the chair. Then, quite suddenly, her bosom swelled in an audible sigh and her words were a question.

"You know why I come?"

BOX 991   249

Dual had resumed his seat also. "*That* you were coming and why?" he replied.

"I—I just can't understand," she faltered.

Semi Dual smiled.

"You are Venus—woman," he made answer. "Your influence affects deeply the destiny of two lives. It is because of that you are here—to throw your influence in the scale of justice, to prevent a wrong from being done if so be you may, to set your own soul at rest and perform your duty to cosmic right."

Suddenly her eyes lighted. Her lips parted. With a quick gesture she threw off the fur she was wearing, unveiling the trim lines of her upper figure and the sweep of her throat.

"I do not understand," she began, "but I feel that you know. I—I suppose Mr. Glace must have told you what happened to-day at the bank where my father is cashier, but your words seem to indicate a deeper knowledge, so that I hardly know how to begin."

Dual leaned slightly toward her.

"Listen, Miss Gibson," he said in his soft, compelling tones. "I know all that happened at the bank. Dismiss that. Tell me rather the personal reason which brings you here at this time—which led you to seek Mr. Glace, because you thought the case entirely in his hands. Place in my hands the burden of doubt you now carry. And in so doing speak as freely as you would to your own soul, secure in the knowledge that what you say will be weighed and judged for its value in this matter only. Come, Miss Gibson. Speak."

I thought she swayed the least bit. I know she grew paler and her eyes darkened and grew wide.

"Who—who are you?" she questioned and then— "Oh, forgive me. I do not mean to be rude. But this—this is all so unexpected."

Dual smiled softly.

"There is nothing, my child, to forgive. I am, like thyself, a seeker of the truth. Come."

She glanced about her, at the room, at me, at Bryce and back to Dual.

"I must," she said. "I must!"

And with that she began:

"Mr. Dual and Mr. Glace, I was at the bank this morning as you know. I heard my father cry out to arrest a man—a Mr. Farr—a Mr. Neville Farr, who is employed at our bank. He cried out that he would swear out a warrant for that young man, just as I was about to rap on the door or his room."

Briefly she paused and then rushed on.

"I know Mr. Farr—have known him for years. What I heard made me think, worried me greatly, because—because Mr. Farr and I were very good friends and I had always thought him the soul of honor. I could imagine nothing for which he should be arrested. I could not remain at the time and ask questions, although, of course, I know a great many of the people at the bank. I left, but I couldn't forget what I had heard, especially after Mr. Mack opened the door of my father's room, and I had seen my father's face, darkened by the anger I saw he felt.

"But after I got home, I called up Mr. Mack, whom I know very, very well, and I asked him what was the real trouble, and he told me that some one had rifled a box in

BOX 991   251

the vault and that Mr. Farr's arrest had been ordered—for reasons which I suppose you know."

Dual bowed, but made no other reply.

Miss Gibson paused and seemed to be collecting herself for a moment.

"As I've told you, I have known Mr. Farr for some time, and I never thought for a moment that he was a man who would be guilty of anything like that. I told Mr. Mack so, and he was very nice, but said that he thought the main reason was that Mr. Sheldon had said Nev—Mr. Farr had asked for leave yesterday and taken something from his own vault box, and that, taken with the fact that he *could* have known that this Mr. Hood was coming home, had thrown suspicion on him. I asked him why Mr. Farr had wanted to leave, and he said Mr Sheldon claimed he had said something about some personal business connected with some real estate holdings of his own."

Again she paused, and went abruptly on.

"It isn't pleasant for a girl to do what I feel I must in this case, Mr. Dual. My father has always been so good to me, that I do not like to criticize him in any way whatever, and yet I must confess that he is a man of very strong temper and opinions and likes and dislikes as well—and he doesn't like Mr. Farr.

"And it's just because of that very real estate Mr. Farr has, that he has taken his dislike to him—I think—at least that is one reason." She flushed slightly as she qualified her statement.

"That is also the reason why I know that Mr. Farr actually has property. You see, some time ago, father became interested in a small plant up at Little Falls and wanted to move and enlarge it after he took hold. In order to do that they needed new land, and some of it was this land Mr. Farr owns. He offered to buy it and Mr. Farr didn't wish to sell—or held out for more than father offered—or—at least there was some trouble.

"Anyway, father became very angry about it at the time, and I really think that except for the fact that Mr Carlton, the bank's president, and Mr Sheldon both took the view that a man need not sell unless he wished to, Mr. Farr would have been discharged from the bank. You see, father made it a personal matter rather than one of business. And to-day when I heard that he had ordered the—the arrest. I couldn't help feeling that perhaps his attitude toward Mr. Farr caused him to be more ready to suspect him.

"You see, aside from the fact that he was out of town, there was really no more reason to think him guilty than there was to accuse any other of the bank's employees— and against that he may really have gone away to attend to some business of his own, just as he told Mr. Sheldon he wished to do. And anyway"—her voice grew suddenly more incisive—"I don't think it's right to slander a man behind his back, or order him arrested without giving him a chance to say a word for himself like that. And I don't care if it is my own father who does it—it isn't right, or kind, or just. They can all say what they wish, I know Neville Farr, and I don't believe he's a thief."

She was panting the least bit at the end, and her color had crept back and actually heightened under the force of her final vehement denial. She seemed to sense the fact, and caught herself up.

"So I thought and thought, and after a time it came to

BOX 991   253

me that as Mr. Glace was handling the matter for the bank I just must come and tell him not to be too sure that Mr. Farr was the guilty man. I—I didn't want father's temper to make that boy a victim—and—well, I knew I was the only one here to say a word in his defense."

Dual sat silent for some moments after she had finished.

"You have known Mr. Farr for some time, then?" he queried at length, with his eyes full on her face.

"For about eighteen months," she said quickly.

"And Mr. Mack?" said Dual, in a positively insinuating tone.

Miss Gibson flushed, swiftly, deeply.

"Mr. Dual," she said in a voice almost choked.

"What does he think about Farr's guilt?"

"He doesn't believe it, I'm sure!" she cried. "He says Neville is caught in an unfortunate circumstantial net— those were his exact words to me myself. Why," she lifted her eyes, "he even came here with me in the car. He's waiting for me downstairs. He wanted to come up, but I wouldn't let him. Of course he knows what I came for—I told him that. But he's sorry. He even 'phoned me to destroy a photo I have of Neville. He said father was going to demand it to give to the police."

She lifted a bag which had lain on her lap since she sat down and opened its cord-closed mouth. "I didn't destroy it—I brought it with me. I—I thought maybe Mr. Glace would be able to use it—I hardly know why. It—it just occurred to me."

She drew out a small photograph mounted in a folder and held it toward Semi Dual.

He gave it a glance, nodded slightly and passed it on to me.

"Just about how long ago did this land matter come up between Farr and your father?" he asked.

"About six months now," said Miss Gibson.

"There was no trouble between them before that?"

"Oh, no."

"Mr. Farr, outside of this real estate, is not very well off, Miss Gibson?"

"No." She pursed her lips without looking up from closing the satin bag.

Semi spoke slowly.

"Is it not possible that your father has another reason for suspecting the young man besides the one you name? Other men in the past have found a certain woman attractive—and dreamed of winning her for their own. May not your father believe that this man dared to lift his eyes to you, and, led on by some such desire, has taken the step of robbing that box in order to speculate with the stock in the hope of making a fortune? Is it not true that your father has a different man in mind for your husband—a man he knows and trusts and feels would make you a more suitable mate?"

She didn't look up. She flushed again, as she had flushed before, but she did not shirk the answer.

"Yes. I—I think that once more you are right. But—" there was the absolute pleading of a child in her tone, "there would be nothing wrong in Neville's loving me— no reason why that should throw suspicion on him. If he had wanted money to gamble in stocks he could have sold the real estate he held. He wouldn't need to rob that box."

BOX 991   255

Suddenly Dual smiled.

"You are a good advocate, Miss Gibson," he said, "and a singularly logical one, in that you have picked the one weak spot in that possible suspicion. Now, just why didn't Mr. Farr wish to sell your father that land?"

She jerked the strings of the bag tight.

"Oh, he had a plan," she said, her words running all together. "He—it was his old home place—where he was born. Neville has a lot of sentiment at times. He meant never to sell it. He—he said when—when he was married he was going back there to live, if he were able, and was going to improve it and make it a very handsome place.

"You see, it lies right on the river, and father wanted it for yards and trackage and things like that. Neville held it more because he didn't want factories and warehouses to encroach in that direction. He could have let father have what he wanted and still have kept the house, but that would have spoiled the whole place if a lot of smoky old chimneys had been put up, and as it would have been the first factory in that part of town, Neville just held out and wouldn't sell. Some of his neighbors—and friends, urged him not to. I don't think father ought to have tried to put his plant in a residence neighborhood, myself."

Clearly Miss Gibson had a mind of her own, and a rather good one as her resume of the situation showed. On the other hand, I could imagine Gibson, as very possibly holding some such thought in his brain as Dual had suggested. It was Semi who spoke.

"That would hardly seem sufficient cause, to my mind, for suspecting Mr. Farr of this crime. In fact Mr. Farr's attitude appears natural enough. Such animus as your father seems to have shown would indicate some deeper reason, or the effect of some other suggestion."

"Father is very quick tempered," Miss Gibson repeated. "That is the very reason I felt I must explain, before a dreadful injustice was done. At the time he was very angry and insisted that Mr. Farr be dismissed from the bank, but Mr. Carlton and Mr. Sheldon would not hear of it on such grounds, and I induced Mr. Mack to talk to father about it and get him to withdraw his demands. Mr. Mack has a great deal of influence with father—"

Dual smiled as he interrupted.

"And you with Mr. Mack. Miss Gibson, I think Mr. Farr a rather lucky man, despite the present aspect of things."

That was a typical remark for Semi to make. It might mean so much or so little, and yet when everything was ended you would see that it applied exactly. But Miss Gibson caught at the surface merely, as it seemed.

"You mean everything will come out all right?" she exclaimed, her face suddenly alight, sparkling with hope, brilliant with the fires of youth and her sex.

"Exactly. Everything will come out all right," Dual told her.

She rose.

"You wonderful man," she said slowly. "When I talk to you I feel as if—as if—oh, as if everything just was all right already. And now that I have told you, what I came to tell, I really must go. Fred—Mr. Mack will think I've lost myself or something. But I just had to come, and I'm so glad I did. Good-by." She hesitated and half put out a small gloved hand.

Dual took it.

BOX 991   257

"I, too, am glad you came, Miss Gibson," he replied. "Mr. Glace will take you down, but before you start, spare us one moment longer." He glanced past her and caught my eye. "You, Gordon, need not return. Go do that upon which we had decided, and suppose that in talking to Hood, you learn all the details surrounding his leasing the box, which he can be led to remember."

From me his gaze shifted to Jim. "Mr. Bryce, I shall ask you to remain for a short time, if you please.

"And now, Miss Gibson, Mr. Glace will see you to your car." He bowed in an unassumed courtesy before her, straightened and stood, while I opened the door and permitted her to pass.

And then we were out in the garden again, walking down the path to the staircase, side by side. My companion made a short, inarticulate exclamation.

"What an odd place, and what a strange man," she said in an uncertain fashion. "He impresses one in a most peculiar manner. One doesn't know whether to regard him as a man, or—" she gave a little nervous laugh—"something like a priest. I—I half expected the benediction, I think, right at the last. And he makes you trust him, as you trust a priest. There is something—you *feel*."

I nodded. "I know," I told her. "I have felt it, too."

We went down then and I took her out to her car—a little town electric, standing by the curb. Mack was watching for us and opened the door.

"Hello, Glace," he greeted me smiling. "So she found you? Just what do you really think of this affair?"

"It's a bit early to do anything else," I rejoined, as I helped Miss Gibson into the coupé.

"Gertie thinks her daddy went off a bit sudden in order-ing out the dragnet for Neville," said Mack. "I don't know but that she's right. If there's anything I can do to be of assistance, don't hesitate to ask. Sheldon's dreadfully cut up about the whole thing. Where are you going? Can we give you a lift?"

I stepped back and raised my hat despite the rain.

"Thanks, no. Just now I'm going over to see Hood."

7

ANOTHER LETTER

BUT I DIDN'T go to Hood directly after the coupé ran off
under the rain. Instead I growled at the storm, caught a
car and went home for a bite to eat and to tell Connie that
I would be away all night and probably a part of the next
day at least.

From my own place I telephoned to the Kenton, got
Hood on the wire and directed him to meet me at the
inter-urban trolley station, where we could get a car for
Little Falls about nine. He was somewhat surprised at my
request, tried to ask a lot of questions over the 'phone, but
assented to the journey to the little manufacturing town
readily enough in the end.

I ate a hurried dinner, while Connie packed a suit case
for my needs. Then I kissed her good-by, promised her to be
careful, as she always made me, and set out for the station.

Finding Hood marching up and down the concrete
platform, puffing a cigar, quite independent of the weather
in storm coat and pull-down cap, he greeted me with his
usual grin.

"Nice weather to go hunting," he remarked. "What do
you expect to find at Little Falls to-night—that room in
the Dawson Block?"

I nodded.

"Yes. That and anything else we can turn up in the line of information about the chap who got the letters addressed there in your name."

Hood removed his cigar.

"I'd sort of like to meet that man," he said, doubling up the arm in the sleeve of his raincoat quite slowly and grinning. "I'd give him something to take away with him at least." Then quite abruptly he switched. "Fred Mack called on me this afternoon after you left and wanted to know how we were coming. I told him we'd just discovered I stole my own stock and sold it. Have you found out anything more?"

Our train came in just then and I did not answer until we had found our seats.

"Nothing of importance," I told him, glancing about me.

The car was very sparsely filled on this stormy night, and we had our section all to ourselves. It seemed as good time as any to go into the matter of the vault, as Semi had suggested. This hour's ride with the pound of the wheels to drown our words, and no one near enough to hear, offered just the right sort of opportunity for finding out what my companion could remember.

"There are a few questions I want to ask you, Mr. Hood," I began.

"Shoot," he returned, slipping down in the seat, with his knees against the one ahead.

"You told me you rented this box two years ago this month, and you said Mack arranged most of the preliminary details. Tell me just what really did occur."

BOX 991   261

He turned his head slightly toward me.

"Why, I told Fred I wanted a box and he arranged it for me. That's all there is to it."

"Yes, I know," I said, "but that isn't all there was to it. Just how was it done, and why did you tell Mack anything about it?"

"Oh," he grunted, "that's it, huh? Well, then, I told Fred about it because I wasn't acquainted at the bank and I had known him the best part of my life. When I got this job up north and found I'd have to be away a good part of the time, I decided to leave my papers where they would be safe.

"Naturally I thought about a bank box, and as I knew Fred worked at the Fourth National, I spoke to him about it one evening, told him what I wanted and what for, and asked him to introduce me at the bank. I didn't know, but I fancied that it might be of a little advantage to Fred—such things are, sometimes. Of course, I know I could have gone there and rented the thing myself, but I didn't. That's all there is to that. I can't see that it really makes any difference in this business now; a plain matter of mutual friendship between old boy chums."

The train had started and we were out in the rain-swept country.

"I don't know that it does, the way you tell it," I returned. "But you've stopped with the introduction."

"Eh? Oh—" he grinned. "You want the whole thing, step by step, till I turned the key on those stocks? I see. Well. Fred said he'd arrange it for me and I should come to the bank the next day. I went. I saw Fred. He told me he had fixed the matter, and took me to the vault. He introduced me to the guard—and I signed the card and got the password. Fred told the guard to show me about the keys. The guard got them and explained that there were two—in case I lost one. Fred told me to put one on my key ring and keep the other somewhere safe. Then he went back to his window, and the guard took me in and showed me how to unlock the box I put the papers in and we locked them up. To-day I came back and unlocked it. You know the rest. Want to see the key?"

There was almost a note of raillery in his voice at the last.

"Yes," I said; "I do."

He grinned.

"Well, Glace, you sure are thorough at least," he remarked, as he dug up his keys after some twisting and turning, and handed them to me.

I took them and held them to the central lights of the car. There were half a dozen of various sorts, and the thin, flat blade of the vault box type. I inspected that one closely. It was in every respect like many others I had seen now and then, and numbered quite plainly "991." There was nothing there. I gave them back.

"That the one you used two years ago, or the duplicate?" I asked.

"Same one," said Hood. "Didn't lose it. The duplicate, as I told you, is in my trunk. Fred and I were looking at it this afternoon."

The car swayed and swung as it rounded a corner. I sat and tried to see anything in the details I had just heard that could lead any deeper into the perplexing affair of box 991. I couldn't see anything in them at all. The whole business had seemingly been no more than one man friend might do for another any day in the year.

BOX 991   263

And yet Dual had taken the trouble to emphasize his desire that I learn what I could concerning the events leading up to Hood's taking the box. I had gained all I apparently could. Possibly he would be able to find something in it to help the final solution. It all seemed commonplace enough to me.

"Did your partner find any trace of where Farr had gone?" Hood questioned at my side.

"No."

"What gets me," my companion ran on, "is why that chap should have jumped out, even if he is the guilty party. If he'd sat tight, there would have been nothing more to point to him than any other employee of the bank. Outside of his absence, there isn't anything to point to him now— really. Honest, Glace, I can't help having a sort of gnawing doubt about that youngster being guilty."

"Your friend Mack says he thinks Gibson premature in the matter of the warrant," I remarked.

Hood sniffed.

"Gibson?" he said. "That old bird has it in for Farr, I'll bet. He was too ready to put it on him. He literally jumped at the chance."

He had noticed it, too. I smiled slightly.

"You know Farr? Ever see him?" I asked.

He shook his head.

I took out the photo Miss Gibson had brought and showed it to him.

"That his picture!" he exclaimed. "You're a good one. Where did you get hold of this?"

"Miss Gibson gave it to me," I remarked.

Hood stared.

"Miss Gibson! Lord!" He began to chuckle. "Fred has hopes in that direction, you know. What's she got to do with this affair?"

"Like Mack and yourself, she doubts Farr's guilt," I explained. "She thought this might help me to recognize him, if I saw him, and that as I was handling the case, I ought to have it."

"If she doesn't think Farr guilty, that doesn't make sense," said Hood.

"That will apply to the entire affair, as yet," I returned.

He grinned once more.

"Well, just what *have* you done since I saw you this afternoon? You appear to have seen this girl."

I told him what Dual had discovered concerning the typewriters, and he listened carefully to the end.

"That's right about Fred's machine," he declared. "He uses a Zenith of the vintage of I don't know when. And that's pretty clever work, too, Glace, I must say. Thunder! In this age of the world a man has to be pretty sharp to put something across and get by with it in the end. I'd hate to take a chance. It's pretty heavy odds. Why, in order to get away with a thing the criminal has to out-think a dozen—a hundred other brains, and not slip up once. I was saying something like that to Fred this afternoon. He's a clever chap, too, but this has him stumped."

"Just how long have you known him?" I asked, because I could think of nothing really important to say.

"Ever since we were kids at school together," he replied, settling down once more in his seat, after giving the photograph of Farr back to me. He smiled in a reminiscent fashion. "He was always a great kid to be fooling around, trying

BOX 991   265

this new idea and that. I know along when we were about sixteen he got a great scheme for making our fortunes, or at least enough for treats our folks didn't think we needed. He was going to publish a school paper. We begged and wheedled enough out of our folks to buy a little hand press, and we did run the paper for most of one term. It was some sheet. I think we made several dollars until our subscribers began to default in their payments.

"Then we stopped their papers and that stopped the paper and closed the deal. Afterwards, he was always dabbling with things, till a few years ago, when he went into the bank and got in with old Gibson, and met the girl. He went crazy about her first off, and has the old man to back him in his aspirations. Well—she's certainly some girl, from the glimpse I got of her this morning."

The train whistled and slowed. Outside misty arc lamps bobbed up and began to flit past.

"Pretty near there," I said to my companion, and he straightened in his seat.

We ran into the Little Falls station and stopped. Hood and I picked up our bags and got out.

Experience had taught me that there was only one really first-class hotel in the place. That was the Wilson Hotel, several blocks up town from the depot. We went out and hopped on a trolley which would take us close to its doors.

Neither one of us spoke while we rode along or after we left the car and made our way, through the cold drive of the storm now turning into a damp snow, toward the hotel doors.

And then, as Joe Hood in the lead kicked open the door and we entered the lobby, that grip of unseen force, which

Dual had mentioned in sending me here, took hold without my knowledge and began sweeping me along.

"One room or two?" I queried as we crossed to the desk.

"One suits me," Hood responded. "We bunk close up north. I've sort of outgrown the notion of four rooms, bath and valet."

I nodded.

"And we can talk all we want to without hunting each other up," I assented, as we set down our bags beside the counter.

"Rooms, gentlemen?" The clerk asked the question and spun the register for us.

"Room," I told him as I took the pen from his fingers. Hood was standing right beside me, as I bent to sign, and he uttered a smothered exclamation at that exact instant of time.

I glanced toward him as a matter of course. He had thrust out a finger and was pointing to the last line on the opposite page, where appeared the guest list of the day before. I turned my eyes toward that line, and held them there for a second, before lifting them to my companion's face, and meeting his surprised, widened stare. For the thing which had attracted his attention, and made him arrest mine, was the plainly written signature of—Neville Farr.

"Anything wrong, sir?" It was the clerk's question broke the momentary silence of our surprise.

I turned away from Hood's unvoiced conjectures.

"Nothing," I said. "We merely found the signature of a friend we didn't know was here." I pointed to the name on the wide page of the book. "Is that right? Is Farr stopping here to-night—or has he gone on?"

BOX 991   267

He bent over to look.

"Farr—one hundred and twelve. He's here, sir. His key is not in the box "

I looked at Hood.

"By jove! that's luck," I remarked. "I wonder it we could get a room next him, by any chance."

Hood played up to the lead.

"Fine!" he exclaimed, and glanced at the clerk. "How about it?"

The clerk consulted his records. "Number one eleven is full, sir. I can give you one thirteen."

Joe yawned.

"Oh, we aren't superstitious," he said. "Go on Glace and sign up."

We registered; the clerk called a boy and we went up one floor and down a hall. As we passed, I glanced at the numbers. A light burned over the transom of number one hundred and twelve. Our boy unlocked the next door and ushered us in, collected his tariff and departed. Hood and I turned toward each other, and my companion grinned.

"This thing is getting more crazy as it goes along," he observed. "Shall we go surprise our young friend?"

The same thought had been forming in my brain. I nodded. Throwing off our coats we stepped into the hall and rapped on the adjoining door.

Footsteps crossed the floor within, and the door was pulled open without any hesitation, so far as I could see. There appeared before us a young man of generally blond type, some five feet seven and a half or thereabouts, as closely as I could judge. That he was the man for whom the warrant was out there could be no doubt whatever. He tallied to the description completely, and his face was the face of the picture reposing at that moment in my pocket. More than that, there was the little flesh-colored mole just outside the corner of his eye.

"Good evening, Mr. Neville Farr."

He peered into my face.

"It's—Mr. Glace, isn't it?" he questioned. "I think I've seen you at our bank."

"Quite probably," I agreed. "This gentleman is Mr. Joe Hood, of whom I think you've heard."

He gave no sign of confusion. Instead his face lighted.

"Indeed, yes," he exclaimed. "I've heard of him and what he did up north. That was bully. I didn't know you were in town, but it's fine for you to hunt me up. Now you're here, I'd like to ask Mr. Glace a question. I know he is a detective. Don't stand there—come on in."

Hood's eyes were puckered as we stepped into the room. Plainly he felt that the chap's greeting had been singularly free from restraint for that of a guilty man. I felt the same way myself. However, Farr apparently saw nothing about our manner to attract attention, but gave us seats and offered us cigars from a case of his own.

"When did you get into this burg?" he inquired.

"To-night," I explained. "We happened to see your name on the register as we were signing, and took the liberty of coming over, as we're quartered in the next room."

"Glad you did. It's a beast of a night, and I was sitting here twiddling my thumbs," he replied. "I came over here yesterday—or last evening, to be exact, in order to meet some parties about a little land deal I thought was on. Don't let me force you to talk shop, Mr. Glace, but that brings me

BOX 991   269

to the question I wanted to ask. It's too deep for me; but here it is. Maybe you can see what it means. It may have been just a joke, but I don't know.

"Yesterday morning I got a letter which I thought came from the Johnson Arbiger Real Estate Company here. Anyway it was on their letterhead, all right. They said if I'd meet them here to-day at nine o'clock they had a purchaser for a piece of farm land I own, at a top notch figure, but that the deal must be closed to-day.

"Well, I asked Sheldon, of our bank, for leave for the rest of the week, in case any hitches came up over the deal, as they often do, and I hopped a trolley and came over here last evening, after going to the recorder's and seeing that everything was straight up to the minute with regard to the land in question. This morning I went down to the real estate firm and told them there I was. They said they could see that, but what did I want? I showed them the letter, and they said they knew nothing about it—"

"What?" Hood very nearly yelled it. I looked at him in surprise, and so did Farr.

He flushed under our double gaze.

"I beg your pardon—I was startled—go on." Pretty lame, I thought, but Farr let it pass.

He fumbled in his pocket and brought out a typewritten letter.

"There it is," he said, tossing it over. "Look at it for yourself and see if you can see any sense in the thing."

I took it and spread it out. As Farr had said, it contained exactly the statements he had indirectly quoted. I examined it closely. There seemed to be a remarkable number of letters flying around in this business whose authorship demanded authentication.

Meanwhile Farr himself ran on.

"You can imagine I felt rather funny when I found the thing some sort of a plant. I asked some questions of Johnson himself, and he asked a lot of his clerks. Nobody knew or else they wouldn't tell. After the first surprise I began to get a little bit sore, too. I decided that as I was over here anyway I'd stay, and see if I could find out anything about it myself, and as I hadn't been over since spring, I thought I'd drive around to several of my pieces of land and see how things were, look after any repairs needed and have a talk with my tenants.

"That took all day, and I turned up a little trouble in one place which will need fixing. I decided to stay over till morning and get it arranged before I went back. That's why you found me here to-night. I thought it would save another trip, and I don't like to ask for leave from the bank any too often. Wouldn't have this time, except for that infernal letter you've got there in your hand."

"You didn't find out anything about it?" I asked.

He shook his head.

"No. Might have known I couldn't, I suppose, only I was hot just at first. I didn't know where to begin to look."

But while he talked I had found what was to me a very interesting discovery, indeed, about his letter. I had made a pretty careful examination of the correspondence dealing with the sale of Hood's stock, which I had obtained from the broker. On top of that Dual had pointed out to Bryce and me the essentially distinguishing marks of those pieces of work. Now as Farr paused I held the letter toward Hood.

BOX 991   271

"Do you notice anything particular about this?" I inquired.

He bent down and ran it over.

"Can't say that I do."

"Think," I urged. "Remember what I told you about those Little Falls letters, coming over—what I said about the character of the work, and the type of a machine."

His eyes widened. He snatched the letter out of my fingers and held it under the light, turning and twisting it this way and that. "Good Lord!" he said thickly, and wheeled suddenly back to me.

"You're right, Glace; by the Lord Harry, you're right! I see it now. This thing is the exact duplicate in appearance of the letters to Pearson. I'd take my oath to that!"

"That is my opinion also," I told him. "Unless we are both mistaken, this letter also was written on a Coroya machine of an old model, with a defective 'd' and 'e.' That would mean that in all probability they were written not only on the same machine but by the same person as well."

That was as far as I got. Joe Hood sprang to his feet and toward Farr, so that the young lank employee started back a pace before the other man's scowling rush. Hood's hand came up and he pointed a finger at Farr, leaning forward in a half crouched position.

"And that answers your question and calls your bluff, you damned young thief! You wrote those letters and forged my name and sold my stock. Then when you heard I was coming back you got cold feet and wrote this letter to yourself as a blind. But it don't go. Not with Joe Hood. I admit you're a pretty cool 'un, but there's a warrant out for your arrest, and I reckon I've got you right in hand."

8

ROOM 221, DAWSON BLOCK

"WARRANT? FOR MY arrest?" cried Farr, starting back before the menace of Hood's gesture and words.

Hood's face twisted into a snarl.

"Drop it," he growled. "I tell you the jig's up. You can't bluff, or if you do I'll call you."

Then the fighting blood of Farr's ancestry showed up. Instead of retreating farther, he took a step toward Hood and his own fair face flamed red.

"I don't know what you're talking about," he began, "but if you're drunk—"

Hood doubled up a fist, and right there I got between them.

"Stop it," I said. "I see how it looks to you, Hood, and you may be right or wrong, but whichever way it is, I'm in charge of this thing and it won't do any good to mix it here. Sit down, both of you. I don't think Farr will get away if we want him to stay "

Hood relaxed slowly. Then he nodded.

"I guess you're right. I saw red," he remarked, and resumed his chair. "You can see how it looks yourself."

"How what looks?" Farr shot the question out quickly. So far as I could see he appeared completely puzzled. "What

BOX 991

273

is there about that letter to make this man act as if he were crazy? and what's he mean about somebody's robbing his bank box? Does he mean the box in our vault?"

"You knew I had one, it seems," Hood sneered.

"Of course. Fred Mack was telling us the other day you had twenty-five thousand in it, too."

"He thought I did, and so did I. I reckon you knew better, eh?" Hood's jaw was held at a fighting angle.

"I didn't know anything about it," said Farr, wheeling toward him, "and you want to be careful what you say. Where'd it go?"

Hood's laugh gritted.

"I'm asking you," he retorted.

"Dry up," I broke in again, none too politely, it must be confessed. I waved Farr back to his seat, and then speaking quickly I gave him an outline of all which had happened since he left the bank. It couldn't do any harm to tell him how much we knew. If guilty in fact, it would shake him. But so far as I could judge he wasn't shaken in any such way, although he grew pale when I mentioned Gibson's swearing out the warrant. He listened closely while I explained the situation, and nodded at the end.

"I'll go back, of course," he said then.

"But—but why should they think I was the man who did it. I'm not rich, but I have property of my own, if I had needed money."

"That," I remarked, "is what Miss Gibson said this afternoon."

He swung toward me quickly.

"Gertie? Did she say that?" For a moment his whole face

was lighted by some inner emotion. "She doesn't believe I did this then?" he went on in a more controlled tone.

"She does not." Suddenly I remembered what Dual had said to the girl about this man's having dared to love her, and it seemed to me that I had struck fire for just an instant.

It flashed again on my words.

"Bless her!" The exclamation appeared to escape Farr rather than be spoken, and he flushed immediately after, till his fair skin burned.

I struck home.

"Farr, do you love old Gibson's daughter?"

He eyed me directly.

"That's none of your business!" he said coldly.

"In view of the fact that she came to me to say she believed in your innocence in this, I fancy it is." I returned.

He got out of his chair and began to pace the floor. Presently he paused.

"All right," he burst out, speaking quickly and flushing once more; "I'll tell you. I do love her then. She's the biggest, the best thing in my life, since I lost my mother. And I love her, and there isn't anything I wouldn't do for her—and that's the best reason why I wouldn't steal Hood's dirty stocks. Gertie Gibson is a clean, pure woman, and I love her too well to insult her by a trick like that."

I looked at Hood.

"Well, what do you think now?" I asked.

He frowned.

"I'm past that." He spoke to Farr. "You're going back there and give yourself up? You mean it?"

"Sure," Neville told him without a quiver. "I don't like

BOX 991

275

the idea exactly, but they've got nothing on me, and the quickest way to prove it is to let them try."

Hood twisted in his chair, and finally rose.

"Hell!" he ground out. "Kid, you don't look like a crook or talk crooked either, and I'm damned if I believe you are."

Abruptly be thrust out a hand in conciliation.

And Farr took it. The two men looked at each other and gripped fingers. The least bit of a smile wreathed Farr's lips.

"I *know* I'm not, Mr. Hood," he replied.

Hood returned to his chair, shaking his head.

"Back up the same old tree." He grinned at me as he said it, a rather rueful grin.

"And that's what brought you fellows to Little Falls?" Farr joined in.

"Yes," I admitted. "We were rather surprised when we found your name down-stairs. You can see why we hunted you up at once."

He nodded.

"Rather. Well, what do we do now?"

Honestly, I liked that "we" as he said it. Suddenly it made our interests seem one.

"It's too late to go down to that Dawson Block room now," I decided. "We may as well wait until morning."

"Then I'm going to bed. This day has made me tired." Hood got up and yawned.

I think we all felt a bit the same way. There could be no question that for each of us three in its way, the day had held its perplexities and worries, and such things weary one more than work.

There was a door between Farr's room and ours, and we set it open. Farr went with Hood at his own suggestion, and I occupied his room. But I didn't go to sleep as soon as I turned off the light.

My brain was in too much of a whirl for that. I lay and listened to the drip of the driving storm down the walls of the building, the sticky tap, tap of the wet snow on the panes of the window, trying the while to put together once more the fragments of information at my command. And out of it all there finally leaped a question.

Had Dual known we would find Farr here in Little Falls?

A funny thrill ran through me. I knew he had set up his weird figures of the whole occurrence. I knew he had said *he* knew the thief. His own words had meant he knew certainly something of Farr. Had his calculations showed him where the chap was, and had he really sent me over here to find him, just as he had sent me other places before?

If Farr's denial of guilt were as sincere as his love for dark-eyed Gertrude Gibson—if he were the victim of some peculiar grouping of circumstance and no more— if he were possibly suffering an injustice due to Gibson's readiness to believe the worst of him. I could see why Semi Dual should have stepped between him and a possible injustice—that would be like Semi Dual.

Alone in the strange hotel, the thing came to me, and I smiled. I felt that at last I was getting somewhere, that I had touched the truth, that I had contacted in this hour of quiet the real vital element in the case. And I asked myself if perhaps, lying here listening to the drip, drip of the storm, relaxed after the mental turmoil of the day, I had not perhaps sensed one of Dual's own mental waves, and read it at least in part, as he so often did with mine.

BOX 991   277

Little by little I came to feel myself *en rapport* with him—
to feel that an invisible bond of thought linked me with
the man in the Urania's tower in very truth, and gave me
to see faintly wherein he was silently working—to avert a
sin against a soul. And thinking in that wise, I fell asleep
to wake on a new day, with clearing skies and an early
sunlight outside.

Hood and Farr were speaking in the adjoining room. I
think it was their voices which had waked me. I sprang up
and dressed quickly, calling to them through the door. They
answered me at once, and came in where I was splashing
water on my face. They seemed on excellent terms this
morning. Like the day, the atmosphere of distrust between
them appeared to have cleared up. To have seen us no one
would have suspected that one of us was under the shadow
of arrest for a criminal action.

I finished dressing, and we went down to the hotel café
for breakfast, and we rather hurried through the meal. Both
Hood and I were anxious to get over to the Dawson Block
and see what we could find out about Room 22.

Farr caused a little delay in our starting, however. He
insisted on calling up Gibson's home on the long distance
and getting in touch with Miss Gibson.

"It'll only take a few minutes, and I want her to know
where I am and that I'm coming back to face down those
charges," he explained "Gee, Glace. I don't want that girl
to think I ran away, whether she thinks me guilty or not."

"She said she didn't, and she'll know you're back quick
enough to get some flowers into your cell before night,"
said Hood. "That is, if Mack will let her send 'em."

It was a rather illy-judged speech, I thought, and I could see it flicked Farr badly.

"Mack!" he shot back, doubled up his fist and brought it down on the table. "What's he got to say about what Gertrude does. You mean that yarn about his marrying her and dragging down Gibson's money? You can take it from me, Fred Mack won't do it, because—well, just because I'll marry her myself."

"Well," Hood persisted, "you don't need to waste time calling her up now just to tell her you're coming back."

"As it happens, I want to call her up," Farr persisted, and got out of his chair.

We went with him as far as the 'phone booth and waited while he spent some five minutes inside. Hood grinned.

"I hadn't ought to have ragged him about the girl," he conceded. "It was just ragging, but he's hard hit in that spot all right. Look at his face."

If a little doubt as to just whom Farr really meant to call had nibbled at my brain, it fled away as I glanced through the glass front of the booth. The boy was standing there, the receiver at his ear and a great light in his face. One could see that the words which came to him over the wire had given him courage, hope, determination. His expression was that of a man uplifted—strengthened, nerved for some future he saw stretching dimly before him. And then while I watched he spoke—slowly—with almost a caressing motion of the lips, and hung the receiver on the hook.

He came out of the booth with an actually elastic step.

"You were right," he said to me without any hesitation. "She doesn't believe for a minute that I did it, and she's glad I'm coming back. She's all right—a dandy little girl,

BOX 991   279

and she says for me to do just what you say. Come on now, let's go give that mysterious room the once over and then go home."

I knew roughly where the Dawson Block was. It was a three-story brick on the main street, with stores below and offices above—such a little building as one can find in dozens of the smaller towns of the country.

We left the hotel and turned in the direction necessary to reach it, and after a bit we came to the stairs which pierced the middle of its front and gave access to its upper floors.

We went up and came out on a board-floored hall running straight back, with side halls branching off. A brief inspection showed us the system of numbering used, and we moved on down the hall, scanning each room we passed.

No. 22 was a little inside box, to judge by its location. Outside the number there was nothing distinguishing on its door. And the door was locked. I tried it, and so did Hood. And after that he shook his head.

"My supposed headquarters don't impress me as very much of a place," he remarked.

"Wait till we get in," I suggested.

Hood grinned.

"How *do* we get in?" he inquired.

I didn't know myself, but I was determined to do it. "Wait," I said again, turned and walked down to one of the side halls, which branched off from the main one in which we stood. There was no one there, and I went on to the next—there were two on each side, giving on light wells cut out of the two upper stories. It was in the last that I spied a man with a broom languidly sweeping the floor.

"Janitor! I say, janitor!" I called.

He turned and looked toward me, then advanced after setting down his broom.

"If you're wantin' me, my name's Jenks," he declared.

"All right, Jenks," I accepted. "I want some one who knows about the building. Do you?"

He grinned with a twist of his lips.

"Ought to. Been here six years."

"Then," I said, "come back here with me and tell me what you know about Room 22."

He shot me a shrewd glance.

"Know what about it?" he returned.

"Come along," I urged. "I'll make it worth your while I moved back toward Farr and Hood, and Jenks came hobbling after. When I had rejoined my companions I addressed him again: "Now, who rents this room?"

"Mr. Hood," he said, after an apparent interval of thinking. "Mr. Joe Hood, I believe he said his name was. Yes, sir, Joe Hood."

"This man?" I waved my hand to the engineer. "This is Mr. Hood."

Jenks eyed him for a minute.

"No, sir—not him. It might have been his brother, though. Looks a leetle like him, but not so stout."

"What does he do here?" I asked.

"Don't know. Ain't here much of th' time, only at nights, 'bout th' time I'm leavin' or after. Reckon he jest gits his mail here an' writes answers to it. I've heered him poundin' on a writin' machine. He sure can make it rattle."

BOX 991

281

"When was he here last, or do you know?" I questioned next.

Jenks scratched his head to stimulate his mind.

"Night 'fore last—or no—night 'fore that, I think it was. I ain't right sure."

"Not since?" I wanted some way to be sure of that last. I had an idea I hadn't mentioned to any one as yet concerning that decoy letter to Farr.

"Nope." Jenks shook a positive head. "Reckon he'll come to-night. Mail man left a letter under his door 'bout fifteen minutes ago."

"All right," I said. "Now, Jenks, I want you to open this room and let us in. We're officers, and we've to search that room. If we're right there's some funny work been pulled off by this man. So open up."

He set his jaw.

"How be I know youse are officers?" he inquired.

I took out my pocket folder and produced one of our firm's cards.

"I'm Mr. Glace," I told him. "I'm at work on this case for Mr. Hood here—Mr. Joe Hood. This other man has been using his name instead of his own."

The fellow wasn't very bright, and I think his curiosity was aroused as much as anything else.

"Do tell!" he chuckled as I paused. "I reckon that might be so. He's a right smooth spoken young man. I've learnt you can't trust that sort over much. An' you're a detectif. Well, seein' as that's so, I'll unlock the door." He produced a passkey and turned it in the lock. Then, with a final flaring up of caution: "I hope you'll let me keep this card in case anybody asks questions?"

I nodded.

"Sure, and we'll stand by you if you need it."

He set the door open and we peered in. As I had suspected, the room was merely a box, without windows. I imagine it must have been built as a storage room for janitors or something in the first place. It was dusty, with only the light from the hall, but I saw a single cord incandescent hanging down from the ceiling and the shadowy outlines of an old desk, and then I dropped my eyes to the white oblong of a letter on the floor in front of my feet.

I bent down, picked it up, and we all went into the room. I reached up and turned on the light, and we looked about. There was a battered old desk, a small table with a covered writing machine upon it and a chair, and that was all.

"He bought them things second-handed," said Jenks.

They certainly looked it, and the information tended to show that we were really in the scene where the phony letters had been written. It was just about what one might have expected on first glance. All the fellow had needed was a chair and a desk and a machine. All three were here. I nodded, and glanced at the letter I still had in my hand.

And then my heart turned over. The thing was addressed very plainly in type to "Joseph J. Hood, Room 22, Dawson Block, Little Falls." I tossed it to Hood.

"That's addressed to you," I said.

He took it, looked it over, turned it in his hand.

"So it is," he grunted. "Notice the postmark?"

I nodded. It was that of our home city, dated the day before.

Hood grinned. "I suppose I may as well open it?" he suggested.

BOX 991   283

" 'Tain't fer you, it's fer him, mister, an' it's United States mail."

Hood nailed him with a stare.

"What of it? His name isn't Hood and mine is," he retorted. "This is addressed to Hood." He tore the end of the envelope across.

And there fell out, when he shook it, the folded half of a sheet of cheap, ruled writing paper, which he caught in his hand. While we watched he opened it on the crease and gave it a swift inspection. Then his eyes came up and met mine, and they were once more clouded with dazed suspicion.

"Well, I *am* damned," he got out after a second and held the paper toward me.

I took it. Farr was standing close beside me as I did so. We both read it at once, running over its few badly written lines. It was only a note, without heading or date:

> DEAR FARR:
>
> The real Hood has turned up, and he is raising merry Hades. If you happen to be fool enough to come where you get this, beat it quick.   E.

"My God!" Farr breathed the words in a sick whisper at my elbow. He stepped back suddenly, struck against the edge of the old desk, and remained half leaning, half sitting upon it. His head dropped, and he fell into a pose of complete and overwhelming dejection.

Not so Hood. For a moment he stood staring at the younger man, then he spoke to me.

"The bank vault guard has a machine inside the grill on

his table. He writes the names on cards, as you may have noticed. I saw the thing yesterday, Glace. And the guard's name is Edgar. That begins with an E. Well, by God, Farr, you had me pretty well fooled? What about going back *now?*"

Farr raised his head. "I'm going," he flashed in a tone actually savage. "I don't understand this, but it's some sort of a dirty plant, and I'm going back to show it up."

"You bet you're going back," Hood sneered. "Lord, but you've a nerve to come here with us this morning! You must have this man pretty well fixed." He cast an eye on Jenks.

I turned on the janitor myself.

"Look here," I began. "Remember I'm an officer and tell the truth, if you care for your own skin. Is this young man here the man who's been using this room?"

"Him?" queried Jenks, thrusting a dirty finger at Neville.

"Naw! I never seen him before in my life."

Hood laughed.

"Is there anything else you want to do here, Glace?" he questioned.

"Yes," I decided, "I think there is." I went over and jerked the cover off the writing machine on the table. One glance was enough. I beckoned Hood to my side and pointed to the nameplate fastened to its base. "Coroya, Joe, do you see?"

"Coroya it is. You were right there," he agreed.

"Now, just a minute," I went on. "I want a bit of paper."

I glanced about the desk. Several sheets lay scattered upon it, and I bent over to pick one up. And where most of them were blank, my eye caught one with the dark lettering of a firm business head upon it. My hand seized it

BOX 991   285

and lifted it up, and even as I did so my eyes had told me what it was. There, staring and black, the words "Johnson, Arbiger Company, Real Estate, Insurance and Loans," danced before my vision.

I turned it so that Hood might read. He nodded, without the least surprise in his face.

"A pip—just a pip," he said gruffly. "You'd better keep that, along with the letter."

I folded up the telltale bit of paper purloined somehow from the real estate firm and stuffed it away. It certainly began to look as if Hood had summed the matter up. One could almost reconstruct the scene of the man sitting here and concocting the letter which should seem to offer an excuse for his coming over here.

And yet how clumsy, how flimsy it was! Nobody but a boy would think of doing a thing like that; but that very fact, of course, made it worse for the boy still leaning on the far corner of the desk, his brows drawn into a troubled frown, his lower lip caught into the grip of his teeth.

Well, Dual had told me to come over here and find whatever presented, and certainly in the light of events the trip had been justified. Thus far I had two more letters and the blank letterhead, and I had found a Coroya old-style typewriter sitting here on the table. There remained but the final step of proving beyond doubt that it was the same machine on which the Pearson letters had been written. That was easy. I took up one of the blank sheets I had started to reach for a moment or so ago and fed it into the machine.

Then I dragged up the chair, sat down and hammered off a few lines. And I was careful to make them such that the letters Dual had pointed out would show up plainly. I wrote:

> These decidedly characteristic lines should demonstrate beyond any question that they were composed on the identical machine which was used in the bogus Hood correspondence.

I was satisfied that showed up the "d's," the "e's" and the "t's" and "l's" at least. But it was not until I was taking the sheet out at the end that I noted the final clenching point about the machine. Then, glancing at the margin stops, I found them set for a six-point edge I called Hood over and made him note it.

Once more he accepted it as wholly a matter of course. "All right, I see it, he acknowledged quickly. "Come on, Glace, let's get this young crook over home and in jail."

And suddenly, as Hood spoke, I became aware of an inward urge to follow at least a part of his suggestion. All at once something seemed pulling me away from that dusky little built-in cell of criminal endeavor, where the dirty incandescent glowed wanly, and drawing me out of Little Falls and back to my home city.

In that moment I knew that my mission was ended—that I had accomplished all for which I had been sent, and that Semi Dual knew it and was silently calling me home in his own peculiar way.

From high up in that white tower on the city's highest building his thought waves deliberately projected were bearing his invisible message to my brain. So closely as that was he keeping track of events, by means of his own

BOX 991

287

strange methods. Well, I had known him ere this to set the hour of the ending of an episode to the very minute, and I felt no surprise now as I turned toward Hood, who stood with his jaw thrust out, waiting.

"I think we may as well catch that ten o'clock trolley," I suggested, after a glance at my watch. I put my hand in my pocket, drew out a bill and gave it to Jenks.

Hood viewed the act with a frown.

"What he needs is a few days in clink to refresh his memory," he growled.

Farr spoke for the first time in minutes.

"And what you need is more sense and less temper, Hood. This man tells the truth when he says he never saw me. That will come out in time, whether you believe it or not."

"It'll be some time before you come out, at any rate," Hood snarled.

Farr paled slightly. I saw his hands clench, but he made no reply. We left the little room and with Farr between us made our way to the street and back to the hotel for our bags. From there we lost no time in getting to the depot, where we managed to catch the ten o'clock train with a bare minute to spare.

There was no longer any doubt in Hood's mind that we had found the man guilty of the theft and sale of his stocks. In the train he insisted on placing Farr next the window in the section we occupied, seating himself beside him and making me take the aisle side of the other seat, which he turned so that I faced him and the young bank accountant.

In that way he placed Farr in a pocket from which it would be difficult for him to escape by any sudden effort.

Neville on his part submitted without the slightest demur. He seemed to tacitly proclaim his entire willingness to do what he had previously said in words and return to the scene of the crime and surrender himself on the warrant for his arrest. I studied him closely as we took our seats and after the train had started, and I had to confess that, outside of the expression of worry natural to his position, he gave no actual evidence either of fear or guilt.

I don't remember now that one of us spoke during the entire ride. Hood sat glum and dour, shooting an occasional watchful glance at the man at his side. At another time that might have made me smile, for heaven knows Farr was peaceful enough. As for himself, he spent most of his time looking out of the window, with an evident desire to be left to his own thoughts, which I respected.

If, as the evidence I had gained would indicate, he were guilty, I felt they must be gloomy enough without my adding anything to them by questions he needs must evade or answer with fabrications. There would be time enough for that sort of thing when he was safely lodged behind iron bars.

And though I didn't know it, every turn of the wheels was bringing us closer to a revelation of Semi Dual's supreme insight into the matter and his complete control of the situation from first to last.

If ever anything demonstrated the truth of his astrological computations, the events which transpired before the end of the day certainly did. Because even then by his directions, agents of his endeavor were waiting to take the first step, along the lines indicated by his abstruse calculations, and from the time the first step was taken things

BOX 991   289

moved forward swiftly to a close as dramatic as any picture of the stage.

The first step itself came as a complete surprise to us all, too. The train ran into our home station after due time and we rose to leave the car. We went out and down the steps and so to the platform—Hood, and then Farr, and then I.

"Neville!" I heard a woman's voice speak the word as an exclamation through which ran a quiver of heart-tensed feeling. More than that, the dark-dad figure of a woman left the side of a man and came forward swiftly.

"Gertrude!" The reply was an echo of the girl's cry as it seemed. Before Hood or I had time to do more than sense the thing and gape the two young people were together. Farr's arms came up and gathered the woman to him with an almost hungry gesture. And then, while I stood staring and Hood followed suit, Gertrude Gibson put up her arms and pulled Farr's head down and kissed him on the lips.

"Boy!" I heard her croon rather than speak. "Oh, boy— my boy!"

9

THE LUNCHEON PARTY

I MAY BE a detective. I have been called such and I have even solved some puzzles, but right at that minute I would have been willing to let somebody kick me for a wooden headed ninny.

The thing was so clear, so patent, and I had never seen it. In fact, I had never even suspected that Gibson's daughter *returned* Farr's love—that this was romance in the everyday world on which I had blundered. Not until I heard that note of mingled maternity and passion in the girl's words did I sense the truth. But then I knew, and I turned my head away and encountered the grinning features of James Bryce.

"Hello, old scout," said Jim in a visible assumption of non-observation.

"Hello," I replied. "What brings you down here?"

His grin widened.

"She did." He jerked his head toward where Farr and his winsome sweetheart were now speaking softly together. "We come down to meet you."

Hood frowned.

I thought you were working for me—not for a sentimental girl."

BOX 991   291

Jim chuckled.

"We all think a lot of things now and again, Mr Hood," he rejoined. "Just now I'm workin for Semi Dual."

That was my first jolt in the beginning of the end. Ordinarily, as I have said, Dual did not wish his name mentioned, yet here was my partner not only naming him frankly, but declaring that his actions were inspired by our subtle friend. And the effect was worse on Hood than on myself.

"Semi Dual?" he repeated without the least understanding. "Some other case you mean? I fancied I had retained both you and Glace."

Bryce winked in heavy fashion.

"Steady, Mr. Hood, so you did—an' then Glace an' me found out we'd need help, so we got Mr. Dual to help us, an' he told me to come down here, an' meet you, an' bring Miss Gibson after she phoned you was comin' back. I reckon you won't need very good eyes to see a reason, why Farr mustn't go into a cell."

"But he is going—just there." Hood's tone challenged denial.

And the challenge was accepted. "Oh, no, he ain't. Dual don't want him jugged. It's all fixed, I guess."

Hood's face darkened swiftly.

"Say, who the devil is this man with the freak name?" he demanded.

"Oh, he's a wise guy all right. He's the only man who *is* wise to this thing of yours. You've got to go see him after we get Farr fixed up, too. He told me to bring the whole bunch of you over." I could see that Bryce was enjoying his present position immensely.

As for myself, my heart gave a bound. Such an order from Dual, given to Bryce, could mean but one thing. He knew he was ready to strike—and surely not at the boy and girl who stood there side by side in the sunlight of the morning, no more full of divine warmth and life than the glances from their eyes to each other.

Had I been right last night? Surely it looked so, now. Surely it was these two souls whose happiness had been threatened, and from which Semi Dual was working to turn away the danger.

"Do you know this—this Dual, Mr. Glace?"

"Certainly," I told him. "He is the person who made the discoveries concerning those typewritten letters, of which I told you last night."

"Well, by heavens!" said Hood. "This thing is getting more and more like a nightmare. Why does he want Farr out on bail?"

I looked him in the eye.

"Because he isn't guilty—and the girl loves him."

"Fred's girl," said Hood.

I smiled.

"Not yet, Mr. Hood. Apparently not ever."

Bryce interrupted.

"Well, we got to be getting along. I fixed it to have Judge Harker meet us at his room about eleven thirty an' that's gettin' pretty close. Wait till I put it up to the kid—th' girl was to wise him up accordin' to our agreement." He cleared his throat. "I say, Mr. Farr, you hep to the program?"

"I think so, Mr. Bryce. I am to go with you before the justice of the peace, waive my preliminary hearing and be bound over to the district court for trial, and be admitted

BOX 991   293

to bail in the interim. Is that it?" Farr's voice was without a tremor.

"That's it," said Bryce. "You'll be held to the court on information. I got a copy of Gibson's statement sworn to an' on file with Harker right now. If you want to go up there—"

"Any time you're ready," Farr picked up the girl's hand and drew it through the crook of his arm.

Bryce nodded.

"Come along."

He led the way from the platform into the station, and through that to a large automobile on the town side.

We all climbed in. Bryce by the driver, Hood and I next and Farr and the girl cuddled on the back seat by themselves, and cuddled is right, because I saw Farr's arm slip between Miss Gibson's back and the tufted cushions of the car.

"I got this all fixed," Bryce began again, as we started. "Harker knows me, an it was easy. Farr waives his preliminary an' Harker binds him over to the next term an fixes his bail. That lets him loose an' it won't take over ten minutes at the most. Pretty slick?"

"For Farr." Hood was plainly dissatisfied with the suggested proceeding.

The car drew up before the Budge building, where Justice Harker had his court room. Bryce hopped out and opened the door. He told the chauffeur to wait and we all went in and waited in front of an elevator bank for a car to come down. When it did, we went up to the fifth floor and along a corridor to a frosted door which Bryce threw open in order to let us enter.

We came into a waiting room, and crossed that to a

farther room with a raised dais and desk railed off from the main part. Behind the desk sat a middle aged man reading a morning's paper. A younger man was writing at a small table set below and in front of the desk.

The man with the paper, who I knew to be Harker, tossed the sheet aside and came to attention.

"Good morning, Bryce," he remarked in familiar fashion, and remained waiting with his elbows on the desk.

After that things went through without a hitch. Bryce introduced Hood and Farr. Harker asked the latter a few questions. After that he glanced over the desk at the young man making notes in a record.

"Bail fixed at five thousand," he said.

Without a moment's hesitation Bryce put his hand in his pocket, drew out a long envelope of manila paper and laid it on the table before the clerk.

"Five thousand in currency—cash bail, your honor," he declared.

"But—but—Mr. Bryce. I—I am prepared—" Gertrude Gibson stammered in confusion as she fumbled with the catch of the purse she carried.

Bryce grinned.

"Bail's up, Miss Gertrude."

The clerk had broken the seal of the package and was rapidly counting the contents. "Five thousand, your honor," he announced.

"Enter the amount. Prisoner dismissed to appear in due time before the district court," said Harker, reaching for his paper after a smile in Miss Gibson's direction. "Anything else, Mr. Bryce?"

"Thanks, your honor, I guess not," Jim made answer. "As

BOX 991

I told you over the 'phone this mornin', I'll come back after that coin sometime to-morrow. Much obliged."

But as he turned to leave the room, I asked my partner a question.

"Where did you get those bills?"

And his face wore a puzzled expression as he told me "From Dual—but for heaven's sake, how did he know it was goin' to be five thousand? Honest, that feller gets me."

"If he just gets to the heart of this thing, now," I whispered.

"Get to it?" Jim's eyes began to twinkle. "Son, I'm tellin' you that guinea's as good as got."

I nodded. I did not doubt it in the least, yet for the life of me I couldn't see just how it was to be done.

I held Bryce by my side and asked a question.

"What have you done while I was gone?"

"Sleuthed a bit and fixed this business," he told me.

"Then Dual doesn't think Farr guilty?" I wanted to hear the thing confirmed in words.

Jim grinned.

"Hardly. He says he's a lucky guy."

"Then who is?"

Jim actually chuckled.

Search me. Dual's wise, but you know what he said to me up there yesterday afternoon. He's keeping the lid on a big pot of trouble for some one till he's ready to take it off.

I caught a glimpse of Gertrude Gibson's face as we left Harker's room, and I sensed she had heard what we said. Her whole being seemed glowing as she walked at Farr's side. She turned toward him and began to speak swiftly, and then Hood cut in.

"Well, what's the next step in this farce?"

"We go to see Dual," said Jim, and punched the down signal for a cage.

"What for?"

Bryce gave him a look.

"You want to know what happened to your stock, don't you?"

"Yes. But—"

"Well, we're going to find out."

"From this—Dual?"

"From him and everything that's happened," said Bryce, and led the way into a car which had stopped.

For a moment I think Hood had it in his mind to refuse going any farther, but after a barely perceptible pause he came along. Just the same, it was an oddly assorted party who filled the waiting machine in front of the Budge building entrance some two minutes later.

Hood was plainly puzzled, and as plainly disgusted, with a palpably weakened faith in both Bryce and myself. Farr was beginning to wear a dazed look under his sweetheart's efforts to explain what she didn't fully understand. The girl herself looked to me like a woman, buoyed up and supported by a great, unreasoning faith.

Dual could inspire such faith in women—particularly good women, who followed their intuitions. Bryce and myself, even more, had the same faith strengthened and hardened by experience of the past, and in my own case there was slowly beginning to be a faint understanding of Semi's methods as well. In fact, as the long car shot off in the direction of the Urania, I confess my chief emotion was one of impatience to get up in that tower shrine of eternal

BOX 991   **297**

right, and watch the swift play of Dual's superb mind as he took the final steps in the case.

It was Miss Gibson who interjected the next note into the situation. She leaned toward my client.

"You've never met this Mr. Dual, have you, Mr. Hood?"

Hood shook his head.

"No, Miss Gibson."

"I have," said the girl. He is wonderful—splendid. He makes you feel as if—as if—he knew everything you knew, and thought, or wished, or hoped. You can feel that he's big, and strong—and good."

Hood just stared and kept silent.

"I've been telling Neville," Miss Gibson ran on. "You don't really think Neville is guilty, do you, Mr. Hood?"

That was the direct attack with a vengeance. Hood appeared disconcerted. It was rather hard to look into the winsome pleading of the face before him and stab her faith in reply.

"I—I'm rapidly coming to a place where I don't know what I think, Miss Gibson," he stammered at last.

Miss Gibson uttered a nervous little laugh. She laid a hand over Farr's.

"Mr. Dual will convince you of Neville's innocence," she proclaimed. "Just wait until you meet him." She turned to me with a question. "He gave Mr. Bryce that money, didn't he, Mr. Glace?"

I nodded.

"Yes, Miss Gibson."

"Farr's bail?" Hood turned clear around till he faced me.

"Exactly," I said.

"And he didn't even tell me he was going to do it. He

said it would be five thousand, and I took a certified check with me. He's the strangest man," exclaimed Miss Gibson.

Hood opened his mouth, thought better of it and closed it again just as the car stopped before the Urania's doors. There came over me a desire to chuckle at the expression of his face. If he was mystified now, I wondered how he would take the garden up there on the roof under its yellow-green glass.

I found out before long. He kept watching the floors as we went up till the twentieth was reached. He eyed the stairs in a still mute question, and, like myself the first time I had come upon it—like the willowy girl walking with Farr—like most persons who came there for the first time, I imagine—he balked completely before the annunciator plate. I followed his eyes and knew he had read the message of the inlay as he glanced at me.

"I say, Glace," he demanded, "just what is this place?"

"Dual's residence," I told him, and saw Gertrude Gibson smile.

"But—good heavens! What sort of balderdash to that on that thing?" he went on, pointing: " 'Shall surely find that which he shall seek'?"

"That ain't balderdash; it's a straight tip," Bryce cut in. "You're seekin' to know what happened to your stock. Come on over and find out." He stepped out on the plate.

The chimes filled the air. Hood actually jumped.

"Just what am I up against?" he queried as we followed Bryce up the path.

And just because he was so totally nonplused, I answered him in two words:

"Semi Dual."

BOX 991   299

There was a little surprise waiting for me, too. Henri met us and led us into the sun-lighted great room, where Dual rose to his feet to greet us. He no longer wore his robes of blue and white. Instead he was clad, as I had seen him before, as a man of the everyday world, in gray suit, gray silk shirt, with soft French cuffs and collar, gray tie, in which was thrust a bit of green Chinese jade, and natty tan boots.

That wasn't the surprise. It was a table laid there in the room with silver and glittering china and flowers—a table laid for six. We might have been a luncheon party for the seeming, with Dual the host bending over Miss Gibson's hand and smiling at some low-toned thing she said into his ear even before she presented Farr.

Then Semi gave Farr his hand and looked into the lad's eyes.

"I am very glad to be able to welcome you here, Mr. Farr," he told him. "It is a very pleasant occasion. Those clouds which obscured your prospects a few hours ago are lifting, even as the clouds of yesterday give place to-day to the sun. Let it give you courage, my young friend."

I presented Hood. To him also Semi gave a hand.

"I am glad to make your acquaintance also in person, Mr. Hood," he said. "It was because I deemed it best to do so before the termination of this matter of your loss that I instructed Mr. Bryce to set that you made one of our party."

Hood appeared actually confused.

"The termination—just when is that?" he inquired, somewhat lamely.

Dual glanced at the great clock in the corner. He smiled.

"The time to not yet in which justice shall tear the cloak from the shoulders of the guilty," he said slowly. "That is yet to come. But as the hour approaches noon, I have dared to hope you would accept a light luncheon before we take any more steps in the affair."

He crossed and pressed a button in the wall, and a panel slid back and a serving table set with tea, milk, fruits and small cakes and sandwiches of various sorts slid in.

It was just such a meal as I had eaten more than once in this room with Dual before—only now the service was for six. Henri appeared through the door at the rear of the room just after the table, and Dual bowed us to our chairs, drawing back that of Miss Gibson with his own hand.

We sat down. Henri served, and Hood spoke again.

"You said you were glad to make my acquaintance in person, Mr. Dual. You mean just what?"

"I mean," said Semi Dual, "just what the words convey, Mr. Hood. We have never met face to face. And yet I have been closely in touch with your personality since yesterday morning, through my connection with your position and my consideration of it under the stars."

Hood paused with a cup of tea half way to his lips.

"Under the—stars?" he repeated.

Semi Dual smiled.

"Yes, Mr. Hood. I think perhaps that before the final steps in your affair are taken it were best for us to arrive at at least a partial, mutual understanding. To that end I wished you to come here at this time. I am one who believes in that science upon which astronomy is founded—one who holds with those who once read the signs flashed from the pinpoints of light in the darkened skies which we call stars, but which are really but the polarized foci of univer-

BOX 991   301

sal forces, and determined the influence of their magnetic radiations upon mundane life.

"I believe astrology to be true. And as in all ages since wisdom first came down to the minds of men, despite all the material strides of our modern science, there have been a few men who still clung to the truth and kept the lamp burning in the shrine of knowledge, so the truths of astrology—of planetary causation in men's fate, have been preserved, for me to use.

"Those ancient wise men determined the character of the influence of each planetary body. They devised a method by which, given the time of the main incidents of an event, they could by a consideration of the forces acting at the time, as shown by the positions of the stars, judge as to not only what had happened, but what would happen, as a result of the influences first bringing it about—and could predicate without any great fear of rebuttal what incidents would happen to the actors in the affair.

"And since I know this science, I could set up an astrological figure of your loss at the bank. In that, Mr. Hood, you appear very plainly as the party injured at the first. And after that appears Mr. Farr, as a man whose moral welfare was vitally threatened in spite of his innocence. And, too, there appears another whose aspects toward you both is malefic, so that him we may take as the real thief, who robbed your box and sold your stock, and sought to divert all suspicion from himself by throwing it upon Mr. Farr."

He paused and turned toward Miss Gibson.

"And there is Venus in the figure, too," he went on.

"Venus—woman's own particular planet—shining with a soft, steady light—throughout the ages. And on one of these men in my calculations her influence is benefic and on one it is malign—and on you, Mr. Hood, it is negative quite. Perhaps now you gain an inkling as to my meaning and the trend of coming events, when the hour of that man's fate shall overtake him."

Hood shook his head. He seemed to me like one impressed against all preconceived conceptions, yet unwilling to admit it.

"I'm afraid I don't," he replied.

Dual glanced again at the clock, and then about the table.

"Whether you do or not, it is time we began the final considerations, in the apparent mystery concerning what happened," he said.

10

A LESSON IN PHOTOGRAPHY

"APPARENT MYSTERY?" HOOD repeated quickly.

"Certainly," said Dual. "All mysteries are so merely in appearance—because we view them from a different angle from that which brought them about. To harmonize the possible and the impossible, all that is needed is to discover not the new, but the unusual angle through which cosmic force has been compelled to act."

"Like the signing of my genuine signature to stocks I hadn't touched for two years, and letters I never wrote in my life," Hood suggested.

"Exactly, Mr. Hood." Dual bowed his head in assent. He turned to Bryce. "You attended to the matters we had under discussion last evening and this morning, but you have not reported beyond saying you were successful. You have, I perceive, something for me."

Jim nodded. He put a hand in his pocket and produced a thin, flat key, which he laid before Dual.

Semi picked it up and read its number aloud.

"991."

"991!" Hood exclaimed sharply. "Why, that's the number of my box. Where did you get that key?"

"Out of your trunk at the Kenton, wasn't it, Mr. Bryce?" Semi returned quite calmly.

"Yes, sir." Jim covered his mouth with a hand and coughed, but he didn't cover his eyes and they were dancing with amusement. "I—I went over there last night, as you suggested, got the officer on that beat an' we insisted on searchin' th' room. This key was in the trunk, just like Mr. Hood said."

Hood's face had grown suddenly flushed, then crimson, then purplish red as Bryce spoke, but he held in until he had finished.

"Of all the high-handed outrages this is certainly the limit," he burst out then. "The way you people act you'd think *I* was the crook and everybody else ready for a coat of whitewash. Did the stars sic your man here on my private belongings, Mr. Dual? Your action is little short of burglary under sanction of the law—using the law as a blind to put it over.

"If I'd known what sort of a gang I was tying up with when I took Sheldon's advice to employ Glace and this Bryce for the case, I'd have let the stock go and run for safety myself. So far they've done nothing but snarl things up, and then ring in a bit of mummery to cloud the issue still more. Now I want action, and quick action at that. Do I get it? And I want that key." He broke off and thrust a hand out toward Semi, and in so doing he met Dual's eyes.

Did you ever put out a hand in the dark and touch, not what you were seeking or expecting, but something else—something cold, clammy, paralyzing by its very feel?

That was how Hood looked when his gaze was locked and held by that of Semi Dual. Not that there was anything

BOX 991

305

of anger, or of passion, or of menace in the deep gray orbs of my friend. Rather there was the blinding light of pure power—strength—unshaken calm in the face of the insulting utterance to which he had just been subjected by Hood's words.

And Hood sat there before that coldly impersonal glance and forgot to draw back his hand, while the color of anger drained from his face, and his eyes widened, and his lower jaw dropped until his lips parted a trifle, and the stiffness of rage went wholly out of his figure and its pose. And not until then did Semi Dual speak:

"As it happens, this is *not* your key, Mr. Hood—although it lay in your trunk. Save for the fact that the affair in hand concerns others more deeply than yourself, however, I should comply with your request and surrender it to you." Very slowly he rose and waved to Henri to clear the table.

"As it is," he went on once more, "and because a far greater crime was intended—a crime which would have blasted a young man's life and future and wounded his soul—a crime which would have pierced the tender breast of an innocent and lovely woman and drawn blood from her heart and robbed her of her birthright of marriage to the man she loves, I shall retain it and with it and the further evidence at my command I shall go down into the world and as one of the agents of the Eternal One's eternal justice, strike down that one who injured you—in the petty sense of money—while he sought to injure these others in their lives; not for you, Mr. Hood, but for them—shall justice be done. And because of them, Mr. Hood, you shall still find that which you came to seek—for they are the pure of heart on whom a divine mercy smiles."

And then he turned to me.

"And now, Gordon, my good friend, give into my hands those letters and the other evidence which you gained in your trip of last night and to-day."

Joe Hood said not a word. I think the man was temporarily beyond it. Certainly Dual's words and intonation had been calculated to make him feel a sense of his own atomic smallness in the cosmic plan of things. He sat in a subdued silence while I gave the several papers I had brought back to Dual; and was still silent while Semi went to his desk and spread them out—and then drew out the Pearson letters and the letter Fred Mack had written to Seattle, studying the whole collection with a huge magnifying glass he sometimes used in such work. Once his eyes met mine and he turned them away quickly, encountered those of Bryce, on the other side, and dropped his gaze to the floor.

Meanwhile Gertrude and Neville had wandered to one side. The girl paused before the great bronze Venus lamp and inspected it closely, with frank admiration.

"See, Neville, Venus and the apple," she said.

Dual glanced up from his work and smiled.

"Venus—and like woman always, when rightly placed, she gives light in the darkness—the breath of sweetness— the breath of life. I agree with Paris about the apple."

Bryce came over and mumbled under his breath.

"Grandma, but I feel a lot better—somebody else got a wallop on the bean, an' it looks like it knocked him silly. He's shy a lot of pep, since Dual passed out the mustard."

"What about that key?" I asked in the same sort of tone.

Jim shook his head.

"I don't know. Dual said go get it, and I got it. You an' me

BOX 991

307

is just retrievin' his birds for him, Glace, in this matter. But I betcha he's getting ready to shoot again pretty quick, an' then somethin' will drop."

He appeared to be right. Dual gathered up all the papers, letters and shares and thrust them into the inside pocket of his soft gray coat. There was an air of finality about the way he did it—a something which said that at last he had gathered all the threads into his fingers and was ready to begin weaving the net of their meaning about the one to blame.

"The number of that other box was—" he addressed Bryce quickly and paused.

"One sixty-six," said Jim.

Semi smiled brightly, and accepted with a nod. And even the nod was final, the mere checking off of an already determined fact.

"One of the letters you brought back was written on the same machine which was used in the Pearson correspondence," he remarked to me. "A machine which you appear to have found."

"In Room 22, Dawson Block," I told him. "It was set to a six point margin, and I wrote off enough to show the character of the defective type."

"You have accomplished your mission ably," said Semi. "As I told you in this room before you went, the criminal mind has made its one fatal move, from which it cannot retract, which shall certainly fasten its guilt."

"One moment." Hood was speaking for the first time since his demand for the key. "As a matter of interest, have I any say in this affair at all? Am I to be in any way consulted or not? As the man who employed you people, it seems to me I still have some rights."

It was a rather pitiful attempt to justify himself I fancy. The man was all right at heart, but impulsive. And Dual answered him without any sign of annoyance.

"Your rights will be wholly respected, Mr. Hood. As for the rest, I am not employed by you or any one else"

"You're workin' for love, I suppose?" It was almost a sneer.

"Yes," said Semi—"for love, Mr. Hood; for love of right, of truth, of the best things in life, which must not be destroyed by the parasites of evil—without favor and without price—therefore in my own way, for the good end."

Hood frowned. He looked at me. I could not doubt he was shaken.

"See here, Glace," he rapped out; "am I in wrong? I thought you said that you'd retained this gentleman to assist you."

"That was me, an' I'm a good deal too careless with my words," Bryce took it up. "Mr. Dual don't work for no one. He helps his friends an' people what need it, like he's doin' for Farr now, and," his heavy face flushed the least bit, "this here pretty little girl."

Hood cleared his throat. It was a struggle, but he rose and took a step toward Dual.

"I ask your pardon," he said as man to man. "I didn't understand—I don't now—but I guess I've been hasty. That's a failing of mine."

"Of a great many, Mr. Hood," said Semi, smiling. "One, however, we can learn to control. And now, if you are willing, I should like to run briefly over the matter of these seeming signatures of yours, before anything else."

BOX 991   309

"Seeming signatures?" Joe Hood repeated. "You mean you've found out that they're bogus?"

"Exactly," said Semi Dual.

He paused a moment, during which Farr and his sweetheart drew nearer and we all clustered about him at the desk.

"Some moments ago, I spoke of the advance of material science and how it had blotted out the occult," he began, when we were gathered at attention. "But the occult may apply to science as to any other activity of life. I have just said that the signatures were false—forgeries in fact—but they are forgeries depending upon that very advancing science of which I spoke.

"They may really be described not as forgeries made in the usual way with a pen either free handed by an expert, or by means of a tracing, but as actual photographic reproductions of the genuine writing itself. And should we look closely—should we measure each signature on each letter—on each share of stock, we should find in that very fact our first proof that the signatures were not genuine indeed, but forgeries in fact—for we would find that on each share, on each letter, *each signature measures the same!*

"Signatures written by hand save for a coincidence merely, would very seldom do that—not only because one signing a document naturally confines his writing to the space at his command, but because while the character of the signer always controls the form of the writing, everything from time and place to mental mood, may affect its size. And so when we find each and all of these supposed signatures of Mr. Hood's to be the same, we know also that they cannot be genuine."

At last Hood was on ground he could feel under his feet. His face lighted at the logical deduction Dual had drawn.

"I see your point there," he gave enthusiastic assent. "I mentioned to Glace yesterday afternoon that the signature I had written for him at the bank was larger than that on the letters and the transfers. I noticed that, but I never thought of the bearing of the similarity of size."

"Yet it is a very important bearing you must admit," Dual smiled.

"Important? I should say so." Hood's interest was increasing by leaps and bounds. He leaned forward. "You know how they were made?"

"Indeed yes," said Semi. "That is a point we will take up after a bit, when we have proven beyond any doubt that the signatures *are* forgeries in the technical sense. After Mr. Glace left them with me last evening, I spent considerable time in their examination. Among the points brought out was one which conclusively fixes the fact that if you have been where you say, during the time you claim, you could not possibly have signed all, either of the letters or the shares."

"So that if I can *prove* I was in Seattle last November, it will positively show that some one else signed the things, eh?"

Hood's eyes contracted slightly, and he wet his lips with his tongue.

Dual bowed in assent.

"And I can do it—I can get a dozen witnesses if necessary," Hood ran on. "And that letter of Mack's sent me at Seattle ought to help some."

"It will help a great deal in the final equation," said Dual.

BOX 991   311

"Fine!" Hood was now in a vast good humor. "What is this second discovery of yours, Mr. Dual?"

"It is one concerning the character of the ink used in the signatures themselves," Semi said. "First, however, let us take up the character of the signatures under the microscope, and one who has made any study of writing will support me in the statement that in words written with an ordinary pen, with ordinary ink, the point of the pen, breaking the surface of the paper even in the least degree, produces a series of flowing lines, running parallel with, the direction of the pen stroke, as well as a slight feathering of the edges of the written lines, imperceptible to the naked eye."

He broke off and smiled at Hood.

"And speaking of chirography, Mr. Hood, when I first saw your signature on the list of stock you gave to Mr. Glace, I deduced from the character of your writing, the heaviness of its lines, the open loop in your 'd', that you were a man of honest motives, frankly outspoken, inclined to be generous and impulsive.

"Hence when I found that, in seeming contradiction to all such characters as shown, you had signed the letters to the broker Pearson, and the transfers on the stock—that told me that the signatures were false, because no man can falsify his handwriting—without that effort's also showing; and the signature Glace brought me was evidently your natural, uninfluenced work. But although I had formed my own conclusions, such proof as they offered would not be taken by any court of law. I therefore set about finding more material proof. Now to go back once more to it.

"Under the microscope these signatures do not show

any flowing of the ink lines such as would be made by an ordinary pen. While to our unaided vision they appear like handwritten words, the lense shows that the ink in their case is evenly impressed on the paper in a uniform manner, with none, or very little, feathering of the edges. Hence they were stamped on the paper without breaking the finer texture of its surface to any appreciable degree."

"Stamped!" Hood exclaimed, gripping the arms of the chair in which he sat.

"Speaking broadly," said Semi. "And that brings me to the feature of which I spoke some time ago—the thing which proves that you had nothing to do with their signing. Ordinary ink, such as is used on a pen, in writing, is quite fluid—it flows easily indeed as is necessary that it should. But the inks used on any stamping device, in order to give a clear impression, without blurring, must, on the other hand, possess an adhesive nature of greater or lesser degree.

"In the case of the signatures in question, however, it was desirable that they should appear to have been written by hand, and with ordinary writing fluid. At the very outset then, the forger was confronted by a difficulty he was forced to overcome. One way of doing so would have been to so change ordinary ink that while becoming somewhat adhesive in its nature, it should retain its ordinary characteristics of appearance when dry. The simplest way to gain that end would be to add to the ink a small per cent, of pure glycerine."

"By Jove!" gasped Hood. I looked at Bryce. He grinned in a satisfied manner. Farr and Gertrude were sitting very close together and shamelessly holding hands. Dual went on.

BOX 991

313

"Glycerine, however, while giving the adhesion necessary for the stamping, takes at least six months to dry completely out of the final print. In that, Mr. Hood, lies the proof that glycerine was used in this case. Under the microscope the later signatures on the letters sent to the broker show evidences of its use—and by the application of a rather delicate chemical test I succeeded in proving its presence. In the earlier letters and in the signatures on the shares it does not appear—but that only goes to confirm my contention, because it has had time to evaporate completely from those earlier specimens.

"In proof of that, it is possible to show its presence in diminished amount, through the series of letters beginning with the most recent and following back through each preceding date, until sometime in the early part of this April past, *it entirely disappears!*"

Hood slapped his knee.

"Well, I guess you've got it all right," he declared. "At that rate you certainly were right and the mystery is no mystery at all. All anybody would need to do would be to get a copy of my signature and make a stamp and go ahead. And see here—" his eyes widened swiftly, then contracted to slits. "I signed that vault card, you remember, and that letter sent to Little Falls was signed with an 'E'. The vault guard's name is Edgar—he knew Farr was suspected and he thought he'd help it along. He never expected Farr to see it, but he thought it would be found, when Glace and Bryce began running down the case. As for getting the stocks, he had every chance to get into the boxes with a duplicate key, and all sorts of chances to have one of them made."

Dual smiled.

"If your presumption is correct, why should Edgar go out of his way to attract suspicion to himself?"

"Eh?" Hood stared.

"If, as you suggest," said Semi, "he did so foolish a thing, why did he sign the letter with his own initial and write as though he were an accomplice of Mr. Farr's? I fear, Mr. Hood, that once more you have judged with too much haste."

"Then—"

"Patience," said Dual. "Having determined the signatures to be forgeries in fact, and having learned that they were not written with a pen, let us now consider in what manner they could have been produced."

"I thought you said they were stamped," Hood reminded. "You certainly went to a lot of trouble to prove it, as it seemed to me.

"My words were 'speaking broadly,' as I remember, Mr. Hood," Dual replied. "I would call your attention to the fact, however, that there may be distinctions raised in regard to stamps. In a case so delicate, so particular, as this, the one perpetrating the criminal act would needs take all precautions to insure a perfect result; for upon the perfect simulation of your own writing would depend the success of his venture and the allaying of all suspicion in the minds of the people with whom he dealt.

"If you will read the correspondence with the broker you will realize that he sensed this fact. In ordering the sale of the first stocks he explains that he—presumably yourself—having been in the West, and having urgent need of money—due to losses sustained in the West—desires the brokerage firm to dispose of the Dunn Mills securities

BOX 991   315

at once. That statement was made to cover any possible knowledge upon the part of the brokers as to your trip to Alaska, and lead them to a belief in your *bona fide* presence in Little Falls at the time.

"If, then, he apprehended the need of making his work appear absolutely authentic, he would have spared no pains in preparing for the attempt. Within recent years the advance of science and scientific arts has made it possible for the engraver to absolutely duplicate any signature, so far as the naked eye can see.

"This is done by a modification of photography, as I mentioned when we began this consideration. Given any signature, written, say, on an ordinary sheet of paper, the first step is to prepare the written sheet by the application to its back of an amount of paraffin sufficient to render it transparent, without causing the written surface to become penetrated by the oil.

"The next step is taken by laying the treated sheet over a gelatine compound sensitized by a four per cent, bichromate of potash solution and spread on a plate of glass. This gelatine is in reality a photographic plate, prepared and dried in the dark like any other plate or film.

"The signature being in place, over the gelatine compound, the whole is next exposed to direct sunlight in an ordinary printing frame, exactly as a positive is taken from a negative film. This exposure renders the part of the gelatine not covered by the writing insoluble to water, while the line of the writing itself remains soluble as before.

"After this sunlight printing the gelatine plate is washed under running cold water, with the result that the soluble portion is rendered faintly transparent, while the remainder retains the yellow color due to the chromate content. At the same time, the line of the signature absorbing water rises above the surface level of the rest of the plate in a softly elastic line, corresponding to the exact form of the signature being taken.

"In order to harden this soft gelatine matrix it is immersed for possibly ten minutes in a solution of chrome alum, which, while hardening, causes it to swell still more pronouncedly, so that it projects as a prominent facsimile of the writing, embossed on the gelatine plate."

Abruptly Semi broke off. His eyes lifted and leaped to those of Gertrude Gibson.

"Exactly," he remarked, as though to some spoken comment. "You, Miss Gertrude, who are familiar with the usual photographic methods employed in developing and printing, will perceive how it is done."

For just a moment the girl turned pale. "Mr. Dual, do you read thoughts?" she murmured. "I *was* thinking something very much like that, and I do dabble with a kodak quite a good deal—but—how did you know?"

Semi smiled upon her. "A concentrated thought, like any other manifestation of force, can be perceived if one knows how, my child," he returned. "I *felt* the projected wave from your brain. Feeling it, I sensed what it was, and responded. There is nothing in that save an application of a natural law to gain a certain result."

"But"—she stammered, flushing—"if you can read thoughts—" and broke off, covered with confusion.

"What matter," he said very softly, almost like a caress, "if what we think is sweet—is happy—natural—in tune with the laws of that One who called all life into being?

BOX 991   317

Why care who reads them? Why trouble to pull down the mental blinds?"

The woman's bust rose in a deep, full sigh, like that of a sleeper awakened. Her eyes turned from Semi to Farr and back to Dual.

"Thank you. I wish that some time—you would teach me—how—to live," she breathed in short emotion-clogged phrases. "I mean how to live, and be happy—and bring happiness—to others."

Dual bowed his head for a moment.

"That is life's real purpose, dear maid," he said at length.

And as suddenly as he had paused he resumed his interrupted subject.

"Having now a raised reproduction of the writing, the next stage is the formation of a matrix, from which to make a mold. This is done by placing a rail about the gelatine plate and covering the whole with perhaps half an inch of thin plaster of paris, and leaving it to harden. After the plaster is set, it is very carefully removed and plunged into hot water, which melts out any particles of gelatine which may have adhered to the lines in the plaster mold. The cast is then taken out and carefully dried of all moisture, after which it is ready to form the final cast, which is to be used as the stamp.

"To make this final cast for such a purpose as was intended in the present case, hard—or vulcanized rubber, so called—would most probably be used. The plaster matrix would be very carefully greased or dusted with graphite, and the substance selected for the printing cast run into the depressed lines to form the final raised and reversed impressing surface. If each step has been successfully performed, the result will be a signature reproduced with photographic detail, from which any number of signatures may be struck."

"Struck!" Bryce stiffened "Say, Mr. Dual, that—" As suddenly as he had spoken he fell silent under Semi's glance.

But his sudden exclamation, his expression showed me that my partner was in possession of some notion or information I had not as yet heard anything about. If ever a man looked as though he had seen the outcome of some baffling thing in a startling flash of comprehension, Bryce certainly did. I wondered just what there was about Semi's closing remarks to make him repeat the last word in that fashion, and I knew at the same time that it was not the proper time to ask. Whatever it was, Dual appeared not ready to have it mentioned. So much his glance at Jim had said.

And while I wondered, Hood nodded, his head slowly a number of times.

"I see, exactly, what you mean, Mr. Dual," he made comment after that. "As an engineer I know something of chemistry and things of that sort. I can see how the thing could be done, in the way you so clearly outline. And I really feel that you are wholly right. Now that we have determined that I did not do it, and also how it was done, is it possible that you know who really did the thing as well? Your words have led me to believe that you do."

Dual glanced again at the clock.

"In that, Mr. Hood, you are correct," he replied. "So far as we may do so here, we have now gone into the preliminary stages of the proof of his guilt. And now, as I see that the

BOX 991   **319**

hour in which it shall be wholly proven approaches, I shall ask you to accompany me where the stars decree the end."

Hood gasped.

"You—mean that you—know—that, too?"

"The time—and the place?" said Semi Dual. "Assuredly, yes."

11

A NOTARY'S COMMISSION EXPIRES

HOOD ROSE SLOWLY to his feet.

"You mean that your study of the stars has told you the exact location and hour for the end of this affair?"

Again Dual assented.

"Yes, Mr. Hood."

"At that rate," Hood said, "your method would appear to approach an exact science in its nature."

Dual bowed.

"Quite so; as exact as the astronomical estimation of the eclipse of a planet's orbit; as exact as the location of the planet at a certain point in that orbit, at a given time; as exact, Mr. Hood, as the estimation of the number of cubic yards, feet and inches of excavation, in a tunnel of known length, breadth and height. The only possible source of error lies with the one who computes the result."

"So that given the date of a man's birth you could literally chart his future life?"

"Exactly."

For a moment Hood regarded him in silence. Then he drew a deep breath into his chest.

"It makes me feel small—like a slave of unseen forces."

BOX 991

321

Dual smiled.

" 'We are but figures in a moving row of magic shadow shapes, which come and go,'" he quoted. "One may suppose that Omar had something of the same feeling, Mr. Hood. Most of us *are* ruled by our stars. And yet—man may learn to throw their influence off and walk among them, no longer a slave, but godlike—free!"

Hood shrugged. Yet in his face there was an expression as of one convinced.

"The thing is interesting, I have to confess," he made reply. "At least it has shown you more of this tangle than any one else has been able to see. Come then—well go to the place the stars have appointed. As you say, I fear most of us are still—slaves."

Dual bowed once more. He turned to his desk, opened a small door in its far end and produced a telephone on a cord, He addressed Miss Gibson.

"Will you, my dear young lady, be so kind as to call your father at the bank and ask him to arrange for us to meet himself and Mr. Carlton and Mr. Sheldon in, say—Mr. Carlton's office, within the next half hour?"

There was wonder in the face of the girl as she took her seat at the desk to comply—but she made no comment, and she did what Dual suggested. Calling the Fourth National Exchange, she got in touch with Gibson and preferred the request for the meeting. From her answers to various murmurs over the phone, I gathered that she was being subjected to a rather severe return interrogation. In the end, however, she hung up and turned back to Semi.

"Father will arrange it," she said.

This time I glanced at the clock. It lacked but a few moments of two.

Dual spoke again.

"Thank you. And now before we go toward the final consideration of all evidence in hand, I shall ask you, Miss Gibson and Mr. Farr and Mr. Hood, to go out and stroll through my garden for a very few moments, while I speak briefly with Mr. Glace and Mr. Bryce."

Hood nodded and walked out. Apparently he had come to the place where he was willing to follow Semi Dual's directions. Miss Gibson and Farr followed him through the door.

Semi turned to me as they passed from sight.

"And now, Gordon, tell me briefly, what transpired on your trip. You found the papers you brought back, in the Dawson Block room, of course, and in possession of Mr. Farr himself."

"Yes."

"What else—Hood's conversation concerning his taking of the box in the vault."

I told him the whole thing, as I always sought to do. I even ran over the seemingly trivial details of that conversation on the train the evening before, and paused only when I could think of nothing I had omitted.

"Granny!" Bryce exclaimed. He had been listening closely to everything I said, and apparently gaining a vast satisfaction from it, as shown by his face.

Dual met his ejaculation with a smile.

"I perceive, Mr. Bryce, that you comprehend the bearing of the discoveries you barely mentioned to me over the telephone this morning, at the time I sent Mr. Farr's bail

BOX 991   323

to your office. We will go into their application later. And now, I should like the list of stock sales you obtained from Mr. Pearson."

Bryce gave me a wink as he produced a folded paper and handed it over.

"Beat you to it this time, son," he chuckled.

Dual put the paper in his pocket with the others, glanced in my eyes and smiled.

"Come, let us join the others, now," he said.

And the manner in which he said it was a bugle call to action, the announcement that now armed and equipped for the final step, he was going forth to confound and convict the one who had sinned, as the agent of that justice, whose priest he was.

Looking into his strong, calm face, I turned without a word and followed him with Bryce, went through the anteroom of the tower, and so to the garden, where Miss Gibson was exclaiming with all a girl's delight, over the beauties it held.

"Come," Dual said again, catching Hood's eye. The engineer spoke to Gertrude and Farr. They hastened to join us, and we all went down with the soft chimes ringing a farewell sign of our passing as we crossed the inlaid plate.

I glanced at Bryce, at Hood, at the sparkling girl and the man she so palpably loved as we waited for the cage.

And this was the end of the tangle, I thought—the beginning of the end, at least, in which Semi Dual by his strange prescience led us to an appointed spot to witness the confusion of the guilty, and the final triumph of right and love.

And so we went down in the cage and came out and

found the car which had brought us still waiting. Bryce gave the word and we were off, heading toward the Fourth National Bank.

Reaching our destination in due course, and leaving the long auto, we pushed through the main doors of the bank. Gibson was watching for our arrival from a seat in Sheldon's station. Both he and Dick rose as we came in, but it was Gertrude's father who came out on the floor and met us half way.

There was an air of annoyed impatience about the man as he spoke directly to the girl.

"Gertrude, what is the meaning of all this, may I ask?" He caught sight of Farr, and paused abruptly with darkening face.

Dual interposed before the girl could reply.

"I shall explain that entirely to your satisfaction as we go along, Mr. Gibson. It was at my request Miss Gertrude called you up. She was in my rooms at the time."

"In your rooms?" grumbled Gibson, caught now in a double surprise.

"And who, sir, may I inquire, are you?"

"I," said Dual, "am the man who has undertaken to discover just how Mr. Hood's box was rifled, and who committed the theft. Also I am the man instrumental in having Mr. Farr released on bail, in defiance of your rather too hasty order for his arrest."

The muscles of Gibson's throat contracted sharply. He appeared to swallow something before he spoke; then:

"You appear to have taken a great deal on yourself, sir. By whose authority, may I ask?"

"By mine, Gibson," Hood suddenly cut in. "I started out

BOX 991   325

to learn what happened to my stocks without waiting a year to do it. Mr. Dual here says he knows the answer. We've come down to tell it to you."

Sheldon had advanced. His face was lighted by pleasure.

"Mr. Dual," he exclaimed with hand extended. "I hardly dared hope you would interest yourself in this, but I'm mightily glad to see you have." He broke off, dropping Semi's palm, to speak to Farr. "Hello, Neville, glad to see you. Feeling all right?"

"Better than ever before in my life," Farr told him, with a face which supported the words.

Dick's eyebrows went up and he glanced at me. I smiled. I think Sheldon sighed with relief.

"So," said Gibson. "Well, Mr. Hood, you may have been within your rights, I suppose, of course, you were. Do I understand then that this Mr. Dual is a detective?"

"He has acted in that capacity for me," Hood made a sort of indirect answer.

Gibson turned on his daughter once more.

"I still fail to see your connection in this matter," he began, "or why you come openly here in the company of a man under arrest."

Gertrude flamed. Suddenly she was all woman—woman with her chosen mate assailed.

"We will not discuss it on a bank floor," she gave back coldly. "When you learn how unjust and mistaken you are, you may perhaps understand."

"I think," Semi suggested, "that Miss Gibson's point is well taken. If, as I directed her to request, we can adjourn to the room of Mr. Carlton—"

Gibson nodded. He appeared undecided as to either

further speech or action. In a way I fancy he was glad to turn the matter over to a general discussion. He turned and led us through Sheldon's railing and so to Carlton's door.

Carlton at least knew Dual. He rose as we entered, and his dark, clean shaven face showed interest as well as recognition as he bade us welcome, dismissed his stenographer and waited until we had found seats. Sheldon introduced Hood, who was the only one of our party with whom the president was not acquainted.

Dual produced the various documents he had brought and laid them out on Carlton's desk, a good-sized square-topped affair. Then he picked us all up with his eyes, very much as a hostess might do a group of guests.

"I presume that you know at least the details of this matter, Mr. Carlton?" he began.

Carlton nodded.

"In it," Dual went on after receiving that assent, "from first to last we are confronted with evidence of a very careful plotting and a very consistent carrying out of the original plan, to the end. In only one instance did the mind which first conceived of the theft fall into a major error, and that after the theft itself had been discovered. We have here practically sufficient evidence to make the entire matter clear, but in order to complete our chain of documentary proof, I deem it advisable that Mr. Hood make a sworn statement as to his whereabouts on—" he bent and picked a letter from the Pearson correspondence—"the fifteenth of November last.

"Mr. Hood states verbally that at that date he was in Seattle. A letter among these in our possession, written by Mr. Mack of this bank, to Mr. Hood, and addressed to

BOX 991   327

him at that city, was surrendered to us from Mr. Hood's possession. The postmarks upon its cover indicate that it was mailed November 10 in this city and received in Seattle November 15 of last year, and Mr. Hood undoubtedly received it at that time and place—or later."

"I got it on that date," Hood interrupted. "I'm willing to swear—"

"Personally I do not doubt your veracity, Mr. Hood," Semi checked him. "My suggestion merely bears on another fact, because as one may notice the brokerage firm of Pearson & Co. are in the habit of using a receiving stamp on their correspondence as a check against any mistakes in dates. Each and every one of the letters purporting to have been written by you to them bears the date of its receipt, and the first letter, authorizing the sale of the canceled shares of stock which we have here at present, is dated in Little Falls, November 14, and bears the Pearson receipt stamp of November 15 for last year.

"Your sworn affidavit as to your presence in Seattle, if corroborated—as you have told me it could be—would conclusively show that you could not have written that letter. What I therefore would suggest is that you dictate such a statement, have it written down and acknowledged by a notary here and now." He shifted his gaze to Gibson. "I believe Mr. Mack holds a notarial commission, and can operate a writing machine. May I impose upon you so far as to ask that he be called in?"

"Sure. Get Fred. He knows all about the business anyway," said Hood. "He knows I was in Seattle, too. He's got a letter I wrote him from there."

I remembered that Mack had admitted the same thing

the day before, during the conversation in the vault, but I said nothing, and after a slight pause, Gibson himself rose and left the room, to return in a moment with Mack.

Apparently he had told him what was wanted, too, because after bowing to Miss Gibson, and giving the rest of us a rather questioning stare, the paying teller went over and sat down before the typewriter Carlton's stenographer had deserted when we came in.

"And now, Mr. Hood, make your statement in your own way," said Dual.

Hood turned around to face Mack.

"It's this way, Fred," he explained. "You know and I know that I was out West when my box was looted, but I've got to make an affidavit to that effect. Slip a sheet of paper in that machine, and I'll reel it off."

Mack did as requested, and sat with his hands ready at the keyboard, waiting for Hood's first word.

Hood cleared his throat and began.

"On the fifteenth day of November, 1913. I was in the city of Seattle, State of Washington, U.S.A. On that date I received a letter written and posted in this city, by my friend Frederick Mack. The letter was a friendly communication in the main, but enclosed a receipt from the Fourth National Bank of this city for the rental of Box 991 in their vaults, for one year. This receipt I still have. The reason that Mr. Mark wrote me was because I had forwarded the rental amount to the bank through him.

"In order to verify this statement, I would refer any one desiring confirmation to Mr. John Burgenheimer, local representative of the syndicate with whom I was at that time engaged as a mining engineer. I would also refer him

BOX 991   329

to Mr. Maurice Todd, of the firm of Todd & Todd, attor-
neys at law, who drew up contracts of transfers of certain
properties from me to Rogers, Jackson & Co., both of the
city of Seattle. I would also refer to Rogers, Jackson &
Co.—either to Mr. Rogers or Mr. Jackson—both of whom
met and conversed with me during several days covering
the above period in November, both before and after. And
I guess that's all, Fred. Fix it up and I'll sign it and you can
put your John Hancock on and affix your seal."

Mack took it down from Hood's dictation, and only
once or twice did he interrupt, and that mainly to ask the
correct spelling of names. He wrote steadily and swiftly,
and jerked the sheet out of the machine by the time Hood
had finished his final remarks.

At the end he rose from his chair, brought the written
statement over to Carlton's desk, and, after producing a
small pocket notarial seal and a small rubber commission
expiration stamp, such as many notaries use, he showed
Joe where to sign his name, stamped it with the date of
his own tenure of appointment, laid the stamp down and
picked up pen.

"You appear to have a certain facility with a typewriter,
Mr. Mack," said Dual, as the teller signed his name with a
little flourish and reached for the seal.

Mack lifted his eyes. "Oh, yes. But I fancy I haven't met
you, Mr.—"

"Dual," said Semi. "You are quite right. You have never
met me before, unless in dreams. But I was watching your
manipulations of the machine."

Mack impressed the seal on the paper.

"One finds it handy to be able to do more things than one," he remarked.

"Versatile ability is admirable in a great many instances," said Semi. He bent over and picked up the rubber communion stamp Mack had laid down. "You use a different machine than this, however, I would be led to believe, Mr. Mack."

"I know how to operate several, if that's what you mean," the teller admitted with something like a smirk.

"That is exactly what I mean," said Semi. "I would even go farther and suggest that in some time in the past the machine which you use for your private correspondence has suffered a broken type bar—that is, that the type carrying portion has become detached from the bar itself."

Mack frowned. His fingers came up and pulled at his pouting lower lip. Then he lifted the paper he had just sealed and held it out to Hood.

"There's your statement," he remarked, picked up his seal and returned it to his pocket. "As it happens you're right, but I fail to see how you arrived at the conclusion," he made final reply to Dual.

Semi turned the little commission stamp he had picked up in his fingers.

"I've made a study of such things to a considerable extent," he returned. "As a result of that I would extend my statement to embrace a correlated addition, that you have had the original type replaced upon the bar."

Mack shrugged.

"You would be both right and wrong," he admitted. "The thing was broken, but I replaced it myself."

"And you failed to give it a proper alignment," said Semi.

BOX 991 331

"It is on that very detail that my entire deduction rests. In writing to Mr. Hood—the letter mentioned in this statement just signed—a letter which I have seen, you used a Zenith machine of an old model without an automatic reverse. In addition to being an old model, it has, as you assure me, an 'H' bar aligned at a slight slant to the right on the bar, so that while the small 'h' strikes at approximately the normal space from any other letter in a given word, the capital 'H' is shifted into very close juxtaposition to any letter written after it has been struck.

"The condition I mention is very clearly shown in the address of that letter addressed to 'Joseph J. Hood' in Seattle last November. In that address the 'H' in Hood is practically in contact with the 'o' in the same word. Following through the body of the letter itself, one can find other instances where the same thing is true. For instance, in the very line of salutation where you write 'My dear Hood.' There once more the line of the 'H' contacts the first 'o.'"

Gibson was frowning. Carlton sat tapping softly on the knuckles of one hand with a pencil held in the other. Purely as an exposition of deductive reasoning, and close attention to detail, Dual's remarks impressed one very strongly, but I could see no particular object to be gained.

There was no question as to the identity of either the sender or the recipient of the letter Mack had written to Hood. I could therefore see small use in reestablishing the fact, or the additional detail that the machine had an improperly adjusted bit of type. In fact, the whole thing struck me as a surprising digression for Dual to make at such a time.

That is, the thought occurred to me for an instant, until my knowledge of the man told me that he never spoke without a purpose, and, as he said of his astrological calculations—if there was any error, it must be due to some lack of understanding in me, and that whether I understood it or not, he had some definite object to gain. I am positive Hood, too, felt wholly confused as to his purpose, because he growled faintly into my ear.

"All very fine, but where does it get us?"

I shook my head in answer and kept my eyes on Dual and paying teller Mack. Semi, still standing, was again turning the little notarial stamp in his hand and Mack was regarding him with a sort of fixed stare. Presently he seemed to sense the need of some comment on Semi's words.

"You appear to be a very observant person," he remarked.

I saw Dual's face alter. It seemed to me that the wings of his nose drew in to make his nostrils thinner, that the warm gray of his eyes suddenly chilled, till his glance, like his voice, became utterly cold.

"One needs pay close attention to details, Mr. Mack, either in the planning or the attempt to detect an action against the laws of man, the name of friendship, the spirit of honor. The detective must pay close attention to discern the act of the man he pursues. The malefactor must pay close attention lest he do something to betray himself and so forfeit the freedom he would fain retain.

"Take the case which has brought us all together this afternoon. Presuppose that after cleverly obtaining Mr. Hood's stock in the simplest and boldest possible manner—that after sparing no pains to make the signa-

BOX 991

333

tures on the shares of stock I have here appear so absolutely Mr. Hood's own work that they should arouse no suspicion, he should, after the theft itself was discovered, and through a desire to throw absolute suspicion on another man in order to shield himself, act on impulse and commit one act, which would react to point an unswerving finger of proof at himself?

"Presupposing all this, do you see how that one faulty bit of detail might work his complete undoing?"

While he spoke, Mack appeared to consider. He still pulled at his lip. Gradually a dusky flush crept into his cheeks.

"I can see your hypothetical conclusion, of course," he assented, "but—" his voice rose the least bit, "what I can't see is the object in drawing me into the discussion. Of course, I helped Joe get his box in the first place, and if there was anything I could do to help him out, I'd be glad to do it, as I think he knows."

Suddenly Gibson nodded.

"Exactly," he said. "I agree with Mr. Mack that all this discussion of non-essential details is merely producing a needless waste of time."

"To which you object? "Dual suggested.

Gibson glanced rather pointedly at a clock on the wall of the room. "With me, time is money, Mr. Dual. And it is now time for closing."

Dual bowed in assent. "Time for closing," he repeated. "Indeed, yes," and turned again to Mack. "Speaking of attention to detail, Mr. Mack, allow me to call *your* attention to an error in this stamp."

"An error—in the stamp? That stamp?" cried Mack, starting to his feet. "What do you mean?"

"Yes," said Semi. "It reads, 'My commission expires May 15, 1915,' Mr. Mack, while as an absolute truth—" With a wonderfully swift motion he tore the soft rubber face from its wooden backing, turned the latter over and shook into his palm a small rectangular plate of hard rubber—"as a matter of fact, your commission *expires here and now!*"

12

THE TRIUMPH

"GIVE ME THAT stamp!"

The words were Mack's, and he snarled them rather than spoke, while the savage menace of a trapped thing distorted his face. He knew—he must have known—in that instant, when the little rubber plate fell from the cunningly contrived hiding place in the hollowed out back of the stamp, that he was caught. Leaning slightly forward, his hands gripping the edge of the desk, he glared at Dual. And then one of his hands came up and darted into the breast of his perfectly fitted coat.

And on the instant the room was in a turmoil. Bryce and I sprang up as we saw that sudden motion.

"Mr. Dual! Fred!"

Gertrude Gibson screamed it. A shadow flashed past me even as I leaped toward Mack and sensed Jim's mass beside me. Dimly even in the urge of effort I realized that the girl also was hurling her slight body toward the teller.

"If you show that I'll kill you!" Mack cried out again in a blind unreasoning passion of hate and fury. His hand came out of his coat in a sweeping gesture.

It swept out and around pointing toward Semi. And then Gertrude was upon the man in desperate attack, seizing that arm and clinging to it with all her frail, yet tenacious force, just as Jim and I closed with the crazy fool in a rush.

The gun went off. I heard the snap of its little report, as I struggled with the man, and panted a command to the clinging girl to let go. I smelled the faint vapor of the powder rising to my nostrils, and fought on, perceiving in a sort of blur that the woman had staggered back and had been caught and held upright by Dual himself.

But the weight of her body had dragged down Mack's arm, who, it came out later, she had known to go always armed, and deflected the gun's muzzle so that the bullet tore into the floor and buried itself in the wood. By that time I had the would-be murderer on one side and Bryce had hold on the other, and Bryce knew something about handling bad men from his years on the force. As a result, although Mack fought back insanely, it was not long until the gun dropped dully at our feet and we forced his hands down far enough for Jim to snap on the "cuffs."

"An' I reckon that will hold you for awhile, you tinkering duffer," he granted when it was done.

The click of the things seemed to take all the fight out of Mack. Without warning he went limp, staggered toward a chair and sank dizzily down to drop his face on his shackled hands.

It was to that seemingly broken thing Hood spoke.

"You—You—?" and stopped, to stand staring at the man he had thought his friend.

Not so Gibson. He got up and walked over, and took the man by the shoulder.

"Did you do it?" he thundered, and shook him. "Did

BOX 991 337

you? Fred—good God, can't you answer! Did you do it? What for?" Abruptly he whirled back to Dual. "You haven't proved anything yet. What's the matter with everybody here? What have you got there—that thing in your hand—the thing you took out of Fred's stamp? Heaven above, man! can't you answer either?"

Dual held up the little rubber plate between thumb and finger.

"The plate from which the Hood signatures were *printed*," he said.

Printed! I saw it. I know Hood saw it, and remembered his story of the little school paper he and Mack had printed as boys. I saw it in his face. Neville and Gertrude saw it, of course, and Bryce. He saw it, too, and grinned as one who has waited a denouement in a great deal of impatience and is wholly satisfied with the result.

"You bet they was printed!" he roared. "There's a press in his room right now. I called at his boardin' house this mornin' early. His landlady told me all about it. She said he was a mighty smart man—said he fixed menus for her dinners on special occasions an' soldered her pans when they sprung a leak. She took me up an' showed me his room. The press is there all right."

And I guess Carlton and Sheldon and Gibson saw it then, too. Conviction grew in their faces. Gibson turned and stared at Farr and Gertrude and his face took on a sickly pallor. He sat down in a chair with a bump and panted and puffed.

Something like a suppressed groan came from Mack.

Carlton cleared his throat.

"You mean then, Mr. Dual, that the thing in your hand is the instrument used in forging the letters and shares?"

Dual bowed.

"Yes." He laid the little oblong on the desk where the president sat. Throughout the entire turmoil he had changed neither his position nor expression. "It is the last bit of evidence," he said.

We crowded about the desk to see it for ourselves. There could be no doubt. There was the signature of Hood embossed on the face in reverse. Hood himself was the first to speak. He glanced up at Semi after he had inspected the little mold of his name.

"It's rubber," he admitted, in a manner almost comically inane at another time.

"As I suggested," said Dual. He bent over and once more picked up the rubber plate. "Some moments ago," he went on, "it was intimated very plainly that I was indulging in a waste of time. As a matter of fact, that was an erroneous statement, for the reason that I was laying the foundation for the final proof of Mr. Mack's guilt. And now with your further tolerance, I shall endeavor to show the exact manner in which a man deliberately plotted to rob, and did rob another, and thereafter planned to throw the blame of his action on a second innocent man, and to that, unless prevented, would have added murder, because he was insanely frightened when unmasked.

"My remarks concerning the broken type bar on Mr. Mack's machine were made for the purpose of proving that peculiarity in the machine he uses, because in the address of a letter discovered in room 22 Dawson Block, Little Falls, this morning—a letter addressed to 'Mr. Joseph J.

BOX 991   339

Hood,' the same position of the capital 'H' appears. It also occurs in the one instance in that letter, where the word 'Hood' is written. And in both letters there is also another similarity which tends to show them as written on the same machine.

"That feature is that in both the machine was set to a six-point margin—an apparent preference of the writer. I may add, also, that on a Coroya machine found in the same Dawson Block room by Mr. Glace and Mr. Hood at the same time as the letter, the same six-point margin was registered on the stops—and in all the correspondence to the brokerage firm of Pearson & Co. the same six-point factor occurs.

"From all of which we may conclude that all of these letters were written by one and the same person at various times. That conclusion is made more definite still by this small rubber cast which I hold."

Hood roused from an abstraction apparently caused by the perfidy of his friend, and as Dual paused, he looked him full in the face.

"What I can't understand, is how you knew where to look for the thing. What made you pick up that stamp? How did you know he was a notary in the first place?"

Dual's lips twitched.

"Your question is more or less pertinent," he replied. "Therefore I shall try to explain. I have told you I had gone very fully into this case. Also, if you will recall the letter written to you in Seattle—a rather boastful letter—you will remember that Mr. Mack states, among other things, that he is making quite a little pocket money by notarial work for Mr. Gibson, of whose favor he was at that time definitely assured.

"Being a notary, it was not unnatural enough for him to choose the inside of his stamp as a place of concealment for the cast of your name, in case he should need it again. As for the rest, you heard me say to-day that a thought wave is as much a force as a ray of light or a vibration of sound. By the nature of the work Mr. Mack was called upon to do, his mind was concentrated on the forgery of your name. I sensed it. By picking up the stamp and turning it in my fingers, I fixed his attention both on it and myself, as also by my remarks about his machine. One who has developed the power may gage the quality of another's thought emanation. Mind reading is what you would call it. Mr. Mack's knowledge of what the stamp held produced a very strong thought directed toward it. You saw the result."

He paused again and Hood accepted with a nod.

"Yes, I saw the result," he said.

"Just how the cast was made I shall not enter into at this time," Semi Dual resumed. "I have already explained the process to Mr. Hood and Miss Gibson and Mr. Farr. I shall say merely that it is an exact reproduction of the signature of Mr. Hood. Its method of use is to place it in a small press and print from it the number of signatures required. And now, with these facts as a preliminary foundation, let us reconstruct the story of this crime. Before beginning, however, I shall ask Mr. Bryce to obtain any keys in Mr. Mack's possession."

Bryce grinned as he moved over to Mack's side and ran his huge hand into one after another of the teller's pockets. While Mack glowered in a helpless rage, the ex-policeman

BOX 991   341

made a thorough search and came back with a bunch of keys in his hand.

Dual extended his palm and Jim dropped the keys into its clasp. Semi took them and ran them rapidly over, finally closing his fingers upon them as he began once more to speak.

"This is the story of a crime against friendship—the betrayal of the trust of a friend, than which there is nothing more loathsome, more deserving of punishment and disgrace.

"And the false friend, conceiving in his treacherous mind the thought of robbing the friend who had trusted and confided in him, deliberately set about its plotting. He agreed to arrange for the deposit box at Mr. Hood's request; and he did. And when Mr. Hood came to the bank bringing his papers with him, his friend took him to the vault where he had already selected the box, and introduced him to the guard. After that he asked the guard to explain the matter of the duplicate keys. What happened then, Mr. Hood?"

Hood started as the question rapped out.

"What happened? Why the guard produced the keys and I kept one and put the other away in my trunk." His brows drew into a pucker. He seemed trying to connect some detail. "Or wait—" he burst out once more. "Fred took the keys from the guard and gave me one to put on my ring."

Dual smiled coldly.

"Besides the fact that Mr. Mack had a printing press in his room, what did you learn about him, Mr. Bryce?" he asked.

"I saw his typewriter, too. It was a Zenith, all right. An' I had a talk with the old lady what runs the house where he boards. She said he was mighty handy, like I've told you, and a great hand at helping with parlor entertainments and such. You know how a woman talks. Well, she said he was great at sleight of hand and parlor magic and things like that."

"Very good," said Dual. "Now, Mr. Sheldon—just what is the number of Mr. Mack's box in your vault?"

"I told Bryce that last evening," Sheldon made answer. "It is 166."

"You devil!" Mack sprang from his chair with his shackled hands lifted and struck like a snake at Dual.

But Semi stepped aside quickly, and the steel circlets fell and bit into the surface of Carlton's desk in a ragged gash as Mack failed of reaching his mark. Then once more Bryce had the fellow in a none too gentle grasp and hurled him back into his chair.

"Stay there now," he grated. "One more break like that and I'll bash your bean with a jack."

"Mr. Mack appears to have anticipated my remarks," Dual resumed in the pause which followed. "Mr. Hood says Mr. Mack handed him a key. What now, about the second key, Mr. Hood?"

"After I'd put the first one on my ring he gave me the second, told me to put it away where it would be safe, and went back to his window, Mr. Dual."

"Did you examine the second key?" Semi's question came quickly.

Comprehension came over Hood in a flood. "No," he

BOX 991   **343**

said weakly. "No, I didn't. I-I supposed it the duplicate of the other, of course"

"As you were meant to think—as you were led to think— as Mr. Mack was sure you would think when he substituted a key of his own box for one of yours, while you were placing the first key on your ring. It was very simple for a sleight of hand performer to accomplish that, and if you will consider, the numbers 166 and 991 bear a striking resemblance to each other if *reversed.*

"It is easy to see why Mr. Mack selected 991 for your box. Having done so, and having exchanged the keys, he would need merely to enter the vault at some time, say near closing, pick up the master key from the desk of the guard, who knew him so well as to offer no objection, go to the box and take out whatever he wished, and carry it away, without the custodian paying any attention to whether he went to his own box or not."

Save for Mack's now audible breathing there was no sound as Dual once more paused. After a bit he opened the hand which held the keys, and went on.

"In proof of all this there are several facts. Primarily, a key kept for two years in a trunk would become dull of surface. A key carried on a ring would remain bright from the friction of daily contact either with other keys or cloth in a pocket. Yesterday afternoon Mr. Mack visited Mr. Hood at his hotel and asked to see his duplicate key. Last night Mr. Bryce went there during Mr. Hood's absence and brought me the key from his trunk. But the key Mr. Bryce found is bright and numbered 991, while of the keys on this ring, one is bright, and one is dull, and both are numbered—166."

"You switched back, didn't you, you merry josher?" Bryce growled with a scowl at Mack.

Dual tossed the keys aside.

"Having arranged to obtain the papers, and being in correspondence with Hood, Mr. Mack next obtained one of his signatures from a letter and made this little rubber plate. From it he printed the endorsements on the shares, and the signatures to letters dealing with their sale, and on drafts received from the broker from time to time. I would call your attention to the fact that Little Falls is only an hour away by trolley, and the janitor of the Dawson Block says the renter of Room 22 was rarely there save at night."

Bryce chuckled.

"An' th' landlady says she thought Mack was courtin' 'cause he'd been out so much at night th' last year."

It was a pertinent interruption, but Semi gave it no attention, save a brief pause to allow for its apprehension.

"But there is another element in the case. Mr. Mack was in good standing with Mr. Gibson. He was in hopes of marrying his daughter. He was also aware of the fact that Mr. Farr was out of favor with Miss Gibson's father. He planned, therefore, to throw suspicion upon Mr, Farr, whom he doubtless knew to be in love with the woman he was scheming to make his own wife. He felt that this would be the more easy, because of what he knew to be Mr. Gibson's attitude toward Farr. He appears to have intended Mr. Farr's conviction of the theft and the removal of a rival at one and the same time.

"In furtherance of that plan he talked with his second victim and learned what he could about him, and when the letter arrived stating that Mr. Hood was returning and he

BOX 991   345

knew that discovery of his theft would come, he concocted a letter purporting to have been written by the Johnson, Arbiger Company, of Little Falls, to Mr. Farr. This letter, which shows clearly that it was composed on the defective Coroya machine in the Dawson Block room, was so worded that it would insure Mr. Farr's absence from the bank and the city on the day Mr. Hood would appear at the bank. The result of that you all know.

"A short time ago I told Mr. Mack that he had never met me save in dreams. That was a figurative statement. For Mr. Mack has never met me in the personality I wear. But as all who sin must do at times, no matter how cleverly they think they have covered their steps, he also must at times have dreamed of one—who would find him out. Because of such dreams, perhaps, and because having seen suspicion light upon the one he intended, and because of a desire to strengthen that suspicion, he yesterday wrote a letter addressed to Joseph J. Hood on the cover—to Mr. Farr, to whom it seemed to convey a warning—on the inside. And he sent it to the Dawson Block room—after signing it with the single letter 'E'—the initial of a man already under arrest as all here know. And that letter bore the fatal evidence in its construction, which showed it to have been written on Mr. Mack's own machine. Save for that—who knows?

"This, then, I think completes the case, and proves beyond any question that Frederick Mack planned in cold blood to betray the honor of his manhood, to blast the life and hope and good name of another, and rob the man who for years had called him—friend."

"Fred!"

Gertrude's voice, full of something like sorrow, like shattered faith, like hopeless remorse, cut through the room, little more than a whisper.

But Mack, slumped in his chair, his locked wrists limp on his thighs, gave no sign that he heard it, by movement or word.

Hood nodded slowly.

"Yes, I guess that's all," he said dully. "I wanted to find out who did it, but now—well—I don't know but I'm sorry that I did."

Gibson shifted in his chair.

"Fred," he began thickly—"you're guilty. Nobody with a grain of sense could look at you and doubt it, so I'm not going to ask you to lie. But why did you do it? What for?"

And suddenly Mack answered. He forced himself up in his chair and lifted his manacled wrists to point with both hands at Gibson's daughter.

"For her!" he cried hoarsely. "For her! I wanted to marry her—I wanted her for my wife. You said the man she married would have to have money. I didn't have, as you very well knew. But when Joe went off and left these stocks—stocks anybody would be glad to buy, I thought I saw a way to get enough to make more. But I didn't do it, till I got this letter last November, saying he struck it rich. Then I knew even if I lost, he could spare, and I went ahead. I thought I had some good tips on the market, and I could make a big profit—and—" he paused to lick his lips with a nervous grimace—"I never expected any cunning devil like this man here to step in and show how it was done. I—I thought I had it all fixed. As for Farr, I didn't have anything against him, only that I knew he was in love with

BOX 991   **347**

Gertrude, too, and I knew you'd grab at the chance to send him over, and that would get him out of my way. That's all there is to it. I did it for her."

"Fred!" There was a sick reproach in the girl's tones now. Gibson flushed.

"For her, eh?" he growled like an angry dog, deep in his throat. "You'd have offered my daughter a thief for a husband, would you? Why, you poor fool, didn't you know that if she wanted you—if she'd married you—I'd have made you rich in spite of yourself? Haven't I showed you enough favors to show you where I stood about the girl? I'd have seen she didn't want for anything after she was married. All you'd needed to have done was to have treated her right and run straight. Here I've petted you up for the last two years, and all the thanks I get is to have you drag her name into a criminal matter; but I'd a lot rather you did it before than after marriage. Thank Heaven we've found you out in time."

He stopped just long enough to mop his face with a huge square of linen, and turned on Sheldon. "Go get our man and have him taken away, Dick; and—tell Hobbs when he gets him over to the station to arrange to have Edgar turned loose."

Mack went deathly pale. He turned miserable eyes about him. The fingers of his hands clasped and unclasped under the stress of his emotion. Quite suddenly he spoke again.

"Gertrude—you—you've more influence with your father than any one else. Gertrude, won't you say a word— for me? I've told the truth. It was for you—just for you, Gertie, I did it. I—I wanted you—I wanted to—to give you everything to which you had been accustomed. I—I meant to make it right with Joe if I'd won. And—and I'll do what I can now. Mr. Dual says he has a list of the stocks sold. I—well, I sold them all. But I didn't spend all of the—money. There's—oh, a lot in my box. There's as much ten thousand there. I'd—I'd lost so much I meant to wait a bit—and—and—get your father to put me onto something—sure. Then I was going to make it all back and fix it up—fix it all up, Gertie.

"You see it was because I wanted you so much, I did it—so—won't you ask your father, and—and—Joe—to give me a chance? Won't you ask them to let me go? I—I can't stand the disgrace of arrest and going to prison. Won't you ask them, Gertie—won't you? Even if you don't love me—we've been such good friends for years."

It was a pitiful thing to hear and see. The man was such a wreck. All his aplomb, all his debonair poise had left him completely as he sat there and begged a woman to interpose between him and the same fate he had plotted for another.

And I think Gertrude Gibson felt something of the pity, the shameless degradation of the man's soul as she listened. I think, too, she must have felt a great sense of her escape from any closer relation with such a spirit. It was such a poor spirit now that it was wholly entangled in the net of its own selfish weaving, the strands of which had been drawn together by Dual.

I say I think she must have sensed something of all that, because her voice held nothing of anger, not even anything of contempt, scarcely anything so much as a sort of impersonal pity as she answered.

BOX 991   349

"I don't believe, Fred, that you are one to offer the plea of friendship. I wouldn't if I were you."

Mack groaned as his last hope departed.

The door through which Sheldon had left the room at Gibson's direction came open. Hobbs, the bank's policeman, came in and laid his hand on Mack's shoulder.

"Sorry, sir, Mr. Mack, but I got to do it," he said in a low-toned rumble. "If you'll just come quiet, 'twon't be so bad, sir, an' you an' me will just take a little walk."

Mack rose and stood at Hobbs's side. Without a word, without a backward glance, he stumbled with bowed head, from the room. Joe Hood sat and stared after the friend he had lost. I saw Gertrude Gibson wipe her eyes. But suddenly she smiled and turned a face like sunlight shining through a mist on Farr. And from Farr her glance traveled to Gibson.

"Father," she began in a broken little stammer. "Father—here is Neville. I—I think you ought to say something—to him."

Gibson pursed his lips. I saw Dual smile softly. While we all sat and waited, the Fourth National's cashier inspected the two young people before him, turning his eyes from one eager face to the other and back again before he nodded as one who understands.

"I guess you're right daughter," he said then at last. "Farr, you young scoundrel, why in time wouldn't you sell me that piece of land?"

And Farr answered him straight from the shoulder, with Gertrude's hand fast in his own.

"Because, sir, I love your daughter and we'd planned to make it our home."

Gibson's jaw came open.

"Eh?" he gurgled. "Eh? Well, bless my soul, so you shall!"

I glanced again at Dual.

Once more the gray eyes were warm and glowing, the smile still on his lips.

And very softly, almost like a benediction, I caught the words:

"Shall find that which he shall seek."

ABOUT THE AUTHOR:
DR. J.U. GIESY

BORN NEAR CHILLICOTHE, Ohio, August 6, 1877. That
makes me a Buckeye, and some people have suggested that
I was a nut. Of my actual birth I have no recollection. So
this is mere hearsay evidence. When I was eight months
of age my parents removed to southeastern Kansas and
took me with them, as I was still unable to shift for myself.

When I was thirteen we again removed to Utah, where
I received my common school education in common with
other youngsters of a similar age. In 1895, I entered the
Starling Medical College, Columbus, Ohio, and received
my medical degree from that institution in 1898.

Returning to Salt Lake, I served an internship in a local
hospital and have practiced medicine in that city ever since,
with the exception of the time I spent in the United States
service during the World War as a captain in the Medical Corps. As regards the Army, I am still a major in the
Reserve, attached to the Division Surgeon's Office of the
104th Division. In 1916 I was instrumental in organizing
the first Plattsburg camp ever held in the State, starting the
movement and acting as secretary of the general commit-
tee which put it over.

I began to write in 1910. Unlike many well known writers, I have had rejections since. At the same time, I've found a lot of editors who liked my work. I have written as an avocation ever since. At present I am associate editor for Utah on the staff of *California and Western Medicine*, and the staff of the *Archives of Physical Therapy X-Ray and Radium*. Because of the latter fact I am a member of the American Medical Editors Association.

I am also a member of the Salt Lake Chamber of Commerce, and a life member of the American College of Physical Therapy, which I have served as an officer for several years. My ancestors made me a Son of the American Revolution, and I have made myself more or less of a nuisance to a lot of people all by myself.

I was married in San Francisco, to Juliet Galena Conwell, in December, 1904, and the marriage took. Personally I think they did better work along those lines, that long ago. Anyway we're still living in the same apartment, with no intentions of divorce.

Just why the editor should want to print this confession I really can't imagine. But that's his business. He's asked for it and here it is!

ABOUT THE AUTHOR:
JUNIUS B. SMITH

I WAS BORN at Salt Lake City, Utah, September 29, 1883, at approximately 3:55:27 P.M., right ascension of the mid-heaven (for the benefit of my astrological readers) 16 hrs. 27 min. 57 sec., or 246° 59' 15"; position of planets, Neptune 20° 45' ret. Taurus, Saturn 10° 6' ret. Gemini, Mars 22° 10' Cancer, Jupiter 0° 26' Leo, Moon 22° 24' Virgo, Uranus 24° 34' Virgo, Sun 6° 27' 23" Libra, Venus 8° 52' Libra, Mercury 20° 31' ret. Libra. Declinations: Sun 2° 34' south, Moon 0° 7' south, Neptune 16° 13' north, Uranus 2° 50' north, Saturn 20° 2' north, Jupiter 20° 18' north, Mars 22° 25' north, Venus 2° 20' south, Mercury 11° 17' south.

With this meager astronomical data, the astrologians will know more about me than I could write in a volume.

For the benefit of you other readers:

I am an attorney at law and practiced for many years, paying my office expenses in the lean years by writing. I never had the bitter experience of having to write years before anything sold. At the beginning of my writing career, Dr. J.U. Giesy and I joined intellectual forces, and our first joint effort was submitted to *Argosy* way back in 1911. It sold, first time out. Rapidly we "dashed" off more and they sold also. We each write separately as well as jointly, at such times as we cannot get together.

Early in life I took up astrology as a hobby and lived to see it recognized in judicial decisions as a science. That I have helped, in some measure, to brush away the misconceptions in the minds of many people regarding this much maligned subject is perhaps testified to by my election to Fellowship in the American Academy of Astrologians, an organization that one can't get into for the asking.

I've wasted enough time playing checkers to have built one of the Egyptian pyramids single-handed. Another hobby is shorthand, which has fascinated me for thirty years. I understand several systems. I can sling a wicked toe on the dance floor, but only dance when my weight crowds two hundred. One year I spent the summer on the desert drying out, where my own cooking, plus the heat, effected a material reduction. But I come honestly by it: my father weighed two hundred and sixty in athletic condition—three hundred when not.

And speaking of ancestors: My grandfather was a brother of Joseph Smith, who founded the Mormon Church, which probably explains why I was born in Utah.